de facto Justice

by
Donald F. Ripley, JD

ISBN: 0-75965-575-8

This book is printed on acid free paper.

1stBooks - rev. 08/08/01

DEDICATION:

To Sergeant George Brison

He always had my back.

PROLOGUE

"There is no odor so bad as that which arises from goodness tainted."

- Henry David Thoreau

Perhaps the book *Peyton Place* caught the attention of so many because it mirrored the story of every community. Whether or not it was true in detail, it certainly was an accurate reflection of how the social structure functioned. It revealed that old Puritan concepts of everyday life were only apparent and not always real, for reality is that society is imperfect, sometimes base, and frequently shocking.

It is no less revealing to examine two other institutions of democratic society: the justice system and the press. Both movies and books have touted these as the last bastions for the protection of the socially disadvantaged.

The real issue is whether the constitutional values of those institutions function fairly and impartially.

An old expression may hold the answer, when examined as to origin and application. The expression "different strokes for different folks" likely originated in ancient feudal England. Supposedly, it is based on the fact that peasants believed that important or well-connected swells and aristocrats, who were seldom convicted of wrongdoing, received less strokes of the whip, applied with less vigor, than those meted out to the less fortunate.

A complicated struggle evolves when corruption is discovered in Shiretown, a typical New England city, and the solution requires the dedication, integrity, and stealth of honest officials and dedicated police officers.

CHAPTER ONE

Conflict

"And, through the heat of conflict, keeps the law..."
- William Wordsworth (1807)

The incessant noise of the telephone, once called ringing but now a more modern, amplified, annoying cricket sound, blasted into the bedroom silence. Dr. Kirk Donald, medical examiner of Sussex County, answered with obvious distress, bordering on belligerence. The room was too dark for him to find his glasses, but he could see the oversized red digital numbers of the electric clock: 3:15 a.m.

His voice was low, as it almost always was, slight compared to his six-foot plus, 225-pound structure. Yet, there was a subtly assertive, self-confident tone when he spoke, which correctly created the impression of his pitbull-like will.

The 911-dispatch operator's voice was exactly like that of Fran Drescher's from the sitcom *The Nanny*. It pierced his ear as he said hello. Her tone was almost a shout, as if she did not believe in the power of the telephone.

"Doctor, the crime lab wants you to come to the back of the Webster Street parking lot, near the railroad tracks. Someone was run over by the train."

Donald paused, thinking, a bit curious why they would want him there when his usual venue was in the morgue, searching for the cause of death.

"Who asked for me?"

She coughed a raspy, cigarette hack into the phone, which hurt his ear. "I believe it was Dr. Foley from the forensic section."

"OK," he replied. "Tell him I'll be there in thirty minutes."

He mechanically pulled on yesterday's socks from the floor by the bed, along with his crumpled tweed pants and a fuzzy white wool fisherman's turtleneck sweater, and stuck his feet into his aged, size twelve, Cordovan loafers.

"What's up?" his wife Dorothy asked as she swung up from her side of the bed next to the window.

"Some poor bastard's been run over by the train and for some reason the forensic nerds sent for me."

Dorothy reached for her kimono as her feet hit the floor. "I'll make you an instant coffee to drink while you brush your teeth."

He did not discourage her as, by nature, he was not an early morning person and he would need the coffee to charge his brain.

He washed his face in cold water and brushed his teeth, pausing to look at his unshaven face in the mirror, and silently promise himself he'd shed ten pounds. When he reached the kitchen, he watched Dorothy nuke a cup of water and then dump in a large spoonful of Taster's Choice instant. She added his mandatory three heaping spoonfuls of sugar and a slurp of skim milk. "Mud," she commented. "How can you justify three sugars and then use fat free milk?"

"Diet," he explained as he pulled on a shabby, old brown leather jacket. He glanced at her still-sexy figure that defied her fifty-five years, and gave her a good-bye peck on the forehead.

"You know," he said, "after Vietnam I specialized so I wouldn't have to deal with mangled bodies anymore, and then I was stupid enough to take the medical examiner's job as a temporary monetary supplement, and now thirty years later, I'm still doing mangled bodies."

Dorothy rolled her eyes and looked amused. "Semper Fi and bullfeathers. You love it or you'd have taken your pension already."

He smiled, a sly guilty grin, one his pal Dr. Horace Foley of the forensic unit would call a shit-eatin' dog look, but said nothing further to contradict her as he disappeared out the side door to his unwashed Dodge van, carrying the muddy coffee like it was gold.

Donald sipped the dark brew as he drove the twenty minutes to Webster Street, located in the older, downtown area of Shiretown, the county seat of Sussex County. It was still composed of an interesting collection of independent merchants trying to keep the fifty-five thousand residents from trooping to outlying shopping centers by promotion, price-cutting, and innovation. The effort was failing as one after another the Mom and Pop operations became blank, tombstone-like reminders of another era.

The locals had made a concerted effort to try to survive the suburban thrust of the Wal-Mart dominated, self-contained malls with their acres of parking. Despite some new storefronts and two new Webster Street parking lots, the street was still typical of the late 1950s Eisenhower era, just before the federal interstate highway program. But the easy access ramps from the super highways had isolated hundreds of cities like Shiretown.

Behind the parking lots on the north side, running parallel to Webster, the railroad tracks still carried commuter trains and piggyback freight trains to convey people and goods back and forth to Capitol City.

Dr. Donald drove westward down Webster and reached the parking lot next to Morse's furniture store, just opposite Dunkin' Donuts on the south side. The lot was secured by restrictive yellow plastic police tape and a bevy of rubbernecking citizens who had magically materialized despite the fact that it was barely four in the morning.

Donald parked in front of the donut shop and crossed over to the tape, ducking underneath. Despite the crowd. the police officer recognized him at once and allowed him to pass to the scene without question.

Dr. Horace Foley, head of the county crime lab, sighted the medical examiner and approached quickly, his lean, six-foot-six structure almost loping like a giraffe. Foley's countenance revealed tension, which was not consistent with his usual cool and detached professionalism. "Kirk," he blurted,"follow me to the meat wagon so I can clue you up."

They ducked into the vehicle and closed the big door.

"This guy," began Foley, "was an undercover state cop planted inside city police headquarters as a janitor with the help of the human resources woman at city hall. He was put there to investigate some pretty serious allegations of police corruption. The reason I know all this is because one of the local cops came to me with some suspicions of his own and I contacted the state police commander in Capitol City."

Kirk sat with his eyes fixed on the railroad tracks and the idling diesel train, which had mangled the victim. Foley, known as Hoss because of his long-legged, gallop-like stride, paused and sighed. It was clear, despite Foley's usual detached attitude and years of seeing bodies in every imaginable gory mess, that this was personal because he was involved with the dead state police officer. He cleared his throat several times. "I contacted the state police guy running the investigation by cell phone and he wants us to treat this like a murder. He's contacting his supervisors to see what their next move will be."

Kirk did not hesitate, "What do you want me to do?"

Foley opened the side door of the van. "I want you to run this deal with me so the exam will be double-checked and verified. We don't want any loopholes for some lawyer to exploit if we ever get to court."

Kirk Donald shivered as he replied, "Bullshit Hoss, you've done hundreds of these jobs and you've got academic credentials up the yin yang, so what can I add?"

Foley ignored the answer and plodded toward the body at the tracks. "I'm getting ready to retire and I don't want the death of an undercover cop I was responsible for bringing here screwed up as my last case."

Kirk nodded more as a sign of comfort than in agreement. "Who's the local cop at the scene?"

"Sergeant Richard Murphy," replied Foley.

"Judas Priest," exclaimed Kirk, "Attila the Hun."

"Don't tell the local PD squat," advised Foley. "We'll act co-operative, but tell them shit."

Kirk moved to the front of the van. "Give me a quick update. What do they suspect is going on with the city PD?"

Foley glanced around them, checking for privacy. "Later. Right now we don't know who's dirty and who's straight, so treat them all with suspicion."

They walked to the tracks where a city generator had been hauled to provide light at the scene. The train engineer stood silently near the train, shivering and wringing his hands as he stood staring at the twisted, sickening pile of dead flesh. A second trainman was trying to comfort the distraught engineer who had driven the train over the victim.

Kirk walked directly to them, where he recognized the driver as a local man, Glen Ells. He advised them to not look at the body saying "It'll serve no purpose for you or him."

The second trainman tried to counter any thoughts of blaming the train crew. "The guy was on the track. There's no way we could have avoided him."

Kirk ignored him and turned to a railroad cop also at the scene. "Get Mr. Ells to the hospital. He can give a statement later." That done, he turned to Dr. Foley and they walked to the body.

"Jesus," exclaimed Kirk, "he's split from asshole to windpipe, but somehow his head's been severed without crushing it. The wheel ran from his crotch right up his spine."

Foley leaned over the head, which lay on the inside between the two rails. "Maybe the head was pushed out of the way by the impact of the wheel on the body." He leaned closer. "There's a strong smell of whiskey, but it's almost too strong, unless he had a bottle in his pocket, but there's no broken glass. What do you think?"

Kirk could smell the alcohol too. "First of all, even if he was loaded, and the blood work will answer that, how many people would fall asleep or pass out straight up one narrow rail, like a cat perched on a railing?"

Hoss shook his head before he spoke. "Conversely, if you're killing a guy by trying to make it look like an accidental death by train, it wouldn't matter which way he was laying, up or across for instance."

Kirk agreed, but then raised another question. "Unless, you wanted to cover up a wound in the back and had to make sure the train wheel did that."

Hoss smiled. "As to being a suspicious fucker, maybe the whiskey was poured over him by a train man. Sort of like New York City cops. When they shoot a guy who is unarmed, they put a throw-away gun next to the body to make it look like self-defense."

Kirk listened intently. "Sounds like a shitty defense-lawyer argument at a murder trial, but pretty far-fetched, although it would make the death look like the victim's fault and not the train crew's conduct." He found the idea amusing. "So you're saying that most trainmen carry a throw-away bottle of whiskey in case they run over someone?"

Horace Foley chortled. "I think we've been at the job too long. Let's try to find all or part of the stomach contents for a toxicology." Then, looking at the torn body changed his mind. "Better yet, let's photograph everything and then bag it all and take it to the lab where we can have a better chance of finding something."

"What about his wallet and pockets?" asked Kirk.

"Already bagged that stuff. When I saw his driver's license I called the troopers and had 911 call you."

As the meticulous, painstaking, and messy collection proceeded, the attending police officers kept their distance. Dr. Foley was noted for almost skinning anyone who interfered with or disturbed a crime scene. Yet, Sergeant Richard Murphy, who Foley considered a deadly surly bully, approached.

"Hey, Doc, the Chief's on his way down here."

Foley never looked up from where he was removing flesh from one of the train wheels. "Well, I hope he ain't in no hurry and can keep from chucking-up his cookies cause I just found one of this guy's balls stuck to this wheel."

CHAPTER TWO

Do-Gooders

"All wars are caused by some moke trying to inflict his version of good on somebody else."
- Lucky Luciano (1939)

In Shiretown, the Sussex County hospital is named the Elliott Chipman Fraser Memorial Hospital because old man Fraser tried at the last to pay his way into heaven. After selling illegal bootleg liquor during Prohibition and later legally after the act was repealed, Fraser was very rich. However, he lacked the respectability he coveted because he was a socially outcast enigma to the Baptists of the West End. While many of them secretly drank his product on Saturday nights, they soundly condemned him at church on Sunday mornings.

When it finally occurred to Fraser, on his eightieth birthday, that the end was near, he first took to regular church attendance, and then gave a hundred acres of land and two million dollars to build the hospital. It was completed in 1950, and Fraser died there in 1952, praying vigorously for God's loss of memory about his Prohibition-era business.

The hospital was perched like a giant brick crab on Park Street Hill, high above the Veteran's Memorial, the city's ballpark, and the swimming pool and tennis courts. It was expanded outwards in 1968 and upward in 1994 with the aid of another huge Fraser bequest, and was now an imposing, if not architecturally significant, landmark.

Situated below the Fraser edifice, and to the south of the hospital hill, the trustees of the institution built a neat row of twenty inexpensive, varied but small, two-bedroom Cape Cod houses on a cul-de-sac named Fraser Lane. The houses were intended to attract top-grade, newly graduated, and student-loan ridden MDs to the Fraser hospital. And they came, staying in the frugal dwellings until their incomes increased to where they could build small mansions of their own on half-acre lots sold to them by the hospital trustees in the impressive, yet overpriced Fraser subdivision.

Then, during the nurse shortage just before the end of the Vietnam War, the hospital trustees decided to compete with the bigger hospitals to attract nurses to the Fraser. They built a thirty-unit brick nurses' residence on the plateau of the hospital hill, within a half-mile walking distance of the hospital. It was not unattractive, perfectly landscaped, and discretely located behind a staggered stand of native evergreens, which provided privacy. And the Fraser hospital attracted top-flight nurses.

Rumors of love nests between young doctors down the hill and nurses at the residence up the hill made coffee shop gossip, but during the naughty nineties, such tales had little impact, even on the Baptists of the West End. To the quiet, introverted, twenty-five-year-old Kathryn Fraser, who had first graduated with a degree in science and then from nursing school, the location of the nurses' residence and the thought of male attention was an inducement. There was also the fact that she was the great-granddaughter, and one of the heirs, of the original Fraser and his estate's fortune. That fact did not hamper her selection as a nurse ahead of other applicants. She would not inherit for fifteen more years until she was forty because E. C. Fraser and his narrow-minded attorneys, Chase and MacDonald, deemed women to be immature until they reached that age. The current executor, Judge Harold "Goat" Chase, the grandson of Willard Chase of the law firm which represented old Fraser, concurred. The less the estate paid out, the more Goat Chase earned, as the legal fee was a percentage of the assets, and the more the estate grew, the more his fee grew.

Kathryn was a big girl, large-bosomed, overweight, but sexy in appearance: flashing blue eyes, blonde to brownish hair, sparkling teeth, and a pleasant personality but dreadfully shy. By her own admission she had never been asked to anything by a male, even at the drunken bashes at university. She hoped that nursing at the Fraser would change that fact.

After twelve weeks of internship and a period of probation, she was assigned to a regular shift and routine. She grew confident in her work and learned to flirt by watching several other nurses who had busy social calendars. She learned to use her blue eyes as a leader and soon she was flirting outrageously with almost every doctor, particularly the attractive ones, and especially if they were financially able. Several doctors, two cops, a pharmacist, and even old Goat Chase were not immune to her growing ability to tease. It was from these encounters that she received her first invitation to go for coffee after the four-to-twelve shift on a rainy night, an event which would add to the mystique of the Fraser hospital for years to come.

She grew more excited as the evening wore on. At 11:30, the relieving nurse arrived early. Kathy Fraser went to the nurse's lounge to kill time and kibitz while she waited. There was small talk and so many introductions as the shift changed that she could not peg all the names, but there was one she knew: Joan Murphy, the surgical nurse supervisor. She had talked to Kathy about studying surgical nursing. Kathy was flushed, red-cheeked and increasingly nervous, because she was anxious to break off the conversation as the time reached midnight.

She excused herself, almost rudely. She put on her dark blue raincoat over her white uniform and left through the side door, frequented by the nursing staff who lived at the residence. She skipped across the puddles, which had formed on the staff parking lot, and headed towards the lane to the residence. At the dark corner of the lot she saw his car. He parked just out of sight of the residence, hidden by a clump of cedars, with his lights out and the motor running.

As she opened the passenger door, the dome light did not come on because he had taped a penny over the automatic button on the door to protect them from prying eyes.

"Lay down on the seat," he instructed, "so nobody sees your silhouette if they recognize the car."

She understood. Her heart pounded with excitement, her mouth was dry as cotton and tasted bitter. She worried about her breath and fumbled in her raincoat pocket for a Lifesaver.

He drove down the hill, paused, turned left and headed west towards the wooded plateau where new houses were being constructed on land sold by the hospital. He turned left again then up the newly constructed residential street onto the plateau high above Park Street. He had planned well because he turned into a rough driveway and circled behind a partially constructed new house. He shut down the car and she snuggled into his arms. He kissed her, a long, deep, exciting, wet kiss and caressed her hair, nuzzling her neck and her passion exploded. "There's no room here," he said. "Let's go into that new house."

"What if the contractor has a security guard"? she asked. "Forget it," he replied, "there's no one coming here tonight in the rain."

They entered through an opening in the basement, and he led her to a corner where the contractor had stored a plastic-covered pile of vapor-barrier.

"Looks like a bed," she said, and he eased her down onto it. She could feel his hand as it slid up her thigh in a slow, tantalizing motion until he reached her panties. She had worn black bikinis because he had told her he like black panties, but in the dark, private corner it did not matter. He pulled her uniform's zipper down the front. She raised her hips as he slid her underwear off. He opened her bra and she could feel the fire of his tongue on her nipples.

And then he was in her and she made a soft almost purring moan as he pressed his lips to hers. Slowly at first and then almost violently he thrust himself into her until all too quickly it was over. Suddenly she arched her body upwards, gasping for breath as he slid the double-edged, sawtooth, Navy Seal knife upward under her ribcage and into her heart. He thrust the knife again and again, all the time uttering slurred threats and insults.

"You fat fucking slut. You big-titted cow," he said like a ten-year-old boy on a rant with new swear words. "I know your type and you won't do this again."

He stood up and backed away staring at her dim form in the darkness. Reality seemed to set in because he unfolded a piece of plastic he had left nearby during the planning of the ritual. He placed it over Kathy's body and then, reaching under it, he grasped her breasts, and hacked a big portion of each one off with his knife: first the left, then the right one, protecting his clothes from the blood with the plastic.

He rushed to the trunk of his car for a gas canister and, returning quickly, poured it over her body and the surrounding area. "No forensic evidence," he thought. "No pubic hairs, no finger prints, and no semen because he had worn a condom.

He slopped the gas generously toward a pile of newspapers he had spread in the corner, but stopped without wetting the papers. He moved back, well away from the gas fumes, to the cellar opening. He lit a cigarette and sucked the flame well into the tip. Opening a pack of penny matches, he placed the cigarette into the fold of the cover just above the match heads before closing the cover. The fold in the cover held the smoldering cigarette on a burning path to the matches, making a crude but effective incendiary device. He tossed it gently into the newspapers knowing it would take about one minute for the cigarette to burn down to the matches, and then it would light the strewn newspapers, causing the flame to travel the dozen or so feet to the gas soaked body. He was destroying her again, as well as the evidence, and likely the new house too.

His eyes glistened and his mouth was pungently dry; sweat ran down his back in a torrent as the excitement engulfed him. Sadly he knew he had to be gone from the scene before the fire was really big, but by that time it would attract others and be reported. He charged away, headed home to change his clothes and vacuum the car so there would be no trace of her there. As he drove away, he burst into tears, ashamed that he had been tempted by another loose sluttie woman, and blurted the same words over and over, "another fat slut, with big tits," but the words did nothing to quell his conscience.

CHAPTER THREE

The Facts

"Observation is a passive science..."
- Claude Bernard (1865)

Dr. Horace Foley listened to Kirk's initial report on the two bodies over the phone. He then relayed the opinions to Colonel Alex Kendall at the state police. He next headed to Kirk's office at the morgue. He walked from his office at the connecting crime lab, down the hall, past the refrigerated storage facilities where the bodies were kept in temperature-controlled drawers. As he walked past the autopsy lab, the smell of disinfectant chemicals wafted into the hall. The lab staff, perhaps as an emotional shield to the constant exposure to violent death, called the autopsy facility the "meat market" in the dark tradition of occupational humor.

Foley entered the medical examiner's office, located near the front of the building. Kirk's secretary Sharon Marshall a crafty, mature ex-army nurse acted as sentry, medical assistant, and den mother, and had done so for ten years. She was efficient, officious, and could lie to the press and visitors without a twitch evident in her beautiful, black face. Foley called her Sergeant Schultz, mimicking her usual response to questions, "I know nothing."

"Inside," she instructed before he even spoke.

Kirk sat at his desk where twelve small, insulated, cold-pack shipping containers were stacked. These contained samples of partially digested food, feces, blood, hair and flesh from the mangled body of State Trooper Mike McCurdy who had been working undercover as Harvey Gates, while investigating the Shiretown PD for corruption.

"I made two sets of samples as you requested," Kirk said by way of a greeting. "These go to the state lab and your set is over there on the table."

Foley's expression revealed his eagerness to hear what Kirk had discovered. "You said on the phone that you found something?"

Kirk reached for a plastic evidence bag and passed it to Foley. It contained a small shiny sliver of metal, the end of a broken syringe, the tip of a needle.

"It broke off at the base of McCurdy's skull. I almost missed it."

Foley smiled a wry, knowing, Halloween pumpkin grin. "The train missed it, but you didn't."

Kirk got up from behind his big oak desk and walked towards the autopsy room door. Foley tagged close behind like an eager puppy. Inside, the corpse lay on a stainless steel table, looking more like a tangled assortment of parts and pieces than a body.

"Look here," said Kirk, pointing to the skull, which had escaped the wheels of the train. "I photographed the needle mark with the Polaroid but it isn't too good. The toxicology will likely prove he was either poisoned or drugged. Either way the train was to be a cover-up, but it missed the head and both his legs too."

Foley leaned forward. "Look at those knees. All scraped and full of dirt, like someone dragged him on the pavement to the tracks."

"Possibly," replied Kirk, "if he was on his belly and someone tried to drag him by his arms, then the knees would make contact all right."

Foley circled the table, shaking his head, lost in his thoughts. Finally he spoke. "After you phoned, I called Colonel Alex Kendall at the state police. He's coming down here today at three o'clock and wants to meet both of us and my police pal Bear."

"OK by me," Kirk said. "Before you go, come look at the Fraser girl." He rolled out the refrigerated drawer to reveal her burnt, blistered body; and the smell of cooked flesh oozed into the room.

They stood silently at first, and then Kirk spoke. "There's some sick hump out there Hoss. He killed her with a knife to the heart, then cut her breasts off. He obviously burned the place to cover any forensic material."

Foley agreed. "You don't have to be a shrink to figure the killer is a weirdo who hates women, or his mother, or some abusive aunt, or maybe he just hates tits."

Kirk rolled the drawer back. "Did your guys find anything useful at the scene?"

"A wet Kleenex tissue," replied Foley. "Someone discarded it, but it could belong to anyone: a fire fighter, a cop, a worker, or even the victim. Matching it to a killer with DNA is pretty remote at this point unless we find some other evidence and a suspect. How about you?"

"So far I've only done a cursory swab for semen up inside her, above the burns, but I think it's spermacidal. It looks like signs of penetration and latex so he probably wore a rubber. My guess is that he burned her pubic area in case his own pubic hair was present after intercourse."

"She's old man Fraser's relative," said Foley, "so I expect that the hospital trustees and the press will be screaming their empty heads off."

Kirk made a clucking sound with his tongue. "Well, the best of British luck to them. We can't find what ain't there, and besides it's the PD who'll take the heat."

Foley reached for the wall phone and punched in the direct line to the crime unit. "This is Foley. Who's doing the Fraser homicide?" He paused, listening. "Thanks," he said and hung up. "Sergeant Richard Murphy was the scene supervisor, and he and another cop are picking up the facts for the investigation, but homicide will take over," he reported.

Kirk whistled through his teeth, "Murphy strikes me as a weirdo who doesn't like people."

"Yep," agreed Foley, "but he's not stupid, just an asshole."

Sharon Marshall entered the autopsy room. "Murphy and another guy are outside, but I wouldn't let them in here, and they're unhappy they didn't hear from you," she said.

"Bullshit," Kirk replied. "Hoss just found out who was on the case. They never phoned us, and then they show up with no notice looking for a report."

"I'm out of here," said Foley. "I'll pick up the autopsy samples later." He disappeared through the side door to the hall to avoid the two cops.

Marshall escorted West and Murphy into the room. Kirk put on his best face "Sorry guys, I told her no visitors but I just meant the press."

Murphy stood there looking sour and made no comment. He had been senior man by rank at the scene, but Kirk was glad Murphy wouldn't be running the case.

"Anything to report?" Murphy questioned. The other officer stood silent like a statue.

"Not yet," replied Kirk, "except it's definitely a homicide. She was killed with one of those military Special Forces type, double-sided saw blade knives. Shoved it directly up into her heart. I should be done on this by tomorrow. The guy Gates from the train yard will be a complicated autopsy, and I may not be able to give you anything for a week."

Murphy scowled. "Can't do it sooner, Doc?"

"Impossible," Kirk stated. "It's a tough one because of the condition of the stiff. All we know so far is that he smelled of booze and was cut up the middle by the train. It's a real hard call, but I gather the train crew had no chance to avoid him, but it's for your department to figure that one out."

The two officers grudgingly accepted Dr. Donald's excuse and departed. They were no sooner out the door when Sharon threw up her arms like a Bible-thumping preacher, rolled her eyes upwards as if praying to Heaven, and shouted. "Hallelujah. Crime hath many tools and a lie is a handle which fits them all."

Kirk suppressed his smile, but she noticed his slight grin and knew she'd struck his sick sense of humor. "Back on guard," he said to her and then disappeared through the door to the meat market.

Horace Foley and Officer Noel Bear arrived shortly before three for the meeting. Bear, who was born on the Six Nations Reserve in upper New York State, represented a new breed of university graduate in law enforcement.

He had attended Cornell on a scholarship and graduated from the Industrial and Labor Relations School. He played professional hockey for two years in the American Hockey League, where his crashing, six-foot-two frame commanded respect. He married a photo-perfect model, Shania, and they had twin boys who were carbon copies of his fine native Seneca features. By his own decision, he chose to leave hockey at the age of twenty-eight as he believed he would not reach the NHL and it was time to make another career. The Shiretown Police department had accepted Bear with open arms because of his background and education.

Bear had been a police officer for only two years when he became suspicious that at least two officers were corrupt. He struggled to reach that conclusion, tormenting himself with worry for weeks before finally confiding in Dr. Horace Foley one night when they were playing handball. They had become friends and worked out together. Added to this was the fact that Foley and his wife had lost a son in a car accident and found Shania and Noel Bear like a substitute family after the tragedy.

Kirk Donald was curious, even eager, to meet Bear and hear his account of the PD before the state police commander arrived. Bear was cautious as usual, shy, always reticent to say much, and the three of them were uncomfortable as they attempted to make small talk. Foley, sensing Bear's reluctance to speak in front of Kirk, whom he did not know well, told Vietnam stories about Dr. Donald and other old war stories to relieve tension.

Bear slowly relaxed, but before he told Kirk anything, Sharon Marshall entered the inner office and announced the arrival of Colonel Kendall and another state police officer, Lieutenant Sam Folker.

Despite his civilian attire, it was evident that Kendall, in a dark blue suit and conservative striped tie, was either a cop or a military type. Folker was the opposite; he looked sort of like a teacher, six feet tall and slender, thirty-five plus years old, and geeky in a brown tweed suit, which revealed his lack of attention to sartorial matters.

There was almost no small talk after the introductions. Kendall cut to the chase.

"There are a number of problems as a result of this awful incident," he began in the curt manner of a training lecturer. "We want to honor Trooper McCurdy and his family, but his sacrifice will mean little if we compromise his undercover work. To preserve the integrity of the investigation, we have to be careful."

At this point, Kendall's stern-faced facade seemed fragile. It then became obvious that he was deeply affected by the death of the young trooper. His lip trembled and he had to pause to maintain self-control. His curt manner disappeared.

He continued, "If we bury McCurdy with the full honors he deserves, it will attract the attention of the media, and when they go after the details of his death, the facts, or the lack of facts, will become an issue of controversy. But it is pretty callous not to pay tribute to one of our own who was killed in the line of duty."

Kendall paused again as if waiting for a reaction, or at least a comment. "McCurdy's parents have made it clear that they don't want his work to be for nothing, so they suggested we wait to hold a service, or announce that he was killed out of state in an accident, or basically whatever we decide is best."

Foley interrupted, "Listen, those shit flies from the press would be on that like beetles on manure. Someone obviously knew he was a cop or else why would he have been murdered?"

Lieutenant Folker spoke up, "Exactly, but we can't reveal an undercover operation now because it would turn into a political shit-pit and accomplish nothing except to put the dirty cops on notice to be careful, and it would tarnish the reputation of all the good officers. The chance of getting another person in there by some ruse is now remote because the killer will be expecting another undercover trooper. Therefore, we think we should delay the funeral and the honors, and the family have agreed to whatever is best for his investigation."

Kendall and Folker had clearly thought the issue through. Kendall spoke again, "We suggest you leave the remains under his undercover ID, Harvey Gates, and report your findings as an accidental death to the Shiretown PD We'll have someone pretending to be a relative claim the remains when you finish the autopsy." He hardly paused to draw a breath. "That may make the killer think he got away with murder. You can send the actual reports to us for the real investigations because the needle you found proves murder." Kirk and Foley exchanged glances and nodded their agreement.

Folker opened an old, weatherworn carpet-bag-style leather briefcase and removed a thick file. "These are McCurdy's reports." He passed them to Noel Bear. "We want you to be our inside man, to take McCurdy's place."

There was silence as they waited for some reaction from Bear.

Noel Bear was on the spot. He had started an investigation, which resulted in the death of a state trooper; now he would look bad if he refused to place himself in the same dangerous position. His reaction was easy to read because he fairly stammered trying to give an answer. "I've only been a police officer for two years," he stammered. "I know what McCurdy was up against, and I wonder if I'm capable of pulling this off."

Folker opened a second file from his old-fashioned bag. "We have your background since grade school on the reservation and we know you're capable, both mentally and physically, to handle tough situations."

Bear was not comforted, nor convinced. "But I don't think I could fool anyone, and I have no undercover experience."

Kendall interrupted. "This is a case which initially will require a lot of passive observation and maybe some wire work. Mostly, you keep your ears and eyes open. Just remember that observation is a patient science."

Bear still felt on edge. They had made it difficult for him to refuse. He was dealing with internal doubt and honest-to-God humility about his ability to pull it off, and he was given no chance to consult his wife. He said almost to himself, "Who was it who said: 'Many men are heroes in their mind but few have the opportunity to face the real test?'"

Kendall laughed, "I think that was General George Patton before he counter-attacked the Germans at the Battle of the Bulge."

"OK," sighed Bear. "I'm in. Give me an hour or so to read McCurdy's reports."

Folker passed him another file. "So far it appears there are only two or three bad apples and maybe someone up the command ladder too. But, is there anyone else in the department who you would trust? And remember, there's been one murder already, so think carefully."

Bear did not hesitate. "Sergeant Shirley Reading. She's the officer in charge of the juvenile division. She once alerted me to a potential mess when a young offender she busted told her that drug investigators Hunter Stent and Frank Nichols had once let him go on a drug bust on the condition he would sell pot for them."

"OK," agreed Kendall. He stood up. "See if she'll help, but don't tell her much till she proves herself. Now, let's get this show on the road."

CHAPTER FOUR

Chase's Magistrate's Court

"Not that the story need be long (in court), but it will take a long while to make it short."

- Thoreau (1857)

Harold "Goat" Chase, who reveled in the title of judge, was in reality a Sussex County police court magistrate at Shiretown. He was the offspring of old money, had practiced law in the firm of his father and grandfather, and had managed to maintain his executorship of several big estates and trusts when he received the magistrate's appointment as a political boon. Knowledgeable attorneys, who rated magistrate's court as the legal equivalent of the plague, could not understand why a snobbish old boy like Chase would not aspire to progress further up the judicial chain. Unknown to them, he had at first lobbied vigorously for an elevation to a higher court, but that had been a dozen years ago.

Chase's very appearance certified the nickname "Goat" which had been bestowed upon him by an unhappy drunk who had noted the similarity. Chase's white hair, which was slanted slightly upwards from his head in a semi-Don King coiffure, and his beaked face and bleating voice were, in fact, not unlike that of a goat.

Chase's court, where he judged the dregs of society, was relegated to petty crimes, drunk and disorderliness, public nuisances, and traffic offenses. It was usually overburdened with drunks, street people, repeat offenders, and a smattering of people from higher society who were plagued by addictions to alcohol or other mind-altering chemical substances. The word trial in conjunction with magistrate's court was usually a stretch; by necessity induced by the sheer numbers, it was really a system of plea bargains as experienced perps, defense attorneys, and especially prosecutors seldom wanted a trial. A guilty plea and a penalty agreement usually resulted in a fine of fifty dollars or less, plus costs. The ability to pay the fine was very important because failure resulted in a seven-to-fourteen day stay in the antiquated, filthy, foul-smelling city section of the county jail, where cockroaches and perverts made life miserable. A brief stay in that known cesspool of a facility was all the incentive necessary to all but a few street people to beg, borrow, or steal the funds to pay the fine.

The jailer, a county deputy named Crowell Roscoe well-known for his trademark bad breath, dirty shirt, and beard-stubbled face, was a second incentive to avoid the place. Roscoe received a per diem of three dollars to feed each prisoner. According to experienced prisoners, the food he served proved that his profit was huge. It was a jail joke that Purina Dog Chow cost more than the prisoners' meals.

Roscoe, like the old chain gang bosses, made prisoners voluntarily work on his own various moneymaking projects. "Or else!" one captive said in describing voluntary.

Roscoe was the brother-in-law of prosecutor David MacAdam, whose performance was usually limited to negotiating plea bargains.

Chase's court was filled five days a week because of the Shiretown chief of police, John Pineo. He had been appointed chief years before for his political connections when brawn, not brains, was the standard. He was long past retirement age, if such a rule was enforced, but like the late J. Edgar Hoover of the FBI, Pineo had something on, or was connected to, the people of power and influence. Pineo understood that the public usually believed you can never find a cop when you want one, so wisely he insisted upon frequent, visible police patrols and demanded a daily round-up of all drunks, and panhandlers. He was especially hard on traffic offense perpetrators.

"The mission," he preached to the police force, "is to keep the streets free, crime down, and increase city revenues from fines, without riling the decent tax-paying citizens."

And that is exactly what the public seemed to want. Pineo re-enforced his sterling image by visiting magistrate's court daily, schmoozing with merchants and business owners, enjoying free coffee with shoppers, and playing golf with the socially advantaged on Saturdays.

Pineo's second-in-command was Major Lester "Sonny" Brown; he was the chief's Sancho Panza, or bum-boy according to detractors. He carried out all Pineo's dirty jobs, errands and edicts. Brown was, in the opinion of those who disapproved, sort of a nasty Corporal Radar with a gun and attitude. But he knew the chief wanted no citizen provoked to the point of litigation, so as a rule, Brown did not rock the public's boat.

At first, the case of juvenile Donald Frank was a nothing issue. Major Brown assigned the file to Juvenile Officer Sergeant Shirley Reading. As she read the police report, her casual curiosity moved from low to tilt. Because Major Brown had made the off-duty arrest, Reading became interested in what would normally pass without question. Reading did a brief check on the background and nature of Donald Frank and the incident, which had resulted in his arrest.

The boy looked like a pretty average sixteen-year-old high school student with no record of difficulties with school authorities or the law. He was a fair student, held a part-time job, was a better-than-average athlete and came from a good, hardworking, middle class family.

Donald Frank and several pals were at Wendy's on School Street after a high school dance. The parking lot between the fast food place and the CVS drugstore was a regular hangout for the kids. An altercation of some nature started between two cops, Tom Kierans and Greg Clarke, and a pathetic, drunk, homeless guy. The cops were using pretty rough methods, and of course, many of the kids gathered to make catcalls. All of a sudden, the officers forgot the drunk and grabbed Don Frank. The other kids claimed that Frank was only a docile observer, but Kierans and Clarke held on to him, and when the crowd became boisterous they called Major Brown, who was off-duty at home.

Brown arrived in civilian clothing and arrested young Frank, handling him so roughly that the boy's shirt was ripped off as he dragged Frank to the police car. Brown then took Frank to the adult jail where the jailer, Roscoe, placed the teen in the adult bullpen. Sergeant Reading shuddered when she realized that during the night the young man had been raped and there were no suspects.

Reading completed her cursory inquiry into the report and the youngster and was disturbed enough to press the direct line to Major Lester Brown. He answered in his usual curt manner, which quickly melted to civility when he discovered it was Reading. "The Donald Frank case," she began, "it's a nothing issue at a glance. Do you plan to proceed with it or can it?"

Brown, known for his volatile temper, responded quickly; there was no civility in his tone or answer. "Absolutely, to the fullest," he snapped.

She knew from experience that Brown was often tough, impetuous, and difficult to persuade about changing a decision. She maintained her low-key manner but did not drop the discussion. "Major, I think we might reconsider because this thing is riddled with loopholes and possible civil rights issues, plus there seems to be a lot of civilian witnesses."

Whatever diplomacy Brown started with on the phone call was now depleted. "That kid's a wiseass," Brown yelled. "He challenged the authority of two police officers and embarrassed the department in front of the public. I was called and had no choice but to back the officers and maintain the law in front of onlookers."

Reading could tell the discussion was useless. "Yes, sir. I only wanted you to know about the legal pitfalls in case you hadn't had time to consider the potential issues."

Brown now displayed umbrage at the questioning of his decision. "What are you? Some ACLU lawyer or a cop?"

Reading did not hesitate in her reply. "No, sir, not ACLU, but yes, I do have a law degree. This case is weak and it has a lot of potential for the department to be sued."

Brown paused, and she hoped it was to reconsider. He did not. "Bring that file up here at once. You're off it and it will be prosecuted outside juvenile devision."

Reading photocopied the file and delivered the originals to the top floor where Brown's office was located. She then took the elevator to the ground floor and walked to the back of the building to the detective division of the crime unit. She walked between the crowded desks to the cubicle where her boyfriend, Sergeant Jack Baptist, was wrestling with a computer.

"Coffee," she stated curtly and walked towards the back door. Baptist snatched his suit jacket and followed her into the police department parking lot.

In the car, as they drove down Webster Street toward the West End Lunch, it was obvious she was pissed.

"OK," he said. "Spill your guts, what's up?"

"Listen to this," she replied and read him the Donald Frank report and the background. "That asshole Brown is screwing this kid over and it spells lawsuit. It's a nothing case and they stuck him in the adult slammer with that creep Roscoe. I get a strong feeling that there's some reason, petty or otherwise, that Brown is pushing this. Even if I'm wrong, we're gonna get sued."

Baptist let her vent. Finally he spoke, "And, you gonna be just as unreasonable as hell and want me to do something to get my ass wrecked in your crusade."

Reading ignored his facetious answer. "My question is why? Why does Brown want to create a potential incident over nothing?"

She hardly drew a breath before charging on. "Do me a favor and dig around a little and see if there's any history between Brown and the Frank family? I can't because he ordered me to give up the file to him."

"I reckon," Baptist mused, "he didn't order you not to give a copy to me, and when he sends me up on complaint, you figure that technicality can be my defense."

CHAPTER FIVE

Quid Pro Quo

"A friend in need is a real pain in the ass."
- Redhorse (1999)

Reverend Kenneth Solomon paced back and forth like a caged lion, but his feet paced on the posh paisley multi-colored Persian rug in his office at the back of the Lutheran Church on Bishop Avenue. His bulky, two hundred pounds bulged over his low-hung black ministerial pants, displaying ample evidence that a five-foot-eight man of that weight, in a tight suit, looks like two-hundred-pounds of potatoes in a hundred-and-fifty-pound sack.

Solomon's panic grew as he waited impatiently for the arrival of his old Army buddy and life-long pal, Chief of Police John D. Pineo. He had called the chief's private line and had spoken to the secretary who promised she would immediately locate the chief and send him to the church. In the meantime, he paced. His clerical shirt and white collar were soaked with sweat, and a crimson, two-finger scratch was evident on his left cheek, just under his eye where she had clawed him when he pawed her like a horny goat. He knew she was only sixteen, despite her mature, voluptuous appearance, but his sexual urges carried him away. He knew she was worldly and hardly a virgin in this day and age, but her response to his brazen touching had been to fight back. Now she sat sobbing on the visitor's sofa near the office fireplace, holding a poker at the ready in the event he tried again. None of his pleading, whining, excuses, or promises had dispelled her terror, and until she heard him phone for the chief of police, she had been near hysteria. She had settled into a defensive position waiting for the chief's arrival.

For Solomon, the situation was dire. The girl was legally a child, beautiful despite her slight plumpness, with a perfectly shaped sexy figure, which more than one male schoolmate wished to experiment with in reality rather than in nocturnal dreams.

Little did the girl know that the horny clergyman had chosen her for summer employment because of her breasts, nor did she realize the old pervert and the chief of police went way back. They had been buddies since the peacetime draft in the period just before Vietnam, when the army was fun and consisted largely of dice games, bar crawling, and whoring with the local hookers in the segregated South. They were just boys when Pineo borrowed an army sedan from the motor pool without authorization, and while driving drunk - roaring, almost blind, falling down drunk - struck and killed an old black man on an isolated rural road.

The cover-up consisted of Pineo and his good buddy PFC Ken Solomon putting the body behind the wheel of the stolen car, shoving it over a steep bank, and setting it on fire. They were never suspected by the fat, stupid local sheriff who deemed it an accidental death by misadventure because he believed the victim had stolen the car and died when it rolled over and burned.

It was the1960s in the South, and the good-old-boy sheriff said, "Who really cares about the death of an old nigger? Case closed."

Solomon and Pineo were thus bonded together forever, and while they chose different fields, it was an ironic coincidence that they both ended up in the same northern city, and seemingly on the side of the angels. However, the careers of both, upon proper examination, lead to the definite conclusion that what is born in the bone can't be excised, or even beaten from the flesh. Despite their chosen careers, they were both flawed to the core.

Chief Pineo arrived at the historic fieldstone church, and parked out of sight in the back. Upon entering the office and seeing Solomon and the sobbing girl, he immediately realized that his guess that the urgent call was trouble was correct. The crying girl, Mary Anslow, presented a problem that would be difficult to keep quiet. The chief realized his own conflict, the result not only of his connection to Solomon but also of the errant clergyman's hiring Pineo's wife Ruth, despite her Church of Scientology allegiance, as the Lutheran Church organist. Although Pineo knew at once what had happened, he still asked for an explanation, hoping he was reading the obvious signs incorrectly.

Young, blue-eyed Mary confirmed Pineo's worst fears in a halting voice, interspersed with sobs. "This old pervert tried to get me to have kinky sex with him." Pineo reckoned her version of events would be the correct one, and knowing Solomon as he did, he had no doubts after he heard her bleak account.

She had been sitting at the new Dell computer typing his Sunday sermon while he stood beside her making corrections. Ironically, it had been on the subject of adultery, which had been suggested by Solomon's matronly wife Rosealy, who was most noted for her bad teeth and putrid breath. Mrs. Solomon had just left the office when the preacher's sex drive kicked in.

Pineo listened to Mary with a sense of dread. She said she had first noticed that Solomon had moved closer and closer when his hip butted against her shoulder. As she related the sordid details to Chief Pineo, Solomon stood biting his lip and wringing his hands.

She blurted out the story. The minister had grabbed her breast and massaged it roughly, then planted an unwelcome, sloppy, wet kiss on her mouth, ramming his tongue deep inside. She cringed in disgust and shivered as she continued her narrative. "He opened his fly," she said, "and he tried to stick his thing in my mouth." Pineo cringed as he listened, and she related how she had managed to repel his attack by sinking her fingers into his bulging face.

Pineo's stomach had a sour, almost vomit-inducing reaction as he listened. It was classic Solomon, the horny bull, trying to relieve his excessive sexual urges brought on by his fascination with large, firm breasts. Pineo remembered that Solomon had expressed his sex theory repeatedly in the old days. He had claimed that even when women resisted a sexual advance, they all liked sex once you managed to "get it in."

Solomon, now cooled by the seriousness of the incident, babbled on, offering stupid, asinine and unreasonable excuses, which sounded as weak as those of a man facing execution who blames the victim for the crime.

"She kept sticking those big tits out," he said to Pineo. "She wanted it. I can tell. She's been banging a football player at school."

Pineo shook his head in disbelief. He took Solomon by the arm and led him away to the minister's private bathroom. "Shut the fuck up," he hissed. "Get cleaned up. Put on a Band-Aid to cover that scratch. Say you cut yourself shaving. This is the mess that could ruin us all, so just shut the fuck up." He closed the door, leaving Solomon in the bathroom.

Pineo walked back to the girl and asked her if he could get her a doctor or anything else. She shook her head.

"Where does your father work?" he asked.

"He's dead," she replied.

Pineo, still hoping to manage and mitigate the damage, continued, "Where does your mother work?"

"At the Fraser; she's a nurse."

Suddenly Pineo could imagine the breath of gossip drifting this story through the halls of the hospital, and he knew, in light of the recent sex murder of Katherine Fraser, the press would go nuts. He also knew Sergeant Richard Murphy's wife was a supervising nurse at the Fraser.

"I'll get someone to drive you home," he said, and called dispatch on the direct unrecorded line. "This is Pineo. Don't log this. Send Sergeant Murphy to the Lutheran Church on Bishop to do an errand for the minister. Tell him to stay off the radio so the whole city doesn't think were UPS."

That done, Pineo walked back to the teenager. "Would you like to go to the ladies' room and wash your face, and would you like me to call the doctor?"

She shook her head no and shuffled off toward the office door to head to the washroom in the hall.

It was only a five-minute drive from the PD and it would not take much longer than that for Murphy to arrive, but Pineo was already impatient. By the time

Murphy showed up Pineo was deeply troubled and stood in the middle of the office between the two key players like a wrestling referee fearful the combatants would start their battle again.

Before Murphy could ask, Pineo spoke. "Is your wife on duty today?"

Murphy nodded. "Yes, but she might be in the OR by now."

"Shit," muttered Pineo. He knew from experience that unexpected events always seemed to mess up battles, crimes, and love affairs. Events like a sleeping sentry, or a getaway car with a flat tire, or a husband arriving home at night a week earlier than expected ruined many foolproof plans. The doomsday thoughts were already in Pineo's head. "Call and see," he instructed Murphy. "If you get her, ask her to find Ellen Anslow and get her to the phone without making any waves or drawing attention."

"I know Ellen," Murphy said, "I can call her directly if you like."

"Do it," Pineo ordered curtly.

After an agonizing wait, Murphy was finally connected to Ellen Anslow. He identified herself and asked her to wait for the chief. Pineo took the phone, and spoke in a controlled, low voice. "John Pineo, Mrs. Anslow. There's been a misunderstanding here at the church between your daughter and the minister. She wants to go home. Would you like to pick her up?"

Ellen Anslow was used to stress from her stint in Vietnam and working in the emergency room, but it was not usual for the chief of police to phone about her daughter. She rattled off several questions, not allowing him to answer one at a time. "Is she OK? What kind of misunderstanding is she involved in? Is she in trouble?"

Pineo did not go into detail but felt he had to comfort her or the whole incident would blow up before he had a chance to seek a solution. "She's not in trouble, Mrs. Anslow. I'll wait here for you, so relax."

Ellen Anslow was not convinced yet. "I can't come now because we have a full ER and I don't have my car. Is there any way you could take her home?"

Pineo paused before answering. "We're supposed to have a female officer present when a child or female is involved, and your daughter is both. There's only Richard Murphy here with me."

"I know Richard," she replied. "I work with his wife. I'm OK with that if he'd drive her home."

Pineo sighed. "I guess it would be OK since you asked, but I need to talk to you too." Mrs. Anslow paused then said, "Would it be possible for me to wait and come to your office late this afternoon because there's a backup of patients here? I get off at 4:30."

Pineo did not want that. "I'll pick you up at 4:30 at the Fraser, if that's OK?" he said.

She agreed, and having settled that, he hung up and turned to the girl. "Your mother wants Sergeant Murphy to drive you home." He then directed Murphy into the hall so that their conversation could not be heard.

"Take her home; try to buy her a coffee or a soda and see if you can find out what makes her tick: boyfriends, school hobbies, the whole nine yards. Don't log this and stay off the radio."

Sergeant Richard Murphy, a twelve-year veteran of the force, a pure sycophant, a six-foot-two, one hundred and ninety-pound department brown noser, knew whose ass to kiss. Here was the main ass, a chance to ingratiate himself and have a get-out-of-jail-free card with the chief.

"Gotcha, Chief," he said, fairly oozing with charm.

Murphy and the girl departed and Pineo turned to Solomon. He was disgusted by the very sight of the fat, dirty old man who had such perverted lust that he couldn't resist molesting a sixteen-year-old girl.

"I'm meeting Mrs. Anslow later this afternoon, and I don't expect she'll be filled with forgiveness for you. She'll want your balls for bookends and I can't say that I blame her, and if she does I can't save you. But I would guess that as a single parent she could be hard-pressed financially, and she might respond to a settlement, but she'll more than likely press charges." As he said this, he tried to guess if Solomon comprehended the seriousness of the incident. "How much money could you raise if I can soothe her into a settlement?"

At first, Solomon did not respond, but then, hoping money could be a solution, answered, "Only five, maybe eight thousand."

Pineo was frustrated. "You're nuts. Nobody would go for that. As it is, I'll have to scare the shit out of the girl's mother to convince her that money is better than revenge. So, here's what you do. First, go draw out your money from the bank, in cash. Don't take out more than ten thousand because the banks are obligated to report withdrawals over that amount to the DEA."

Solomon acknowledged the instructions. "That's not a problem because I only have a little over eight thousand in the National Bank. So, what will I do if they ask why I'm withdrawing it?"

Pineo realized the question might be asked. "Ken, you're a minister, act like one. Charity and not business is your forte so tell the bank you're assisting a parishioner who's in financial trouble. And whatever you do, don't babble on with too much of an explanation."

Solomon agreed. "But what about the rest of the money? How can I raise the rest?"

Pineo was keenly aware this was an iffy proposition: full of traps, loopholes and damaging questions. Pineo had to convey a level of confidence, which he really did not have, to Solomon. Calmly he said, "You must have some other banker or parishioner you know from church. So draw your eight at your own bank, then go borrow seven more using the same excuse. They'll think you're a fool with your money but will likely lend it to you. The more I think about it, the more I think fifteen might catch Ellen Anslow's attention, especially if I can convince her that prosecuting you will cause a media frenzy."

Solomon now seemed to grasp the fact that a prosecution would be his undoing. "I know a woman from the church who is fairly well-off. She's offered me money before."

Pineo immediately knew by that revelation that it was the classic Solomon pattern: he was boffing some church widow. "I don't care if you screw it out of her or steal it but raise it and have it here by five o'clock so we can try to settle this today. And don't discuss this with anyone not even your lawyer because attorneys have secretaries and that's how stories leak into the press."

Back in the police car, a bright flash of hope shoot through his mind. Maybe his pain-in-the-ass friend would be so depressed he'd choose to commit suicide. That would certainly end everybody's troubles. It was a fleeting thought though because he realized that Solomon was, despite his education, dreadfully dense, and the thought of suicide would likely never occur to him.

"Pity," Pineo said out loud, and then drove away, dreading the rest of the day.

Sergeant Murphy reported to Pineo in mid-afternoon after spending time with Mary Anslow on the way home. He was armed with the girl's gossip and a brief history of her high school social life with several boys, especially the football player. Pineo hoped that these facts might be enough to fake the mother into worrying about embarrassing things coming out if she pressed charges against Solomon. That was Pineo's plan: he intended to use subtle innuendo to persuade her. He decided to take a police car to meet Ellen Anslow, so there could be no future allegation that he was attempting to hide his participation in the incident, or the cover-up.

When he reached the main doors of the Fraser just before 4:30, Mrs. Anslow was already waiting. Pineo got out and boldly walked around the car to open the door for her. He joked with two people nearby whom he knew and said, "Mrs. Anslow isn't under arrest, she's just giving us a hand."

When he got back behind the wheel, she hardly waited for the door to close before she unleashed a torrent of words about charging Solomon. "I heard the details from my daughter on the phone," she shouted. "I spoke to Mary just a few minutes ago, and she told me what that Bible-thumping pervert did, and I want him in prison." Her anger mounted. "The pig! He tried to get my daughter to perform oral sex on him and he mauled her breasts."

Pineo had known she would be angry, but the degree of her emotions exceeded anything he had expected. He had a sinking feeling in his chest. He had to be very careful lest she smell a rat and suspect that he was protecting Solomon. The truth was that because of his own old sins he had no choice but to defuse the scandal. He also believed, as Mrs Anslow apparently did, that Solomon was seriously flawed: a real pervert. He suspected that if the Anslow case hit the papers there would be other victims out there who would garner the courage to come forward.

Criminal history shows that unknown victims always appear when a man with a sexual perversion is caught. In fact, he recalled the earlier sudden resignation of a young, buxom woman from the church choir, which was a subject of curious gossip at the time. Experience had taught Pineo that when the jail door closes with the clang of finality almost all prisoners sing their guts out, ratting out all their associates. He expected it would be the same with Solomon, so he had to keep the minister out of the courts.

He listened to Ellen Anslow attentively, interjecting brief statements of agreement and offering sympathy. He did not interrupt because he believed that letting her vent was therapeutic. Finally, she seemed temporarily relieved of her understandably deep, emotional anger.

"Mrs. Anslow," he said quietly, "I'm obligated to file any complaint you make, and I can see that this is a serious issue here. I'm no lawyer, and I'm not supposed to advise or arbitrate disputes, especially when a crime may be involved. It's not up to the police to decide a matter; we just file reports and the DA decides if the incident warrants prosecution. But I wonder if there may not be a less painful way to deal with this."

Pineo now thought it best to reveal that he had known Solomon for a long time, and, in the event that she did not already know it, that his wife was the church organist. He made these comments in an off-hand way and then, to defuse any negative impact, he said, "I've often had an uneasy feeling, almost a gut reaction, that Solomon was weird or flawed, but that's hardly a professional theory and it's sure not evidence."

He watched her carefully to see what her reaction was, and he felt he had her confidence, so he continued. "Solomon is at the edge of a cliff right now, and if there's a trial, the publicity would ruin him, even if he's found not guilty. So, it's my bet he'll be pretty dangerous with his own accusations about Mary because he's a desperate man and will say almost anything."

He spoke slowly, pausing to gauge her reaction. "What I'm saying, Mrs. Anslow, is that this type of trial is a mud-slinger and I wonder if it's necessary to drag your daughter through that stress?"

Mrs. Anslow considered his words but was still seething, "I'll just bet that deviant would say anything to try and lie his way out of this."

Pineo decided to play his trump card. "Exactly. You're in a powerful position here, so you should concentrate on what's best for you and your daughter. You have choices; Solomon doesn't, and at trial he's bound to have some greasy defense attorney try to cast Mary's reputation into disrepute." He noticed that she had relaxed some, but he knew from experience that in sex crimes the victim's anger and need for revenge often overcame reason. Yet, embarrassment and guilt were also present, and he hoped to exploit that fact.

She set her lips is a cruel expression, "I thought there were rules to protect victims from accusations about their reputations?"

Pineo nodded. "There is a rape shield law, but there is always innuendo and gossip, even with a youngster." He knew he had caused her to consider his suggestion.

She looked at him with a strained expression on her face. "What would happen if he was convicted?"

"As I said, Mrs. Anslow, I'm no lawyer, but this offense doesn't seem to rate any severe legal punishment like a rape. He'd likely get a few months or a suspended sentence at worst. But he would be worried about being listed on the state registry as a sex criminal, and that might make him more conciliatory to finding a way out of this mess." Pineo realized his words were sinking in because she became quiet. He hoped she was turning away from the idea of prosecution, so he made his key pitch.

"Wouldn't it be better for your daughter, and for you as a single working parent, if you got a quiet financial settlement? You must be facing a horrendous expense for her to attend university in a couple of years."

Ellen Anslow nodded. "I couldn't stand to see her hauled through the media circus with her reputation sullied. The first year at University alone will cost me about ten thousand dollars, and she'll still need a student loan."

Pineo knew he had to be very careful at this point to avoid sounding as if he were pushing her into dropping a prosecution. "I wonder," he mused, "what would happen if you walked into his office and confronted him?"

She shuddered. "Oh God, I could never do that, and if I did, I'd want to kill him. But, maybe I could do it if you came with me?"

He was now on the spot as he had hoped to keep his distance from any future accusations of a cover-up. "I don't mind helping you, but if this ever got in the papers it might be said that I was either playing lawyer, or suppressing crimes, or favoring you, and in my job that's a death knell."

Ellen Anslow was very quiet now. Pineo knew there were two serious weak spots in his position. The first was obvious: the possibility of a future accusation that he'd exceeded his mandate. The second was how to explain to Ellen Anslow how Solomon just happened to have all that cash on hand. It was way too much of a coincidence for anyone, including her, to believe.

"OK," he answered. "I'll go in and see how conciliatory he is. If it sounds like he wants to settle with you, I'll suggest he better do it as soon as possible before you change your mind, and I'll tell him he has to pay up now."

As Pineo turned the car onto Bishop Avenue, he had the foreboding fear that this mess would eventually suck him under like quicksand. "Are you sure this is what you want?" he asked her as he pulled into the church parking lot.

"It's the best solution," she replied, "but I'm not waiting for him to debate this. If he makes an offer he's got only until tomorrow to settle it. Is that reasonable?"

"I hope so," Pineo answered. He felt comfortable that as a mother she had made a good decision for her child's welfare, and one that would likely cover his butt too. It was better for him than having to take Solomon to trial. Pineo thought about the old adage about mothers and their offspring: "Never get between a tiger and her cubs." That fact better impress Solomon or he was ruined and Pineo knew he went down if Solomon went down.

The chief disappeared into the church. Time seemed to stand still. Ellen Anslow looked at her watch almost a dozen times between 5:00 and 5:10; the hands seemed so slow she checked to see if her watch was working. Pineo finally returned just before 5:30.

"He's agreed to pay you fifteen thousand in cash. He made some phone calls and he'll give you the money at ten tomorrow morning." Pineo lied; he knew the cash was already in the church safe, but it would be too suspicious to pay her on such short notice. No clergyman just happened to keep fifteen thousand dollars in cash at a church office.

Pineo could see that she was relieved. "I want you to phone me at the office when you finish here in the morning," he instructed. "If you get the money, just say `my daughter is feeling good today,' but if there's a hitch, say `I need you to handle a complaint'."

"No," she said, "you must come with me," and he knew he had no choice and agreed.

"God bless you," she said, and in his heart, he knew he'd need that too.

CHAPTER SIX

Freedom of the Press

"Freedom of the press is a great theory, but in reality, it best serves the owners, editors, and the good old boys in the halls of power."

- Attributed to an ACLU attorney when Richard Jewell, an innocent man accused, was pilloried by the press during the investigation of the bombing at the Olympic games in Atlanta, Georgia.

Noel Bear, as a new officer, was assigned to sleepy old Willow Street for the roadblock checkpoint because traffic was minimal there. It was a quiet, postcard-like residential street where 1930s-style Dutch Colonial houses were evenly spaced on large lots and separated from the river only by a litter-strewn greenbelt and a row of mature, messy willow trees. At the north end of Willow, just at the right turn onto Wade Avenue, there was an opening in the trees. It allowed anyone who knew the city streets to cross the green strip to a dirt road along the river and then escape into the countryside, without the hassle of city traffic.

There had been a major drug robbery. Two armed men, dressed in coveralls and wearing masks, had entered the Walgreen distribution warehouse on Fifteenth Street just before eight that morning and efficiently stripped the controlled drug section of multiple thousands of bottled anti-anxiety pills known as mellowers by street users. The Walgreen company's cursory inventory check revealed more than fifty thousand missing pills: among them alprazolam (Xanax), chlorazepate (Tranxene), chiordiazepoxide (Corax, Librium, Murcil Novopoxide, Tenax), and an entire lot of fluoxetine (Prozac) – a favored and expensive anti-depressant medication. The street value of the drugs, according to the DEA evaluation chart, was approximately two hundred and fifty thousand dollars, or about five bucks a pill retail on the street.

The checkpoint on Willow Street was a boring, one-man detail with no other officer to talk to and no traffic except for one car driven by an old lady, which had turned into a driveway down the street about thirty minutes earlier. Bear paced back and forth behind the patrol car, which he had parked at an angle, with the blue and red roof lights flashing to notify an approaching car that it had arrived upon a checkpoint.

Finally, Bear noticed a car nearing him slowly from the far end of the street. He moved into the open lane but remained close enough to the cruiser to escape behind it if the car tried to hit him or run the stop.

The approaching vehicle was an old Ford, a real clunker, which slowed and then stopped nearby, but still at a respectable distance from his position. Bear edged forward cautiously to check the occupants, and then recognized Detective Sergeant Hunter Stent behind the wheel. As he moved even closer, he could see Stent's omnipresent partner, Inspector Frank Nichols in the shotgun seat. He did not recognize the car as one of the undercover PD drug section vehicles because the department used an assortment of seedy looking civilian cars.

"Which is it?" Stent asked, "an exciting one-man checkpoint for drugstore robbers or a watch for an old lady bootlegger using the cow path?"

Bear smiled. It was really his first direct conversation with the two drug officers because drug section people operated separately and remained aloof. They were generally considered weird in both appearance and manner.

"An exciting rookie assignment," answered Bear, "no cars and nobody to talk to. It looks like rain, and I have to stay outside the car in case the patrol supervisor shows up."

Nichols chimed in, "All the good boring assignments like school intersections and road construction traffic sites for the new guy, right?"

Bear was pleasantly surprised that they were friendly, yet he was uncomfortable because he knew that Sergeant Shirley Reading had been informed, admittedly by a street punk, that the two drug officers had tried to push the kid into dealing at the street level for them.

Bear sized them up. Nichols was about five-ten, slightly overweight, forty-seven years old, with rounding shoulders that suggested an out of condition body, and a saggy jowl face, salt and peppered with the stubble of yesterday's beard. Although he had a fair police arrest record, he was sort of a social leper because of his wife, unkindly but accurately called Fucking Fay. She was a plump, frumpy, artificial blonde who reportedly maintained an open legs policy once she had a drink. It was openly gossiped that her promiscuity prevailed all the time but especially when she'd been drinking. She had once humped the leg of numerous officers on the dance floor, including the chief's, at a department Christmas party while dancing, and none of the wives were amused. Worse, at the next year's party, she was accidentally discovered in a broom closet doing a standing hump, a knee-knocker, with the wily old property clerk. It was after that the chief announced, at the insistence of his wife, there would be no more Christmas parties. From then on, all personnel received a card and a five-dollar Dunkin' Donuts gift certificate from the chief.

Forty-two year-old Hunter Stent, in contrast to Nichols, was a shorter man with oversized feet, which pointed outwards when he walked. He closely resembled the silent movie star Charlie Chaplin, including the funny little mustache. His attire and sloppy sartorial appearance fostered his nickname, the Little Tramp, based on Chaplin's famous movie. Stent was certainly Nichols' alter ego, and wherever one went, off duty or on, the other was sure to be close by. If most longtime police partners seem as close married couples, these two were like Siamese twins.

Stent passed Bear the morning paper, the *Daily Bugle,* out the car window. "Take the paper. Keep it folded, and lay it on the passenger side fender, and you can read to kill the boredom. Keep your eyes peeled for the supervisor, but at the distance from here down to the corner, the hood of your car will hide the paper anyway."

Bear was amused. "Pretty cool. Thanks for the tip."

Nichols spoke. "An old cop trick. We gotta go. We're interviewing a guy in the country. We only came this way to avoid the traffic and the hassle of the road blocks."

Bear retreated behind his car as they left and placed the folded paper on the fender. The headline was exactly what the state police had feared to see in the death of the undercover officer working at the PD as a janitor. The *Daily Bugle* reporter, Steven Jobb, had devoted a quarter of the page to the death under the headline: "Train Death a Mystery."

As Bear opened the paper, he noted that the sex murder of the nurse Kathryn Fraser had rated only a small column on page three. Bear dialed Lieutenant Folker's direct line on his cell phone.

Folker had seen the story and expressed his concern. "This guy Jobb is really trying to create a Pulitzer Prize story, and all he's going to do is stir up interest that will damage an investigation. Can you get Dr. Donald or Dr. Foley to butter Jobb up a bit, perhaps do an interview and gently switch his interest to the Fraser girl's murder?"

Bear was skeptical. "I'll try but both of them know Jobb as having no hemorrhoids: he's a perfect asshole."

"Too bad," Folker said. "That should be an additional incentive to fool him ."

Bear clicked off, then dialed Foley's office. "I'm at a road block. Did you see the *Bugle*?"

"Yes," replied Foley. "The *Daily Blow*, and I can just imagine Kirk Donald bouncing off the walls."

Bear decided to get right to the shittie request. "Folker wants you two to divert this guy's attention to the Fraser killing: to give him something to get him off the train death."

"I'll try," answered Foley, "but Kirk's not an easy lay. He despises the press."

Bear hardly let him finish. "Look at it this way. It will be fun to fuck Jobb over; it'll help keep him off the train story; and more important, it might assist the Fraser investigation by focusing attention on it."

Hoss Foley looked at the news article again after Bear hung up. The prose contained no real news, only speculation and Jobb's own opinions. It was clear sensationalism, which concluded that a poor man had died on the tracks and hinted that no one really cared about it. Foley cursed softly and called Jobb a professional "agin-it", a person who invented controversy in an attempt to achieve fame.

Foley decided to visit Kirk, expecting his old friend to be in a rage about the poorly written news article. He was not disappointed. Kirk sat at his desk, a mug of steaming coffee resting beside him and the newspaper spread before him. His usual low-key manner was absent, and his anger was revealed by his tone as he spurted adjectives of derision about papers, and about reporters being liars.

"Jobb," he roared, "is dangerous. He's like chlamydia: he causes a lot of damage before people even realize the disease is present."

Hoss Foley had suffered from Jobb's vengeful nature himself. Instead of trying to placate Kirk, he decided to throw gas on the raging fire of his friend's anger. "Jobb said you didn't return his call, and he implies the autopsy is slow because the victim was only a janitor. That's a direct poke at you."

Sharon Marshall, who had silently observed without commenting, came to life on hearing that Jobb claimed no one had returned his call. "He called at six last night and we close at four-thirty, at least in theory, and he knows that. He didn't want to talk to Dr. Donald; he wanted to pretend there was no response in order to bolster his lies."

Foley decided to ease into the requested interview. "Bear called a little while ago. The state police saw the article too. Lieutenant Folker apparently would like this guy cooled on the train story and wondered if we'd play along." Foley paused, "Basically, it's your ball of wax as ME, so I told him it would be up to you, but I'd like to stick it to Jobb."

Kirk had known Foley too long to be conned. "I know, gawddamn well you already agreed to something, so let me in on what you signed me up for."

"Well," replied Foley putting on his best country-boy act of false humility, "I thought you might want to return Jobb's call and invite him over here to see a real body and find out how an autopsy works."

Sharon exchanged glances with Foley. Kirk saw them. "OK, I get the message. Call that asshole and ask him over for a tour, but you better call the guy from the *Chronicle* too because they'll be pissed off if we give Jobb an exclusive."

"Let's do Jobb first," Sharon said. "I'll set the second paper up for later today. What about me taking a picture or two?"

"Be my guest," said Kirk and took a sip of his coffee. "But Jobb got one thing right. The body sure is a mess, and Fraser is even worse in terms of being a stomach turner."

Foley agreed, "I think a peek at Fraser would make an impression on most folks."

Sharon dialed the *Daily Bugle*. To her surprise she not only got Jobb on the phone, but when she told him she was returning his call from the day before, he was suddenly quite nice. She pretended she had not seen that morning's paper. Her second surprise was when he responded hungrily to her invitation and said that he would be over within thirty minutes. She hung up.

"Mr. Jobb is on his way. We better be ready because I get the impression he's only so eager cause he thinks we're stupid."

Steven Jobb had asked many times, nagged even, to be allowed in the morgue and to interview Dr. Kirk Donald, and now that he had the chance, he rushed over. He arrived looking disheveled, and his appearance reminded Kirk of when he came home on leave after basic training during the Vietnam War to see all the protesters dressed in used clothing and wearing their hair longer than his mother's. One of those young people had spit on him back then, just because he wore a uniform. He would have retaliated, but his father asked him not to. Jobb brought that painful memory flooding back.

Jobb's hair was long, unkempt, and oily and frequently fell across his eyes. He habitually brushed it out of his eyes, in a losing battle. His pants were shiny, but his shoes were not. He wore an old plaid lumberjack work shirt, but his hands looked soft like real work would damage them. It was difficult not to prejudge him because of the way he looked and because of what he wrote. It bothered Kirk that his own lifelong habit of treating everybody equally was challenged by this man's appearance.

Jobb shifted the notebook he carried into his left hand and accepted Kirk's offer to shake with a firm grip.

"Mr. Jobb," Kirk began in his usual soft voice, which forced most people to strain to hear what he had to say, "this is Ms. Marshall, my assistant, and Dr. Foley; I'm sure you know of him. You can take notes as we tour, and you can ask questions, and Ms. Marshall may get a suitable photo on her Polaroid that you can use, but I'm not sure we'll be able to answer all your questions because these are official autopsies." Jobb nodded and Kirk proceeded.

"Dr. Foley is also an attorney, and if he thinks it inappropriate to answer any question, he'll tell us."

"OK," Jobb agreed.

"Now," Kirk asked, "how do you wish to proceed?"

"Q and A first," Jobb replied. "How would you classify Gates' death by the train?"

"Accidental death by misadventure. There was a strong presence of alcohol."

Jobb scribbled on his notepad. "Why has it taken so long to reach that opinion?"

Foley watched for any sign of emotion on Kirk's face but saw none.

"I think we should proceed to the storage facility in the autopsy lab," Kirk said and avoided answering Jobb's question.

They walked into the sterile, stainless steel atmosphere of the room; the sudden smell of antiseptic and chemicals made breathing uncomfortable. Jobb continued his questioning.

"Is the train driver at fault? Was the train traveling at the proper speed?"

Kirk was leery of such queries and usually considered that subject one for the police. "I only have a verbal opinion from the railroad police on that. They say the driver's conduct was proper and the speed of the train slower than allowed."

Jobb continued, "What about the alcohol level?"

Kirk ignored the question. "Step over here," he instructed Jobb and moved to the stainless steel doors of the refrigerated body lockers. Foley looked at Jobb while Sharon Marshall fidgeted with the Polaroid camera.

"Mr. Jobb, this is not a pretty sight. I don't want to suggest you can't look, but believe me, it is very distressing," Foley cautioned. The warning came across as sincere and not at all like a put-down, which is what both Kirk and Sharon thought Foley intended.

"It's fine," Jobb replied. "I've seen a lot of bad stuff as a reporter."

Sharon asked Foley and Jobb to stand to the left of Dr. Donald so that she could take the photo when the body drawer was pulled out. Without more discussion, Kirk opened the door, grasped the handle, and slid the drawer holding the body mangled by the train out of the wall. As the cover was removed, the body and the detached head, with one eye half open like the victim was peeking at them or perhaps sighting a rifle, created an eerie aura and an emotional jolt. The face was ashen, tinged with a bluish tone, and the mouth was tightly drawn back into a cruel expression, partially open with some teeth showing in what looked like a grimace of anger.

"The train," said Kirk, "missed the head. The torso, however, was split up the center from his groin to his neck. The legs were also not struck by the train's wheels." Jobb stared, his eyes wide open.

The torso was a hamburger-like mess, a mixture of flesh, bone, organs, feces and greenish stomach contents. The smell, despite the cold storage, was putrid beyond description. There was a plastic bag, almost like a sandwich bag, containing one lump of flesh taped to the severed right leg near the hip. It was labeled simply: testicle; the only part of the genitals recovered, according to Foley, who had found it stuck to the side of the train wheel. The severed legs were relatively unscathed and looked rather like those of a store window mannequin awaiting trousers. They had an offbeat, pasty-beige color tinged with a bluish hint, typical of severed limbs.

"You see, Mr. Jobb," Kirk said in a flat voice, as if he was giving an autopsy lecture, "it is difficult to rush an autopsy in some violent deaths." He fixed his eyes on Jobb, who by this time, was very quiet. His trance-like stare ended only when Sharon snapped the picture.

"Next," Kirk droned, "step over here please to locker thirty-one where we have the remains of the Fraser girl. The body is mutilated and burned with gasoline, but both the cause of death and sexual penetration were obvious because the fire did not destroy all the evidence." He then opened the door, rolled out the drawer, and removed the cover.

The body lay like a blistered, overcooked piece of fat pork left forgotten on a barbecue. The breasts, severed in jagged cuts just behind the nipples, gaped like huge burnt fat bubbles. The face was cooked tight to the facial bones like a baked Halloween horror mask, and the scalp was black and almost completely destroyed, the hair burned away by the intense, gas-fed heat.

Jobb, whose face now was the same pasty color as the severed head he had seen in the first drawer, suddenly power-puked a stream of sour stomach contents down toward the floor, splashing the pant legs of both Kirk Donald and Horace Foley. At the same instant, more by instinct than design, Sharon pressed the button and the flash of the Polaroid captured God only knew what until it developed. Jobb then sagged downward in a dead faint but was saved by Foley who managed to grab him and drag him purposely through his own rancid vomit.

Steven Jobb slowly wakened, his nostrils filled with the smell of his own sour stomach contents, coupled with the chemical odor of the lab. He was laid out on the stainless steel autopsy slab, where Foley and Kirk had placed him after his untimely faint. He heard voices and managed to raise his swirling head a few inches. He could see Foley and Marshall standing near his feet, examining a Polaroid picture. Dizziness forced him to lay back. He heard the mellow voice of Kirk Donald.

"Mr. Jobb, do you want me to call your office and have them come and get you?"

"Jesus, no," moaned Jobb. "I certainly don't want that."

"OK," said Kirk, "rest here until you feel better, and then I suggest you take two aspirins and a bottle of Pepsi." Kirk then walked towards his office with Marshall and Foley following, leaving Jobb where he had wanted to be for so long: in the morgue.

CHAPTER SEVEN

The System

"With justice for all, (sometimes)."

- Redhorse (February 1998) speaking about the case of Leonard Pelletier, a man wrongfully convicted of murder, to the law students at the New England School of Law, Boston.

Detective Sergeant Jack Baptist punched in the direct line number of Sergeant Shirley Reading and when she answered, he said only, "Coffee."

He walked through the maze of desks in the investigation section and out the back door to the parking lot. He waited near his unmarked police car. As she approached, he noticed she was flushed, her cheeks rouge red, except she didn't wear any.

"Are you upset?" he asked with concern.

"No, no," she replied. "It's stupid, but when I wonder when I meet you what kind of gossip it generates."

"Who cares? We're both single and as long as they know we're dating, it won't seem odd that we go for coffee. The union agreement with the city allows coffee breaks."

That amused her because he was union born and bred, his father a steelworker and union officer. "You're a Calvinist at heart," she teased.

He winced, "Long as you don't call me Baptist because the Baptists are prudes. Know why Baptists don't screw standing up?"

"Go ahead; give me the squad room groaner of the day."

"Cause someone might think they're dancing."

"Oh barf!" she said, "that's not even a groaner."

They drove the five blocks to Dunkin' Donuts and went to the drive through window. They ordered two black coffees and parked in the side lot, back against the fence in plain view, yet private for conversation.

Jack started, "You asked me to poke around about the kid Donald Frank who Brown and those two other bozos busted. Well, he checks out pretty well, but a schoolteacher told me of a strange incident involving him at school. Another boy reported that Frank tried to sell him a Valium capsule for five bucks at a school dance. Young Frank denied it, but the school rules call for a disciplinary hearing on drug accusations. Then the poop hit the fan. Frank's father Harold, who owns a family shoe store and is a community volunteer, and his wife Lucy are both active in the ACLU. When the hearing was held, they showed up with Dale Dunlop, the trial lawyer, to defend the kid."

Shirley was impressed. "Geeze, bringing Dunlop to a school hearing is like taking a lion to a cat fight."

"It gets better," Jack replied. "Dunlop not only punched holes in the other kid's accusations, he gently and completely tied the kid up in his own tongue. It was pretty obvious his claim was false and finally the other kid admitted he had lied about Frank because he was threatened into doing it."

Shirley was puzzled. "But who would do that, and why?" Was it some petty school jealousy or did it involve a girlfriend or what?"

"Not likely. This kid was scared; said that someone that he refused to name threatened to castrate him and admitted at the hearing that they also forced him to sell pills. Now the plot thickens. Donald Frank told the hearing someone tried to force him into selling pills and when he refused, they informed him he'd be very sorry. But neither boy would name names; they were very scared. Next, Dunlop informs the hearing that the law provides that if a person's life is threatened to force them to commit an offense, the duress is a legal excuse, and, therefore, neither boy was guilty of the offense. Dunlop recommended that the school call in the police, but both boys refused to talk to the drug officers, and so the school decided the issue would be dropped."

"Wait a minute," Shirley interrupted. "What's all this got to do with the arrest in the Wendy's parking lot?"

"Likely nothing; it could be just a coincidence, but the fact is, it happened after the school hearing. It almost seems like lightening striking the same guy twice."

Shirley didn't buy that. "I'll grant you the arrest was stupid and ill-conceived, but I can't believe anyone would be stupid enough to try and scare a kid into keeping quiet by doing that in a public place, in front of multiple witnesses. Besides, why would they call Major Brown in; that's strange."

Baptist also had an opinion on that. "I can understand that they'd call Brown if they were in over their heads, and it started to look like a riot, but here's the crunch. The drunk and disorderly guy who started all this was not booked, and the incident is not logged in the blotter or incident book, nor does it appear in the radio log, and now nobody knows who he was."

"Oh boy," Shirley said. "Then it seems Donald Frank was arrested for criticizing an arrest which never took place. Probable cause is pretty flimsy when you try to make that out more than poor police judgment."

"Yeah," Jack agreed. "I suppose I'm looking for funny stuff ever since you told me about the street moke claiming Nichols and Stent were peddling pills."

When Reading arrived back at her desk, the pink telephone message slip confirmed her premonition that the Frank arrest would be a public relations disaster. The slip showed a call from Joanne MacDonald, a reporter from the *Chronicle*, and in the space for comments, the secretary had printed *re: the Donald Frank arrest.*

Reading called Major Brown first. His response, curt and condescending, revealed that he either did not grasp the potential of the arrest to create a controversy, or else he believed it was just business as usual, and he'd just plough through it.

"We're handing the case as we would any other incident where there is a potential interference with police function. The case comes up in magistrate's court on Monday morning."

Shirley tried to get his attention by suggesting he might want to return Joanne MacDonald's call. It did not work.

"No, you do it," he said "It's a run-of-the-mill arrest, and you should tell her that. I'm not talking to her."

Joanne MacDonald had been a writer at the *Chronicle* for almost ten years. Her calls were always troublesome because her tone and questions gave the impression she was an attorney doing a cross-examination. Even if it was just her manner and not her intention, her questions usually suggested that the last answer given was a lie. MacDonald lived with Steven Jobb, who worked for the competing *Bugle,* and their combined opinions of themselves, according to experienced cops, made Muhammad Ali look modest. Jack Baptist had warned Shirley. He said, "the only difference between a hooker and the press is that a hooker's honest, but they both get paid to fuck you."

Reading dialed the number for the paper. The secretary who answered the call, upon hearing who was calling, directed the call to editor Allan Tobin. He was icky-sweet and told Reading that she was on his speaker phone and that Joanne MacDonald and the paper's lawyer, Jane Parrish, were both present discussing the Donald Frank matter.

Reading knew at once that the call was a trap. If she had not returned the call, the *Chronicle* would have announced the lack of response and made the department look bad. Once she returned the call, the questions would undoubtedly be the usual, double-edged kind, such as, "Are you still masturbating?"

Shirley bit her lip and expected the worst but resolved to use the cops' best method of avoiding a blind-side lie.

"Sergeant Reading," Tobin said, "what's the story on this young Jewish kid being arrested?"

Shirley hearing the word Jewish knew at once that their theme was going to be the persecution of a minority, and sadly the public would have every reason to believe it.

"I know of an arrest," she replied, "but I'm on something else and the enforcement division handled it."

Jane Parrish's patronizing tone was heard next. She had been at law school with Shirley, but they had hardly known each other and had had no contact since the bar exam, which they both passed. Now, she was all gushy and spoke to Reading in familiar tones, using her first name after all but ignoring her at law school and in all the years since.

"Shirley," she said sweetly, "this arrest is generating a lot of attention and to avoid media speculation I thought the department might want to present their version before the media present it as it looks."

Reading made no knee-jerk response and answered with coolness and control. "I'm sure, Miss Parrish," and she emphasized the Miss, "that as an attorney you can explain to those lay people at the paper that it would be improper for me to discuss the charges, even if I knew the facts, which I don't."

Parrish was not deterred. "Isn't it unusual that your juvenile section is not handing the case of a juvenile?"

Shirley realized Parrish and the paper would try and put their own spin on any answer she gave. "Not at all. We're pretty thin here because of budget restrictions, and like the Marine Corps, we all improvise and cover each other's duties when called upon." Her gung-ho response would be difficult for the paper to twist to suit its own agenda.

The paper's editor Allan Tobin was no fool either. He must have known the call would accomplish nothing because he suddenly became polite, almost respectful. "Thank you, Sergeant, for returning our call. Perhaps Joanne will be phoning you again."

The evening edition of the *Chronicle* reached the street about five o'clock p.m. Jack Baptist appeared at Reading's desk carrying the paper and looking grumpy. He said, "Well, they put the lies on the lower half of the front page and, innuendo and speculation notwithstanding, it's pretty hard to argue with them. Brown and those two did cause all this with poor judgment."

Shirley unfolded the paper. The title was also hard to disclaim. "Arrest Civil Rights Issue?" The article was littered with phrases like, "Jewish youth arrested" and "innocent onlooker." There was questioning about the identity of the drunk who caused the incident and why he hadn't been arrested. "Why Donald Frank?" the paper asked, and used provocative buzz words like First Amendment.

The ball breaker for the PD, and those three police officers, was the report that attorneys Dale Dunlop and Ray Wortman would represent the Frank family. Dunlop's presence spelled a tough fight; he had a spotless defense record and was a nationally respected attorney. Wortman was a litigation expert and his involvement pointed to lawsuit for the PD.

Reading was not given to using the rough adjectives that are common in most stress-ridden law enforcement organizations; she did not try to be one of the boys, yet she was respected. However the arrest, the apparent lack of cause, and the media attention would cast the whole department in a bad light and she responded with anger. "That asshole Brown dug a hole with his temper that may cause us all grief," she said. And events at the Courthouse on the following Monday proved Sergeant Reading's forecast accurate.

Magistrate's court after a weekend was a typical Monday morning zoo. The court was filled with DUIs, drunks, domestics beefs, petty shoplifters and an assortment of the socially disadvantaged whose unwashed existence added a musty and unsubtle aroma to the ambiance of Magistrate Harold "Goat" Chase's court. In harmony with the court's denizens, Crowell "Stinky" Roscoe, full-time jailer, part-time deputy, and magistrate's court bailiff, dressed in an old, obviously dirty, baggy uniform, and clearly reveled in his glory as he called the name of each accused to be tried by Chase.

The cases, by sheer necessity of numbers, were cranked through and usually plea bargained, lest the impasse of an actual trial result in an unmanageable backup. If it appeared that some accused person might impede the flow, Chase warned them to take a five-minute recess with the prosecutor, which usually led to an immediate plea bargain. Accused people received about as much due process in Chase's court as sheepherders tried in a saloon by a cowboy jury for stealing horses.

At eleven a.m., the whisky-roughened voice of Crowell Roscoe called out the name, "Donald Frank, charged with public mischief under city by-law thirty-two, section B, subsection twelve, to wit verbal abuse of a police officer in the performance of his duty, blah ... blah ... blah." Chase perked up. He read the papers like everyone else, so he knew this was going to be a hot one. The presence of the media, including TV reporters, in the smelly courtroom would have alerted him even if he hadn't read the news.

"Is Mr. Frank present?" Chase asked. When no one stepped forward, Chase scanned the room, looking like a chicken hawk, his pointy nose trying to locate the victim. Then there was rustling and a faint stir among those assembled as attorney Dale Dunlop stood and announced himself.

"I represent the Frank family and the accused. Donald Frank is in the hospital, and I have his medical excuse from the attending physician stating that the reasons for his absence are physical and mental trauma. That is a result of rape and abuse suffered while incarcerated at the city jail due to an arrest by police officers Lester Brown, Thomas Kierans, and Gregory Clarke."

Dunlop did not pause and Chase couldn't seem to interrupt or stop him as the attorney's clear voice dominated the courtroom.

"We enter a plea of not guilty to the charge."

Chase was now visibly distressed. "Mr. Dunlop, have you and the prosecutor met to discuss this case?"

Dunlop was polite and succinct. "Your honor, I have not met with Mr. MacAdam, and if you mean are we willing to entertain a plea bargain, the answer is no. We wish to go to trial, and we feel the matter will take at least a week as we have forty-two witnesses to call." He paused. "So far."

Chase gave it another try. "Mr. Dunlop, this sounds like a very minor incident, a small fine upon conviction, and I wonder if there isn't room for a compromise here?"

David MacAdam sat at the prosecution's table in silence, knowing the issue was laced with legal land mines, and also realizing there would be no plea bargain, as he had previously tried to reach Dunlop all week. Finally, a clerk in Dunlop's office had returned those calls only to ask for a potential trial schedule. MacAdam was now on the spot. Chase had put the ball in his court.

MacAdam was a slight six-footer with greasy hair and a hint of an impediment in his speech. He was a legal drone who was best known for his vindictive and turgid nature.

"A minute, Your Honor," he said and walked over to Major Brown where a quiet but obviously strained whispered conversation took place before Brown stood and left the courtroom. MacAdam returned to the prosecution's table.

"Your Honor, the prosecution moves to dismiss the charge against Donald Frank."

"Dismissed!" Chase roared. "Next case."

Officers' Kierans and Clarke were not as quick to leave the courtroom as Major Brown. TV anchor Arthur Johnson had stuck a camera in their faces, and unfortunately for the PD, the microphone picked up Kierans as he told Johnson to fuck off.

Shirley Reading, who had attended as an observer, managed to depart and headed down the wide courthouse steps unfettered by the media. She sighted Noel Bear who, as junior officer, had been assigned to keep the traffic moving in front of the building. As Shirley approached Bear, she paused to hear Dale Dunlop's report to the press.

"My clients are considering suing the police officers, the city, the jailer, and the police department. The actions and conduct of all concerned have caused immeasurable damage and mental suffering to my client Donald Frank. But for those actions and misconduct, the damage would not have occurred. I should mention that the actions of those officials go beyond their written code of conduct and are certainly not discretionary but forbidden acts and conduct."

Shirley smiled. As an attorney she knew what Dunlop was really saying. She was aware that, in some states, suing any government at any level was very difficult because the court would examine the conduct of the official challenged to see if the act was discretionary.

Dunlop was serving notice that this case looked like it was headed for federal court where he could prevent it from being heard by a politically appointed good-old boy judge.

At curbside, she joined Bear as he gave a taxi driver "what for" because he had double-parked.

"I'll wait by the car," she told him. "I want to talk." Shirley trusted Bear because he was a new man, so no stain of corruption had reached the idealistic young officer yet. He trusted her because she had warned him about the drug officers. He had observed them enough to report the issue to the state police, mainly because he did not know who else was tainted.

Bear decided to hint at a few of his suspicions to her but did not reveal that he had picked them from the dead trooper's reports or that he was undercover. When he joined Shirley, he first let her vent as they sat in his police car.

She ranted about the Frank matter. She was clearly a conscientious officer who played by the rules. She also relayed Sergeant Baptist's theory that Kierans and Clarke, and maybe Major Brown, were connected to Nichols and Stent.

Bear listened without interrupting her. Finally it was his turn. "Let's pretend, purely for speculation, an absolutely hypothetical scenario. Suppose there were four or five dirty cops in our department, and maybe they've come to the conclusion that they're being watched or are under surveillance. The next logical questions for them are who and why. Possibly in building a distribution network for their drugs among the street punks or the school kids, the tainted cops run into one kid like Donald Frank who won't co-operate. Right after he refuses, something causes them to believe they're being watched. Wouldn't it be natural for them to blame the young guy and so try to get him into a mess to ruin his credibility?"

Shirley listened with interest. "Your theory, or speculation, is about as wild as Baptist's suspicions, but yours at least make sense, even though I don't buy it. Who would be stupid enough to pull an asinine arrest in front of all those people at McDonald's just to get a kid in trouble?"

"OK," replied Bear, "here's a flash for you. I know Dunlop because we hunt together. He told me that after Frank was put in Major Brown's personal car, and before he was searched at the jail, he found drugs in his coat pocket. Somebody who was in on the arrest or perhaps at the school dance planted them."

Reading was not convinced. "Wait a minute. Officers always search an arrested person for weapons, so why didn't they search Frank in the parking lot?"

Noel Bear held up his hand. "They did. Dunlop asked each of his witnesses from the scene and all agreed the two cops did a search on Frank and so did Brown before they put him in the car. Brown was the last person to touch him before shoving him into the back seat."

Shirley still wondered, "So they either missed the pills or ..."

Bear interrupted, "Or they wanted someone else to find them, namely Roscoe at the jail. All new prisoners are thoroughly searched before being placed in with the other prisoners. It would have been more difficult for the kid to deny the pills if a third party found them."

Shirley was slowly changing her mind, but some doubts lingered. She speculated out loud, "The idea would be that young Frank was cleared of selling pills at school but once drugs were found on him at the jail, he'd be so discredited that nobody would take any claim he made seriously about cops trying to get him to distribute pills." She paused in the argument with herself, debating both sides of the issue, as she had learned to do in law school. "Maybe the pills did belong to Frank," she said and looked smugly at Bear.

"Not likely," Bear replied. "He discovered them because he noticed that Kierans stuck his hand in his pocket during the scuffle. He ditched them by kicking them under the front seat of Brown's civilian car before they got to the jail. And Dunlop later made Frank take a lie detector test, and he passed with flying colors, so that's the truth."

Shirley was almost completely convinced, then she smiled, "Hold on, wise guy. How did the cops know Donald Frank would be at Wendy's that night?"

"Simple question: simple answer. His Uncle Aubrey Frank owns the restaurant and young Donald goes there with a couple of pals in tow for a free treat every week after the school dances. Dozens of people would know that."

Shirley was fascinated by Bear's theory. "Can I try this hypothesis out on Baptist, if I don't tell him where I got it?"

Bear looked doubtful, "How well do you know him?"

"We're engaged," she said, "and if that's a Biblical question, the answer is very well; if it's an ethical question, more so!"

Bear smiled, shook his head, and said, "That's more information than I need."

CHAPTER EIGHT

Seeking Facts

"Learn, compare, collect the facts."
- Pavlov (1936)

Dr. Foley scrawled his usual unreadable signature at the bottom of the last page of the two reports and added his credentials: MD, PhD, and JD. The first was the extensive toxicology report on the body of undercover Trooper Mike McCurdy aka Gates for the state police. The second was a well-crafted fake that had been prepared at the request of the state police to be given to the city police department so that the killer would not be alerted that the authorities were wise to the murder. The fake one stated that the cause of death was accidental misadventure, an alcohol-related death by train. It gave the victim's name as Harvey Gates.

Foley phoned Kirk at the other end of the complex. When he had to wait while Sharon connected him, he became annoyed and tapped the table impatiently with his long powerful fingers. Finally, Kirk's soft voice, which Foley called the purr of a tiger, answered, "What's up, Hoss? And in your case, I know it's nothing below the belt."

Foley did not let the remark pass. "Actually, Dr. Donald, the condition I have is a state of perpetual priapism, and I am in constant demand by many women, and my social calendar is very full. And why does it take you bastards so long to answer the phone?"

Kirk replied, "You're dick daffy, Old Man, and why don't you just walk down here instead of phoning, you lazy old fucker. It's not that big of a building."

Foley added, "Do you know what has just been described in the Medical Journal as the ultimate sexual rejection?"

Kirk Donald knew he would get the answer whether he wanted it or not. "No, I must have missed that article."

Foley continued, "The ultimate sexual rejection is: you're playing with yourself and your hand goes to sleep."

Kirk concealed his laugh with a weak guffaw, "I'll use that as my own and you'll get no credit unless it flops."

Foley interrupted, "I finished the toxicology on McCurdy, and as you figured, there was an extract there, which I think was from the castor bean, but we'll need the state lab to identify it for certain. They have all the toys to prove my informed guess for court with the spectrometer, chromatograph, and such to prove my analysis."

Kirk smiled. "Or disprove it," he said, "but why would anyone go to the trouble of using such an old-fashioned, cumbersome poison?"

Foley fumbled through a thick file of papers. "Listen to me," he said. "I have before me a british medical journal article from years ago. The Soviets killed a Czech defector in London by stabbing him in the calf of the leg with an umbrella point holding a tiny amount of the core extract from the castor bean. British MI5 were suspicious, but the hospital people were mystified for a long time, before a shrewd old university medical professor identified it. It is very difficult to detect and any ordinary lab tech would never think of it".

Kirk replied, "Does that mean you are extraordinary? And what about alcohol in the blood stream?"

Foley answered,"Yes, I'm quite extraordinary, and yes, there's some alcohol in the contents of the stomach, but it's not processed, so it was likely funneled down his throat after he was dead. His blood alcohol level was almost nil, so he was not drunk. It's like you guessed: someone wanted us to believe he was drunk to create the idea that he stumbled onto the tracks and was killed. His clothes likely had more booze on them than he had in his body."

Kirk pondered the reply, "How could anyone be that stupid, especially if the killer was a police officer. How could he possibly believe that you'd buy the accident theory and not do a toxicology?"

"Not so stupid based on the old days," Foley replied. "And I'm not talking that long ago. It was only about a dozen years ago that the lack of trained personnel and tight budgets meant there had to be suspicious circumstances to spend much time on a body. If the death looked like an accident, we had little choice but to label it as such. For instance, I've looked back at dozens of ancient accidental death rulings, and they're riddled with questions. We certainly can't pursue the old ones now because it's tough enough to handle today's volume, without raking up the old shit. In a case where a train ran over a guy who smelled like booze, it would not likely have received too much attention. It would have been labeled accidental death – alcohol related. That's exactly what we put in the false report to the police department, so they'll think we were fooled."

"Granted," agreed Kirk, "but if a crooked cop killed McCurdy, and logic and motive advance that theory, surely he'd know a wily old fox like you would be suspicious?"

Hoss was silent for what seemed like ages as he considered Kirk's question about the murder. "Maybe, maybe not. In fact, I wonder if I'm sharp enough sometimes. What if I hadn't known that the dead man was a trooper, or if you hadn't found the broken needle in his neck? Would I have just been lazy or lax and signed off on the appearance?"

"Bullshit," Kirk snapped. "You didn't sign off, and you're naturally inquisitive, nosy even."

Foley was pensive, troubled, thinking about what he might not have done. "I hope you're right, but this is a good lesson. We shouldn't ever accept what is too obvious, for what is apparent is not always true."

Kirk asked, "What about the swabs I sent you from the Fraser girl's body?"

"Yeah," Foley replied. "Some good news there. The Kleenex found at the scene wasn't used on a nose; it was stained with fluid, but it probably is a chemical found on condoms, a spermacide. We didn't find the rubber, but he dropped the tissue he used when he took off the condom. There are remote traces of semen, but I'm afraid it's contaminated by the spermacide."

Kirk still thought the sex was consensual. "I figure the killer's a whacko, maybe latent most of the time but a dangerous fruitcake. He likely made a date with her, and after he laid her, he went nuts over guilt, or because he was almost smothered when he was a kid in a big pair of some female relative's breasts."

Foley considered the idea, "You mean, like he was mentally killing his kinky old aunt who used to play with his dick when he was ten, while holding his head between her hooters?"

Kirk screwed his face up, as he asked, "What about DNA? Do you think you got enough from the swab or the Kleenix to do a positive ID on a suspect for comparison?"

Foley replied, "As I said, there's some fluid and the big labs can now get a lot from a little, but contamination kills proof, just like the defense claimed in the O. J. Simpson case."

Kirk responded with his usual cynical approach, playing devil's advocate, "That sounds remote. I just read an old case, *New York v. Castro,* where the lawyer and experts confused a stupid judge into ruling the DNA evidence was inadmissible because of alleged contamination of the semen. And, as you say in the *Simpson* case, Johnnie Cochrane and Barry Scheck attacked the lab, claiming contamination of the samples. So what I have to worry about is two key points. First, there is no suspect to compare the results with, and second, if and when there is a suspect, will some fuckin' silver-tongued defense attorney convince the judge that shit is peanut butter and rule it inadmissible?"

Foley replied, "That's always possible, but the body was in the immediate area, and I just discovered a trace of the same chemical from the condom on the swab you did inside her, so the prosecution can prove linkage, which will be difficult to refute. By the way, Noel Bear just arrived and we're coming over for coffee."

Sharon Marshall poured the remainder of the stale, re-heated residue of the morning coffee into three mugs. It smelled like the boiled powder found in army field rations according to Foley.

Kirk refuted the comparison, "Army coffee wasn't so bad; GIs only thought it was because they believed it was laced with saltpeter."

Foley agreed, "My wife believes that, but she says the saltpeter I consumed all those years ago was slow acting and is just now taking effect."

Bear listened with amusement, having never been in the Army, but when he tasted the over-boiled brew, he screwed his face up, but said nothing.

"Tell us about court this morning," Foley asked.

"Well," Bear began, "you guys heard about last week when Dale Dunlop got the Frank kid's mess dismissed. This week there was another flap. There's a local character named Don McDougall who makes his living hustling pool and dice. He's been up a few times on minor beefs: two DUIs, D and Ds, and gaming one or twice. But, he's harmless and certainly not stupid. Saturday the great officer Kierans claimed there was an outstanding arrest warrant on McDougall for non-payment of a previous fine. McDougall vehemently denied it and claimed he had a receipt for the paid fine back at his apartment. But Kierans wouldn't listen or check and ran him in to Crowell Roscoe's hotel and the poor bastard spent the weekend there."

Bear continued, "Monday morning, I'm in court and McDougall is brought up before Goat Chase. When the case was called, Dale Dunlop was there to represent him. That's the second time in seven days he's represented someone in Chase's court, and judging by Goat's red face, it's clear he's unhappy about it. Dunlop produced McDougall's receipt, proved the fine was paid, and said there must be some confusion in the court records. He added that any citizen might suffer the same fate as

McDougall. He explained to the open court, including a reporter who was making notes, what McDougall suffered by the terrible incarceration at the jail. A 'buggy weekend,' Dunlop called it, 'and a threat to the liberty of every citizen'.

"Chase reacted quickly - and without any motion from MacAdam for the prosecution - and dismissed the charge. That made Mac Adam look bad, and Dunlop wasn't buying the dismissal without comment. He said in that clear loud voice of his, `we want to examine the public records of fines, the copies of receipts for paid fines, and the court conviction records to compare the results.' Chase was a lovely shade of purple on hearing that bit. His morning was backed up like a telescope. He yelled `I don't keep the books. You'll have to see the people at the prothonotary's office.' But Dunlop pushed on and said that he had tried that already, and despite the fact that they are public records and supposedly available, they were not forthcoming. He wanted the court to issue a subpoena *duces tecum* for him to see the records."

Bear paused in his story, "I looked that up. It means show me the records, all of them. Right?" he asked Foley.

"Absolutely correct," Foley replied. "He wants all the records."

Bear went on with the tale. "Chase tried to stonewall. He said, `A subpoena for documents arises out of litigation and your client's case has been dismissed.' Dunlop never even missed a beat. He answered, `Your Honor, I filed a written motion, which must be with the clerk or on your bench, for production of those records to see if there is cause for civil or criminal action. It would be less disruptive to the court for me to see if there is an issue here or simple incompetence in the system rather than start a suit without checking.' Chase was obviously buffaloed. He likely knew that getting into a legal pissing match with Dunlop over the rules of civil procedure might be embarrassing because Dunlop dealt with the rules daily and Chase only dealt with DUIs and petty crap. So then, Dunlop continued. `Your Honor, these records are public and are especially important to an officer of the court who is trying to determine if a cause for litigation exists. More important, they are necessary for any citizens who might be subjected to the outrageous treatment suffered by Mr. McDougall.' Bear added, "It sure was obvious that Dunlop was rubbing Chase's nose in the inevitable, and Chase must have realized it would only get worse, while time was being wasted, and cases were backing up. Chase was obviously flustered. `Mr. Dunlop,' he said, `I'll issue the order giving them a month to produce the documents and records. That gives them a chance to catch up on the workload.' Dunlop thanked him and walked out."

Kirk and Foley were enjoying the story. "I don't know much about this guy Dunlop," Kirk said, "but he sounds like a winner. I read the story in the paper about how he freed those wrongfully convicted Vietnamese, by proving their innocence through DNA testing."

"Bear knows Dunlop well," Foley informed Kirk.

"I knew him when I played hockey," Bear explained. "He was coaching a kid's team and invited me to do a teaching clinic. We saw a lot of each other, and we hunt and fish together. He used to be a state trooper and after law school an assistant prosecutor. Then he moved here to open a private practice, just after I came here two years ago. We're back and forth quite frequently. He's a straight arrow."

"I wonder what Dunlop's planning," Foley said.

"I gotta go," Bear answered "By the way, Dunlop told me that something's not kosher in all this."

"Is that an Indian word?" Kirk asked.

"Absolutely," Bear replied. "It was used by the great Indian philosopher Tonto Levine, and it means something stinks."

CHAPTER NINE

Prayers

"Prayer may help but in the meantime, I'll keep on shootin'."
- U.S. Calvary folklore: old sergeant to conscientious objector during attack.

Chief John Pineo, according to Sergeant Jack Baptist, was drawn to the press like flies to manure. But thanks to the media furor caused when Major Lester Sonny Brown and the two officers, Kierans and Clarke, arrested the Jewish boy, the department was now the center of a media whirlwind and the heat was on. In addition, the boy was the child of upstanding community volunteers who had connections to all the right people. And it was becoming clear that in hiring Dale Dunlop to represent them, the parents had unleashed a force who would find out if the police department of Shiretown were political, half-ass incompetent, or corrupt.

Therefore, Pineo couldn't run around the streets sucking up to the good old boys because some reporter would corner him and ask embarrassing questions about the rape of the innocent Jewish boy. It was pure hell and the mayor was calling several times a day offering impossible suggestions on how to run the PD. In the end, conversations always drifted to Major Brown, the jail, the press, and Donald Frank.

Those who followed the court house scene knew that Pineo was used to tight spots and had survived them for years by a wink, nod, and a promise or outright lies. But the rank smell of this mess required that someone's head roll. And the mayor didn't worry him because, just like the late J. Edgar Hoover's files on elected officials, especially presidents, Pineo had uncomfortable facts on file on all the city fathers, or their loved ones, so he'd have some favors due if there were ever career-threatening troubles.

There was also Chief Pineo's wife Ruth. Mrs. Pineo was a matchless political operator where the chief's position was concerned. To keen observers, she was an ever-vigilant lobbyist for the chief's well being, even though in private their marriage was dull, boring and, certainly listless. She clearly understood that threats to the chief's position were threats to her own well being.

Ruth was the image of propriety at the Lutheran church organ on Sundays. She thought she got the job as church organist because of her running twelve-year sexual relationship with the Reverend Ken Solomon. Her husband thought she'd been hired because he had enough on Solomon, and vice versa, so that he could count on favors being given without his even asking. And Solomon thought he had to give her the job or be ruined by her; he understood that hell hath no fury like a woman scorned, and Ruth was certainly not one to scorn.

Ruth was an experienced and able political survivor, an organist of renown, a vocalist, a community volunteer, and the minister's slut. In fact, if her shrink could publish his assessment of her personality, he might say she was oversexed to the point of nymphomania, and her husband seldom delivered what she desired all day, everyday: 0sex, hot passionate sex. She could manipulate people, especially men when necessary, because she kept a favor-bank in her memory. She was also a social activist, who combined a gracious smile with the ability to listen to fools without looking bored. In fact, she was all things to all people, and what she really thought was hidden behind a facade of benign innocence. She was the perfect wife and a great asset to the chief.

John Pineo and his wife had many diverse interests but one common goal: his career. While they had slept in separate bedrooms for over a dozen years, they both knew that his job success was their mutual objective. He was busy and had lost interest in sex, and then his old pal Solomon came calling on Ruth, a regular part of his pastoral duties. One thing Solomon was wonderful at was discovering lonesome women, and Ruth was available. He had enormous success charming the panties off lonesome women because he could usually recognize which matrons had an ache, a yearning, a heated desire for blatant, earthy sex with bad words and smutty talk. Solomon found Ruth attractive, foxy, and despite her maturity, shapely and, above all, always horny.

Solomon professed his affection for her and his understanding, and in return thought she was addicted to him and loyal to his church. She was neither, but she did find both convenient. Solomon was easy to manipulate and the church was a suitable social platform where she was paid five hundred dollars a month to play the organ. Besides, she was a closet Scientologist, a confirmed, audited member of the Church of Scientology.

When the trouble started over the little Jew, as Ruth privately called the Frank boy, the chief spent more time at home, unlike his usual habit of staying away to avoid her

Scientology visitors. He did not disappear to imaginary meetings, or the Lions Club, the golf course, the American Legion, or the Elks lodge because everywhere he went the press were sure to go too. He sat in his big chair night after night drinking copious amounts of Bacardi's golden rum. Ruth ignored him at first, but then she realized it was time to act. Usually when she approached him, she offered him advice on the benefits of Scientology, trying to enlist him, speaking of the Reverend L. Ron Hubbard, Dianetics, auditing, and how it cleared the mind. He regarded the program with the same disdain he held for the Jehovah Witness movement.

Ruth's keen instincts and common sense indicated that action and not religion was required to save his job and her lifestyle. Pineo had consumed almost a combat-sized jug of Bacardi's, so she knew he would be hostile to platitudes. She moved the footstool close to his chair and spoke gently, trying to comfort him. Normally, he would not discuss the job with her, but she could glean most of the events from his phone calls and other police wives. He was receptive this time because he was worried, so he did not reject her sudden attention and affection. He was, it seemed, in a vice, the handle of which was being turned by the press, and Sonny Brown was their handle.

"It's time," she began, "to distance yourself from Brown or you'll go down in his wake."

Pineo stared at her and suddenly, maybe due to the rum, she seemed as comforting as his dear departed mother had been. He recalled the old wives' tale that boys married a woman like their mother, and finally he understood the theory.

His mother had become pregnant when she was young, and she was abandoned by Pineo's father long before being a single parent became fashionable. She had not only been beautiful, a shapely, buxom Marilyn Monroe look-alike but also savvy enough to understood that the first rule of life was survival by whatever means necessary. The second rule was to protect her cub like a mother bear. She accomplished both by force of personality and flirting outrageously with her physical assets.

Pineo's thoughts returned to the time when he had failed ninth grade, and heartbroken, he rushed home to avoid his friends' asking about his marks. When his mother arrived home from the bank where she worked and found him crying, she took charge. She called the principal, who she knew as a bank customer, and invited him over. Then she sent John to the movies, and when he came home, she informed him that his marks had been revised, and he had been promoted to grade ten. It was typical of his mother.

The worst fright of his life was when he stole a carton of cigarettes from Gerald A. Greenspan's tobacco store and was caught red-handed by the old man. It was common street knowledge that Greenspan was a pervert who sold porno magazines to kids from under his counter, tried to convince high school girls to pose for nude photos, and offered them money for kisses of which he received almost none. He was unforgiving over the stolen cigarettes and called her saying he would inform the police. When Pineo's mother heard of that she drove immediately to Greenspan's store just at closing time. John waited in the car. After an hour, she came back to the car and told him that Greenspan had not only dropped the charges but also given her the cigarettes.

Now Ruth, the wife he had ignored for a dozen years, seemed to be stepping in like his mother: being helpful and resourceful, admittedly domineering but also wise and effective in her manipulation.

"John, dear," Ruth said in a patronizing tone, which she often used when she wanted to negotiate for rather than force the results she desired, "how much could Sonny hurt you if you cut him adrift and he goes down the drain?"

He looked into her blue eyes and knew she had surmised the very crux of the problem. "Lester knows far too much for me to antagonize him. If I abandon him, he'll blab his guts and ruin me."

Ruth hardly let him finish, her clock-like practical sense illustrated by the logic of her questions, "Does he have facts or just gossip? Would anything he say be grounds for investigation or even publication?"

John Pineo felt suddenly like a child seeking his mother's intervention to save him, so he confided in her. "Everything. He knows all the business, plus I think he has some kind of scam that he runs with two drug officers, Nichols and Stent. If I'm right that would come out and it would make me look at best like an incompetent fool."

Ruth was not shaken for she knew more about his police department than he could have guessed. "Where do those two stooges Kierans and Clarke fit in?"

"They're only bum boys for Sonny. Nichols and Stent are the real trouble," he replied.

"Nichols and Stent may not pose an immediate problem because they have to worry about Sonny, in case he starts singing to save himself from prison." Ruth continued. "Sonny is the problem right now." She stroked John's cheek as she spoke softly. "You know, in ancient Rome, when an officer stood to embarrass the emperor, it was considered the honorable thing, a matter of protocol, for him to kill himself to protect the emperor."

Pineo pulled back wondering if he had heard her message correctly. "Sonny Brown isn't about to kill himself, Ruth, if that's what you're wishing for."

"What is he likely to do first?" she asked.

Pineo knew exactly. "He'll give a slanted story to Steven Jobb. He owns Jobb because he squashed a DUI charge for him and Jobb is his puppet. You noticed that Jobb never dumped on Brown in the Frank mess, only me."

Ruth noted that John was very drunk and he was starting to fade. "Go to bed John, sleep away the rum and your worries, and when you wake, things will work themselves out."

He trundled off to his room like a child, hoping his mother, or in this case Ruth, would somehow solve his problems. He was very tired of the burden he carried.

The sun sneaking through the crack of the bedroom blinds awakened him. He stirred and moved ever so slightly. The throbbing pain in his head, the jungle-rot taste in his mouth, and the nausea in his gut reminded him he was alive. He was rum-sick but alive and so was the intolerable mess at the PD. He slowly eased over to the edge of the bed, hesitated briefly to allow the dizziness to subside, and then scuffed barefoot to the bathroom.

He glanced at his red eyes in the mirror, a clear advertisement for the volcano in his brain. He wavered as he tried to hit the toilet with a rotating stream of urine. At that instant, his stomach rejected its contents and he heaved on and around the seat, splattering the sour bile and phlegm over his feet, the wall, and the side of the tub. He fumbled for toilet paper to wipe his chin and lips and then groped for the cold water tap of the shower, which he turned on full. The thundering sound of the water hitting the plastic shower curtain pierced his ears like a probe. Before he could step into the shower his bowels rumbled and then, prompted by the previous night's excessive consumption of rum, exploded in a disgusting avalanche.

Pineo was finally able to maneuver awkwardly behind the shower curtain into the icy-cold water, hoping the shock would dissipate his atomic hangover and restore his balance. It did not.

"Ruth!" he bellowed. "Ruuthh!" There was no answer. He glanced at his Rolex. 7:00 a.m. "Where the fuck is she this early?"

He glanced out the window and saw that her car was gone. "That goddamn church organ. She's gone to practice like nothing's wrong, and everything is fuckin' wrong." On top of that thought, he couldn't for the life of him see where playing the organ, or any religious crap, would convince Sonny Brown to off himself. He remembered that much of the conversation from the evening before. He toweled gently and put on his old bathrobe.

Pineo limped weakly to the kitchen broom closet, fetched the mop and some cleaning rags, and headed back to the bathroom to try and clean it up. His head was paining him, and his stomach was sour. The bathroom smelled like the hyena vomit at the zoo mixed with human feces, and his stomach almost heaved again. He had to leave it. He needed coffee and retreated to the kitchen where Ruth had left a pot of black Colombian perking. He gulped the dark brew, paused to swallow three Tylenols, and then started back to the bathroom for another go at the mess. Before he reached the door, he power-puked the coffee down the hall, catching both the walls and a lot of the floor.

His pride finally overcame his distress, and he spent a painful hour cleaning up the evidence of his hangover. He would not arrive at the PD on time this morning. He sprayed pine-scented Lysol bathroom cleaner to drown the smell, re-showered, and shaved. He dressed slowly, put on his Polaroid sunglasses to cover his red eyes, and left for the office at nine thirty. On the way he chewed breath gum hoping the chlorophyll would camouflage the smell of his sour breath.

When he arrived at headquarters, he instructed his secretary Heather that he was not to be bothered for any purpose except an emergency. He latched his office door open, slumped onto his sofa, and fell immediately asleep.

It seemed like only a few minutes had elapsed, but a glance at his watch showed it was eleven thirty. He rushed into his small personal bathroom, washed his face in cold water, and combed his short gray hair. He could hear Heather, fat nosy Heather, pounding on his door.

"What is it?" he asked.

"Major Brown is dead. Sergeant Baptist is on the phone."

Pineo picked up the handset. "Hello," he heard Baptist's soft voice.

"The major's dead. Looks like gas from the furnace. The coroner and the lab guys are on the way."

"Who called it in?" asked Pineo.

"Reverend Ken Solomon was doing church visits and went into the sun porch. He thought he smelled gas and tried the inside door. It was unlocked and when he opened it he knew it was gas. He went next door and called 911. They found Brown dead in his bed."

"Listen to me, Baptist," ordered the chief. "Unless it's a murder, it's an accident. Do you understand me?"

Baptist replied quickly. "Listen, Chief, Hoss Foley and Kirk Donald are on the way over, and there's no fuckin' way they will say it is what it ain't."

Pineo slammed down the phone without further comment. Then it dawned on him. How Brown died did not matter. Anyway you sliced it, it was not bad news, and his hangover was suddenly less troublesome.

CHAPTER TEN

The Obvious

"[belief] ... to mistrust the obvious and to put one's faith in things which could not been seen."
- Galin (199)

Reverend Ken Solomon reported to the police at the Brown death scene that he had been making church visitations at the expensive homes of his parishioners on Roosevelt Drive. He knew Major Sonny Brown was a member of his church whom he had never visited, nor had Brown often visited Solomon's church. Yet, seeing two cars in the yard, and believing he might effect a miraculous conversion, the patronizing preacher decided to stop in. If nothing else, he figured he'd see the inside of the house and maybe shock Brown's conscience and receive a guilt donation. Upon entering the sun porch, he recognized the putrid, rotten-egg smell of gas and, troubled by the potential danger, he rushed to a neighbor's and called 911. Two emergency medics arrived, followed almost at once by two police officers, and they entered the house through the already unlocked door.

Inside, they opened windows to disperse the gas, and when they searched the house, they found Brown in his bed, the covers pulled up to his neck and his blue lifeless face suggesting carbon monoxide poisoning. Despite extensive medical procedures, the medics were unable to revive Brown, who they guessed had been dead for hours.

Sergeant Jack Baptist, as homicide duty investigator, received the call in his car. The message from the dispatcher was short, "See the officers at 3002 Roosevelt."

He proceeded at once because he recognized the address. It was not until he arrived that he learned of Brown's death from the two officers at the scene, Sergeant Richard Murphy and Officer Roy Black. Wisely, they had not reported Brown's suspicious death over the police radio, so when Baptist discovered what had happened, he was surprised. He knew that since the press would have heard the radio dispatch for the homicide duty officer they would soon follow out of morbid curiosity.

Baptist immediately secured the crime scene, and called Dr. Kirk Donald, Dr. Horace Foley, and the chief of police. The medics gave him a list of the procedures they had used in their vain attempt to revive Brown so that any marks on the body made by them could be sorted out from marks made previous to their arrival.

Sergeant Murphy called for a traffic unit to keep control of the rubberneckers who always materialize at emergency scenes.

Kirk Donald was surprised by Baptist's phone call. Normally, he did not speed to death scenes because he figured the danger to pedestrians from the trip exceeded the value to the dead person, but this time he rushed because he knew there would be a media circus surrounding the death of an officer involved in a controversial case. As a general rule, Kirk hated to rush as he figured it stressed his heart and digestion.

He met Baptist in the driveway after parking his car on the sidewalk to keep the street clear. "Until Foley arrives, I don't want anyone in the house but you," he instructed Baptist.

Baptist was uneasy about this demand because the chief was on his way. "One problem," he said, "the chief's en route, and he sort of outranks me."

"OK," replied Kirk, "if you have to; let him in, but no one else, and if I was the chief, I wouldn't want to enter the house because the press shitbirds will pounce on him for answers when he goes back outside. His best public relations ploy would be to stay out of here and say only that the experts are handling the scene, and until it's resolved, he knows nothing. The press is already arriving in torrents already out there."

"Here he comes," Baptist said. "You go make that suggestion 'cause he'll take it better from you."

Kirk walked quickly to head Chief Pineo off at the mouth of the driveway. They had a brief conversation. The chief agreed with his advice and turned to leave when the media leeches ran across the street, cornering him near his car. There were cameras and recording devices, and he noticed a TV truck down the street by the corner where the traffic officer had closed the street to vehicles. Chief Pineo held up his hand for silence, as they all seemed to be talking at once. "Listen to me," he said.

"The medical examiner, who is also acting coroner, is in charge of the scene, and we have decided that an outside police agency will be called in to ascertain if this is an accident because it involves the death of Major Lester Brown, a Shiretown police officer."

The news people reacted like a bunch of magpies all squaking at once, as they peppered him with questions. Pineo was no novice in dealing with them.

"That's it. I know nothing else."

The press were unhappy, and some of the remarks were unpleasant, but Pineo smiled and was very polite. He turned and whispered to Sergeant Murphy, telling him, "Get their asses outta here."

Kirk was waiting in the sun porch for Foley. When he arrived accompanied by the lab technicians, Kirk spent almost ten minutes bringing them up to date. Foley instructed the techs to start collecting evidence in the basement and to fingerprint the furnace. Foley and Kirk, along with Baptist, decided to start in the bedroom with the body. Inside, despite the now-opened windows, the sulfur dioxide-like odor of gas was still present.

"The furnace is off," Kirk informed the other two. "The medics cut the power."

In the bedroom, the body of Lester Brown was an unsettling sight: his skin was a terrible blue color, his lips sagged, and his face, perhaps caused by lividity, was sunken like melted wax. It looked like a horror mask. At a glance, it looked like carbon monoxide poisoning, but an autopsy and toxicology test would be needed to confirm that assumption. Despite the public perception that autopsies are intrusive and shocking, they are needed to determine if death under suspicious circumstances is accidental, self-inflicted, or homicide.

Baptist was a keen student of crime scene forensics and was impressed by the professionalism of the doctors. He watched closely and gave them the list of procedures the medics had performed. "Their guess was carbon monoxide too."

"Looks like it," replied Foley.

Baptist was curious about the smell of the gas, a definitely unpleasant stench. "I thought carbon monoxide was odorless, so how come we can smell the gas?"

Kirk replied, "The gas companies add an odor-producing agent to the gas to alert people to a leak or malfunction. In order to create heat, the gas is forced through a nozzle, mixed with air, and burned. The burning process is what creates carbon monoxide, which as you know is called CO, and if the flame is not efficiently ventilated, say by a flue, then the odorless gas carbon monoxide is produced and that is what kills you if there is enough of it. Under some circumstances, it can happen quickly. The gas may still smell if the furnace is not functioning efficiently because the flame may not be properly disposing of what's coming through the nozzle, so there can be odorless CO and a gas smell in the air without a complete breakdown."

Foley joined in, "It's like a car in a closed garage with the motor running. When the CO fills the place, it replaces the oxygen in your blood, and you die."

Baptist was thoughtful, "Then, in a case like this, it would seem odd for him to commit suicide by furnace when he could have gone to the garage and simply run the motor to accomplish the same result."

"Right," agreed Foley. "Not conclusive but not likely a suicide. For one thing, a big house like this ain't exactly like sticking your head in the oven because there is a lot of oxygen in this large a space and it would take longer than filling a car with CO."

Kirk nodded. "And that moves the cause more toward accidental or maybe murder." He said to Baptist. "Go call Lieutenant Folker of the state police and tell him Hoss and I want the investigation run by them because that's what the book calls for in the death of a PD member. Ask him if he can bring that professor from State who's an expert on gas furnaces."

"What we want from him," Foley added, "is to determine if there is a malfunction in the furnace, and if so, is it from deliberate damage or just wear and tear?"

Kirk moved to the bed and checked off the procedures and marks made by the medics in trying to revive Brown. He paused for a long time examining the facial area around the mouth and nose. "There's some slight residue like Vaseline or cream on his face. I smell booze from his mouth, and there's a mark on his neck like a hickey."

At that moment, Baptist returned from phoning Lieutenant Folker and heard Kirk speaking. "Brown was as horny as a two-peckered goat according to my information."

Kirk said, "I smell soap on his hands and his genitals, and he has no drawers on. I suspect both have been recently washed. The question is why? I keep thinking of what you said the other day, Hoss, that whatever is obvious should be questioned. There's something suspicious here."

Foley knew Kirk's penchant for minute detail and his instinctual ability to read crime scenes, and especially bodies, like a map. Foley asked him, "What's your theory, and why did you smell his privates to see if they smelled like soap?"

Kirk made a fake grimace. "My gawd," he said, "it's a trip to work with you, Hoss, cause you're a real perv.

"I've got an idea, but it's far from sure. It's only a guess, Hoss, more like a hunch, but I smell a woman. The place is too neat to start with, especially if he was getting laid. I can't believe he'd take the time to fold his drawers and lay them over that chair over there. And then putting his scuffed slippers neatly over there on the floor is not like a horney man. He would have pitched them on the floor.

And, he's still got his T-shirt on, except it was torn to shit by the medics. It ain't natural for a horny-guy to put his drawers and slippers over there by the chair and keep his T-shirt on. But, if someone's gonna wash his dick off, they might not want to wet the drawers, and then, there's the grease residue on his face, what's that all about?"

Foley was impressed, but joked, "Maybe she sat on his face and smothered him. What else?"

"What else do you think, Dr. Know-it-all? Well, he smells of booze and that's a question for your expertise. Tell me later if he has alcohol in his blood stream. And did someone hold a rag soaked in ether, which comes from alcohol, or rubbing alcohol, or whatever over his face? Was he knocked out with something like either first? Will the toxicology test distinguish whether it was ether or whatever, or would the presence of one alcohol cloud the issue and ruin the testing?"

Foley replied. "I see where you're going. You wonder if they put him to sleep before the furnace was fucked up, will the chemicals show up? The answer is almost certainly yes because the chromatography will detect and distinguish between the various chemicals."

Baptist askled question, "But alcohol is alcohol isn't it? If he's loaded, how will the machine pick up ether or rubbing alcohol?"

"A fair question," Foley answered, "but chromatography picks up on any alcohol and it will pick up ether. Because alcohol is a group of compounds that the machine can recognize, like monohydric, hydroxyl, dihydric and even wood alcohol, which is now produced synthetically by using hydrogen and carbon monoxide. In the test, blood is vaporized at a high temperature, and the resulting blood gas is sent through the various chemicals in the blood and will detect what's present. In other words, the chromatography process will determine if the alcohol is ethyl alcohol, that's alcohol from booze, or ether: no matter if they were mixed, and no matter what other chemical may have been used, and no matter whether they were inhaled or injected."

"That's what the grease on his face may mean," interjected Kirk. "Maybe the killer held a saturated rag over Brown's face to make sure he stayed asleep for the furnace to kill him, and they feared the chemical on the rag would abrase the skin, so they put Vaseline on him first."

Foley was dubious, "That's a lot of trouble to go to, but who said killers are rational?"

One of the techs came up from the basement with two plastic evidence bags. "We found residue of a chemical which smells like surgical gloves on the furnace valves and vents. We also found a broken fingernail with red nail polish on the stairs, plus there's a hair present."

Foley said, "It's good stuff if we can connect it to a suspect. Maybe the nail got broken in the surgical glove while screwing with the furnace, and as the perp ran up the cellar stairs, they pulled off the gloves and lost the nail."

Kirk too was thinking murder, not accident. He spoke to Baptist, "Do you think it may be wise to have some officers canvas the neighborhood to see if anyone saw any visitors in the last twenty-four hours, and then we can turn this all over to the state police if anything's found. And Hoss, let's comb his pubic hair to see if there's a second type of hair present. Bag his hands for a fingernail check and have the sheets bagged for semen and body fluid checks."

Foley agreed and asked the tech to collect the used vacuum cleaner bag and to search the outdoor trash cans to ascertain if anything was unusual, suspicious, or supported Kirk's theory of the crime. "Take lots of photos and look for the usual: fibers, hairs. Start here in the bedroom. It's likely too late for fingerprints after the medics were in here, but just the same, print everything in this room, and all the furniture, and door knobs."

Lieutenant Sam Folker of the state police arrived with two homicide officers, John Amirault and Bernie Lewis, plus Professor Roy Jodrey of State University who was introduced as an expert on energy and heating furnaces.

Professor Jodrey and Lewis were lugging a huge box containing the technical instruments for the furnace exam. Baptist and the two troopers went to the kitchen to bring the two late arrivals up to date and to report that several city PD officers were canvassing neighbors looking for witnesses who might have seen visitors to Major Brown's home.

Foley, Kirk, Folker and Professor Jodrey, a tall bespectacled man who looked exactly like a nerdy Jimmie Stewart, went to the basement carrying the equipment trunk. The professor opened the box of equipment and removed gauges, a laptop computer, and an assortment of tools. He removed his jacket, shirt, and tie and replaced them with an old stained T-shirt, an apron, rubber gloves, and safety goggles. He said, "This all looks very mysterious and professional, but it's just to get my fee up because it's really all pretty simple."

He placed the laptop on the work bench. "I have all the statistics and date for many trade name furnaces programmed into the computer. Then, on this old baby I measure air flow, mix, ventilation, and assorted functional measurements with the gauges and feed the data into the computer. The computer tells me where the malfunction or inefficiency is and how serious it is, plus it indicates the probability of it being manmade or a malfunction from time, or wear and tear.

"Very impressive," said Kirk. "In other words, you're saying that the likelihood of wear compared to tampering can be fairly well determined."

"Quite often it can be determined," Jodrey replied. "While lawyers will attack some aspects of this system, there are yards of scientific data that confirm it."

While Professor Jodrey worked on the furnace, Folker asked Kirk about his theory on the death. Kirk outlined his ideas and reasons with both circumstantial evidence and the elements which caused his suspicions.

"What about you?" Folker asked Hoss. Dr. Foley was watching Professor Jodrey but listening at the same time.

"I told Kirk some woman sat on Brown's face and smothered him," replied Foley.

Folker smiled. "Anyone come to mind?"

"Nope, but he may have a few scorned women after him if his reputation is accurate. He supposedly had more tail than a kangaroo."

Professor Jodrey was half-listening to the banter. He said, "My wife's been dead for ten years. Is there any chance I can borrow Brown's address book?"

Kirk chimed in, "Well, the publicity Brown got for being an anti-Semite Nazi over the arrest of Donald Frank sort of excludes the skinheads as suspects, but his sex life does suggest a female."

Jodrey stood up, holding a good-sized piece of soot-stained, fireproof fiberglass insulation. "I'm far from done here, but to start here's what was blocking the ventilation, and it was added because it's not part of the furnace, and it would send the carbon monoxide into the house instead of up the chimney."

Kirk was not surprised, "How long would it take for the house to fill with CO?"

Jodrey answered, "After taking measurements and reading a lot of gauges, and depending on how airtight the place is, I'll be able to tell you almost exactly. But based on experience, I can tell you it wouldn't have taken much time: a couple of hours at the very outside. As you know, CO replaces oxygen in the blood and is a favorite method of suicide. But going to all this trouble with the flue is not a likely way to kill yourself: too much trouble. As a rule, the suicide will just go to the garage, and turn on the car, and die. It's much simpler and quicker: takes from five to thirty minutes usually. My bet is this one was murder."

Foley said, "Sergeant Baptist said the same thing about using a car being simpler. I wonder if there are any statistics on suicide by furnace? You know what I'm getting at: in court, some defense lawyer will cite statistics to proves the world is flat. Are there any stastics on suicide by furnace?"

Kirk answered, "There are lots of stats on weird suicides and many about using a car in a garage, but I never saw any stats on furnaces. I think most investigators would start out thinking it was accidental, but guys like Professor Jodrey can prove malfunction. I've never seen a furnace used in a suicide, and I've done hundreds of suicides. Plus, he already found this furnace was tampered with by blocking the flue. It's a murder. And, say, Hoss, if a guy killed himself by hooking up to a car exhaust is the cause of death 'exhausted'?

Foley couldn't surpress his grin, "Tension at death scenes makes old people corney," he said.

"Dr. Foley," the professor asked, "has anyone fingerprinted the upstairs' thermostat?"

Foley replied, "I'll check on it. Why do you ask?"

Jodrey said, "I did the science on a murder in New Hampshire a few years ago. The killer had to be sure the furnace cut in to create the CO. That required the thermostat to be turned up higher than room temperature. In that particular case, the killer was careless and left fingerprints on the heat control, but nowhere else in the house. He forgot to wipe off that one little termostat and that contributed to his undoing."

CHAPTER ELEVEN

Gossip

"Gossip is a cross to bear but it's fallow ground for an investigator."
- Lt. Dismas Rhodes (2000)

The dispatcher's robotic voice sounded like someone speaking while holding their nose. It was as canned and lifeless as those computer-generated, phone-call-voices that remind people of appointments or tout investments or life insurance.

The message, however, was clear and exciting for Noel Bear because, as one of the newer officers, he was usually assigned to a dull district where the biggest deals were traffic offenses.

"Shots fired" and "robbery in progress" were relayed by the ten series code and the address was the People's Drug Warehouse at Seventieth and Martin Luther King Drive. That district was formerly the slum section of the city which had been renewed over several decades to become a garden-like industrial park. As a patrol district, it usually required little policing.

It was eleven in the morning when Bear activated his roof lights and siren to wheel up Seventieth Street with his heart pounding in expectation of the first felony to which he was assigned. Because he was the officer for that district, he would be the first at the scene until backup arrived. As he turned up the driveway of People's, his anticipation escalated, and he prepared for any exigency.

He reached the front door and skidded to a halt. A uniformed security guard, his weapon drawn, burst through the glass door screaming, "My partner is shot; my partner is down!"

Bear tried to calm the distraught man to ascertain the pertinent facts, but the guard was hysterical. He shook the man and shouted at him, "Tell me what's going down!"

The guard, still babbling, managed to blurt out that there was a robbery and his partner had been shot. Bear's thoughts centered on giving first aid to the wounded person. But he drew his weapon, and cautiously entered the door, and slid along the wall toward the back.. Visualizing a man bleeding to death as a result of a gun fight, he knew time was of the essence. To speed up the process, he yanked the fire alarm as he advanced because he knew an ambulance was always dispatched on a fire alarm, and it was more efficient than pausing to radio for one. He reached the glassed-in reception area, and through the window at the back of that space, he could see into the warehouse where a group of workers were clustered around someone on the floor. There was no sign of gunmen, and he hoped they had departed.

He eased through the hall door marked Employees Only and out into the warehouse where he saw a second security guard laying on the floor. The fire alarm was clanging with an ear piercing clamor, yet the crowd stood as if helpless, offering no help to the guard on the floor. "Are the gunmen gone?" he asked.

"Yea, gone," someone said. Bear holstered his weapon and eased into the circle of people, expecting to see a badly wounded, profusely bleeding victim. But instead, the guard writhed on the floor with what appeared to be an injured foot; with only a small amount of blood visible as it seeped through the toe of his old army boot.

Bear tried to comfort the man while he removed the boot to survey the damage and stem the flow of blood. He moved the crowd back and secured the guard's weapon, which lay on the floor near him. Once the boot and the bloody sock were removed, it was clear the wound consisted of damage to the inside of the big toe and to the second toe, which suggeted that a bullet had passed between them and likely had not broken any bones. Bear thought of old combat movies, where GIs claimed being shot in the foot was the million dollar wound. He doubted the guard would agree with that idea because of the whining sounds of his pain.

He asked for a first aid kit, and when it was delivered, he pressure bandaged the toes and calmed the man, and then for the troublesome report he'd have to write, he started asking questions. Finally an older man who seemed calm and collected stepped forward to help. He reported that two masked men in coveralls had entered through the side entrance, grabbed the foreman from his desk by the door, and proceeded to the secured section where prescription drugs were stored for shipment to the company's retail stores around the city. They forced the foreman to unlock the door, and they then loaded a pushcart with cartons of anti-anxiety drugs, like Valium. The man relating the story seemed to have catalogued the incident into his memory. His detailed report continued.

"They made the foreman push the cartload of pills back to the loading dock, and one man stood guard on the platform forcing the foreman to pass the boxes down to the second robber who stowed them in the back of an old van."

Bear was anxious to hear how the shooting had occurred.

The white-haired witness suppressed a smile, but it was obvious he found some amusement in the question. "It wasn't no gun fight. What happened was that just as the loading finished, the lone ranger here," and he pointed at the guard, "came charging through the door from the office like lightening, reaching for his gun, and screaming `freeze mutha-fucker!' just like them TV cop shows."

"What did the robbers do?" Bear asked.

"They didn't hafta do nothing, cause the guard musta squeezed the trigger as the gun cleared his holster and he shot himself in the foot. Then he went down like a sack of potatoes yelling, `Oh God, I'm shot!'."

Bear thought this was like a script from an old Keystone Cops movie, but continued collecting the facts. "And the robbers?"

The old man laughed out loud, "The one up top just here shook his head, jumped off the loading dock, and they drove away."

Noel Bear realized that his first felony case had just turned into a comic opera, and there would be yards of paperwork required to complete the report. He decided he would exclude the part where he activated the fire alarm because the decision might appear flawed in light of the actual facts, and as a newer officer, he could imagine the squad room jokes.

Shortly there appeared firefighters, two trucks, an ambulance, the patrol supervisor, several backup officers, and even the chief. Noel Bear felt like the switch that turned on the farce. He decided to play it cool, nonchalant even, like his first game in pro hockey, when he accidentally scored a goal in his own net. He was embarrassed, but an old pro advised, "Fuck it; play it cool; no sweat, and never explain too much." Bear decided that strategy applied here, and it passed muster without question.

As he took statements and assisted the investigators by taking photos with his own Polaroid, he was even complimented for his cool efficiency. One female employee interviewed by the detectives mistakenly claimed that the ringing fire alarm had scared the robbers off, and while Bear knew the perps had been long gone by the time he pulled the alarm, he did not feel compelled to contradict her erroneous conclusion.

The press had cornered the chief in a scrum outside the loading platform. While the event was serious because of the drug robbery, as a news story it was more an excuse for the press to badger the chief about the death of Major Brown. While the chief fielded questions, Bear walked by, en route to his car. The chief, anxious to escape the throng said, "There's Officer Bear who was first at this scene and applied first aid to the victim."

As the press people crushed in, Bear noticed the chief jogging away to his car, saved by the diversion.

The reporters all talked at once. A TV camera was stuck in his face. Bear played it cool, "You'll have to see the PD information officer because I'm not authorized to comment."

One reporter corrected him, "The chief referred us to you, so how about it?"

Bear had considerable experience with the media from his hockey days. He knew a polite response was best, even when the question was rude, and that the less said, the better: low-key humility to the point of self-deprecation worked best.

"Wait, wait, you're all talking at once. This is all new to me, and you're razzle-dazzleing me with too many questions at once."

A female reporter wearing the ID badge of a local TV station shoved a mike in his face, "I interviewed you when you went up to the Flyers for three games, and the manager told us you could have made it in the NHL, but you said you decided on a law enforcement career. Do you have any regrets?"

"The team manager was very kind with his words," replied Bear. "I understand he's got cancer now and I wish him the best. But I'm very happy with my choice of career."

The woman reporter pushed on, apparently trying to elicit a negative answer, "Aren't you sorry about losing the chance to make big bucks in hockey compared to the salaries in the police department?"

"No," Bear replied patiently. "This has always been my ambition, and I have a wife and twin boys I see every night: no travel required, like hockey."

The reporter continued, "Officer Bear, Native Americans have descriptive names. I note yours is Noel B. Bear. What does the "B" stand for?"

Bear was used to stupid, stereotypical questions asked by fans and reporters because he had been one of the few Native Americans in professional hockey. He usually stayed low-key and spoofed them. In the case of his middle name, it was Benjamin, after his father, but he knew the press wanted an Indian answer so he gave them one.

"My middle name is Black. Noel Black Bear."

Noel then blew the rest of the reporters off as politely as possible and escaped to his patrol car.

It had been a long day by the time Bear had completed his reports. He finished shortly after five p.m., and while his shift did not end until six, the sergeant told him to take off early. He went to the squad room, stuffed his gear in his locker, and decided to go visit Shirley Reading. Two other officers, Collins and Marvin, from his shift had also finished early and were relaxing on a bench near the lockers.

"Hey Bear," Marvin said, "I hear you did a great job today."

Collins chimed in, "When the robbery was called, I was assigned that Willow Street checkpoint and never saw a fuckin' car except for two drug dicks who went through."

That statement by Collins rang a bell in Bear's memory from when he had the Willow Street roadblock during the previous hit on Walgreen's. Two drug squad members had gone through his checkpoint too. He kept quiet about it and instead asked, "Who were the dicks?"

"Nichols and Stent," Collins replied. Bear did not react. He said goodbye to the two officers and headed to a quiet place to call Foley on his cell phone.

Hoss Foley's scratchy voice squawked a hello. Bear asked how long he would be there. After he heard the answer, he told Foley he would visit on his way home.

"By the way, your wife called," Foley announced. "She saw you on TV and she loved the Noel Black Bear routine. What a crock. If you wanted to pull their chains why didn't you claim the B stood for Bigdick?"

"That's very true," answered Bear. "Contrary to what all you black people boast about ..."

"Hey, I'm not black," Foley interrupted, "I hate that. I'm brown, African, or a person of color, but I'm not fuckin' black."

"Whatever. My point is that it's really the Native Americans who have extraordinarily large dicks. All my family have been well hung."

"Or hanged," Foley added.

Bear headed for the detective division to see Shirley. When he arrived, he saw Jack Baptist sitting on her desk, his tired face revealed the quality of his terrible day.

"Heard you handled yourself well today," Baptist commented as Bear approached.

Bear did not feel compelled to report either the fire alarm or his disappointment with the incident. "Except for the chief feeding me to the press, it was OK, but I hear you had a real bad one."

Baptist said, "Let's go for a beer." Shirley agreed.

Noel did not drink, but he knew some socializing with his co-workers not only kept him from being an outsider, it helped build trust. He trusted Reading, and since he knew she trusted Baptist, he felt comfortable going with them.

They drove to the Pig & Whistle, a combined restaurant and bar where off-duty cops congregated. Reading and Baptist ordered beer, and Bear asked for a Pepsi.

"Not a beer drinker?" Shirley inquired.

"No," replied Bear, "I always wanted pro sports, so I never drank or smoked."

Baptist grinned, "How many kids you got?"

Bear laughed, "That's a hobby that helps athletes and cops."

"Tell us about the warehouse," Shirley said to Bear.

"It was like a Keystone Cops' movie." He related the whole story, less the fire alarm portion, ending with the guard shouting, "Freeze mutha-fucker" – BOOM – "Oh God, I'm shot."

Baptist had just taken a mouthful of beer as Noel delivered the punch line, and he sprayed it over Reading. They were roaring with laughter, and everyone was staring at them.

Reading now prodded Baptist about Major Brown. Baptist wiped off the beer and looked serious. "Damnedest thing you could ever imagine: death by carbon monoxide. He was actually blue. [Lividity] The medics were pounding on his chest trying to revive him. His face looked like a soft blue rubber mask, and Man, those medics are cool. They tried everything; he got three bags full plus. It was an awful sight. He had no pants on; his bare ass was sticking out; his hands were hanging over the side of the bed like lifeless flippers; his dignity was gone, and the medical supervisor was giving radio instructions to the guys on the scene. What a fuckin' scene. It's the first CO death I ever attended. I've seen hangings, which aren't fun, and shootings, and throat cuttings, but this ranks as surprisingly ugly."

"So what's the death theory?" Bear asked.

Baptist was suddenly quiet. He was not a man to prattle nor did he have loose lips. Finally he spoke. "My guess is suicide is not a consideration in the death theory." He offered no more information, and neither Shirley nor Bear attempted to violate his silence.

"Gotta go," Bear announced, and as he stood, Baptist repeated the punch line from the robbery story: "BOOM – Oh God, I'm shot." Again everyone stared at them when they laughed, and then Bear left to meet Hoss Foley.

It was 6:30 p.m., and Foley finally had time to open his morning paper: twelve hours late. By the time Noel arrived, Foley was on the sports section and into another cup of foul black reheated coffee, his umpteenth of the day.

"That shit must be great for your heart," Bear said. Foley ignored him. Bear continued. "Here's a little gossip for you which strikes me as more than a coincidence. The day of the Walgreen's robbery, I drew Willow Street for the road block. It's a sleepmaker, and the only people who came through were Nichols and Stent of the drug squad. Claimed they were avoiding traffic en route to an interview in the country. Today when People's was hit, the road blocks went up, and the guy who got stuck on that checkpoint told me the same two officers went through with a similar story."

Foley perked up, "It's worth passing along to Lieutenant Folker."

Noel was eager to hear about Major Brown's death, and Hoss was in his element when it came to crime theories, forensics, and evidence issues.

"Kirk and I pretty well agree that the initial facts indicate murder. It's possible that a woman killed him. The canvass of the neighborhood for witnesses turned up an old guy who was walking his dog just after midnight. He saw a dark figure go in Brown's door, and then the lights came on in Brown's sunporch. Brown let whoever it was in the house, so he must have known the person. Unfortunately, the witness can't say if it was a man or a woman, and he didn't see a car in the yard except for the two Brown owned."

Noel said, "That's not surprising when you think of how Roosevelt borders on a park-like strip of land. Behind that there is a church parking lot, so a visitor, especially one who didn't want their car seen in Brown's yard, could have parked in back of the church and walked directly across the green belt to Brown's house."

Foley replied, "And Brown certainly knew the person or he wouldn't have let them in." Foley outlined the bedroom scene in the house, including the fact that it was possible Brown had sex with someone.

Noel mentioned that he had heard that Brown's pants were off, and he speculated that whoever visited must have been there when the drawers came off because it was a fair deduction that Brown had not answered the door in his bare butt.

Foley agreed, "Not likely to answer the door naked, unless of course he was roaring drunk, and there was a strong smell of alcohol, but we haven't got the toxicology yet."

"What made you guys think the killer was a woman?"

Foley related finding a broken fingernail and that Kirk suspected that a woman had folded Brown's drawers. "The scene was too neat," he said, "but the fingernail doesn't mean much cause Brown was a stud-puppie and banged many women according to scuttlebutt. It could be anyone's nail."

"Listen Hoss, you guys forgot more about crime scenes than I'll even know, but think about this. A lot of closet gays who work in jobs where their sexual preference would be a real disadvantage make a big show out of how much female company they have, and they let people think they're banging a different girl each night. Maybe Brown was gay, or even bisexual."

Foley was fascinated, "I say everyday that the obvious shouldn't be accepted without question, and then I didn't consider that. The killer could be a man but we stopped thinking when we decided it was a woman."

Foley reached for the phone to call Kirk. As Bear left, he said, "It could still be a female, Hoss, I'm only speculating."

Foley put his hand over the mouthpiece, "Now I'm gonna drive Kirk nuts with speculative gossip."

CHAPTER TWELVE

Happenstance

"The thief doth fear each bush an officer."
- Shakespeare

William Bates Lewis was young yet seemed mentally old. He was barely fifteen, but streetwise and too mature in worldly things. By most adult standards he was a weird dresser. His pants were baggy and hung down in the crotch; the oversized pantlegs halted just below the knees as if either there had not been enough material to make them long pants or there had been too much material to make them into short pants. In fact, Lewis looked like a child wearing Wayne Gretsky's hockey pants. His sneaks were Air Jordans and cost more than a suit of clothes for most working people. His hair looked like he cut it himself: uneven, and too short to cover the bumps and hollows of the bones of his skull. He wore an extra large T-shirt, big enough to fit George Foreman, more like a sweatshirt with the arms hacked off in an irregular manner to reveal his flimsy muscles and hairy armpits. The printing on the shirt proclaimed Born to Love on the front and the number 69 on the back. Lewis had a tattoo of a serpent on his left forearm and a silver stud through his face just below his lower lip. He wore a stud in the lobe of each ear and he was, at least in his own mind and likely in the opinion of his pals, a stylish dude.

It was a freak encounter that brought him into conflict with the police: a childish disagreement over a pool game at the local downstairs hangout under the East End Pizza and Pool Hall on Church Street. It had started as a chicken-and-egg argument over a called pool shot. Then anger and pride provoked the use of cues as swords, like Zorro with pool sticks. The owner, usually a man who honored the street code of silence, became concerned as the fight escalated, and fearing injury or death, he reluctantly called the police. They responded quickly, despite their busy schedule, because the chief was concerned about negative public opinion created by the newspapers. Conservative folks, the chief believed, believed pool halls were dens of thieves where muscular ne'er-do-wells did drugs while planing crimes.

One participant escaped out the side door, but Lewis was caught. While it was really a nothing-beef, Officer Collins decided otherwise because he was of the opinion that Lewis was an effeminate trouble-maker who would grow up to spread AIDS. It was one of those freak happenstances that foul up the affairs of man. A happenstance is an accidental event caused by the gods that criminals can't foresee and fill the prisons. The arrest of young Bill Lewis would trigger a happenstance, which affected the status quo.

Officer Collins decided to take Lewis in, more due to his own bias than for any other cause. Arrests lead to searches, and this search revealed fifty Valium pills in a plastic sandwich baggie tucked into Lewis' pocket. Collins cuffed him and then, as the law dictated because of Lewis' age, turned him over to Shirley Reading in Juvenile.

Collins removed the cuffs and plunked the defiant young man onto the hardwood chair next to Reading's desk. Lewis continued to display attitude: a mean stare, leaning towards the insolent look of a nasty pitbull . Yet there was fear in his eyes and Reading knew how to exploit that fear after lots of experience with underage street punks.

She was well qualified for juvenile, both academically and because of her fondness for kids, plus the fact that she remembered the weird sartorial get-ups of her own student days. Once in her university freshman year, she had dyed a bright green strip down the center of her beautiful blonde hair, which almost gave her parents an apoplectic seizure. Her fads had passed, and she and her parents had maintained a loving relationship. In fact before her mother died, she had confessed to Shirley that she and Shirley's father had conceived Shirley in the back of a Volkswagen van, known in their hippie days as a baby-maker. With this background, Shirley didn't find today's kids too shocking nor was she judgmental.

In Lewis' case, she was already thinking of bigger fish, hoping to telescope his street level distribution bust backwards to the suppliers and honchos. She knew he was not going to be a push-over. He wouldn't co-operate. He lied about his address and his personal history. She ignored his attitude and realized he was likely already in the system records, so she ran his name through the computer and found him there. William B. Lewis: born in 1985, guardian was Sue Sweet, address was 16 Berwick Street. Several minor encounters with the system were listed but no convictions.

Shirley then ignored Lewis as she read the summary opinion, which had been provided by one of his former teachers. Lewis was considered astute, street-wise, likely abused. He constantly sought attention and acceptance, especially from his peers. He was rated a smart but poor student.

Reading continued to ignore Lewis as if she had little interest in him. To add to that image, she casually placed the front page of the newspaper on her desk as if he were not even present and read silently. The front page of the *Chronicle* proclaimed "Police Officer Suicide". She was struck by the article's presentation, which relied heavily speculation, was laced with innuendo, and used carefully structured words that were crafted to lead readers into believing that what the paper conjectured was factual. The article portrayed Brown's death as a suicide over the Donald Frank arrest.

Shirley watched Lewis out of the corner of her eye and then casually asked him if he wanted to read the *Chronicle* while they waited, but she did not mention the Brown story. Her plan was to thaw his attitude. It did not take long to see that he was interested in the Brown story. While he read it, she reached for her copy of the other paper, the *Daily Bugle*. She noted the different slant of this paper's article compared to the previous one. The headline stated "Distinguished Officer Dead". The accompanying story extolled the virtues of Brown and suggested accidental death. The writer, Steven Jobb, didn't mention the arrest of the Frank boy, or any controversy, or suicide.

Reading did not respect the paper or Jobb, based on bitter experience, but she did at least admire the fact that Jobb had written kindly, paying his debt to Brown in his generous portrayal. Most people at the police department knew that Brown had saved Jobb from a DUI charge, his third one, and in general, Jobb was considered Brown's bum-boy.

Shirley disregarded Lewis and read for about fifteen minutes, playing the waiting game in an attempt to get him to talk. Finally, she put the *Bugle* down and turned to him, asking him what he thought happened to Brown, as if she valued his opinion like she would that of another adult.

Lewis apparently could not resist, "He was a pervert. A bad son-of-a-bitch who hurt people for fun. I hope he's in hell if there is one."

Reading was intrigued by his answer, "Explain yourself."

Suddenly, he became reticent and nervous. He looked around, a furtive glance like a shoplifter. "You must think I'm nuts. He's a cop; you're a cop, and that's what got me into the corner I'm in. I know what happens when you fuck with cops."

Shirley knew that to try and patronize him now would not work because he was suspicious. She backed off slightly, "I heard things about Brown. In fact, I heard he was a sleaze."

Lewis did not comment. Her strategy did not work so she decided to move the pressure up a notch, going from carrot to the hint of the stick.

She picked up the plastic baggie, "You got fifty pills here." She then pretended to know more than she did. "I know these pills came from the Walgreen robbery, and I think it's time you took stock of the mess you're in and co-operate."

Lewis tried to talk his way out, "I got those pills with a doctor's prescription and I never robbed anyplace."

She looked skeptical, "Really? Then you give me the name of the doctor, and I'll phone him, and we can clear up this robbery mess."

Lewis looked worried, maybe because he had not considered how easy it would be to refute his claim, or perhaps because he was shocked that she knew the pills had come from the robbery. Shirley turned up the pressure.

"Doctors don't give prescriptions for fifty Valium at a time, and drugstores don't put them in plastic sandwich bags with no label on them, Billy-boy, so you better stop bullshittin' me. This is distribution of a controlled substance, which spells time in an adult facility."

The final statement caught his attention, "What would happen to a person who was forced to do something, if they helped the police?"

She shrugged, implying that she wasn't too interested, "I can only tell you what I've seen in other cases, but with no parent or guardian present, I can't talk deals with you."

He was suddenly upset. "My parents are dead; my aunt's my guardian, and she's a falling-down drunk who couldn't give a shit."

Reading stood up, "Well, that's it. We'll end this and call social services."

"Hold it," he blurted. "Does that mean I'll go into the system?"

"Looks like," she replied.

He became slightly but noticeably conciliatory. "What if I volunteer to help you?"

"Well," she replied, "I'd have to get a judge's permission and get you a lawyer to be present to protect your interests and rights but no more bullshit or I don't bother."

"How long would all that take?"

Shirley acted doubtful, "If I can catch the people we need, you might be shooting pool again by sundown."

"I don't think I'll bother with the pool hall," he said. "If I help you, word will leak out and, I'm gonna need to hide out. One more thing, I want a woman lawyer because I don't want no faggot pawing at me."

Shirley found the remark puzzling but she did not pursue the matter.

Judge Gertrude Curry, whom Shirley had known and appeared before since her law school intern days, was a crusty defender of the Constitution and a no-nonsense, fair judge. Had she been a male, she might have been labeled a curmudgeon.

Shirley outlined the entire matter to Curry over the telephone, explaining both sides of the problem as she saw it and asking for permission to get a lawyer for Lewis and then to proceed. Curry listened patiently then asked to speak to William Lewis. He was surprised but took the phone and listened. He then loosened up; whatever the questions were that Curry asked, he replied, "yes" numerous times, then thanked her and passed the phone back to Shirley.

Judge Curry instructed Shirley to call the public defender, and once Lewis was lawyered up, if he wanted to co-operate, that was fine.

The public defender's office is overworked, and the lawyers and staff are underpaid. Most of the people who work there do so because of personal dedication, because there is no hope of wealth and little of fame. Their mission statement states their responsibility is to defend those who are socially disadvantaged.

Shirley Reading had never acted like public defenders were the enemy, and she understood the burdens of the job: too many problems, too few resources, not enough lawyers, and a never-ending line of people needing help. Their phones never stopped ringing.

Reading transported Lewis to her former classmate, Lydia Corkum, who worked in the Public Defenders office. Lydia's desk looked like a salvage dump. There were open law books, a computer, files, papers, a pile of pink unanswered phone message slips, half a sandwich, and a styrofoam Starbucks coffee cup. Shirley kidded with Lydia about the police department not being able to afford Starbuck's coffee, only the stuff from Dunkin' Donuts.

Shirley introduced Lewis. He and Lydia touched hands, but the shake was a standoffish defensive motion while they sized each other up.

"Let's go into one of the client rooms for privacy," Corkum suggested.

Inside, she sat across from Lewis, with Reading at the head of the small table separating them. "If you want me to be your attorney, then I'll represent you. I'll be your lawyer, not hers, and your well-being will be my responsibility."

Lewis' expression revealed his doubts. "Don't give me the `I'm your attorney shit, I've been screwed over by the system before when they stuck me with my aunt when I wanted to go with my father's family up north, so show me your magic."

Corkum was no green intern; she had faced doubtful clients many times. "Tell me what you want," she said to him.

"A walk," he snapped.

Corkum turned her attention to Shirley, "How can we accomplish a walk?"

Shirley was equally blunt, "We might arrange one if, and I mean if, he gives me something worthwhile and no more bullshit."

Lewis was still not ready to cave in without comment. "How do I know anything I give you won't end up with the same cops who pushed me into this mess?"

"Hey wise mouth," Corkum replied, "Reading and I may be on different teams, but she's straight, and do I look like I'm on the pad and being paid by the mob?"

Lewis sat silently for several minutes. Finally he spoke, "I guess I don't have a lot of choice. I hope you people are for real, 'cause the bunch I'm dealing with make people disappear."

Both women were intrigued. The tension in his voice suggested he was scared and telling the truth. He sagged back in his chair, resigned to the fact that he had to co-operate. "It's real bad. A couple of cops roust certain kids, usually people like me from broken or troubled homes. I think they pick carefully and likely get the names from some of their contacts. Then you end up meeting with that prick Brown in a room at the jail."

Shirley was surprised by his statement. "At the jail," she asked, "do the cops take you to jail to see Brown?"

He nodded, "You end up alone in a room with him, and he makes it very clear what your options are. You have sex with him, or you distribute pills for him, and if you refuse, you end up being arrested and enough drugs will be found on you so you'll be up the creek."

Shirley was noticeably appalled, "You mean Brown forced the young women to have sex with him or distribute drugs?"

Lewis laughed a bitter laugh, "Young women, young men; he'd do it with a dog, and agreeing to deal the pills didn't protect you from him in the future either. He was like one of those Australian poison toads I saw on TV. There was this science show on horny toads and it said that some of them do it five times a day to females or even other male toads They had a film of one big old toad humping another male for over an hour and the interesting thing was that the second toad was dead. That's why we called Brown a horny toad."

Reading and Corkum looked at each other with disgust for the story in their eyes.

"What cops?" Shirley asked.

"I met four. Kierans, Clarke, Nichols and Stent. Nichols is a mean son-of-a-bitch and he slapped me around once."

Shirley continued with her questions. "Did they all have sex with the kids?"

"Only Brown did that I knew of."

"Have they all been brutalized by Brown?"

Lewis was embarrassed, his face red. "Yes, same story, at the room at the jail."

Shirley pushed on. "What did Brown force you to do?"

Lewis shook his head, tears filled his eyes, "Everything. It's too disgusting, no details."

"OK," Shirley soothed. "I understand. Can you think of anyone who would want to kill Brown?"

Lewis did not hesitate, "I can't think of anyone who wouldn't."

Shirley was deeply moved, and Corkum's disgust was evident. It was obvious that Bill Lewis had had a lot of baggage forced upon him by people who had violated positions of trust.

"Tell me how the drug dealing works," Shirley asked.

"They supply the pills. I sell them for five bucks apiece: I get a dollar, they get the rest."

"How do you meet or arrange to get the pills?"

Lewis was more comfortable with this line of questioning. "They rotate the pick-up points, a different spot each week. One week I meet Nichols at the church parking lot, the next week at the Publix parking lot: always out in the open but every week a different location. Nichols never talks; he's afraid of someone being wired. I get in his car; we settle up; and he replaces what I've sold. He told me once that if I'm ever questioned, I'm to pretend I'm his snitch, and that would explain my getting into his car."

"What about the other kids?" Shirley wondered. "How do they control them to keep them quiet and prevent gossip?"

Lewis' expression became even more serious. "One guy, Donnie Randall, got too noisy and shot his mouth off and poof ... we never saw him again."

Shirley remembered Randall's name from a missing persons report. He had never been found in over six months of looking. "Maybe Randall just wanted out and moved away."

Lewis considered her suggestion, "I don't think so. We heard they killed him. They beat him to death with a chain and buried him in the county landfill."

Shirley was skeptical. Not of the fact that the people involved would kill, but Lewis had provided nothing more than rumor. Double hearsay was what a judge would call the story.

"Could they have just leaked that yarn to you guys to scare you into keeping quiet?"

"I hope so," Lewis replied. "Then they tried to do a number on that Frank kid."

Shirley's heart skipped a beat, "Tell me what you mean."

"They put the heat to Frank to distribute and he refused. Then they tried to get him into trouble at school to make him look bad in case he ratted, and when that didn't work, they arrested him, and you know what happened to him at the jail."

Reading leaned in, "Do you think it was Brown who raped him?"

Lewis laughed, "Maybe Frank doesn't even know who it was cause the room would be dark. My bet is on Brown."

Shirley and Lydia sat silent, stunned by the dreadful facts they had just learned. It was too macabre to be a bullshit story unless Lewis could put together better tales than Stephen King. They had no doubt it was true but whether it qualified as admissible evidence was questionable. It required action but what and how?

"William," Lydia said. "Do you have anyone, any relations out of state, where we could send you?"

"My uncle, my dad's brother, lives in Portland, Maine with his wife. He tried to get me to move up there when my father died, but the court stuck me with my mother's sister here. I wanted to go to Maine because I liked them and my aunt here is a drunk."

"What's your uncle do?" Corkum asked.

"He gets a veteran's pension and he has a little fishing boat."

Corkum leaned forward and the tone of her voice revealed her concern, "If your uncle will still take you, and he checks out as clean by the authorities up there, you better go."

Lewis nodded and reached into his pocket and removed a fancy wallet. In the small pocket of it, he retrieved a folded piece of paper and passed it to her. "That's his address and phone number, but where can I hide until it's arranged?"

"With my mother," Corkum said without hesitation and reached for the phone.

Shirley was still troubled, "At least you can trust your mother, and you can check out the uncle, but who can I trust at the police department?"

CHAPTER THIRTEEN

Alliance

"Trust few, and always cut the cards."
- apologies to Shakespeare

It was eleven in the evening, not very late for TV addicts, yet nighttime phone calls still made her uncomfortable. "Why do people phone at this time of night unless something's wrong?" Shania Bear asked, knowing full well the answer to what was a stupid question from a police officer's wife.

"Mrs. Bear," a silky-smooth female voice greeted her. "This is Sergeant Shirley Reading. May I speak with Noel please?"

Shania politely asked her to wait and then indicated to Noel that the call was for him. He had been almost asleep on the sofa, ready for bed early because he was on the six a.m. day shift and would have to be up early, by four-thirty, to make the pre-shift inspection an hour later.

""Hello?" Noel said in a sleepy voice. Then he said nothing else for a while, and just listened. Finally, he said, "OK" and hung up.

"Reading and Baptist are coming over," he said to Shania. "They have something they can't discuss over the phone."

"Should I make coffee?" she asked.

"Make it for them," he replied. "I'd never get to sleep for the rest of the night if I drank some now."

When the police officers arrived, Bear sensed the tension emanating from their facial expressions and no-nonsense manners. It was certainly no social call with the time approaching midnight. The couple exchanged introductions with Shania, and then Reading started the story.

Shirley told Bear the facts given to her by Bill Lewis and related his version of the corruption and predatory sex drive of Major Brown. She went on to tell about the disappearance of Donnie Randall and Lewis' claim that he had been beaten to death by two police officers in order to silence him. By the time she got to the part involving Brown's arrest of Donald Frank, and why, and the jailhouse rape, Noel Bear and his wife were sitting in shocked silence.

Shania's eyes were big and brown, deep and beautiful like a work of art, a picture of innocence, but as she listened, her eyes registered revulsion, and the disgust she felt was evident in her stare. Reading, seeing that reaction, now regretted that they had not asked to speak to Noel alone. Perhaps she should have been sophisticated enough to excuse herself when they had arrived, but hindsight was useless, and she could not now erase the awful facts.

Noel said very little, almost nothing, but he paid close attention and periodically nodded or asked a brief question purely for clarification of some aspect of the facts. Silence while others talked was a courtesy required in the Native culture of his childhood, and it was natural for him to be polite and attentive because he had been taught the Indian way by his mother. Sometimes he found that remaining silent provided a stimulus for a speaker to reveal a tale in more detail. In some interviews of suspects, the use of periodic stillness by Bear seemed to cause the person to prattle and reveal useful information. His mother had taught him those old ways, things passed down from the elders: like respect for others and for the earth. Often as a youngster he had wondered about some of her teachings or was secretly amused because the ideas seemed old fashioned, but age and experience had taught him the value of those teachings. One thing he particularly remembered was his mother's frequent warning, "When the mouth is open, the ears are shut."

As Bear sat listening and watching Reading and Baptist, he sensed their sincerity, their distress, and their angst over learning that police colleagues had violated the sacred trust of public service and responsibility. Yet, Noel did not reveal his undercover connection or what he knew about the murder of the undercover trooper, Mike McCurdy. He trusted Shirley more than the others, mainly because she had befriended him and tipped him off about her suspicions of corruption in the department, but he did not divulge that he was also uncomfortable and worried about whom he could confide in. Another hockey player's edict came to mind, "Trust few and always cut the cards."

In practical terms, there were several reasons for him to be cautious at this meeting. The first was that he had not yet confided in his wife because he did not want to worry her. To do so now, with no warning, would prove her claim that he mislead her by silence. Second, he did not want to compromise the productive efforts of the dead trooper by speaking prematurely and revealing too much. Finally, he did not think it judicious to trust them completely at this stage just in case they were lying in order to set him up.

Before the Europeans came to America, there was no Indian word for liar. After they came and broke treaties, one tribe adopted the word bacana, which meant both liar and white man. The words became interchangeable to the natives.

Reading obviously had an objective in mind for telling her story to a new officer like Bear. It made little sense for her to do so unless she had an agenda. That was the reservation Bear held: was her objective as honorable as it seemed? As for Sergeant Baptist, he seemed trustworthy, and he was someone Reading had expressed confidence in, but he was also her lover, so Bear would be cautious about him too.

Finally, after Shirley had spoken for over an hour, she paused and said, "We came to you because you are new to the department, and we believe you are not involved. Your speculation to me about various aspects of the Frank arrest and the drug distribution story Dale Dunlop gave you makes us think you're suspicious about corruption in the department. Frankly, we don't think just the two of us can dig into this alone, and yet, if we get too many involved, our suspicions will leak out."

Baptist spoke up, "Do we involve some outside law enforcement agency? And if so, which one? That's the circular discussion we've been having between ourselves for hours, so we finally agreed to check with you for a third opinion."

Bear was comforted but not convinced enough to reveal anything. He was still mentally cutting the cards to make sure the deal they discussed was honest. He decided on a simple test based on their quandary. He hesitated long enough to formulate his thoughts and words and then spoke. "An outside agency is almost mandatory because how deep and extensive this mess is precludes spreading the word among others in the department, so it better be the state police, besides I hear the chief is thick with the sheriff, and nobody gossips more than cops."

Reading smiled, sort of a sour grin. "Don't forget the press as the biggest gossips. If this leaks to them a lot of good officers are going to be tarred with the same brush as the few bad apples."

Bear decided to make his test suggestion specific so that he could see how they reacted. If they carried out his idea it would be a fairly good indication that they were honest. He said, "Dale Dunlop has a friend at the state police you could contact. His name is Lieutenant Sam Folker, and he assists the commander. I've also heard Foley speak of him, and it appears the guy is a winner."

Baptist liked the idea, "I think that's a safe plan to start. We'd be less likely to cause a public stink, which would hurt us all."

Reading was still concerned but realized they had to start someplace. "OK, that's where we'll begin, but what about you? Can we count on your help?"

Noel did not hesitate, "Just remember this. If I'm in - and with my limited experience, I don't know what I can do - but with all due respect, if I'm in, wherever this goes and whoever it uncovers, there are no exceptions, excuses, or exclusions. Any dirty cop goes down."

Shirley smiled, "Absolutely." She turned to Baptist, "I told you he was a cool straight guy."

Bear held out his hands, one to each of them, and as they grasped them he said, "A troika, like the Three Musketeers."

Shania had taken it all in. She said, "I hope your swordsmanship is as good as your intentions."

Bear walked Shirley and Baptist to the door. "You phone Folker and if you have to leave a message, maybe you should ask that he return the call to your house so no body gets curious at the PD."

After they left Shania went upstairs. Noel went to the kitchen and used his cell phone to call Folker at home. Folker answered himself. It was almost one in the morning.

"Sorry about the hour", Bear apologized , "but I've just had visitors." He then related the events and facts he'd heard from Reading and Baptist. Folker listened attentively, and after Bear finished, he said, "I agree with your caution. They sound OK, but your safety may be at risk as whoever it is has killed once already. We don't want to compromise what McCurdy accomplished or the investigation."

"Last point," said Bear, "did Hoss tell you about the two drug officers going through the same roadblock on the same days as the robberies?"

"He did. Last night he gave me the rundown on Brown's autopsy, and he told me that the state lab is also doing an autopsy to satisfy Dr. Foley's concern for any court challenge on his and Dr. Donald's conclusions."

They signed off, and Noel dragged his tired frame upstairs and slid into bed next to Shania. She raised herself up on her elbow and faced him, "I know you and your every facial reaction, Indian, and you were on the defensive down there. What's going on?" she asked.

Bear was impressed, "I don't know if you're a shrewd Indian like the movies' Injuns or just the average sly smart woman, but you read me right. I have to make sure they're for real before I trust them. Now go to sleeep, unless you want to ..."

"G'night," she replied.

Despite the shortness of his night's sleep, Bear made it to the shift inspection at five-thirty a.m. There were the usual lists of crimes, and wanted felons, and the reading of events from what police call the pass-along book, a list of occurrences on each shift's watch, where incidents, which may or may not be related to crimes, are noted for future reference. An event might be chronicled just because it was unusual or perhaps an anomaly. The entries might result from an innocent act such as a person with perfectly proper ID being found snoozing in a car. If the hour was late or the location unusual, the person's name and the place would go into the pass-along book. Sometimes the entries were simply the names of street people or panhandlers and their locations. In Shiretown, the parochial name for beggars was road-agents because they often stood with a sign stating, "will work for food," but in reality upon being offered work, they usually hit the road.

The book had provided clues to crimes on many occasions. Today, the pass-along book contained two entries from the previous night that Bear would later remember. The first was a bunch of road-agents hanging around the war memorial on the eastern approach to the ballpark. The second was an informal call from a concerned mother to an officer she knew about her sixteen-year-old daughter not coming home by midnight, when the mother had to leave for work. She was concerned because it had never happened before. The officer involved noted the incidents in the pass-along book. At the time the information seemed of little value.

Following inspection, Bear headed his police unit number forty-two toward his assigned patrol in zone three. He traveled to West Park Street near the hospital hill and set up his radar for the early morning speeders. He sipped the hot black coffee Shania had prepared in his Thermos bottle. Traffic was jammed up and slow for over an hour, then he heard a call for district four next to him on the north side of Park Street, which included the ballpark where Officer Collins was assigned.

The police dispatcher's voice was flat and unemotional in the ten-series code, which almost anyone who watched TV cop shows or owned a police scanner could understand. "Unit forty-three Collins, in zone four, point two, secure and confirm, do you copy?" The dispatcher used a slight bit of double-speak and the nuance in her voice on the call made Bear curious.

"Copy," Collins replied, and he knew he was to secure a crime scene. The reference to point two was significant. Each week the department assigned numbers to specific points in each patrol zone to identify a place without naming it. The numbers were changed frequently to fool the public and the press who monitored police calls. This week, point two was the outfield bleachers, scoreboard, and fence at the ballpark.

Procedure required that an officer near a crime scene call in giving his location for use as backup. Bear announced his availability as unit forty-two. There was an immediate response by the dispatcher.

"Forty-two!"

"Go!" he replied.

"Ten-ninety-nine, point two, zone four, copy."

"Ten-four," Bear answered and slowly proceeded toward the location in a safe but efficient manner, because ten-ninety-nine was an unofficial department code used to confuse eavesdroppers. It meant to proceed to a location with no lights, no sirens, attracting no attention. It translated to, "Get your ass there without fanfare."

Bear arrived at the back of the ballpark scoreboard and stopped next to Collins' patrol car which was parked so it could not be seen from Park Street by the prying eyes of passers-by. Three young boys were standing next to the car. Yellow police tape ran around a wide circumference starting at the outside corner of the bleachers using various off-field shrubs and trees as supports. Then Bear saw what it was all about: just between the walkway of the scoreboard and the bleachers. Two bare feet stuck out from under a square of plastic sheet, covering a body. The homicide detectives would soon arrive.

The crime scene techs and the medical examiner had not yet shown up, and Bear figured it would take them thirty minutes.

"What's the deal?" he asked Collins.

"Those kids found a body, a white female; looks like rape-murder. Her panties and pantyhose are over there, like someone tossed 'em. She was stabbed up under the ribs, likely right into her heart, and her breasts were hacked off, then the sicko burned her. It smells like gas. The kids found her purse over there. Her name is Mary Anslow and she just turned sixteen, according tothe ID in her purse. The motive certainly didn't include robbery 'cause there's eighty bucks in the wallet."

Bear shook his head in sadness. "Just like the Fraser girl, same MO."

Collins stood gazing at the bare feet, his face a pasty-gray like a sea-sick sailor. "First time I ever saw a burnt body. It's fuckin' awful. I woofed my breakfast." He began to spread more of the police tape. "Do me a favor, Bear, get statements from those kids."

The three boys were leaning against the police cruiser on the driver's side, away from the view of the body. Bear was mindful of their sickening experience.

"Hi guys. Help me out with your names, ages, addresses, and how it happened, so we can get you out of here quickly."

The smallest boy, known as Mouse, was twelve and the other two, who were thirteen, seemed to defer to his leadership. Mouse was as pale-looking as Officer Collins. His eyes displayed his emotional shock, yet he sounded worldly, streetwise, as he spoke.

"Man, she's burnt. Looks like big blisters and blackened flesh. I never wanna see no burnt body again."

Bear recorded how they had discovered the body on the way to throw a ball around on the big field before they went to school. It was their usual shortcut. Bear was completing his interview notes as Dr. Donald and Sergeant Baptist arrived.

The two new arrivals asked Collins for the details and then uncovered the corpse. Kirk walked over to Bear and suggested that if he was finished with the kids, he should send them on their way. "I don't think their memory of this scene will be forgotten in a hurry so let's not prolong the agony."

Foley arrived at the same time as the forensic techs. He walked slowly around the scene while Kirk examined the body. Finally Foley spoke, "Looks like a car drove to and from here by the depressions in the grass. There's not enough marks to get a tire mold, but the flattened grass shows the direction of the vehicle. Let's assume that the killer and the girl came in here by car, and he drove out the same way."

He paused, then pointed toward the northwest corner of the park where the tire tracks headed. He continued to talk to no one in particular, almost as if he were just thinking out loud, using deductive reasoning to explore his idea. "The field ends up there near the playground, and there's a dirt connector road from the field across to old Main Street. It wouldn't be the first time someone used that street to sneak in here with a woman. Now what would he do with a condom if he used one, and since the MO is like the Fraser murder, he likely wore one."

Then, as if providing an answer to his own question, he replied. "He wouldn't throw it away near the body. But it's about a mile from here up to that old connector road, and by the time the perp got there on his way out, he might be careless and think it was safe to dispose of the condom, because there's a big storm drain channel that runs beside the road. He might just pitch it out the car window into the ditch."

Baptist liked the scenario enough to follow it up. He turned to Bear and Collins. "How about you guys start searching along the car tracks from here up to the ditch. Pay particular attention to the ditch all the way over to Main Street."

The two officers walked along, one on each side of the car tracks, scanning visually for the used condom. It took almost fifteen minutes to reach the drainage ditch and they estimated it was almost a mile. From where the dirt road and the ditch which ran parallel started, it was about five hundred feet to Main Street. The ditch originated on the high ground and passed downward to the side of the dirt road and was only accessible by car from that short dirt track. The ditch was three to four feet deep during this reasonably dry period, with only a trickle of water running through a maze of old wine bottles, beer cans, and assorted refuse.

Bear took the far side and Collins the narrow path between the road and the ditch. There was an endless assortment of discarded items in the foul-smelling stagnant water. Collins sighted a dead Christmas tree that revealed its former glory with several faded broken ornaments still attached to its bare limbs. As he looked closer, he saw something else. He waded into the smelly water and finally groaned, "Aw fuck! There's at least two rubbers caught here and the opening in one is above the water on the tree but the other one may be contaminated by the water."

Bear, who had stepped in some dog poop, was scraping the sole of his police boot with a stick, his face contorted from the unbelievable smell. "I hear you. But if there's two condoms, you're supposed to say, `aw, fuck, fuck'."

"Very funny," Collins replied. "Or I might say, very funny shit-heels."

Bear stuck his boot in the water trying to clean the smell off. "Did you bring surgical gloves?" he asked Collins.

"Nope, did you?"

Bear was now scuffing the sole of his boot in the sand beside the bank. "I'll go back and get some, but remember you're in charge, and if they start to float away, you'll have to dive in because they're potential evidence."

Collins shook his head, "Between seeing the body and smelling whatever you stepped in, diving in would be easy."

Bear jogged back to his patrol car down at the crime scene. "Hey guys," he yelled, "we might have what you want."

Both Foley and Baptist looked puzzled. Foley spoke first. "I don't get it. Is it there or not?"

"There's two," Bear replied as he walked over to them. "I came down for gloves and bags."

Foley looked sour, "That's bad news, 'cause some fucking defense attorney will argue that whoever threw the second rubber away was the killer and that, my friends, is reasonable doubt."

Bear took the evidence kit and started back. When he arrived, he jumped down the back of the ditch, passed Collins the gloves, and held out the evidence bags. Collins leaned over the tree which held the two condoms and gently retrieved the one above the water and dropped it into the bag. He then slowly picked up the second one which appeared to have some dirty water in it. Bear labeled the bags and both men started back to the crime scene.

"Your pal Foley is a shrewd student of human nature, figuring out where the perp might throw the condom away," Collins said.

"That's true," Bear said. "But these condoms might have no connection to the murder. They could have been there for a week."

Collins seemed to consider that before he spoke. "All this DNA shit mystifies me anyway. How'd it all get started?"

"I read a book called *The Blooding*," Bear said. "An American named Joseph Wambaugh, an ex-LA Cop, wrote how the English first used DNA in solving two rape murders in England."

Collins was interested, full of questions. "But how did they use it?"

"An English scientist named Jeffreys wrote a paper on DNA in 1980, according to Wambaugh's book, and then in 1984 there were these two rape murders in the English midlands, and a Brit detective called in Jeffreys to help. The first suspect was an inmate at the mental institution and Jeffreys compared his DNA with the semen found at the scene, and he actually cleared the guy the cops had liked. They were pretty frustrated by this time, so they asked all the males in the village to volunteer to submit to blood tests."

"Holy shit!" exclaimed Collins. "If you volunteer, there's no rights violation, and if you don't, you're automatically a suspect."

Bear laughed, "Something like that. Anyway, they tested over three thousand males and no match was found."

Collins shook his head, "Did they ever catch the guy?"

"Yup. Because the real perp feared the blood testing, so he had a pal go in for the test using his name. He almost got away with it until the pal told someone he'd taken the perp's place for the blood test, and when they finally tested the proper guy, bingo, they got a conviction."

"What about here in the US?"

"It was a battle here about the admissibility of DNA, including a submission by some defense lawyers' group who claimed that DNA was fallible. But science prevailed, and subsequent research papers provided empirical data, and apparently the court requirement for admissibility is that there have to be scientific articles on the subject. One scientific opinion won't do."

Collins was warming to the subject. "What about the O.J. case? Do you think that case will hurt the chances of admissibility in future cases?"

Bear shook his head, "You'd have to ask Hoss to get a legal answer to that because he has a law degree and is good on admissibility questions, but as I understand it, the Simpson lawyer Scheck claimed contamination of the sample at the lab, he didn't really attack the science of DNA."

Collins held up a bag with a condom in it. "What about our sample from the ditch, this one with the water in it?"

Bear was dubious. "Possibly, but I'm just a reader, not a technical person and I don't know if water, especially polluted stuff, affects the sperm or simply dilutes it. Maybe the other condom will be cleaner and will work for us."

By the time they reached the crime scene, Bear had developed a friendly feeling and respect for Collins and his common-sense curiosity. Kirk had finished the preliminary examination of the body, and the techs had collected fiber and a cigarette butt, and had found a black substance on the ground between the victim's feet. Foley surmised that the substance was shoe polish from where the rapist had dug in with his feet on the turf.

Foley was still cogitating, trying to equate what they knew with what they thought. "No overt signs of physical force, so it may have been consensual sex, and then he killed her, and used the fire to destroy the evidence, but we'll have to wait until we do the lab work to be sure. It's almost certainly a case just like the Fraser girl, and of course, the question is how come a sick fucker like this suddenly does two victims in a row?"

Kirk listened intently, "Maybe there are similar cases in other cities maybe even out of state, so the two in Shiretown could be just two in a string of others."

He turned to his assistants, "Sack her up. We'll do the rest at the morgue."

It was a long depressing day, as the autopsy progressed slowly; Kirk was determined to be very thorough. There were traces of a chemical used on condoms in the victim's vagina, just like the previous murder, so a rubber had definitely been used. The murder wounds were also similar, made by a serrated military weapon. The burns on the body had reduced the chances of forensic evidence such as pubic hair from the perp being caught in the victim's hair, but Kirk did find one clue which had not existed on the first victim. This one had a clear bite mark, an imprint of teeth, on her cheek which had not been obliterated by the fire. Possibly, the bite could be matched to the tooth imprint of a potential suspect, if one was found.

Kirk had just finished the awful task, with Hoss present and assisting, when Sharon Marshall entered the lab. "The victim's mother is here to ID the body."

Kirk looked worried, "Stall. Give me five minutes to get out of these scrubs. I don't want her to see the kid's blood all over my clothes. It's bad enough without that."

Usually Kirk was a cool professional, a consummately detached medical person who revealed no emotion despite the fact that he had great compassion for the victims, but this was particularly bad. He entered the office where Ellen Anslow stood fidgeting nervously. Her pale, grim face above her austere nurse's uniform revealed her sorrow. Kirk knew that even though she was an experienced nurse, she could not possibly imagine what it would be like to view her own daughter's body. He shook her hand and explained what they were about to do.

"This is not pleasant anytime, and this one is particularly bad."

She rolled her eyes and nodded agreement but he knew that she still had no idea what she faced.

"Let's get it done," she said, and Kirk agreed. They walked through the door into the morgue. Foley stayed on one side of her and Kirk walked on the other in case she fainted. Kirk had already decided to only show the head to try and avoid revealing to Ellen Anslow the mutilated body of her daughter.

"Are you ready?" he asked her. When she said yes, he removed the plastic sheet from her child's face. Ellen Anslow was stunned. She wavered, almost losing her balance, weaving back and forth as the impact registered.

"That's my daughter Mary. I want you to uncover her."

Kirk exchanged glances with Foley, "I urge you not to."

She insisted, "I have to see her, she's my baby."

"It's very bad," Kirk warned her, hoping she would change her mind, yet his experience was that mothers always wanted to see it all, because it is their baby, regardless of the age. Mothers are compelled to look.

Reluctantly he removed the rest of the sheet. The full appearance of the jagged wound, the severed breasts, the badly burnt and blistered flesh, and the autopsy's intrusive cuts presented a view from hell. Ellen Anslow's legs buckled; her eyes rolled back, and she slumped like a rag doll, as Foley and Kirk grabbed her before she hit the floor.

Sharon Marshall placed a pillow under Ellen's head and propped her up slightly on the office sofa, as she came around. Kirk reached over and placed some smelling salts under her nose, and she snapped back to reality. She raised herself up slowly and swung her feet to the floor, leaning back against the sofa in a sitting position.

"Do you know Reverend Ken Solomon?" she asked. Without giving them time to acknowledge that they new him, she hurried to relate the story of his sexual abuse of her daughter at the church and the subsequent events with Chief Pineo, Sergeant Murphy, and the money from Solomon.

Foley forgot propriety, "That filthy perverted old bastard. What the hell was Pineo thinking? I'm filing an official complaint with Sergeant Baptist about this as it relates to the homicide."

Ellen Anslow did not really comprehend. She sat, gently rocking back and forth like a child, her arms crossed defensively as she cried. "My baby, my only baby."

CHAPTER FOURTEEN

Questions

"There's more to questions than answers; even silence can be revealing."

- Redhorse (2001)

Jack Baptist arrived at the morgue to meet Ellen Anslow in Kirk's office. If the eyes mirror the soul or the inner thoughts of a person, his revealed a man in pain. His expression was that of a deeply distressed person, someone so troubled that no words were needed to reveal his grief. He was so obviously burdened that Kirk Donald would later say to Foley that Baptist's shocked response to the young girl's rape-murder and the possibility of the involvement of crooked cops made him resemble the Vietnam vets who suffered post-combat stress disorder. The grief of Ellen Anslow and having to interview her were also factors contributing to Baptist's anguish.

Baptist was curious by nature, and he sought every detail possible in his investigations in order to compose the facts into an evidential profile. There was not much in the way of small talk he could offer in the face of her tragedy, so he first attempted to get her to open up, to tell the general facts in her own way. He listened attentively scribbling notes on a yellow evidence pad. Ellen Anslow told how her daughter was sexually assaulted by the Reverend Ken Solomon at the Lutheran Church office.

Her description was thorough, and the account sounded as if were taken from a paperback porn novel, except, sadly, it was not fiction. She told the story in sequence, which is something some witnesses cannot do because of the stress. She related the phone calls from Sergeant Murphy and the Chief of Police from the church to her at the hospital, the fact that Murphy drove her daughter home, and that the Chief of Police had later picked Ellen up at work. And she told how the matter was settled. Baptist let her speak without interruption until she suddenly paused, understandably exhausted.

Her story had raised questions. He was curious about how the chief had become involved and the way the incident had been handled. Police procedures had not been followed: a female officer had not been called to the scene involving a minor girl, and the two officers had not gone by the book. Murphy had driven Mary Anslow home alone.

There were so many questions that Baptist decided to explain to Ellen that the best method of proceeding would be a police procedure called Q and A, questions and answers. He did not want to further upset her or seem callous, so he apologized and said that it was a proven method of stimulating the memory and clarifying the facts, plus it would take less time. Q&A was best.

Ellen made it clear that she would do whatever it took to help him. He started the questions with the thing which troubled him the most.

Q: "Who called the police? Was it your daughter?"

A: "I don't know, I never thought of that until now."

Q: "What time did they phone you from the church?"

A: "Midday, I was on days that week."

Q: "Did the chief tell you it was a sexual incident?"

A: "No, he said it was a minor incident and asked if it was OK for Murphy to drive her home. I work with Sergeant Murphy's wife so I was comfortable with that. He also told me he needed to see me.

Q: "Did you go to the church then?"

A: "No, the day shift is hectic, and I said if there's no emergency I'd see him at five and he offered to pick me up then."

Q: "Did you phone your daughter later that afternoon at home?"

A: "Many times over several hours, but I never reached her until four o'clock."

Q: "When you finally reached her, did you ask her where she'd been?"

A: "First, I asked what had happened and she told me about Solomon. I went nuts. Then I told her I'd been trying to reach her for hours and she told me Murphy took her for coffee to calm her down."

Q: "Did you ever ask her exactly what she and Murphy discussed?"

A: "Yes, she said mostly he asked questions about school and he was a good listener and was very understanding."

Q: "How did Mary seem on the phone about all this?"

A: "Disgusted by Solomon; she was really disgusted."

Q: "Had there been any signs that Reverend Solomon was flirting with her before or hitting on her?"

A: "She never said anything, but maybe she didn't recognize the signs because she was pretty unworldly about sex."

Q: "Was there any sign of male interest, any school suitors or boyfriends?"

A: "Never, that is not until after this mess, then there were a lot of phone calls, funny calls. They started about two days later."

Q: "What makes you say funny calls? Jokes or strange?"

A: "Sort of strange. When I answered they hung up."

Q: "Could they have been wrong numbers? How often did they happen?"

A: "At least twice a day."

Q: "Did Mary get hang-ups too?"

A: "No'. That's what gave me the feeling it was a boy, because before the church mess, the only calls she got were from her girlfriend Diane Taylor."

Q: "Did you question her or ask her who she was talking to?"

A: "Yes and no. I sort of made a joke out of it, because I didn't want to violate her privacy, as she hadn't had any great number of friends calling before. She only laughed when I asked and said, 'I never date, so who'd call me but Diane?'"

Q: "Did you ever ask Diane if she was calling a lot?"

A: "I tried to ask her in an indirect way, and her reaction suggested she wasn't calling very often."

Q: "Back to Chief Pineo. The day he picked you up at the hospital, what did he say to you?"

A: "I exploded before he could say much of anything. I wanted to put Solomon away. He listened, and then said maybe there was a better way for everybody."

Q: "And what was the better way."

A: "He said that a trial would be a reputation killer for Mary, and he suggested that it might be better for us if we accepted a settlement from Solomon. He thought Solomon would be agreeable, and it would pay for Mary's education."

Q: "What did you say?"

A: "I didn't like it, and I said I'd have to ask Mary if court would upset her."

Q: "Did you discuss money, or suggest an amount?"

A: "No. Chief Pineo suggested fifteen thousand dollars, and said I should consider it no matter what Mary said."

Q: "And did you go to see Solomon?"

A: "No, we drove to the church, and the chief went in to see him."

Q: "How long did that take, and when he came back, what did he say?"

A: "He only stayed about fifteen minutes, and when he came back out he said Solomon would pay fifteen thousand, and if I accepted, I'd have to sign a secrecy agreement."

Q: "How long would all this take, according to the chief?"

A: "He said the next morning at ten a.m., and he'd make the arrangement and drive me down to the church."

Q: "Did you ever discuss this with Mary?"

A: "The minute I got home, and she definitely didn't want to go to court, so I called the chief's cell phone and told him OK."

Q: "What happened the next day?"

A: "The chief picked me up, and we drove to the church, and we both went in to Solomon's office. He passed me the money in cash, and I signed an agreement promising to keep quiet."

Q: "What time did all this happen?"

A: "Ten in the morning, just like the chief told me the night before on the phone."

Q: "Did Solomon say anything to you?"

A: "No, he looked wimpy, guilty like an old pervert. He just passed over the money without a word."

Q: "Did Mary know the details of the settlement?"

A: "Definitely and then suddenly she decided she didn't want to go to college. She said she didn't want to go away and thought she'd get a job instead."

Q: "You phoned Murphy last night just before you went to work and expressed concern about Mary not being home, is that correct?"

A: "Yes, she'd never done that before, and I had to leave for work for midnight."

Q: "Had she indicated where she was going before she went out?"

A: "She said she and Diane were going to the library, and then she was baby-sitting with Diane."

Q: "Were there any phone calls to your house yesterday?"

A: "There was a call about six p.m., and Mary giggled and acted coy on the phone. I sort of suspected it was a boy, but I really didn't know. That's when she told me about going with Diane."

Q: "Did you phone Diane's house after you started worrying?"

A: "I phoned there about eleven, and her father said she was baby-sitting, but he didn't know where."

Q: "What made you decide to phone Sergeant Murphy?"

A: "He was the only one I knew besides the chief, and I certainly wouldn't call him after the other mess."

Q: "Did you call Murphy directly?"

A: "No. I called the police number, and they had him phone me back. It only took about ten minutes for him to call."

Q: "What did he say to you when you told him about Mary?"

A: "He was very nice, very understanding, and he said all kids go through a stage of staying out late, and he'd have a look around. He also said he'd make an information entry in a log."

Q: "Can you think of anything else that happened over the weeks since the church incident that now seem strange to you?

A: "Those damn phone calls. I think they were connected."

Baptist finished his notes. "I need the address of Diane Taylor, and I want you to write me a permission slip to the phone company to check the computers to see if we can pick up on any numbers who have called you on a repetitive basis over the last few weeks. Maybe, if they're cell phone calls or long distance calls from out of the county, the computer will have them." Ellen complied with both requests and then Sharon Marshall drove her home.

After Ellen Anslow had left, Baptist asked Kirk to phone the department and ask for Noel Bear to be dispatched to the morgue. "Don't say it's for me. Just act like you want him."

Kirk punched in the direct dial to the police station and made the request to the desk sergeant. While they waited, Baptist raised the question which bothered him the most about the church incident.

"Who called the police from the church? Are there entries in the log? How did the chief get involved? And how did Murphy get into the act?" Baptist decided to review the desk entries at the station and question Murphy and the chief on those points, but he didn't want to speak to either man yet.

When Noel arrived, Kirk and Baptist outlined what had happened with Ellen Anslow's Q and A, the autopsy, and a few of the tests from the crime scene even though they were not all complete, as the state lab had yet to do the DNA forensics. Kirk explained that time of death was at first difficult to establish because the front of the victim was burnt. Foley expressed concerns, because the time of death would be crucial in court if a suspect had an alibi for the stated time. Kirk explain that when he had turned the body over he discovered parts of her back which were not burned, apparently because her own weight against the ground had prevented the killer's gas from seeping under her. Without oxygen to feed the fire, the back of her had large unburned areas.

Kirk had estimated the time of death at six or seven hours before it was discovered by the three boys. He had determined the time by the lividity, insect activity on the body, and other usual tests on the portions which had not been burned. Foley, realizing how important the question might be, acted as devil's advocate. He tried to provoke Kirk into changing his opinion. Kirk was not shaken.

"Fuck you, Hoss. I am not allowing some gawd-damn snake of a lawyer to shake me."

Baptist snorted as he listened to the two old friends try to provoke each other, as usual. "I do hope you remember to use less rough language in court," he said to Kirk.

"Right," Kirk answered. "I know some lawyer will try to make me say piss is lemon juice, but I'm not buying."

Bear had listened to the experienced veterans discuss the case without offering his opinion, but he was curious.

"What about the Fraser girl's case compared to this one? Are you satisfied it's the same MO?"

Baptist answered, "The major difference is that there is better evidence this time. There's a bite mark on this girl's cheek and two condoms, which may yield something. The first murder scene had only the Kleenex with the chemical from the rubber on it. I think there's no doubt the same nut did them both."

Bear couldn't suppress his curiosity anymore. "I don't want to ask stupid questions, but here's an idea you've likely already thought of. There are two condoms. First, is there a similarity between the semen found at the current scene and the stuff found on the tissue at the first one? Secondly, are the two condoms from the Anslow scene by the same manufacturer? And can that be proven by some manufacturer's mark or number for ID? And last, was the chemical from the condoms found inside both victims the same or was it the same as the chemicals on any or all of the condoms?"

Foley liked the questions, "What I think you're asking is can we cross-reference the chemicals from the victims' vaginas to the Kleenex from the first scene and the two condoms at the second scene? The answer is: probably, and the results might kill a reasonable doubt argument, if we ever get a suspect to court."

Bear now looked thoughtful. "The bad news is, there are some flaws in my theory. For instance, what if the condoms are all made by the same manufacturer? Or what if all manufacturers use the same chemicals on condoms? Or what if the ditch water washed all the chemical away?"

Kirk had listened with great interest, "All those questions can be answered. Even if the water washed the chemical away, it wouldn't matter because the manufacturer could certify what chemical they used and tell us whether it was the same as what we found on examination of the bodies."

Foley was enjoying the session, "Another lesson for me to remember. Stay curious. I have all the sophisticated training and equipment, but if I don't ask the right questions, it's all wasted."

"Yeah," said Kirk. "You're an old fart, and maybe you should commit hari kari."

Foley stood up. "Too busy today."

Baptist outlined his first theory for Noel, "In both cases, we assume the girls went with the killer and had sex voluntarily. That's a positive for Reverend Solomon's innocence, because Mary Anslow would not likely go anywhere with him after the incident at the church, but I'm still going to interview the pervert. I'm also going to speak with Mary Anslow's friend Diane Taylor, and later, it's mandatory that I question Murphy and the chief. Likely Murphy's first, but for now, I'll stay away from them until we get our ducks in a row. Now here's where I need you to help me. Murphy wrote in the pass-along book the time and names of a bunch of road-agents he found at the war memorial near the time of the murder. I'd like you to take the names, hunt them down, and interview them. Somebody, including that bunch, must have seen the gas fire. Even though it was outside the outfield seats, there would still be a bright glow."

Bear agreed, but just as he started to leave, Kirk asked the question that each of them had secretly thought. "After listening to Ellen Anslow and the story of how Chief Pineo handled that church thing, I wonder if he's a crook or has Solomon got something on him or is he incompetent?"

Baptist responded, "It doesn't much matter which the result is the same. It's wrong."

Foley agreed, "If nothing else, he's lost perspective and is confusing enforcement of the law with dispensing justice."

Bear started for the door again but stopped for a final thought. "I think Murphy is cast in a shadow here too, and whether he just did what he was told or is in deeper, he's just as wrong as the chief."

On that note, Bear departed and headed out West Park Street to start his search for the road-agents named in the pass-along book. He knew that during daylight hours they hung around well-traveled places to panhandle. His first point was to be the Park Street ramp to the state highway. As he approached, he saw a local legend, Skeeter Greene, a long-time road-agent. He was an unwashed, foul-smelling, unshaven fifty-eight year old male who was known for his impatience and inability to suffer fools. Bear thought that might be the reason Skeeter didn't have a job.. He had dropped out, or more likely just failed out, of society. As Bear moved closer, he could see the brooding hulk of Greene holding his sign. "Will work for food." Bear marveled at the sign, because he knew that it only took a mention of labor to send Greene rushing away, pausing only to curse your ancestry.

Noel pulled the police car up over the asphalt curb onto the green strip next to the on ramp and got out. Greene, upon seeing the car, expected a police roust and turned to walk away.

"Hey, Skeeter!" Bear shouted. "No problem, Man, wait! I got a proposition for you."

Greene paused then turned around and faced Bear. His sour look suggested he was skeptical. Bear decided to bluff him. First he reached in his pocket and took out five dollars then held it so Greene could see what it was.

"Last night you were at the war memorial over at the baseball park. Who was there with you?"

Greene sat his backpack down on the ground but did not come closer. "So what?" he said in a grumpy, challenging manner.

Noel held the fiver up with both hands to make sure Greene could see it. "Answer my questions and Lincoln goes with you."

Skeeter advanced a few feet in Bear's direction his eyes fixed on the money. As he came nearer, Bear could smell him, an odor so strong and bad that he wondered why Greene was not surrounded by his very own manure flies.

Greene held out his hand for the money.

"Not so fast, Skeeter. Tell me what you know first."

Greene now looked even grumpier, proving he had several degrees of temper. "I know the drill. Five Ws. Who, what, where ... but how do I know you'll pay me?"

Bear lowered his hands and held the money by his side. "It's up to you," he said in a take-it-or-leave-it tone. "Either move your lips or move your feet and take your sorry ass outta my face."

Greene now decided to answer, "I was there with some people. We stayed from about eleven till a few minutes after one."

Bear decided to keep the five dollars in view but to ask questions which suggested he did not understand the impatient Greene. "How'd you know the time when you don't have a watch?"

Green responded with agitation, "No, I don't have a watch, but I got ears and Sweet's got a watch."

Bear knew George Sweet was another homeless man who was also well-known at the PD. He was a man who gave the impression of superiority yet had little to be superior about. He was a bullshitter, whose bravado was illustrated by the omnipresent used cigar butt stuck in his mouth.

"Did you ask Sweet what time it was?"

"Nope," Greene replied. "A cop came by and hassled us and said by the time he came back we'd better be gone. After he left, Sweet said it was eleven o'clock and the cop wouldn't be back there on his patrol until after one, so we had no need to rush."

Bear kept fingering the five dollars, moving it from hand to hand. "And you didn't know who the police officer was?"

Skeeter took the bait, his sharp tongue moving quickly, "I know most of them. It was that prick Murphy who hassled us, but that was at the front of the park."

Bear pretended he had not heard correctly, "And you say that was about ten o'clock?"

Skeeter was frustrated by the question, and he wanted the five dollars. His legendary bad temper was starting to show, "Have you got fuckin' Alzheimers? For chrissakes, are you deaf? I said eleven o'clock. What are you trying to do? Change my story? Gimme my money."

Bear kept a passive face and continued, "I was just testing you, Skeeter. What about the fire behind the bleachers? What time did you see that?"

Skeeter was experienced with the police, and he also had the disposition of a pitbull with a sore butt, according to local legend. He wanted his five dollars and Bear was not delivering, "Who said I saw any fire?" he bellowed.

Bear lied with a straight face, "George Sweet said so."

Greene spit, revealing his disgust, "That's what I think of that rat-bastard. If I don't get the five now, I answer no more questions."

Bear said nothing in reply but held the money up as if he was ready to deliver and Greene softened slightly, "It was closer to one in the morning 'cause Sweet reminded us that Murphy's patrol would be back soon. But we all saw the fire, a glow behind the bleachers."

"And did Murphy come back about that time?" Bear asked.

Skeeter shook his head, "No, we watched for about fifteen minutes, but because of the scoreboard and the bleachers, we couldn't see more than the glow."

Greene then tried to divert Bear's attention to speed up the process, "Why don't you ask that fag Hicks? He fruits around over there, and most nights he sleeps behind the scoreboard platform in the back."

Bear made notes in his note book. Even though he was sure he knew who was present, he wanted confirmation from Greene. "Who else was there?"

Skeeter was close to losing his famous temper. His face reddened. Bear continued to bait him by holding out the five dollars, closer but still out of reach. "C'mon Skeeter, out with it."

"Would you like their social security numbers too?" Greene replied sarcastically.

Bear supressed a smile, "I'm listening and I want full names and if I get them, I might add a couple of bucks."

Those were the magic words to stimulate Greene. "Mindy Hallet, Borden Hart, Rob Feters, Jorge Dunn, and some prissy-ass new guy named Harwood. All of them were hanging."

Bear scribbled down the names, taking too long in Skeeter's opinion. Finally Bear spoke, "Here's your money. I upped it to eight bucks. Now, if I were you, I'd move along before some hard-ass cop comes along."

Greene picked up his shabby old backpack and started to shuffle away under the load of his own junk. Then he paused and turned back, because he had to have the last word, "How come they allow you out without the fuckin' Lone Ranger?"

Bear returned to his cruiser, circled under the ramp, and headed back downtown. He swung onto Church Street past the pool hall, parked by the electric commission's lot, and walked up the hill to the Salvation Army soup kitchen where he knew some of the drifters would be in the chow line. He sighted the lanky Lee Hicks talking with another ne'er-do-well named Rob Feters who always had an old pipe clamped between his yellow teeth. Bear knew them both from numerous encounters during his two years on the force.

Hicks was only forty-five but looked older, pasty-faced, tall, square-jawed. He wore glasses like a professor and claimed he had been a bookkeeper driven to the street by the stress of numbers. Other road-agents claimed he was a kiddie diddler.

Hicks was Bear's first interest because Greene's tip that he may have been behind the scoreboard meant he might have witnessed something.

Bear walked up to the two men and instructed Hicks to move out of the food line, so that he could ask questions without everybody hearing. Hicks was unhappy and sulky about losing his place in line.

"Tell me about the fire at the ballpark," began Bear.

Hicks' surprise registered on his face, and he was flustered. Finally he answered. "I don't know about any fire. I slept under the interstate overpass last night."

"Bullshit," Bear snapped. "Several people put you behind the scoreboard."

Hicks was nervous maybe even afraid, "I can't talk here. There's too many eyes on me. I'll meet you about eight o'clock, after dark at the little ballpark behind the courthouse."

As he turned away, walking fast, Bear said, "For your sake, I hope so."

Bear then decided to try to interview Feters. He had first encountered Feters when he was a new officer interning with an older cop for training purposes. He and the older cop caught Feters smoking grass in his pipe behind the pool hall. The senior cop let Feters go. When Bear asked why, the older cop laughed, "First, he's a snitch, a suck-ass rat. Second, he's already a burden to the taxpayers and couldn't pay a fine. Third, the sooner he smokes himself to death, the better. Besides, he's so stupid some dealer likely sold him dried horse shit as grass and we'd never get a conviction on smoking manure."

Bear called Feters out of the line. He moved toward Bear, his phony smile signaling his ass-kissing attitude.

"Mr. Feters, what time were you at the ballpark last night?"

Feters was uncharacteristically reticent, a 180-degree change from his usual effort to curry favor with the police. "I don't know anything." Despite his usual smile, he remained silent and then turned away abruptly and headed back to the chow line.

Bear was not pleased. He decided to embarrass Feters. He spoke in a loud voice. "Thanks, Rob, for your help on the ballpark fire last night. You'll get your money later." It worked. Feters slinked back into the food line with his face a scarlet red.

Bear headed for the patrol car satisfied, thinking, "Suck your sycophantic ass out of that rap, Mr. Feters."

CHAPTER FIFTEEN

Searches

"Nothing's so hard but search will find it out."
- Robert Henick (1674)

In Shiretown, the courthouse of Sussex County was located on Wallis Street near the Snake River Bridge just across the meadow from St. Anthony's Roman Catholic Church, which stands like a sentry above it on Church Hill. The courthouse record section, a tomb for old legal records, was situated on the ground floor and in the basement under the main building. Two huge vaults, one on each level, provided safe storage, but lack of space, multiplied by time and population growth, had caused some records to be reduced to microfiche and others to be stored at outside facilities.

Modernization and computerization of the system had been resisted by some of the older employees, most of whom had worked there for years as a result of their appointment by county bosses under the political patronage system. The slow influx of younger employees hired for their ability, as opposed to their voting habits, had wrought some improvements.

Attorney Dale Dunlop, representing Donald McDougall who had been charged with not paying a fine, even though he had a receipt proving otherwise, requested access to the court records. He had been stonewalled by the court clerk, Mabel Morash, who several times had refused, offering some transparent excuse for not complying. When Dunlop raised the issue in court, Judge Harold "Goat" Chase attempted to deflect the request. But Magistrate Chase underestimated Dunlop, who was not only capable, from his experience as a prosecutor, but could not be bullied like some Shiretown attorneys who regularly toadied to the dictatorial Chase. Dunlop was determined to examine the public records of the Court House..

The prothonotary's office is the office of the Clerk of the Court. The office is, in effect, the manager of various court functions, especially record keeping. The courthouse is one place where county political machines retain their influence, at least in the appointment of some employees. Within that office, there are specific record-keeping entities, one of which is the Registry of Deeds. The Probate Court is another. All court trial records, transcripts, findings, and sentences are also held under the court clerk's preservation. This system originated in the time of William the Conqueror in England, when in 1081 a survey of all land in the country was compiled in volumes called the *Doomsday Book*. From that, the system of legal record-keeping evolved, and many of the practices in American courthouses derived from the English system.

Courthouses, especially those in New England, are usually impressive brick or granite edifices located near the center of a community, sometimes in a small park-like setting but always in a prominent place. The records' section is usually on the lower floor in large storage vaults, where dust-laden, musty-smelling, hard-cover key ledgers, and scads of old files are housed. Shrewd investigators know the value of these records. A wealth of information exists here: such as who owns what land, from whom did they acquire it, who was found guilty of what, and the nature of the punishment, either fine or jail time. An experienced researcher can glean yards of historic and useful data, and more than one crime had been solved by delving into the records.

Most record sections have grown crowded and this has led to storing some records on microfiche and others in outside locations. Courthouse record sections are historically viewed as places with coveted political jobs, positions of power that also provide opportunities for enterprising employees to ingratiate themselves with various searchers, usually lawyers, who need the information they guard. This is particularly true in the Registry of Deeds, where clerks learn quickly that a lawyer in a hurry will drop an undeclared fifty bucks in their hands for a fast property title search, which lawyers should do themselves. The fifty dollars paid to the clerk under the table is a pittance compared to what the lawyer will charge the client.

Attorney Dale Dunlop decided to pursue the records, especially those on convictions and fines. He was relentless; it was obvious he had an agenda, the nature of which was not yet clear to the people at the courthouse, who responded in a defensive manner. It was against this background that Noel Bear realized that his friend Dunlop had a plan.

Bear had just left traffic court and was headed through the lobby which was congested with a variety of people, some of who were waiting to feel the wrath of Judge Chase, when Dunlop called Bear over.

"How about coming down to the records section with me? You don't have to do anything but stand there, because your presence will convey a message to that Nazi who runs the place."

Bear agreed. He admired Dunlop and he guessed this was Dunlop's challenge to a system which had become an oligarchy, no longer dedicated to the public interest.

Noel and Dunlop entered the double, glass-framed hardwood doors into the inner sanctum of the prothonotory's office and walked to the old-fashioned window opening, where a clerk sat behind an antique oak counter. There was a worn section in front of the cage-like opening, where years of wear by the elbows of visitors had actually left a slight depression in the wood. The clerk was young, maybe twenty-five, and according to the plastic photo ID hanging from her blouse, she was Taureen McIntyre.

Dunlop stepped up to the counter which separated him from the attractive young woman, his military-like presence conveying a message of power. "I'm Dale Dunlop, an attorney, and I'm here to do a search of court records," he said in a firm but not unfriendly voice.

The woman suddenly looked apprehensive, "I'll have to get Ms. Morash." She pushed her wheel chair away from the desk and disappeared into the back of the inner room.

After a five-minute wait, the court clerk, Mabel Morash, appeared, walking with a determined pace to the window, her face revealed a scowl that predicted her mood. She was a not unattractive sixty-year-old, despite the fact that time and calories had added pounds that had produced slight body bulges, a giant bosom, fairly pronounced jowls, and a double chin. Even the style of her hair, gray streaked with fading black and pulled back into a bun, added to the aura of a stern first sergeant who had just tasted an unripe persimmon. Bear stood back, silently observing the impending clash of two strong personalities.

Most of those who were forced to deal with Mabel on a regular basis were reduced to docility, even humble subservience, to avoid her wrath. Sycophants and those who kow-towed, however, fared only slightly better than people who by nature were gutless drones and who,therefore, made their requests to her as if they had had a lobotomy and only grinned when she met their requests with a rude delay or absolute refusal. According to most people, Mabel Morash had the social skills of a shithouse rat.

She reached the counter where Dunlop stood. With no sign of civility, "Yes?" she said.

Dunlop drew himself up in response to her curt greeting, and prepared to answer in kind. "Yes, I can come in now and search the records, or yes, you wish to cooperate, or yes, you know why I'm here?"

Morash was not used to insolence and while Dunlop's tone was not belligerent, his meaning was clear and unmistakable. He would not be bullied by a public servant. Mabel must have realized by his answer, if not by his reputation, that Dale Dunlop was not one of the sheep whom she could dominate with attitude, but she would try.

"Not today," she told him, as if that were the end of the matter. "We're too busy."

Dunlop raised his eyebrows and fixed his steely gaze on her eyes, like a traffic cop who was about to give a ticket to a defiant driver. It was a message and he delivered it without flinching. "We can do the search today, or I can go over to federal court and get an order under the authority of the Constitution of the United States to protect my client's right to access to public documents, which could provide exculpatory evidence in his right to due process."

Mabel may have known a fair bit of street law, and the meanings of almost all the words in Black's Law Dictionary, but she was not prepared to challenge the obvious steel will of Dunlop, nor the federal court.

She made one last attempt to save face, "Who is your client?"

"That's privileged for now," he replied.

Morash was wise enough to yield, albeit without grace. "Fine," she stated with matter-of-fact coldness. "You can have access to the files, but we can't assist you."

Dunlop was not bothered by her reply as he knew from experience the layout of various courthouse systems and document storage.

Morash was not finished, "One person inside at a time," she said looking at Bear. "You both can't go in."

Dunlop winked at Bear, "OK, I won't need the police officer now that you have agreed," and Bear departed, amused at finally having seen Mabel Morash put in her place. He, like most other police officers, had suffered her insolence many times in the past.

Dunlop moved to the security door on the left of the area in front of the clerk's window and was buzzed inside the big office. McIntyre led him to the proper vault, while Mabel disappeared into an office at the back. The records of those who had been convicted were filed first by year, then by month, and then alphabetically by last name.

Dale first decided to scan the records randomly, so he started with 1990, January. The files and key-ledger were dust-laden relics of pre-computer days. The disturbed particles induced sneezing, and he thought what a burden the search would be for an asthmatic. The file that he first selected had a list of forty names of those who had committed a variety of offenses in the first week, the second to the fifth of January: DUIs, assaults, speeding, and other minor offenses. Among the names he saw: Abbott, Earle W. Guilty plea, section III, exceeding the posted speed limit. Sixty dollars plus ten dollars costs or thirty days. Paid fine.

Next was Arenburg, Frank M. Guilty plea, driving under the influence. Two hundred dollars or ninety days. Paid fine. Most of the forty offenses were obvious plea bargains upon which Judge Chase thrived as trials took too long.

Knowing how the system worked, Dunlop next moved to the fines' account book to compare the entries in the record of payments book with the fines levied and recorded in the conviction book. He wanted to match the entries, then total the amounts paid and then compare the gross proceeds with the court's bank deposits for that specific period. It was a simple audit procedure that would balance to the penny in most courts.

Dale pulled the ledger marked Fine Payments and turned to the first section, but January 1990 was missing. There was no list of fines paid. The payment book should have had a list of all who had paid their fines and the amounts paid, plus the date when they were paid and a case number. Then the payment could be compared by case number to the conviction book as a cross-reference.

He decided to leave January 1990 as a possible anomaly and moved his attention to March 1992. When he checked, it was the same problem: no list of fines. He then looked at April 1993, May 1994, June 1995, July 1997, August 1998, September 1999, and finally November 1999.

None of the fine payment sections for those months were on file in the book. His curiosity was now intense.

He walked out of the vault to Ms. McIntyre's desk and explained what he had discovered. He asked her to request that Mabel come to the vault with him. McIntyre was uncomfortable with the request because she knew of the friction between the two.

"Ms. Morash has gone upstairs to Judge Chase's office."

Dunlop was amused, "Who is the posting clerk for the payment of fines?"

"Sometimes it's me," she replied, "but sometimes it's another person."

"OK," said Dunlop. "Let's suppose a person comes in to pay a fine. What happens?"

McIntyre reached into the center drawer and removed a receipt book. She showed him that it had consecutively numbered, dual pages. "Writing a receipt automatically creates a duplicate. I write the person's name, address, amount paid. and case number on it. Then when I have free time, I post the receipts: first in the conviction book then in the fine payment book, by name and number of the case."

Next, Dunlop wanted to know about slow or non-payments. "Do people pay promptly? And by check or cash?"

"We take checks but we prefer cash, because sometimes checks bounce, and then there's a double hassle. Our fine-collection rate is about ninety percent, and we prosecute anyone who's check bounces. We also collect on bad checks, and we charge an added twenty-five dollar processing fee on bad checks."

Dunlop explained his discovery in greater detail so he could be sure she understood. "The problem is that I checked payments for the past ten years randomly, and there were missing sections. Even in 1999 some are missing."

McIntyre looked surprised. "Perhaps those pages are on someone's desk for reference or late payment?"

Dunlop smiled, "You surely can't mean there are late payments that are ten-years tardy, after just telling me you aggressively collect the fines?"

She agreed, "No, Morash wouldn't wait ten years for an unpaid fine, but I don't understand what's happened."

Realizing that McIntyre was uncomfortable, Dale backed off. "Here's my business card. Perhaps you could give it to Ms. Morash and tell her what I reported."

McIntyre was still curious, "Perhaps those records are in storage. We store completed records at Security Records across town."

Dunlop was packing up his belongings, "How long have you worked here?"

"Two years," she replied.

Dunlop was very careful not to sound aggressive, "Thank you. If you think of anything I should know, you have my card." As he walked out the door, he was sure that his message for Mabel Morash would result in stress.

The parking lot at the back of the courthouse was adjacent to a green, manicured, landscaped miniature park with several benches for the public to sit on and enjoy the space. The seats were set among a few majestic elms, some of that fast diminishing breed of trees, which were disappearing due to Dutch Elm disease. In the daytime in good weather, people enjoyed the restful area. At night, police often had to roust the road-agents who sought to hang out or sleep there.

Dunlop saw another sight. It was Mabel Morash and Judge Harold Chase sitting on one of the benches having what appeared to be a heated discussion, judging by the hand gestures.

Dunlop dialed Bear's cell phone number, and when Noel answered, Dale related a shortened version of his experience in cryptic sentences designed to foil any eavesdroppers. He added that he was looking at Mabel and Harold on a bench as he spoke.

"It could be that they're only talking about golf, baseball, or even sex, but my guess is it's about our visit."

Bear snorted, "Sex! That's a mind-boggling thought. Those two having sex would be like buffalos mating."

Dunlop agreed, "Maybe, but that is what other lawyers tell me, that Goat has been humping her for years."

Bear was amused, "What's your take on that place?"

Dunlop cleared his throat, "It makes me think of my first year of literature at university: Shakespeare, the play *Hamlet*."

"Yeah, right," Bear replied. "I get it. I remember the quote. It starts out `Something is rotten ... ,' but I suspect it's your humor."

CHAPTER SIXTEEN

Revelations

" – the virulence of the National appetite for bogus revelations."
- Henry Louis Mencken (1917)

According to radio station WIRR, which broadcast such daily trivia, sunset was at 7:39 p.m., which in reality meant that it was fairly dark by 8:00. In the little park behind the courthouse, it was only dim due to the replica antique, wrought iron carriage lights standing in several places. The period lights had been installed as part of the city's Bicentennial refurbishment project. The result was that while the lights looked old and charming, they provided inferior light, creating an eerie gray area between the courthouse parking lot and the meadow, which ran along the river at the extreme back of the courthouse land.

Road-agent Lee Hicks had reluctantly agreed to meet Noel Bear there at eight p.m. because Bear had purposely embarrassed him and made a public spectacle of him at the Salvation Army food kitchen. Hicks was obviously afraid of being questioned about the ballpark murder in full public view at the Salvation Army by a police officer. So Bear took advantage of that fear to force the night meeting in the privacy of the courthouse yard. It was a last ditch effort by Bear to attempt to get information out of the strange man who roamed the trails of the homeless in the city.

Bear did not necessarily believe Hicks would show up, but the potential for evidence was too important to ignore.

Bear, Reading, and Baptist discussed what Hicks might have seen. Hicks' fearful reaction suggested he had possibly witnessed something terrible and was afraid for his safety. Bear's plan was for the three police officers to dress in old clothes so that it would look like they were road-agents meeting Hicks. The Courthouse park bench was not an unusual place for that social set to congregate. They met at the back of the park, just at the edge of the meadow. Reading and Baptist were to act as back up for Bear, one on the east side and the other on the west. Bear wore an old floppy hat like a road-agent would and decided to saunter into the center of the greenbelt area on the riverside from the north. That way he could approach the bench where Hicks was supposed to be from the rear.

At five minutes to eight, they all checked their radios and cautiously moved forward. Bear hung back so he did not reach the park bench until he was sure Hicks had arrived. He advanced slowly, and in the dim light, he could see what looked like a fairly tall person, who resembled Hicks, sitting on the center park bench. As he reached the middle of the green area, he could see better and it appeared that the person on the bench was sleeping or perhaps just resting as the angle of the head was forward. As Bear neared he was reasonably sure it was Hicks because he saw the same old red baseball jacket that Hicks had worn earlier that day at the Salvation Army kitchen, but he couldn't be sure.

Bear reached a spot about ten feet behind the bench and placed his hand on his weapon. "Hicks," he said in low but audible voice, "it's Noel Bear."

There was no reply. Bear moved in closer and as he came within a few feet, the gut-wrenching smell of Hicks unwashed body and fouled pants engulfed him. Then he saw it, a pencil-thin black steel rod sticking out of the back of the man's neck just below the skull. Bear moved around the bench to the front and saw that it was indeed Hicks, quite obviously dead, his open eyes bulging in a frozen stare. He had been shot from behind with a crossbow, and the steel shaft had passed downward, completely through his neck at the spine, piercing it, and protruding about six inches from the front of his throat.

In death, he looked like a grotesque mannequin, similar to a human, but more like a horrifying wax replica. Hicks' constant quest for coins and begging for food was over. He sat lifeless, like a petrified statue. Bear said, "Amen, this is a tribute to the fact there is still great poverty and suffering in America despite her abundant wealth."

He spoke into his radio, "Come in guys. He's gone; if you get my drift."

Reading reached Bear first, "Jesus, Mary, and Joseph, spare me," she gasped and then blessed herself. "Is this the weird-murder capitol of the state or what?"

Upon his arrival, the smell and the sight immediately bothered Baptist and his pasty expression was evidence. He called the death in, ordering the necessary units and crime lab nerds. He called Kirk Donald on his cellphone and asked him to bring Foley to supervise his lab techs as opposed to the usual practice of letting the underling techs start a body case alone. It was not long before the sound of sirens filled the night air. The area would rapidly become a zoo, populated by police and sightseers.

There were uniforms, blue roof lights, red medical unit lights, the meat wagon, and yards of yellow police tape. Instantly there were a bunch of rubber-neckers who seemed to materialize as if by magic, as they usually do at such somber events. There were lab nerds flitting around with lights and evidence bags, searching for any material that could be connected to the murder. Then the press arrived, as if by parachute or from some nearby happy-hour bar, like vultures over a rotting body. There was a TV crew from the news channel: the usual gear, camera, battery packs, and a mouthy, frizzle-haired female commentator, rudely sticking a mike into the faces of various officers.

Joanne MacDonald of the *Chronicle* was there, her beaked, bird-like face poking through the tape like a hungry crow trying to steal food. Steven Jobb of the *Daily Bugle*also arrived. He wore his usual out-of-date Harris tweed jacket with leather patched elbows, which gave evidence to either his lack of sartorial awareness or his frugal wardrobe practices. His attire did not enhance his bespectacled, geek-like appearance.

"The media," Baptist said. "has arrived with their usual self-righteous belief that they shape public policy."

Reading found that amusing and said, "granting your bias against the press, it's evident that they do believe demanding information is a right, regardless of the police function."

As they became more unruly in their demands, Baptist said, "the press suffers a Jesus-complex," and then he stepped forward to confront them, his flushed face revealing a not-so-latent anger. "You people of the media, this is not some TV show. There is a serious incident here and certain police functions have to be completed, so you either move back and behave yourselves, or I'll run you off."

Some of the press people knew Baptist as a man of few words and that he meant what he said, so they moved back, and then the less experienced followed like sheep.

Foley and Kirk arrived and pushed past the throng of people, passed under the tape and walked directly to the death site. Foley checked with his crime lab techs and then issued direct instructions in rapid sequence as to what he wanted done. Kirk immediately examined the body and seemed preoccupied by the arrow that had killed Hicks. Knowing his nature and Baptist's power of observation, Reading and Bear moved off to one side, out of the way, to discuss their next move.

Bear spoke first, "If the person who snuffed Hicks assumes that his running buddy Feters knew everything Hicks knew, then his life isn't worth squat either."

Baptist and Reading knew Rob Feters as one of the long-time road-agents who traveled with Hicks. Reading speculated that the two homeless men were gay partners. Bear was surprised, "I don't think so. I heard that Hicks had kids."

Reading was skeptical, "Maybe Hicks was bisexual."

"Bisexual," Bear snorted. "Yeah, he smelled so bad the only way he could get sex was to 'buy' it."

Reading kept nervously looking over her shoulder back across the parking lot. "Maybe I've seen too many spy movies, but I'm worried some press person will use an electronic device to monitor our conversation. "So humor me and watch what you say," she cautioned. "Don't talk loud and keep your back to the shit-birds."

"Well, I'm with your paranoia because a news story that reveals Feters' name will either place him in danger or make him disappear like the dodo bird."

"We'll have to initiate a grid search of all road-agent hangouts quickly," Baptist said, "but it'll be tough to find him because there's too much territory to cover and too few of us. And until we know who we can trust in the department, we can't involve much help."

Reading said, "I don't suppose there a hope in hell we could shut the story down or ask those reporters to cooperate and run a sanitized version?"

Kirk walked into the conversation just in time to hear her remark about press cooperation. He scoffed as soon as the press was mentioned. "Anything you want the press to do will never be done because they confuse the greater good with their own opinion. If you don't want something in the news, you can be guaranteed it will appear, and they'll fuck it up."

Baptist motioned to Foley, who was talking with a lab tech near the body. Foley ambled over, and after he listened to their problem, agreed with Kirk's assessment. He looked at Kirk, a whimsical, almost mischievous grin on his face. "There's little hope of sanitizing the story. Unless of course some person who almost never talks to the press, a notoriously shy and honest person, a respected professional, a distinguished war veteran – like Dr. Kirk Donald – were to walk over there and let those fuckers draw the wrong conclusions from his mumble-speak and circular non-answers."

Baptist particularly liked the idea, "I think they'll view you as a virgin Kirk and will just love seducing you into revealing too much. Of course, it might not work but it's about all we have, and you can get away with speaking to the press as the coroner, while we can't due to departmental policy. After all how many times do they get to interview the bashful coroner."

"Acting coroner," Kirk corrected him in a dry voice.

Bear hesitated at first in deference to their greater experience with the media. He finally cranked up his nerve and said to Kirk, "If you were to go over there to your car, they'll swarm you, and your poker face will induce them to love everything you say."

Kirk shook his head, closed up his instrument bag, and removed his surgical gloves, dropping then into an evidence bag. "I couldn't fool anyone. They'd know for sure I was bullshitting them in a New York second."

"Sure," Foley answered cynically, "you're just a poor country boy at a loss for words among these big city slickers."

Kirk picked up his bag ready to leave but agreed to nothing. "I'll meet you all at the morgue," he said, "as soon as you can shake loose here, and then Hoss can clue you up on the lab stuff from the other cases." He walked away towards his car. As he got close, the press crowded around.

Steven Jobb shoved a small recording device into Kirk's face. Foley, watching the scene from a short distance away, cringed. "Oh God, I hope Kirk doesn't stick that recorder up Jobb's ass and ruin the whole deal."

Bear watched with interest, "I thought Jobb would be more polished. Doesn't he teach part-time at the community college?"

Baptist laughed, "That's why all of them are rude. It's been passed down by their teacher."

"Dr. Donald," Jobb said in an authoritative tone, "who is the deceased and what was the cause of death?"

Before Kirk could formulate an answer, a TV reporter and his camera-toting assistant who needed a shave and a shampoo for his oily hair, crowded into the limited space in front of Kirk. The circle was getting smaller and so was his patience.

Kirk's frustration with people lacking personal hygiene coupled with the stress of dealing with a batch of rude people tested his self-control. But somehow he managed to hide his feelings despite the seething emotion that engulfed him, and his anger remained hidden from the assembled throng. To add to his consternation, he sighted Allan Tobin, the editor of the *Chronicle*, literally bullying his way to the front of the scrum. For Kirk, Tobin hit a hot button. He regarded Tobin as a paper tiger, a phony, a self-proclaimed liberal but, in reality, someone who had sucked his way into the editorship of a poor newspaper by inventing controversies.

The most memorable of those stories for Kirk occurred long after the Vietnam War when Tobin wrote a negative article claiming US Army nurses in Vietnam were simply glory seekers. He accused the Army of trying to put a nice spin on a nasty body-mangling war by glorifying the combat zone nurses. Kirk knew differently. He had served there and knew the nurses distinguished themselves under horrible conditions. He also wondered how Tobin had avoided military service. He suspected the editor's wealthy father had pulled strings for him to stay out of the draft, like so many connected Americans had done.

As he saw Tobin pushing closer, Kirk still maintained his personal control, his countenance not revealing his growing anger. Finally, he addressed the questioners, "If you all talk at once, I cannot answer the questions, so why don't you try it one at a time."

Tobin was in front of Kirk as if he had first dibs. "What's going on? Who is the dead person?" he shouted.

Kirk was almost self-deprecating, bearing himself humbly as if he were at a loss to understand their interest, and by his very nature, he exuded trustfulness, which he did not, however, intend to deserve from this bunch. He replied, "This is really a police matter, and you can meet with the police press officer, because I only deal with the body, not the issues."

Jobb was more aggressive, "As coroner, Dr. Donald, you are the person who drives the case, so who it is and what caused the death?"

Kirk set his heavy gear bag down, "It's a homeless man, one of those street people you locals call road-agents, and I don't know his name."

The TV person named Nunn and his camera operator was next. Kirk could hear the buzz of the camera and see the red light indicating he was being filmed. Nunn loomed tall with a cynical expression and seemed to exhibit a condescending attitude that reminded Kirk of the TV anchor Sam Donaldson without the hairdo.

"Do you consider the death occurred from natural causes?" Nunn asked.

Kirk hated having been lured into this bear pit of questions, "I'll be unable to help on the cause of death until an autopsy is completed. It's never possible to come to a conclusion about cause until the autopsy is finished and that will be done at the morgue."

Nunn was not giving up, "Would you consider the death or the appearance of the body as unusual or typical?"

Kirk paused only briefly, "OK, I guess at a glance I could hazard the opinion that it was typical of the way homeless people live and die in their unstructured lifestyles."

Nunn was going for the full monty, "Would you say it was a natural death?"

Kirk became suddenly philosophical, "What is unnatural with a homeless person? Is it too much alcohol? Or poor nutrition? Or sleeping outdoors? Or poor medical attention? I think your question as to what's natural is a how-long-is-a-piece-of-string type endless question?"

Tobin again claimed his attention, "Could you be more specific?"

Kirk said, "I think I mentioned that I can't be specific until after an autopsy."

"Last question," interrupted Jobb, "what would kill a homeless man unless it was poor health, bad booze, or a dispute over territory with another road-agent?"

Kirk smiled, "An interesting speculation, which I'll take into account. I'll hold that thought because that's how many street people die."

Kirk now unlocked his car door and picked up his equipment bag. Allan Tobin was still closest to him and tried to maneuver himself into position so Kirk could not get into the car.

"Pardon me," said Kirk. "I really have to get to the morgue, so no more questions."

"Wait," Tobin said. "Could there be any weird cause of death here?"

Kirk's heart skipped a beat but he answered anyway, "What's weird? A rocket launcher, a bow and arrow, napalm or choking on a fish bone?"

"Right," Tobin replied. Kirk got into his car and drove off, knowing he would live to regret his answer when the real story leaked out. The press would roast him.

He arrived at the morgue still wondering what the morning news would bring out. But fooling them, even if it was for a brief period, was satisfying. He went inside, and by the time Foley and the three police officers arrived, he was in a struggle with the coffee machine, a problem usually solved by his caustic assistant Sharon Marshall.

Foley offered unsolicited advice on the way to brew coffee, which Kirk ignored. "C'mon Hoss, clue them up on everything to date from the lab perspective so I can go home," Kirk said.

Foley loosened his tie and leaned back in the only comfortable chair, which was Kirk's, and sipped the terrible coffee. Kirk was tired. "For chrissakes, Hoss, will you get on with it?"

Foley replied, "OK, OK, it's not bad news, nor is it good news, but there's not much evidence. The chemical found in the vaginas of the two rape victims is the same spermicide, Nonoxydol 10, which is used by a condom maker called Naturals Inc. They seem to be the only manufacturer using the ten strength so we can likely prove it's their rubber that was used in both cases. Now, on the Kleenex found at the first scene there was the same ten strength spermicide, female vaginal fluid, but I'm not sure about there being semen. The problem with the semen in both cases is to separate it from the other substances. Other substances are called inhibitors and when there is only a small amount of ejaculate, it is difficult to separate the DNA from the inhibitors."

Bear, who was a lay student of DNA, interrupted, "I thought DNA was so specific it was like a fingerprint."

Foley agreed, "It is, but that's not the problem. According to scientists, including Genelex Labs, which is an authority on DNA testing and inhibitors, contaminates can be a problem especially certain kinds. For instance, the spermicide and the female fluids might be separated normally, but a Kleenex is so fibrous, so absorbent, that separation is difficult, if not impossible. Some substances which are absorbent defy separation because current methods in use are not foolproof."

Reading listened with fading hopes, "But what about the Kleenex? Is there semen or not? Can't they use thermal imaging or some other lab process to solve the question?"

Foley indicated his pessimism, "Thermal imaging is useful on chemicals, and the heat generated by various chemicals shows up on a computer screen and can be compared with the image of all known individual chemicals. The process is invaluable in identifying poisons and other chemicals from a known information base, but I doubt it would work on separating semen from contaminates. But I'll ask the lab, because it's an interesting theory. Incidentally, the lab reports there is such a miniscule amount present that it will be almost impossible to be definitive or probative. The problem is that with a weak sample and, therefore, a questionable result, some lawyer will be bound to punch holes in it, like Barry Scheck did for O.J. Simpson. Some judge won't admit it if it's weak evidence, because it's prejudicial to fairness."

Bear's frustration was growing, "Then how about the condoms we found at the second scene?"

Foley looked no happier, "The rubbers appear to be by the same manufacturer and the same spermicide chemical is present, but the semen is inhibited and what was found is likely impossible to separate from the dirt of the ditch and the stagnant water."

Kirk chimed in, "From what I've read, there are sources of DNA which are always effective: blood, roots of hair, flesh even after years of burial, and of course semen, the root of a tooth, saliva, and sometimes even urine, but certain surfaces are not conducive to separation of the DNA. Dyed materials, Kleenex, and other porous substances such as concrete and dirt or earth are almost impossible to isolate as an inhibitor."

Foley added a thought, "When there are two blood types mixed, perhaps even female fluid and semen, it may present another complication for the lab and create arguments for defense lawyers."

Baptist had listened passively bu finally spoke, "I think we should keep it absolutely secret that there no clear DNA evidence.. We might even leak the story that we found DNA. We can use some of the facts as circumstantial evidence such as the same rubbers, the same spermicide, and the same MO, but the less we say the better chance we stand of getting improved evidence, especially if the perp is worried about DNA being found. Let's lie a little, spread a subtle rumor as if we got more than we do have."

Foley liked the idea, "Yes indeed, let's leak a little news."

Kirk was almost dozing, "Tell us about what you got on Brown from Lieutenant Folker," he mumbled to Foley.

Foley stood up, "It's late so I'll give you a capsule report. It was murder. The state police are treating it as such. The body was zonked with booze and pills, plus ether was held over his face to make sure he remained unconscious. The state lab found proof of it. He certainly took the booze and pills, but I don't think he administered his own ether. There were several fingerprints: two on the thermostat, which was turned up to ninety to make sure the furnace cut in. The flue was closed with insulation material to make sure the carbon monoxide filled the house. There was also a fingerprint on the wall by the cellar light switch and a broken, painted fingernail on the steps."

"That's great," Reading said, "but the finger nail polish will inhibit the DNA, right?"

"Let's go home," Bear said before Foley could answer, "I need a rest. No more tonight."

CHAPTER SEVENTEEN

Guilt?

"Secret guilt by silence is betrayed."
- John Bryden (1687)

Ruth Pineo had never needed nor wanted a gun. Yet her loving husband, the chief of police, insisted she not only have a gun but that she apply for a carry permit especially for her walk across the big dark church parking lot on Wednesday nights after choir practice. To get a permit to carry a weapon, Ruth was required by law to take a gun safety course, qualify to fire her weapon, fill out a detailed application for investigation, and submit her fingerprints to the state police where they would be kept on file.

She did all that voluntarily to put her husband's concerns to rest, but equally important to her, she needed to be left alone on Wednesday nights to be with Reverend Solomon without fearing that her husband would feel compelled to show up to protect her. She correctly reasoned that carrying the twenty-five caliber Beretta would accomplish that, and it did.

There was nothing unusual about the gun and after her training, practice, and qualification, she never fired it again. But her fingerprints remained on file with the state police.

Sergeant John Amirault, a six-foot-two, two-hundred pound, forty-year-old veteran homicide investigator, was assigned to the murder of Major Sonny Brown. His partner, Corporal Bernie Black seemed totally the opposite to Amirault's military presence. He was shorter, at five foot ten, slightly pudgy at one hundred and ninety, and had a more relaxed personality exhibiting none of Amirault's rigid nature. But his relaxed appearance was not a true indication of his thoroughness, and he was as stubborn as an Army mule.

At the Brown death scene, two sets of fingerprints were found. The cellar light switch contained a female print, and there was a male print on the temperature control in the main hall, next to the master bedroom where Major Brown's body was found.

As a matter of routine, Amirault ran both sets of prints through the FBI in Washington and his own state fingerprint database, hoping for a match. At the state level, the files matched the prints of Ruth Pineo's gun permit, and the FBI matched the male prints from military records to those of Reverend Ken Solomon.

It was Friday afternoon, just after lunch, when Ruth Pineo returned home from church. She removed her dress shoes and slumped into her comfortable easy chair to contemplate what she would prepare for the evening meal when the front doorbell rang. Ruth did not immediately respond, because almost no one used the front door except the Jehovah Witnesses, and she was in no mood for a religious assault. After a minute, her curiosity provoked her and she peeked out the window and saw two neatly dressed men in business suits carrying briefcases. "Mormons maybe," she thought, "but not the Witnesses, they're too stylish looking. She decided to answer the door, and if they were Mormons, she would argue Scientology to them.

At the front sun-porch door Sergeant Amirault showed her his credentials and state police shield, just like in the movies. "Are you Ruth Pineo?" he asked cryptically.

"Yes, I am," she replied in her most graciously patronizing manner. "How may I help you?"

Amirault introduced Black, "This is Corporal Bernard Black, my associate. We would like to have a brief discussion with you. May we come in?"

Ruth made a polite gesture with her hand and led them inside to the den at the back of the center hall. She offered to make coffee but they declined.

Amirault was all business offering no small talk to patronize her and wasted no words. Black acted more friendly, courteous with a comforting manner.

Amirault began, "We are investigating the murder of Major Lester Brown. We would like to ask you some questions. I think under the circumstances we are required to read you your rights," he said.

Ruth did not display her thoughts but believed Ameriault was a cold, condescending stuffed shirt. "Does that mean I am a suspect?" she asked.

Amirault did not answer immediately. Instead he opened his briefcase and took out a yellow evidence pad to take notes of the conversation. "I think I'd classify the questions I'll ask as designed to eliminate you as a suspect. However, it is proper for me to Mirandize you: to read you your rights as required by law."

Ruth Pineo could read people. Her social skills were honed from years of the politics of being the wife of the chief of police. She realized that an improper reaction, or even silence, would make a bad impression even though it was her legal right to refuse to answer. She also suspected, correctly, that Amirault was testing her to see how she reacted. She maintained her passive expression but silently thought him a bore, perhaps even conceited, with an overbearing attitude in which he saw himself as too clever.

"Poor Lester," she said as if ignoring the real issue, "Sonny as we called him. We knew him for a long time. He was a charmer, a tough police officer but an active social animal by nature." Then she paused, expecting Amirault to read her the Miranda warning, but he did not.

Black now played his role, a softer and friendlier approach. "How long would you have known Brown, and did you see him socially?"

Ruth suspected the two troopers had worked interviews so often that they developed a routine like the cops on *NYPD Blue* with each knowing exactly when to chime in on cue. She replied, "We were not socially connected except on occasional official events. He had his own friends, but recently, probably a few weeks ago, he was very ill with the flu and off work. Because he was a bachelor, my husband had me make chicken soup and some food that I delivered to his house."

Amirault scribbled on the evidence pad and was quiet. Ruth suspected that the silence was designed as a pregnant pause, where an experienced interviewer uses silence to make the person being questioned nervous. She knew the silence was to stimulate her to prattle, giving away more information than the question was worth. It was a fishing expedition with silent stress as the bait.

Amirault continued writing. Finally, after painful minutes of silence during which Ruth did not speak, he looked up. "Mrs. Pineo, there are indications that you were in the Brown house. You say that you were there to deliver food when he was ill. Is that correct?"

It was the same question over again. Ruth knew that his facts were not lacking, and also that experienced police interviewers repeat questions on purpose. He was making detailed notes, so she played along without rancor to seem cooperative. "Yes, a few weeks ago he had the flu. If the exact time period is important, the PD records will have the dates because he missed work."

Black was up again. He smiled. He knew it was a mind game and appeared to enjoy the interview process. He said, "Then the fact that your fingerprints were found in the house is not unusual?"

Ruth was curious. She replied, "I certainly was there, but how do you know the fingerprints in his house are mine?"

Amirault removed a copy of her gun permit and her fingerprints from his briefcase and passed them to her. She thought he looked smug as he said, "Your prints are on record at the state police data center because of your gun-carry permit."

She was angry that her prints were on file, but she knew she had to hide her feelings. And her Zen-like state of self-control, which she attributed to her Church of Scientology training, worked perfectly. She replied, "Well, I was certainly at his house, so that's not surprising."

Amirault's actions indicated he was far from done. He unbuttoned his suit coat and leaned back in the chair. "We also found a woman's broken fingernail at the house. Did you happen to break one?"

Ruth replied, "I doubt it. I have short nails, so I can play the church organ, and for any occasion where I might want fancy nails, I use false ones."

Black looked at his hands, as he asked the next question. "Your prints, Mrs. Pineo, were found in what might be considered an out of the way place, in the cellarway, just outside the kitchen door at the top of the cellar steps. Can you explain why you were in there?"

Ruth understood the game plan perfectly. It was to shock or bait her to test her reaction and to elicit information they were only guessing about. She decided to be direct, yet not volunteer too much. She would not stall, as it would create a poor impression. She also realized it would be wise not to act too smart because many men thrived on believing women were stupid. That was her advantage because she was anything but stupid, and she knew how to size up men.

She spoke softly, with confidence, "Yes, his cellar door was open and I noticed the basement light was on so I reached out and shut it off."

Amirault continued writing. "Our investigation really centers on the furnace, as it was tampered with," he explained casually. Now Black leaned forward, his elbows on his knees, looking folksy and friendly, displaying a soft approach.

He said, "The killer stuffed some fireproof fiberglass insulation in the pipe leading to the chimney, so the carbon monoxide was forced back into the house. It might be useful here to explain the gas furnace system. The law requires an emergency shut-off switch for a furnace to be located at the top of the basement stairs. That's where your prints were found."

Ruth was not stumped. "We have the same system here," she replied. "The contractor put the furnace switch in on one side and the light switch on the other. Unfortunately, I'm left-handed and instinctively and automatically I almost always hit the wrong switch. So recently, we put a piece of removable duct tape over the furnace switch to alert me that I've touched the wrong one. Besides, why would a killer turn off the furnace if it was supposed to produce the carbon monoxide?"

Amirault now outlined his crime theory. Ruth Pineo had heard numerous crime theories from her husband for years. In fact, she felt police officers were like old people playing bridge: they had more theories than cards. She knew Amirault would take great pride in his hypothesis, and he did.

"The killer would turn off the furnace with the emergency switch at the top of the steps. Next, he goes down ... ," and Ruth interrupted.

"Excuse me, you said he. Were there other prints found, and is that part of your theory?"

Amirault avoided a real answer. "A figure of speech," he said and continued. "Next the killer goes down the stairs and stuffs the flue with the insulation. Then the killer comes back up but does not yet turn the emergency switch to on. Instead, he first makes sure the thermostat in the hall outside the bedroom is set high, higher than the room temperature. Then, when he goes back to the cellar door on his way out through the kitchen, he throws the switch, and the furnace is electrically prompted to cut in as the thermostat calls for heat. He's near the door, the flue is plugged, the house is filing with carbon monoxide, yet he's in no danger, because he'll be out the back door before the house has filled with the gas."

Ruth knew exactly what he meant. She also knew that the more he talked to her, the less questions she would have to answer. "Just explain the thermostat theory to me again," she asked.

Amirault explained. "Example, the house temperature is seventy degrees, so the killer sets the thermostat at eighty so there will be a demand for the furnace to cut in to create more heat. But the killer leaves the system off until he gets near the rear door so he's on his way out right after he reactivates the emergency switch."

"Fascinating," said Ruth, "but I have one more question. What was Sonny Brown doing all the time the killer was roaming around his house?"

Black was up, "Good sensible question. I figure if the killer was a woman, she might be his lover and she could roam the house at will."

Ruth smiled a pleasant, innocent look, "That is, of course, if you assume that Brown was not gay. It is no longer reasonable to assume that all police officers are straight. Don't ask, don't tell," she said almost casually.

Amirault actually looked surprised, almost as if such a thought had never crossed his mind. Black replied, "Again, Mrs. Pineo, very good."

Ruth now decided to offer a counter-argument to see what she could learn, "Of course, that speculation may be weak if you found no fingerprints or other signs of a male at the scene." Neither officer commented.

Ruth continued, "I guess I can't picture the Sonny Brown we know dozing off or not being vigilant."

Amirault hesitated as if weighing what he was about to say. "Someone administered ether to him, and he was already intoxicated. His blood alcohol level indicated approximately three times the standard point zero eight, plus he had a great deal of prescription downers in his system."

Ruth shook her head, "I'm very sorry to hear that."

It was clear to Ruth by the glances exchanged by the two officers that they had run out of questions and theories for the present. They stood and moved toward the front door. As they neared it, Ruth said, "Call me if there's any way I can help," and they bid her goodbye and departed.

As soon as Ruth saw the troopers drive off, she hurried across the back yard to her long-time neighbor's home. She knocked and then entered in one motion. Nel Schaffner, who was sitting at her kitchen table with a glass of red wine, was temporarily surprised at Ruth's speedy entrance.

"My phone is out," Ruth lied. "Can I use the one in your den?"

"Be my guest," Nel offered. "Do you want a glass of wine?"

She accepted the offer, more to distract Nel than for the wine. Ruth went into the den and dialed John's direct line, praying he'd be at his desk instead of roaming around the city some place.

He answered on the second ring. She spoke in a low voice, "Can you hear me OK?"

When he replied yes, she went on. "Listen to me. Two troopers just visited me about Sonny. Just so we're on the same page, don't say where you're going, but meet me at the back of the Publix parking lot on South Street."

John Pineo was frustrated by her demand, "Is that really necessary?"

Ruth paused saying nothing and her husband, knowing her disposition, then agreed. "OK, OK, I'll be there." Just then Nel Schaffner entered the den as Ruth hung up and placed a glass of red wine on the small desk.

Ruth took one large gulp and sat the half-empty glass back down.

"Have to run, dear. I'll explain later."

Amirault and Black headed to the Lutheran church to interview Reverend Solomon, because he had discovered Brown's body, and they wanted his impressions first hand. "What did you think of Mrs. Pineo?" Ameriault asked..

Black pursed his lips, "For one thing," he said, "I think she was at Brown's house more than once, maybe even boffing him if he wasn't gay, and secondly, I think she's very wise, and a tough experienced conversationalist."

Amirault smiled, "Quite possibly. I also think she's a deadly, capable operator with experience in manipulating social situations who would do whatever was necessary to protect her husband from the mess Brown got him in with the arrest of the Jewish kid."

Black replied, "You mean she might have been dicking around, but she'd still go to the wall for her husband?"

"Absolutely," Amirault replied. "She has an important position, and she loves it. I think she's cold and shrewd enough to be part of the grassy knoll theory."

Black laughed, "I'll bet she called her husband before we were even out of the driveway."

"I hope so," agreed Amirault. "The phone tap on the house started this morning."

At about the same time the troopers entered the door marked Ministers' Study at the back of the Lutheran church, Chief Pineo pulled up next to his wife's Volvo in the Publix parking lot. Ruth ran to his car and once inside quickly explained what had transpired with the troopers.

Pineo's face was lined and tired-looking. His brow carried the creases of worry and his wife's tale caused his heart to race. Ruth continued, now giving him instructions.

"I want you to remember two things to the letter when you're asked. First, you drove me over to Sonny's place a few weeks ago with chicken soup when he was sick with the flu. Second, remember that on the night Sonny died, you and I played cribbage until well after midnight. Say nothing more and don't say anything on our phone."

Pineo suddenly realized she was creating an alibi, and he was it. The question was why? "Jesus, Ruth, what do you know about this, and I hope you're not involved."

She glared at her husband like a stern school teacher and said, "Absolutely nothing, but we can't afford to have any connection with Brown, or we'll get dragged into his scandal." She hardly drew a breath. "Now, rush back to your office in case they're there because they will be coming sometime soon. I have to make a payphone call right now," Pineo only nodded as Ruth got out. He drove off as she headed towards the outdoor telephone booth outside the Publix store.

Small talk and introductions were completed in a lifeless form but only because of the Reverend Solomon's position. The two troopers were seated in front of Solomon in the musty old church study. Solomon was in a perplexed state, believing they were investigating his touching Mary Anslow's breast. When he finally heard that they were there in regards to Major Brown's death, he sat back in his chair, only slightly less stressed.

Black spoke first, "I notice your church parking lot is right next to the green strip park, which runs behind Major Brown's residence on the other street. A person could get from the church parking lot to Brown's house without being seen through the trees and shrubs."

Solomon quickly tried to compose his thoughts. "Poor Major Brown. A terrible thing."

Amirault went directly to the next question, "Doesn't Mrs. Pineo work at the church?"

"She's the organist," Solomon replied.

Black spoke again, "When you went to Brown's house, would you have touched anything inside?"

Solomon was not clear about the question. He paused before answering. "I don't understand."

Black tried a different approach, "With your hands. Would you have touched anything to leave fingerprints?"

"Oh," Solomon replied, "quite likely because I was in a state of excitement."

Amirault was making notes, "I'm curious. What made you suspect gas was present. Carbon monoxide is odorless."

Solomon smiled, "I worked my way through university at Jeta Gas and Appliances. I know that gas producers add a chemical to create an odor so that people will be alerted by the bad smell. I also know that when a furnace is not functioning properly, some gas escapes. When I went in that sun-porch, I could smell gas. I also guessed that meant the furnace wasn't working right, and there was danger."

Before Amirault could continue, the phone rang. Solomon excused himself and answered it. Ruth Pineo spoke to him in a low voice.

"Don't say it's me. If there are state troopers there, break it off. Make an excuse. Do not answer any more questions. Just make up a story and leave. And don't use your home phone and don't call my place. I'll see you at the church this evening."

Solomon said goodbye and then turned to the two officers. "A minor problem. I have to leave right now." He was polite but hardly hospitable and, saying nothing more, headed for the door in a hurried walk and departed without seeing them out and without locking the door.

Amirault looked at Black. "What the fuck was that all about?" he asked.

Black was apparently mystified too. He said, "Maybe nothing, and maybe a sign of guilt by silence. But for certain, this is a weird bunch of people in a strange little city."

CHAPTER EIGHTEEN

Hearsay

"Of facts seen, divide by two. Of those heard, divide by ten."
- Redhorse (2000)

> The City Police training manual declared that being a police officer's spouse is a burden. The stress is not limited to the officer; the pressures affect the families too. There are more emotional issues than the dangers on the job or fear of violent death. Burnout, depression, cynicism, sleep disorders, and sometimes a dependence on pills or alcohol are everyday threats. There is also the omnipresent pressure of relatives and friends to intercede with or advise on various problems, and this adds another dimension of strain. It contributes to social isolation in the already solitary existence of a police officer that must choose friends very cautiously or avoid people altogether.

Noel Bear and his wife read that section of his training book together, but only the reality of actual duty would bring that lesson home with impact. Many people would have an angle in pretending friendship with a police officer or their family.

As a police wife, Shania Bear, mother of twin boys, learned the ropes quickly. Simple everyday transactions, which are nothing-deals for the average citizen, have an added possible significance for the police officer. Most citizens can complain at the market about a tough roast they purchased the week before or give their mechanic what-for when the expensive motor job is flawed, but the police family's complaint will be viewed as trying to take advantage of the badge. Even dickering over the price of an a expensive purchase like an appliance or a car is subject to criticism when done by a police officer. Shania's life with Noel, the twins, a few police wives, Hoss Foley and his wife, and more recently, the rekindled friendship with Dale Dunlop and his wife were protected areas. Sadly, they both came to realize the huge potential for misunderstandings in social contacts, so they limited their socializing to a few real friends.

Shania said, "All Indians have Indian names, and I'm applying for a new one 'three pigs living with' on the grounds that the twins require a ton of diapers, food, laundering, and associated problems and products, and Noel isn't much more self sufficient, sort of like a big twin. And usually those needs surface in the middle of the night."

Hoss Foley, hearing that pronouncement from Shania replied, "If something hadn't come-up in the night, you wouldn't have those twins."

Noel shared his work with Shania, especially for relief on bad days like the Hicks' murder, and the story of Dr. Donald reluctantly attempting to mislead the press to protect another possible witness. After Noel left for work, she scanned the newspaper for articles about Hicks' murder. The papers were featuring the death, and despite the withholding of facts by Kirk at the scene, the journalists implied it was an event rating the same space as a recent disastrous air crash.

"Oh Lord," Shania said to herself as she tucked in for a morning nap, "I'm dying of exhaustion," and then she slumped onto the foldout cot in the nursery near the snoozing boys to catch the luxury of an hour of uninterrupted sleep. She snuggled down, drifting off in that wonderfully floating, pre-sleep aura of well being, her mind and body at peace with the world. The spirit and thoughts descended into the golden realm of sleep, wonderful, marvelous much needed sleep.

At first it seemed like part of the dream, a distant pounding noise, more of a disturbing thump, a far-off sound accompanied by a muffled voice which seemed designed to annoy her, which it did. She slowly wakened, alerted to the sound, confused, fuzzy-eyed, and dysfunctional in a semi-conscious state between sleep and reality. The noise seemed to originate at the back of the house. She eased off the cot in an attempt to locate the sound. She moved down the upstairs center hall to the window, which overlooked their back door and patio. There she saw a man in old, almost indescribably dirty clothes: a seedy, unshaven man with matted dirty hair. He was obviously a beggar, a road-agent who bore the standard small cardboard sign around his neck stating he would work for food.

Shania would not go downstairs and open the door for a stranger, especially one that looked like he had escaped from a poorhouse in a Dickens' tale. The man continued to pound the door.

She was by nature a peaceful, considerate person who possessed great compassion for the socially disadvantaged, but she had an urge, a compelling need to drop something on the man's head from the upstairs window for disturbing her precious sleep.

"Yes?" she commanded through the partially opened window. Her tone conveyed in only one word the not-so-subtle message that his reason for the noise had better be good.

He pointed to his sign, "Is this the Bear residence?"

Suddenly she understood that the white man's folklore that claimed her ancestors had unique methods of punishment. She visualized this nut at her back door tied over an anthill. That thought did not strain her conscience because sleep deprivation breeds a strong motive for extreme crankiness. Then she remembered the necessary restraint of being a police officer's wife. "What is it you want?" she said without civility.

He glanced around like a sneak thief searching for the source of her voice and, finally realizing she was in the upstairs window, answered, "I can't go near the police station. I need Noel Bear and I know he lives here."

Shania was dubious and did not warm to his plea. "My kids are asleep and I can't talk. Leave your name and where he can find you and I'll phone him."

The man frowned and it was obvious he was growing impatient and frustrated. "Your phone number's not in the book and I can't call him at the station. I had a hellava time finding out where you lived. I have no address because I live on the street. I need to see him here."

Shania was becoming nervous, afraid and increasingly angry. "Tell me what it's about and I'll phone my husband on his cellphone."

He screwed up his face into a bitter scowl, a look of disgust. "Tell him it's Rob Feters. He's lookin' for me and I need help."

Shania nervously dialed Noel's personal cell number and he answered at once. "A man named Rob Feters is here at the back door looking for you and I wouldn't give him your cell number and I sure won't let him in the house."

Noel was excited, "Keep him there. Make coffee or something. Ask him to wait. It'll take me about five minutes to get there. He's harmless but he's a pain."

Shania returned to the window. "He wants you to wait, he's coming over. I'm going to make you something to eat."

"Yeah, yeah, that'll be good but I'm worried about my safety so I can't hang around too long."

Shania realized he was not a normal person, perhaps more than eccentric. "Sit on the patio. No one can see you from there. It'll take me a few minutes but I'll feed you."

She made instant coffee, grabbed a handful of cookies, put them on a plate, and delivered them to the back patio. He tasted one of the cookies and then put the rest of them in his pocket. He swallowed the coffee and while he did not ask, she knew he wanted more.

"I'll make you a sandwich and a bigger mug of coffee." He did not discourage her. It seemed like a long wait but once she returned with the food and the hot drink, he seemed to relax.

Noel drove into the yard. His arrival had taken less than ten minutes, but it had seemed longer to Feters, at least until he had hold of the sandwich and the second mug of coffee. He and Shania were now seated side by side at the outdoor table on the patio, perfectly relaxed. Shania got up to leave them in privacy, but when Feters saw that she intended to leave, he pouted and acted disappointed. She was not sure if he had become fond of her or her food.

"I have two little guys upstairs to look after so I can't stay." Noel sat down in her place.

"We were hoping to talk to you," Noel said by way of greeting.

Feters finished the coffee in one long slurp and then burped. "What do you know about the witness protection program?" he asked.

Bear was not sure if the question was a result of some nutty mental whim or if Feters had some important information that made him so terrified he wanted to disappear.

"Let's put it this way," Noel answered, "if you have something to help us, the police will protect you."

Feters looked wild, terrified, and shook his head back and forth. "The police in this berg are who I'm afraid of, because I know some stuff about them."

"Then how do you know you can trust me?" asked Bear.

Feters did not hesitate, "Because Dale Dunlop told me you were clean. I spoke to him and he sent me to you."

"Fine. How about the state police if I could set you up with them?"

Feters appeared interested, "How long would that take if I agree?"

Bear had no idea, but he decided he'd better comfort Feters, or he'd lose him. "I could make the call right now."

Noel dialed Lieutenant Folker's direct line at the office. Folker responded on the first ring and Bear identified himself. "I have just met a new friend," Bear began. Realizing that Feters could hear the conversation and would likely undestand any double talk, Noel decided to be circumspect with the message.

"This friend is concerned about speaking to the locals but has agreed to talk with you. I don't know if it's probative or speculation, but if you have time he'd like to go up there today."

Folker was definitely interested. "Will you bring him?"

"No, I'm on patrol," Bear replied. "It would be bad if I disappeared. I could call Baptist, and he could do it with no explanation required."

"Agreed. I'll be here all day."

Bear clicked off the call and punched in Baptist's number at the department. When he answered, Bear used the word that Reading had told him meant privacy was essential. "Coffee, at Shania's Roost," he said and then hung up.

Feters had listened without interrupting, but now he spoke. "If you're not able to take me up there, who is?"

Bear knew that the question was crucial because of Feters' fear. "Sergeant Baptist. But don't worry about him, he was with me the night Hicks was killed."

Feters did not object but still looked worried. Bear sought to put him at ease. "You're going to meet Lieutenant Folker of the state police in the investigation section. You get a promise from him to offer you a safe place to stay before you tell your story. Do you understand what I'm saying, because this might be your ticket off the street if your information is any good?"

"I understand," Feters responded. "I'd like to get outta here and someday maybe I could get a job as a bookkeeper or something like that. I took accounting at university."

Bear's curiosity was aroused when he heard Feters say he'd been to university. He was also interested in Feters' mental state so he decided to change the subject in an attempt to hear first hand what made the homeless man tick.

"Rob, tell me about yourself and how you ended up on the streets and why."

Feters looked mournful, and Bear was sorry he'd asked because it looked like Feters would have an emotional reaction. He remembered his father's advice, which was, "never ask a fool what are his troubles for he will tell you them all in great detail."

Feters regained control before answering. "I got a degree from BC in Boston and went to work for the old E. F. Hutton investment bank. I got to be a VP and had my own section, short-term. I hired a guy named Fraser. The sunuvabitch not only fucked me out of my job but he took my wife. I broke down, lost my job, and went bankrupt. I ended up drifting mentally and physically and came to this berg about two years ago."

Bear wanted more, "Booze or drugs involved?" he asked.

"Neither. I just cracked up and the poorer I got, the less I had for medication, so it was like a snake eating its own tail. I just fell apart."

Bear decided to try to give Feters hope. He knew it was almost impossible to rescue street people, and without knowing what was wrong with him, it was a pipe dream, but he needed to try. "I know a guy from hockey who works with H&R Block at the capitol. If you get cleaned up, I may be able to help you with a bookkeeping job. Now tell me what it is you know that puts your life at risk?"

Feters leaned forward and lowered his voice as if he was in a surveillance zone. "Hicks was behind the ballpark that night, the night the girl was killed. There's a small space between the support walls at the base of the scoreboard. It was sort-of Hicks' special bedroom, and he spent every night there because he was big enough to drive off anybody who tried to invade his space. He told me he was disturbed by the noise that night and he saw what went down with the girl."

Bear couldn't decide whether Feters was a witness or a paranoid gossip reciting hearsay. He also realized that the killer wouldn't care which label fit Feters because the risk of his blabbing was an obvious threat. "Who was the person Hicks saw?" he asked.

Feters bristled, "He only saw the car."

Bear was now doubtful. He said, "If Hicks saw what went down he'd have seen the killer. What kind of bullfeathers is that you're feeding me?"

Feters pouted like a child and remained silent.

Bear was growing doubtful as to Feters' value as a witness. "Rob, get to the point. What exactly did Hicks see and how did the killer find out Hicks was there?"

Feters was becoming more agitated, "All the homeless people at the park knew he was there."

Bear was now tempted to call Folker back and cancel, and to send Feters on his way because his story was unremarkable speculation. But he decided to wait for Baptist before making the decision. Perhaps Baptist could extract some information that might provide a lead if nothing else. In the interim, Bear decided to try a new tack.

"What did you see at the ballpark?"

Feters' expression never changed. "Nothing."

Bear was now sorry he had phoned Lieutenant Folker because Feters was clearly a fruitcake and needed medication, but he decided to continue probing, hoping for helpful facts. "How did the killer find out Hicks was a witness if he didn't see Hicks out there behind the scoreboard?" he asked.

Feters became even more agitated at the question and Bear could imagine a defense attorney turning him into a confused, useless idiot on the stand. "You remember coming to the Salvation Army that morning, and you spoke to Hicks, and I wouldn't talk to you?" Bear nodded, because he remembered the scene clearly.

Feters continued, "Well, Hicks told me who the killer was, and the crazy bastard had cut the girl's tits off."

The mention of the breasts caught Bear's attention. He didn't think that fact had ever been published and the fact Feters knew it was a sign he had some reliable information. Yet he still realized that Feters' story was hearsay, hearsay from a nut even though Hicks likely had seen the killer.

Baptist arrived and Bear gave him a heads up on Lieutenant Folker's interest and the fact that, so far the interview had been a frustrating, circular exercise in hearsay. Baptist sat down at the patio table and introduced himself to Feters.

"Mr. Feters, the main thing is that you seem to have some information we want, but we'll have to ask some questions, because we don't know everything you do. Officer Bear will pick it up where he left off, and if I think of a question, I'll interrupt. OK with you?"

Feters agreed and Bear continued his questions. "What happened with you and Hicks at the Salvation Army the day I came there?"

"Hicks told me who the killer was. It was the same guy I saw at the railroad tracks that time," replied Feters.

Bear glanced at Baptist. He did not wait for Baptist to interrupt with a question, because he had some information on the track killing which Baptist did not yet know.

"Who did you see at the tracks?" Bear asked.

There was a deadly silence and it appeared for a minute that Feters did not plan to answer. He rolled his eyes toward Baptist, and asked Bear, "Do you trust this guy Baptist?"

"Yes, he was with me the night Hicks was killed, so I'm sure he is not the killer," Bear assured Feters.

Feters answered in a whisper, "I saw Sergeant Murphy there at the tracks, and when I told Hicks that, he was terrified of Murphy and said it was a cop at the ballpark.":

Baptist was shocked and confused and so was Bear. "Did Hicks see Murphy at the ballpark?" Bear asked.

"I'm not sure," Feters said. "I'm off my medication, but I know it was a cop."

Bear was frustrated and showed it. "Listen Rob" he said. "How the fuck would Murphy know Hicks was a witness?"

Feters fumbled with his filthy watch-cap, started to mumble, then answered. "You came to the Salvation Army kitchen, and after you left we discussed it all, and that fuckin' Hallet was nearby listening. She started asking questions, and we shut up, but it was too late. She's a snitch for Murphy, plus she gives him head."

Baptist now interrupted, "So you figure Hallet told Murphy what she heard?"

Feters smiled and answered sarcastically, "Well I didn't tell him, and Hicks didn't tell him, and Hicks was killed for some reason."

Baptist agreed. It was a logical conclusion. "The problem, Mr. Feters, is that your facts about Hicks seems to be hearsay. What did you see at the tracks?"

Feters responded more politely than he had at any point in the interview, "I was across the tracks, under the warehouse platform, settling in for the night when a police car drove up on the other side. Murphy and a man in civilian clothes, some guy I didn't recognize, got out and opened the trunk. They had one helluva time getting something out of it. It sure was dead weight. They finally wrestled it out and then dragged it to the tracks. When they got it there, they put it on one of the tracks and left. After they went, I ran over to see what it was. He was dead as a fence post, lying on one of the rails with a leg on each side. I knew I couldn't help, and I could already hear the train coming and see its lights, so I ran back across the tracks and stayed there. I saw the whole thing. The train stopped and then the police and meat wagon arrived. It went on for hours. I stayed under the platform in my old sheet of plastic and never moved."

Baptist was confused. He did not know that the janitor killed on the tracks was in reality an undercover state trooper, so he could not imagine why Murphy would be involved in his death. "It doesn't make sense," he said.

Bear was not prepared to reveal his undercover role, especially in front of Feters. "You may want to ask Lieutenant Folker that question when you take Feters over to Capitol City," he said to Baptist.

CHAPTER NINETEEN

Procedures

"No battle is so surely lost as one stifled by procedure."
- Attributed to General George S. Patton

Dale Dunlop entered the prothonotory's office at the courthouse and presented himself at the records counter, guarded as usual by the petite Taureen McIntyre. She knew when she saw Dunlop that his visit would generate an interesting time; his last visit had provoked court clerk Mabel Morash into a frenzy that lasted all week.

Dunlop smiled graciously at McIntyre, his eyes sparkling. She noticed how handsome the forty-year-old was, yet at that moment; she thought he looked like a devilish teenager about to play a Halloween prank.

"Ms. Morash, please," he requested in a mildly authoritative but not unpleasant tone. McIntyre was secretly sorry that Morash was out of the office. She guessed correctly that Dunlop was forcing the issue of the court records being made public, and she knew from his reputation that he was not one to back down. When she informed him that Morash was out, she expected him to show some emotion, perhaps a flash of anger. Instead, he presented her with an already prepared, blue-covered document, which was a federal court order addressed to court clerk Mabel Morash.

It was worded eloquently in legalese, stating that reasonable notice had been given to view the court records, and that the clerk Mabel Morash had not complied with the verbal order issued by Judge Harold Chase. The federal order would be difficult to ignore, because the document declared: "failure to comply within ten days is a violation of the order of the Federal District Court, order number 2001, 119, 7b, followed by notice that action would follow in said Federal District Court of the United States."

McIntyre cracked a thin smile, almost imperceptible but friendly, as if it pleasured her to view this aggressive pursuit of the records. Dunlop was sure that McIntyre was also of the opinion that Morash was a courthouse dictator, a legal dinosaur who was now finally being hunted by someone who wouldn't retreat.

Dunlop completed his business and was just closing his legal case when McIntyre asked him to wait. "You gave me your card the last time you were here. I don't have a card, but here are my two numbers, home and office, if you should need information."

Dale smiled, "I'm sure we will be talking."

In the courthouse parking lot, Dunlop paused by his Jeep and punched Noel Bear's cellphone number. When Bear answered, Dale asked him if he could possibly come to the courthouse parking lot to meet him and Noel agreed.

When Bear arrived ten minutes later, Dunlop was standing near the back door. He looked frustrated, but not angry.

Dunlop said, "I've issued notice to take them to federal court, but I need some actual cases to support my complaint. That's where you can help. Can you get me some police information sheets from the record section for a bunch of misdemeanors that went to court and resulted in convictions and fines, say over the last ten years? If I could get those sheets, it will show in the disposition section the amount of each fine. And then, if there is no record showing the same information in the courthouse records, I'll have grounds for a complete investigation and audit."

Bear was not reluctant, but he was a little nervous. "How will I justify the request without it seeming strange that a rookie officer would be asking?"

Dunlop understood his concern. "Speak to Baptist. Ask him if it's OK to say he sent you for the records. That should pass muster as he's always working on cold cases as the head of the homicide section."

Just as Bear nodded agreement, Taureen McIntyre walked out the back door headed for her car. It was impossible for her not to see the two men standing nearby.

"I wonder what plot she'll put together in her mind now that she has seen us together?" Bear asked.

Dunlop was not concerned. He said, "The faster the word spreads, the better. It will make them wonder. By the way, the information Feters gave you about the Anslow murder is useful, I'm sure, but it's likely inadmissible for court. But the stuff he gave you on the railroad death might be good, but he's such a Martian at times that we could never be sure what he might or might not say under the pressure of a cross examination."

Bear was clearly disgusted, yet he understood. He was frustrated, it showed in his face, and Dunlop felt the same turmoil. He said, "I know, it's the hardest thing to learn at law school, to adjust your personal views and opinions to recognize the *The Federal and State Rules of Civil Procedure.*

But if it weren't for the court procedure rules on hearsay, every gossip would be on the stand, and pretty soon, a jury would be so poisoned by opinion that a fair trial would be impossible. My professor explained it like this: Believe half of what a witness sees, because eyewitnesses are notoriously unreliable. Divide what you hear by ten, because hearsay is useless, except as intelligence data."

Bear was not completely satisfied, "Sometimes the judge makes an exception on what sounds like hearsay to me. Does that depend on how well the prosecution can argue the law?"

As a former prosecutor, Dunlop understood Bear's confusion. He replied, "Sometimes, but there are even written rules about what is an exception in the *Rules of Criminal Procedure*. But in that respect, your local prosecutor, David MacAdam, is a dork and if he's prosecuting I wouldn't plan on a stalwart legal presentation."

Bear's bafflement about hearsay and court procedures was now bleeding into mild anger; he hated legal rules, which sounded like loopholes for the guilty. "Great, we got a nutty road-agent for a witness and an asshole prosecutor. I have to go call Baptist. If one more person tells me about hearsay, it's war paint time"

He reached Baptist by cellphone on the way back to the police department and outlined Dunlop's needs. Baptist agreed to cover Bear's request at the record section. "I'll be about thirty minutes ETA, so you go up to records, and I'll see you when I arrive," said Baptist. "By the way, I delivered the package to Folker and he'll protect it. I'll explain later. Oh, you are in for a unique experience at Records and ID. That's the territory of a police legend,

Sergeant Perry White. It's a bit like visiting Dracula's house."

Bear was already having a bad day. "Yeah, I've heard that before. That's just great, really great. Another dimension of weirdness is added. As for the nutty package you delivered, I understand that information could be hearsay, which sounds like legal garbage to me. I always planned to attend law school some day, but after hearing Dunlop talk about rules and court procedures, I'm now considering becoming a shaman instead. It's more scientific."

Baptist said sympathetically, "I know what you're talking about. Everybody watches *Law and Order* on the tube too much. Every time I see that gawddamn show I want to punch the prosecutor out. Reading and I argue every time we watch it together, because the rules always seem to favor the bad guys."

Bear pulled into the department parking lot and walked to the building. He decided to use the stairs to get to the Records and Evidence section in the basement. He descended to the door marked in Old English scroll: Records, Restricted Area. He opened the door to find a steel wire cage, surrounding a small reception area, which seemed about the size of a house closet. It was clear that departmental funds were not being spent lavishly on the record section. Behind the small reception area, enclosed by the heavy steel cage wire, there was a larger room lined with rows of numbered file cabinets, four drawers high, running the entire length and width of the stuffy records room. A petite black female police officer sat within that secured area, punching information into a Dell computer.

Nearby, a formidable six-foot-plus black sergeant sat with his feet up on a big oak desk reading what looked like the *Wall Street Journal*. Bear was amused, albeit quietly, at the ambiance of the place. Forewarned of Sergeant White's eccentric nature, he decided to play his visit low key, because he had also heard that White could display the disposition of a bull with a sore bag if trifled with, according to department rumor..

White looked up. "What's your case, chief?" he asked.

Bear hadn't heard the expression chief since hockey, when opposing players would attempt to provoke him by calling him Chief Wow Wow. He decided to assume that White was just using an old expression without intent to insult, so he ignored it and answered nicely.

"I need your help. I'm running errands for Sergeant Baptist. It's only background stuff and it's not that important, just a ground ball."

White tossed the paper on the desk and stood up. His imposing structure indicated a man of over fifty, who despite his cigars and sedentary job, had stayed in shape. "That's a switch. Most of them come up here trying to make it sound like they're working on the Ted Bundy case. What do you need?"

"I need a few dozen misdemeanor cases from different years. Petty shit, either convictions or plea-bargains where fines were paid. Maybe road-agent convictions."

White moved to the small opening in the cage near where Bear stood. "No shit," he said as he removed the stinky cigar from his mouth. "What you want is information sheets. Those are the charge sheets the department files with the prosecutor. After trial, we insist the arresting officer return his copy showing the disposition, like the result of the trial showing the fine or jail term for our records. Then we expect a confirming copy from the courthouse. To make the file compete we need both copies of every sheet, but no matter how hard we lean on Morash's fools at the courthouse they seldom return their copy confirming the case disposition. That's why there is bad blood between here and the clerk's office." Bear agreed and said, "They seem uncooperative over there."

White smiled, conveying more an expression of a snide opinion than humor. He replied, "Uncooperative, unproductive, incompetent, maybe even worse. Don't get me started on that bunch."

The reply was what Bear had hoped for. He sensed that White was an efficient person ih whose opinion the courthouse record section was a friction point.

White continued, "I talk about them so much it sounds like my personal albatross, only I got old Morash instead of the Ancient Mariner. We view the records as tracks, and if you research the tracks, you'll often find the animal. By the way, do you hunt?" he asked Bear.

Bear didn't know if White was interested in hunting, or he was an old-fashioned person who thought all Indians hunted and was asking stupid questions based on that assumption. But Bear was pretty tough skinned and ignored words with dual meaning lest he might be constantly on the defensive. And, after experiencing the provocative chatter on the ice during his hockey career, he never responded even if he was sure of a negative intention by a speaker. Besides, Bear thought, White was not likely to be a racist, because he was very African and very clearly black, dark black, like he had no watering down from any sneaky white ancestors.

"Yes, I hunt," he answered. "Hoss Foley and Dale Dunlop, a lawyer we know, we all go every October."

White was noticeably more friendly. "I used to hunt; my wife and I went every year, but she died about ten years ago. I'd like to get back to it sometime."

Bear realized the giant of a man was reminiscing about his wife more than the hunting. He said, "You're welcome to come with us. We're going to Vermont this October fourteenth for a week, if you can get the time off."

The small female officer looked over and smiled, "I'm Doreen Roberts. Sergeant Brains didn't introduce me. I run this place and he can go hunting."

White shook his head, "And I picked her to take my place. Listen, don't ask if you don't want me to go, because I'll go."

Bear grinned, "Deal; you're going."

"OK, young blood," said White, "we'll buzz you in the security door, and you and I shall find some cases." He turned to Roberts. "You heard the query. Where would be most productive?"

"E, row twelve," she replied in a bored tone.

White appeared to understand exactly what Bear needed. It was clear that his memory was sharp when it came to the files, because he recalled small details of each one when it was selected.

White chose twelve cases, made a note of the numbers on a pad he took from his pocket, and passed them to Bear. "I assume this is important so I want to log them. I just made a note in my book."

Bear decided to play it carefully. "Do you think I need to ask anyone upstairs for permission?"

White put his finger to his lips like a grade school teacher, "Absolutely not. Loose lips sink ships, so hold your tongue."

"You won't get into trouble, will you?" Bear asked.

White scoffed at the notion. "Fuck that, aside from young Roberts there, I never hear from anybody 'til they need me to figure out the records. This is not an exciting place to anyone but the two of us. There are thousands of records here, over ten thousand, and with the help of computers, we can sometimes turn up a perp's ID by his records or MO."

Doreen Roberts wrapped the twelve files in brown paper and passed them back to Bear. "If these don't work for you, come back and we'll pry the big guy out of the *Wall Street Journal* long enough to find more."

White perked up when Roberts mentioned the paper. "Do you invest?" he asked Bear.

Bear laughed. "Only in my twin boys."

White smiled, "I got Doreen into blue chips now, so when you're ready, let me know."

Bear left the section, exited through the back door, and saw Baptist leaning against the police car waiting for him. "Have you been waiting long?" he asked.

"Almost forty-five minutes," Baptist replied. "What the hell did you do? Wrestle White for the records?"

"To the contrary," Bear replied. "I got a dozen files, without the records showing I have them, and he'll give us more, plus he's going hunting with my crew in October."

Baptist was stunned, "Christ, he's usually like a wolverine. How'd you get on his good side?"

Bear was curious about the unusual Sergeant White. "What's the story on him? He strikes me as an interesting person."

Baptist nodded, "War hero: fought in Vietnam. Decorated cop: became a computer genius by natural instinct. He didn't even realize he had natural flair for the computer, until Roberts decided to computerize the records. Two adult kids; lost his wife to cancer. He's as tough as a Cavalry saddle, and his memory is unbelievable. I remember a bank robbery we were working, and a witness said the robber had a twitch, an involuntary spastic movement. That meant nothing to all of us, but when White heard it, a bell rang. He remembered an old bank robbery where the perp had a twitch. He found the record; we caught the guy; and he went to jail for fifteen years, all because White remembered a robber with the nickname Twitchie.

Bear was impressed, "OK, you got Feters looked after, now I have to go to the courthouse and face the dragon lady."

Bear headed downtown to the courthouse. He dreaded having to face the cranky Mabel Morash. He wrote down two names and dates from the files White had lent him.

When he entered through the door of the clerk's office, he anticipated an argument and made up his mind to be polite but forceful. Taureen McIntyre greeted him with a smile.

Bear passed her the two names and the dates. "We need the files on these two."

McIntyre frowned, "If I'm not mistaken, these may have been in vault three, and the clerk sent most of that stuff to the warehouse today. I'll go search for you. Maybe they're already on microfiche. It may take a little time."

She went away, and Bear sat down to wait. He leafed through an old *Reader's Digest*, over four years outdated as were most of the shabby magazines in the clerks waiting room. He noted the key article was about personality disorders. He figured Mabel should have been a case study from what he had heard and seen of her. Bear waited patiently, reading the article and killing time. After twenty minutes, McIntyre returned carrying a plastic shopping bag.

"The first day I saw you was in here with Dale Dunlop, and then today I noticed you two speaking outside in the parking lot, so I figured you must be friends. I gathered up a batch of microfiche, which I could loan to you for Mr. Dunlop. There is likely a couple of hundred cases here, and the two you want may be included, but I'm not sure. It's been such a boondoggle of a mess and Ms. Morash shipped a lot today."

Bear was speechless. She disarmed him with a smile. "Well, do you want them?"

Bear nodded, "Yes, but I hope you don't get into trouble over this."

McIntyre looked at Bear with child's naughty grin. "Well I'm certainly not going to tell. Are you?"

Bear quoted Sergeant White, "Definitely not. Loose lips sink ships."

He took the plastic bag bulging with microfiche and skulked out of the courthouse like a sneak thief. When he got back to his car, he punched in Dunlop's number on his cell. "I hit the mother-lode. Call Baptist and meet me at Hoss' office at six-thirty."

It had been a long day. Bear signed out and headed for the crime lab. When he arrived, the lights were on but the public area was deserted. He heard voices in the corner's office that Foley occupied. He announced himself and heard Hoss' gravel voice telling him to come in. As he entered the office, he saw Baptist, Dunlop, Kirk Donald, and Hoss, on both sides of the desk with an oversized liquor bottle in the middle. Each of them had a coffee cup of what smelled like strong alcohol.

Bear shook his head, "By the smell I can tell it's not your awful coffee."

Hoss spoke first, "Lieutenant Folker sent it down by Baptist for me. He picked it up last year when he was moose hunting in Newfoundland."

Bear picked up the bottle, thinking Hoss was joking, and read the label: Newfoundland Screech. Black Rum Overproof. "Good grief, that stuff would clear clogged drains."

Dunlop, who had just tasted his, agreed, "It burns alright. Right down to the soles of my feet. My athlete's foot is already eradicated."

Bear did not drink alcohol, but he smelled the contents of the bottle. "Holy Geronimo's ghost. That's some powerful stuff."

Kirk passed the autopsy report on Hicks to Baptist. "What's interesting is that the arrow which killed him appears to be the same that the Special Forces use, but of course you can buy them anywhere today so that's not significant."

Bear's ears perked up, "You mean like the US Navy Seals use?"

"Exactly," said Kirk. "Why? Does that ring any bells for you?"

"Yeah," Bear said. "Richard Murphy was a Seal."

Kirk looked troubled, "It's hardly evidential, more like Redneck prejudice, but I always get a bad feeling around Murphy, like there's a hidden, cruel son of a bitch lurking just behind that expressionless face of his."

Hoss put the cap back on the bottle, "That's enough of that for one night or nobody will be safe to drive."

Bear passed Dunlop the files Sergeant White had loaned him, and then the bag of microfiche that Taureen McIntyre had given him. "I think she likes you. She said I could loan these to Mr. Dunlop. Now, I'm outta here."

At seven p.m., Noel drove into his yard and thumped up the steps. Shania opened the door before he used his own keys, claiming she could tell it was he, because he sounded like a buffalo. She hugged him and said, "Lord, you smell like coffee breath and sweat. Go see if the twins are asleep and then shower before dinner."

He peeked in on the boys and saw they were both deep in Slumberland. He knew that to wake them would stir them up for the night, so he quietly closed the door and went to the bathroom. As he removed his boots, he could smell the hot sweat wafting up from under his body armor. He took off his blues, or the bag as the police in far-away New York called the uniform, and dropped his underwear as he adjusted the shower.

He could feel the relaxing warm water pelting his head and smelled the clean soap as he lathered. He still had dinner and an evening with Shania to enjoy. He promised himself more time with the twins from now on and not to allow the job to run his family.

That self-promise was no sooner made than Shania entered the bathroom. He knew it was not good news she brought.

"Baptist just called. There's a major fire at the security storage warehouse. He said you'd understand that."

"Shit!" Bear said. "It's an arson, but I know one bag of records they missed." After a pause, he spoke again. "Come here a minute."

Shania, either not guessing what he had in mind or playing it gullible, went closer to the shower curtain. His hand moved like a whip and he dragged her, clothing and all, into the shower. She did not scream because she knew it would wake the twins. She loved it when he acted impulsively, especially after a long tiring day. It seemed to regenerate their strength. "Aren't you too old for this, Officer, and what about that fire he called you about?" she asked. He growled like an animal and replied, "The older the buck, the harder the horn, and the only fire I care about tonight is the flames of wanton lust after we get out of this shower, Little Girl."

CHAPTER TWENTY

Banks

"That's where they keep the money."
- Willie Sutton, bank robber (1951)

According to lawyers who specialize in libel, the media need controversy. On dull news days, reporters often cut and paste old stories from other media, or from TV, magazines, or even academic journals. To avoid the dullness of second hand news, the writers seem to reconstruct them with controversial opinion. Younger or inexperienced reporters, according to Sgt. Baptist, felt safe re-hashing cold stories in the erroneous belief that republished facts are immune from legal action. Ben Bradlee of the *Washington Post* made a reputation for good reporting on Watergate by rejecting poor research, twisted facts, or libelous words, which are not shielded from legal action, even if some other publication printed it first. And the *Washington Post* did not print reruns.

Editors, who have made old bones and who carry the scars of old lawsuits, know the laws of libel, but the Shiretown cadre of editors apparently did not. And dull news days cause a few editors to forget the rules sometimes. The last resort of a reporter who suffers writer's block on a slow day is contrived controversy.

Steven Jobb of the *Daily Bugle* was no exception. Perhaps he could blame it on publisher Dean Turpin for pressing him to dig something up. Maybe if his initial opinion article had gone into the trash bin or the bottom of a birdcage without a follow-up piece, things could have been different. But Jobb provided a second rant, a continuation, which would eventually haunt the *Daily Bugle*.

The first story, more of an analysis by Jobb, was banal and consisted of an argumentative review of a legal treatise by Dr. Walter Corbett, a law professor at State Law School. Jobb read it when it was reprinted in the *Police and Legal* magazine. Dr. Corbett's credentials included a PhD in science, a degree in law, and a medical degree specializing in pathology, forensics, and psychological profiling of criminals and crime.

The Corbett piece was a well-researched academic account on the evolving science of crime scene forensics and the admissibility of evidence in criminal trials.

The piece was bland as it described how DNA and other scientific testing were reducing wrongful convictions, resulting in more crimes being correctly solved.

Dr. Corbett then quoted a 1950s case of the wrongful conviction of Dr. Sam Sheppard, a Cleveland surgeon imprisoned for killing his wife. Corbett pointed out that present-day DNA and scientific methods, which were not available just forty-years ago, would have likely cleared Dr. Sheppard. Dr. Sheppard spent ten years in prison before the famous attorney F. Lee Bailey managed to force a new trial based on the conduct, bias, and cavalier attitude of the press and prosecution at the first trial.

Jobb seemed compelled to take issue with Dr. Corbett without doing any research and attacked him personally without consulting news files, court records, or the finding of the appeal court. It was evident Jobb had not conducted good research because the legal records proved exactly what the Corbett piece asserted.

Dr. Corbett had also written about improvements in forensics, blood analysis, fingerprinting, and crime scene particles. He concluded that science was becoming a deterrent to crime. He cited bank robbery as an example.

He wrote: "The good old days of people like Jesse James, Butch Cassidy, Bonnie and Clyde and Willie Sutton robbing banks with ease were over due to science and electronic surveillance, which had made bank robbery a complicated undertaking, too involved for most criminals today."

The worst thing about the article was that Jobb got personal. He went on to call a man he neither knew nor had researched a bigot. To prove it, he used the now famous case of the wrongful conviction for murder of black boxer Rubin "Hurricane" Carter.

The Hurricane Carter story was topical because a movie starring Denzel Washington had exposed the injustice of a black man who spent twenty years in prison. Jobb wrote that by not telling the Carter story, Dr. Corbett had mislead readers, and the reason he alleged for the omission was that Carter was black. The fact was that science had not exonerated Rubin Carter, but several stubborn attorneys had uncovered the unfairness of the Carter conviction and overturned the verdict.. Sadly for Jobb, he did not know that Dr. Corbett was also black and would hardly omit a legal precedent because the subject was also a black man.

Then, perhaps to fill space, Jobb attacked the blandest part of the Corbett article: the part about electronic surveillance reducing bank robberies. Jobb used incomplete statistics, citing one month's figure out of a twelve-month survey, to claim bank robberies were up in New York City. He did not say that for the other eleven months bank robberies were way down, which totally supported Dr. Corbett's assertions. Unfortunately, the only statistics Jobb quoted were slanted to serve his own purposes.

In conclusion, the issues with the review of Dr. Corbett's article were perhaps fair comment, albeit incorrect, because according to Dale Dunlop the test of libel appears to be malice, and disagreement by itself is not malice. However, Steven Jobb went far beyond fair comment when he accused the noted academic of racism and lies and questioned his ethics.

Dr. Corbett was used to criticism, and did not respond, despite the urging of his friends and associates. He was a respected expert frequently engaged to assist law enforcement agencies and a much sought-after speaker on the lecture circuit at twenty-five thousand dollars a pop. Usually a backwater writer's opinion would not draw such a distinguished scholar from his academic, turtle-like position. But events were to change that. A happenstance bank robbery in Shiretown prompted Steven Jobb to do a follow-up article rubbing the good doctor's academic reputation in the mud with a statistical anomaly.

It started on a no-news Thursday. The morning *Bugle* was spread on Sergeant. Reading's desk. She glanced at Jobb's rant, and like the good doctor, she dismissed it as non-essential and pitched it into the waste can. She was running late for an interview with a juvenile suspect.

She cranked up the old department Ford sedan assigned to the juvenile division and headed east past the graveyard towards Minas Street. As she rounded the gentle uphill curve of Huntley Place, which ran between the big old houses of the rich, the dispatcher's voice alerted all units. The State Bank on the corner of Webster Street in the downtown area was sounding a robbery alarm. In the case of major crimes of violence, all units, regardless of their special division, were to be combat ready to proceed to specific streets to set up roadblocks to seal the downtown section and prevent escape.

Reading flipped on her blue dash light and the blatter-siren and did a bootlegger's U-turn over part of the sidewalk and headed back downtown to her pre-assigned intersection at Crescent and Block. She would not stop the robbers but her powers of observation impacted on another case.

The State Bank branch on Webster Street was an older outlet acquired in one of the many bank mergers of the nineties. It had been maintained as a branch despite its small size and location, because it served the downtown business core and was a profit center. It operated at hours convenient to the culture of the neighborhood, from eight in the morning to six in the evening.

The bank staff arrived shortly after seven a.m. to prepare for customers an hour later. The bank layout consisted of a horseshoe-shaped counter with six teller wickets and a supervisor's office in the corner behind the counter. There was an old-fashioned time vault behind that and a recently added surveillance camera.

At exactly eight a.m. as the door was unlocked to admit the few assembled customers, three men crossed the street from the alley, which ran between the Irish pub and the flower shop. They entered the bank just behind the group waiting to be served.

The men were dressed in black military-like coveralls, wore balaklava ski masks, and carried semi-automatic shotguns. There was much shouting as they quickly herded the staff and the customers into the public space outside the counter and forced everyone to get on the floor. One robber scaled the counter and went from cash drawer to cash drawer scooping the paper money into a giant plastic yard bag.

Later retired police officer Winston Bradley, who was at the bank, said they seemed cool, almost relaxed. The two who did not go behind the counter appeared to ignore the people assembled on the floor and instead concentrated on the front doors, perhaps at the ready if more customers arrived. Bradley also noticed they did not bother with the already opened vault, where they would have found much more money.

Almost five minutes passed before a new customer arrived. A man dressed in a polo shirt and Bermuda golf shorts entered the bank and was forced to lay on the floor, which he wisely did without resistance or comment. Then a second customer dressed in a conservative blue suit also entered but froze motionless when he saw what was happening.

Suddenly, according to Bradley, all hell broke loose. The man behind the counter yelled, "Gun," and while Bradley saw neither gun nor movement by the petrified customer, the two robbers outside the counter suddenly fired point-blank at him. The deafening sound of the two guns exploding and the smoke from the powder turned the small bank into a clouded chamber of horror. Bradley noted that the man who had been shot did not slump or fall to the floor as they depict in violent movies. Instead, he seemed to explode into a pattern of crimson blood punctures in his mid-section, which propelled him backwards and downwards in one violent instant thrust, as if an invisible cable yanked him and threw him to the marble floor. It was clear to Bradley that the victim in the blue suit was absolutely dead.

At this point, the perp behind the counter suddenly yelled, "Go" and scaled the counter carrying the plastic bag of cash. The three men burst out the front doors and ran back across the street to the alley, disappearing toward the back parking lot of an adjacent food market. Bradley reported that the bank customer in the golf clothes ran behind the counter and called 911, as it was not clear if the staff had earlier activated an alarm.

The man who reported the crime on the bank telephone was Dale Dunlop.

The downtown area suddenly became a sealed pocket, a box, as the well-trained police units responded to the general alert, setting up roadblocks at every possible exit street.

Normal crime scene sights and sounds were everywhere: ambulances, police cars, crime lab van, meat wagon. Sergeant Baptist arrived to try to make sense of the confusion and the emotions of the distraught people in the bank.

Baptist first talked to Winston Bradley, whom he had known for years as an observant police officer. Then he motioned to Dunlop who was attempting to calm an elderly woman who was in a state of confused shock. A crime lab technician informed Baptist that the dead man was Carl Mueller, an accountant, and there was definitely no gun on or near the body. Baptist walked over to Dunlop as he turned the senior citizen over to a medic. Dale looked rattled himself.

"Gawd almighty, they fired at least four shots into that poor bastard. Between the noise and the smoke, I don't think anyone will get over this in a hurry."

Baptist nodded, "Four shots is right. The techs recovered four empty shotgun shells on the floor. They're old World War Two era, double-ought buck. Impossible to trace."

Dunlop was surprised, "Strange, I noticed their guns were new, state of the art, with fiberglass handles, so why the old ammo?"

The retired cop Bradley joined them, and Baptist introduced him to Dunlop. Bradley shook his hand and then turned to Baptist. "Why didn't they rob the vault? It was open. Another thing, I was lying on my side and could see the guy they shot. He never fuckin' moved. He was frozen by fear. It almost looked as if they waited for him."

Baptist was intrigued. At first he did not answer, then he walked over to the crime lab tech who held the dead man's wallet. "Lend me that," he requested and headed back to Dunlop and Bradley. He said, "This may be nuts but humor me and play my silly game. Dale, how many times have you been in this bank and about what time of day?"

Dunlop paused before he spoke. "Likely fifty times, almost every Thursday morning for the last year, because this is the day I pay the staff, and they want cash, so the teller makes up the salary envelopes for me."

Baptist frowned, "Stupid question, but how come you're in casual clothes today?"

"Simple answer," answered Dale, "Lieutenant Folker and I are playing golf today; he's waiting in my office."

"Stupider question," continued Baptist. "How many blue suits do you have. I've only ever seen you in blue suits."

Dale laughed, "Five, and, yes, all blue. I've got one gray one I wear to funerals, o they know I change my clothes. Why?"

"Not yet," Baptist responded. ""Now, check this. Your hair is black. How tall are you? How much do you weigh?"

"Five-eleven, a hundred and ninety."

Baptist smiled, "Pay attention." He removed the driver's license from the dead man's wallet. "Carl H. Mueller, five feet ten inches, black hair, and look at him: He's wearing a blue suit, like you usually wear."

Bradley, who had been listening, was impressed. "The dead guy does resemble you," he said to Dunlop.

Dale was deep in thought, his normally placid face showing stress. He shook his head and finally, after what seemed a long time, he spoke, "If they were waiting for me, how come they didn't recognize me?"

"Simple," Baptist explained, "you were described to them, but they had never actually met you up close before, especially in those weird golf clothes, when they were expecting a blue suit, which is your trade mark."

"Doesn't make sense," said Dunlop. "I've been in court a half dozen times, and I've lived here a year, so lots of people know my face."

Baptist replied, "Yep and lots of people don't hang around magistrates court, so they just made a mistake about what you looked like. Let's get the surveillance tapes and go over them to see if this looks like a fake robbery as a cover for a hit on you."

With that, Bradley nodded, "Looked more like a hit than a robbery. Another thing, one of those guys was wearing shiny, spit-shined shoes. I hope the tapes picked that up because it's weird in my view."

Both Baptist and Dunlop found his observation intriguing. "What else is coming back to you?" Baptist asked.

"One of those guys, the one nearest the door, had an ear plug with a wire running down under his overalls, like a two-way radio thing. Plus, the two outside the counter didn't really pay that much attention to the people on the floor, they just kept watching the bank doors."

Dunlop listened to the observations and theories of the other two men. "I'm not convinced they were after me, but I agree with you guys, it was a different scenario from what you'd expect in a bank robbery. But, that's pure speculation."

The bank robbery story was exciting enough, but Jobb wrote more, using the bank robbery to refute Dr. Corbett's theory on bank robberies. Jobb's story in the next edition of the *Bugle* would provoke Dr. Corbett into suing the reporter and his paper.

Noel Bear said, "Jobb opened a whole barrel of worms, and Dr. Corbett will go fishing for Jobb."

CHAPTER TWENTY-ONE

Law Suits

"Into the lawsuit fray like a hungry pig – out like bacon."
- Ray Wortman, lawyer

Dale Dunlop, despite a long association with the legal system and a private practice that had grown by leaps in the short period since he left the state attorney's office, was developing doubts and ethical concerns about the practice of law. The conduct of some attorneys and the court system itself were increasingly difficult to tolerate. He'd begun to feel that many lawyer jokes were justified and perhaps even understatements. When Noel told him the latest piece of anti-attorney humor, a riddle, Dunlop could not disagree.

"What's the difference between four lawyers in a Cadillac and a porcupine?" Bear asked, and then provided the answer, "A porcupine has all the pricks on the outside."

Dunlop was not naive, not an inexperienced bleeding heart, nor a whiner, nor had he entered the fray with illusions of the law being a soft-touch profession. He was still surprised to find that he was developing a healthy doubt about the facts some lawyers advanced as true. He figured that Noel's use of the Indian word *bacana* (liar) was often accurate about lawyers' assertions. He particularly hated the wink-nod legal fictions, and some plea bargains were downright repugnant. He remembered the hallowed words of Professor Robert Ward who had greeted the first-year law students at his former school. Ward had ambled into the group of young impatient students who were seated in the mock courtroom. He was impressive, over six feet tall, dressed in a gray Brooks Brothers' suit, a white silk shirt adorned with a First Cavalry Division striped silk tie, and wing tip shoes. Despite his distinguished facade and soft voice, a first-sergeant-like toughness leaked through. He spoke from the heart and the message was clear for those who heard more than just words of greeting. He said "As an attorney, if you do not serve the truth, justice, and the socially disadvantaged, you may sneak by, but you will not succeed in the long run."

Dale Dunlop believed those words then, and he still put his faith in them, but he recognized that there were lawyers prospering who substituted lies for reality. Professor Ward had used as an example Roy Cohn, the lawyer for Senator McCarthy's damning accusations during the fifties. Cohn got away with breaking the rules for years, but was eventually disbarred, and despite power and connections, he was devoid of integrity.

Those thoughts flooded Dale's mind, and in the midst of his quandary, State Police Commander Kendall invited him back into the fold of the state police. The offer appealed to him. He wrestled with his misgivings night and day. He admitted to himself that he was thinking of returning to law enforcement. He decided he would make his final decision after completing two legal issues for clients.

Before the decision was finalized, Professor Ward called Dale to ask for his assistance. His friend, Dr. Corbett, was suing the *Daily Bugle* and Steven Jobb and wanted Dunlop to represent him. Dunlop was in a spot. The call was like selective service, a draft, a call to action to defend the integrity of an individual against irresponsible journalism. Dunlop not only reckoned the case could not be won, but also feared that he was incompetent to deal with a defamation issue. Yet, Ward was an old friend, an elegant man who made time to help anyone needing him. In his view, freedom of the press was not freedom for reporters to misrepresent the truth, and wrapping libel in the flag while shouting freedom of the press gave a black eye to the Constitution.

No matter how many logical reasons Dunlop advanced as to why the case couldn't be won and why he was not the best attorney to plead it, Ward and Corbett continued to push him to accept. Finally Dunlop told them bluntly, "Libel is a greased pig, which is seldom caught, and the pursuit can make the chaser look pretty ridiculous."

Ward replied, "There'll be no recriminations if we lose; I simply feel it's time to draw the line on liars with pens."

Dunlop agreed to act. He said, "Steven Jobb and a few media outlets use their pen as a sword, and those kind of papers represent the power of the press misused. Some press members attack ideas simply by demeaning the thinker or the speaker, instead of logically offering a counter-view."

Dunlop continued, "Believe me, I know the arguments the media lawyers will hide behind. They will wave the flag and present emotional defenses. You can expect to hear them say what the framers of the Constitution had intended, and they'll try to identify this yellow-trash writing with the right to free speech. The media lawyers, other media outlets, and even organizations such as the ACLU will wrap themselves in the flag and hide behind the First Amendment. That is a tough area of Constitutional law to prevail over in the pursuit of poison pens wielded as weapons by unscrupulous writers"

Dr. Corbett knew the risks and understood defamation and Constitutional law. He said in agreement, "I know it's possible to write or say almost anything, but all writers must be responsible in their art, and a suit will at least show them that they haven't a license to write anything but the truth."

Dunlop replied, "Therein lies the devil, for proving something is not true is about as difficult as proving that any abstract concept is true. And truth can be an indescribable abstract, which necessitates defining a legal amoebae without a microscope."

Later, Dunlop voiced those concerns and legal conflicts to his legal partner, Ray Wortman. "Losing doesn't bother me personally, but this is like trying to push a piece of string. Our chances are poor and probably all we can accomplish is to erect a temporary red light for the media, showing them they don't have a license to say whatever they please without at least suffering a nuisance suit."

Wortman was less idealistic by nature and more practical in the bear pit of litigation, and he knew exactly why he wanted to sue Steven Jobb, "I want Jobb's balls on a pointed stick. He's a shit-bag, and that's my objective."

Dr. Corbett arrived at Dunlop's second floor office at the Morse Building just across the street from the post office. There were the usual greetings, legal gossip, and then Dunlop introduced Wortman as second chair and legal researcher. He said, "Ray is one of the underestimated legal gems in practice, and his input will play a big role in our writing and arguing your complaint."

Dunlop had admired Dr. Corbett since their first encounter at law school years before this encounter. Corbett dressed like a Wall Street attorney in natty pinstriped suits. He was a tall, beanpole of a sixty-five-year-old man who had maintained his physique like a lean basketball player. He was a handsome man who looked as pure and magnificent as his ancestors did on the day they were deposited in Virginia in 1608 to be sold as slaves.

Corbett opened the serious part of the meeting. "It's not about suing for money, but remember, whenever a person says it's not about the money, it always is."

That was the icebreaker, reminding Dunlop of the professor's caustic wit from law school. Wortman liked him at once because of his lack of pretentiousness and his self-deprecation.

"You may not recall, but we met again after law school when I was a state police witness at the trial of two youths who killed a little girl by shooting her in the eyes with a pellet gun after they raped her," Dunlop said to Corbett.

"I do remember that," Corbett replied. "After that, the state Legislature toughened the law on young offenders."

Dunlop took charge, "We need you to try and remember anything from your life that the other side could use to surprise or embarrass us in court."

Dr. Corbett suddenly looked very serious and his concern was evident. "About a month ago, my eighty-nine-year-old father told me on his deathbed that I was not their child. Another family they knew from church had a seventeen-year-old daughter who became pregnant. In those days, being with child outside marriage was a terrible disgrace, so the parents kept her out of sight. The couple knew that my parents were devastated by the recent death of their newborn, and so they offered the teenager's baby to them as soon as it was born, which would have been almost a month later. My parents jumped at the chance. But in the interim, the girl and her parents were deported to Canada because they had no green cards.

Apparently, there were many black families up there whose ancestors had gone north via the Underground Railroad before and during the Civil War. Despite the fact there was no legitimate slavery up there, the black community suffered from poor economic conditions, and so many descendants came back to the United States during the Depression illegally, without green cards. That was what happened to these folks, and the INS deported them in 1935. I was born in Nova Scotia, Canada that year. My birth grandparents still wanted to give me to the Corbetts and so they phoned to see if I was still wanted, and I was."

Corbett continued, "The Corbetts went up to Saint John, New Brunswick on the old Boston and Maine Railroad and then by Canadian train to Halifax to meet the family. In order to get me across the border into the States as their child, the Corbetts used their dead child's birth certificate bearing the name Walter and told the Immigration officers I was their son. It worked. I became Walter Corbett, but I'm really someone else. My father couldn't remember the deported family's name after sixty-five years, plus he was ill and dying, so his memory was very poor."

"Jesus," Dunlop exclaimed, "I expect that news threw you for a loop. It would be a helluva shock to find out everything you thought was true for sixty-five years was not so."

"Exactly," Corbett replied, "I've worried myself sick imagining all sorts of bad stuff for a month since I found out. I haven't even told my wife that it's possible I could be deported. I've read some immigration law, but I get so upset emotionally I can't deal with it myself."

Dunlop could picture these facts coming out in court. He looked thoughtful and then asked, "Weren't you in the US Army, Dr. Corbett?"

"Yes, two years total, twelve months of which were in Vietnam, and I was wounded, got the Purple Heart, and Bronze Star."

Dunlop paused before continuing, "Let's leave this problem in abeyance until we can research it. For now, you must try to leave it with us. You've officially reported it to us for action, so it can't be said that you were hiding it. I have a classmate who is an attorney at the INS in Washington who would also know you from law school: Al Caldwell."

Dr. Corbett did not remember Caldwell. He agreed to leave the research to Wortman and Dunlop. Wortman needed to ask a few more questions for clarification.

"Are you aware of, or do you know of, anyone who might know the names of your birth parents?"

"No," Corbett replied, "I only know the INS deported them in July 1935 at Calais, Maine to New Brunswick, Canada, and then they moved to Halifax, Nova Scotia."

Wortman looked thoughtful, "Maybe," he said to Dunlop," you could get a list of deportations for that period."

Dunlop agreed, "It's a good start, but remember, it will take time, because I doubt if records that old are in the INS computer system, so it would take a manual search."

Wortman stood up. "Do you know of anything else the other side might uncover from your past to embarrass you, Dr. Corbett?"

Corbett smiled, "You mean other than the fact that I'm an illegal, black Canadian wetback? No, nothing approaching that."

Dunlop said, "We'll need to talk with you a lot before we file the statement of claim. Ninety days seems like a lot of time to do it, but as you know, there are always glitches."

Dr. Corbett said, "The other side will try to smother us with patriotic rhetoric and prove I have no reputation to be damaged. If the citizenship mess comes up, they'll succeed. But I still want to do this, so relax and use your legal tools without reservation."

As Dunlop predicted, the ninety-day period to file the suit seemed to vanish in a quagmire of research, phone calls, and long tiring days serving other clients. There were the usual endless meetings with witnesses and experts, hours of tiring research in dusty law books, and computer searches in Westlaw. Finally, Wortman filed the complaint at the prothonotory's office and had a copy served on Jobb and the *Daily Bugle,* as required by the *Rules of Civil Procedure*. He went to the courthouse early in the morning to avoid any enterprising reporters who might be hanging around that office on a dull day waiting for new cases.

The media who haunt the courthouse looking for controversy were quick to discover the legal complaint filed by Wortman. Competing media fed on the story, stating that the Corbett lawsuit against the *Daily Bugle* was an affront to free speech and wavin their literary flags as Dunlop had predicted.

The story made the front page of competing papers. "The bastards," Wortman said, "they cry wolf about free speech, but they're really enjoying the troubles of somebody else because the story fills their front pages everyday.."

The first reaction of the *Bugle* was their announcement that they had engaged Capitol City attorneys Peter Sharpe and Mary Grassmuck Fox to defend them.

Dunlop realized at once that when the *Bugle* selected Sharpe it spoke volumes. He was recognized as an academic authority on freedom of the press and interpretation of the Constitution of the United States. He lectured part-time on those subjects at Harper Law School. Sharpe had graduated from Yale Law School with honors and was actively recruited by major law firms across the country. But surprisingly, he chose to join his university sweetheart, Mary Grassmuck Fox, at the firm founded by her father, Kenneth Fox: the family firm, Fox, Meech and Stern.

Wortman listened to Dunlop outline the details of Sharpe's background. "Never mind how great he is," Wortman said. "What the fuck are his liabilities? And don't tell me he hasn't any. Lie if you must."

Dunlop said, "Yes, he's got liabilities in court. He's a stuffy, opinionated, text-book who puts judges to sleep. And it's the admittedly petty view of some observers that he has no street legal smarts, and his geek-like appearance contributes to that impression, whether it's true or not. He looks like Ichabod Crane."

Wortman replied, "The fact that he looks funny doesn't mean he can't play well you know."

"Listen to this," Dunlop said, "his only good win was for the trash publication *David Magazine,* which carries the sub-banner "David v. Establishment Goliaths". It's a vicious rag with a history of sloppy, vile speculation. Sharpe handled their case when they wrote that State Senator Ernie Boudreau had a mistress. Sharpe turned the case into a law lesson, arguing the obvious case *Sullivan v. The New York Times* . The Judge ruled for *David Magazine*, but a first year law student could have won that one, because State Senator Boudreau is clearly a public figure and as such has little expectation of privacy. "Frankly, I thought Sharpe did a poor job, but he had precedent on his side."

Wortman listened attentively to Dunlops rant, "What about Fox, his second chair?" he asked.

Dunlop replied, "Mary Grassmuck Fox, is not without legal credentials and laurels too. She attended Yale Law School and graduated with honors. She had, and note I said had," Dunlop repeated, "a natural affinity for legal research and a memory like a computer. Her legal research was much like yours. But note I said was, because now, as in all the big firms she's gone soft and lazy using clerks to do the grunt work, while you still do your own." Dunlop continued, "Fox constantly whispers to Sharpe in court, coaching him, which annoys the piss out of everyone in ear shot." Dunlop paused, waiting for Wortman to respond.

"I hear you, Wortman said. "I'll have to be sharper than Sharpe if you catch my drift."

Dunlop replied, "I think he'll argue *Near v. Minnesota* in our issue, because he is obsessed with it, quoting it all the time. And rightly so, because, like *New York Times v. Sullivan*, it is one of the benchmarks of freedom of the press. He often quotes from the decision in *Near v. Minnesota*."

Wortman replied, "I remember that case from law school, and then I also read the book about it called *Minnesota Rag* by that guy Fred Friendly."

"Here, listen to this," Dunlop said, "I've read it again today, because I'm almost sure that Sharpe will try to marry the performance of the *Daily Bugle* to the decision in that case because it goes to defamation, and it's a famous case. It has lots of news impact, so the other papers will support it. Here's part of what Justice Hughs said in his ruling: 'Meanwhile, the administration of government has become more complex, the opportunities for malfeasance and corruption have multiplied, crime has grown to most serious proportions, and the danger of its protection by unfaithful officials and the impairment of the fundamental security of life and property by criminal alliances and official neglect emphasizes the primary need of a vigilant and courageous press.'"

Dunlop paused, then he said, "It's pertinent, but it can be used against Sharpe and his client too. If he uses that emotional shit, and I'm almost sure he will, then you can complete the quote of that same Judge, which says: 'the fact that the liberty of the press may be abused by miscreant purveyors of scandal does not make any the less necessary the immunity of the press from previous restraint in dealing with official misconduct. Subsequent punishment for such abuses as may exist is the appropriate remedy consistent with constitutional privilege."

Wortman looked thoughtful and replied, "Apparently what Justice Hughes meant was yes, the press could print anything they liked and couldn't be restrained from doing so, but if they abused the truth, they should expect a punishment, a remedy for the injured party, and that is the essence of Dr. Corbett's case. We'll argue that the *Bugle* can publish anything they choose but when they shortchange the truth about Dr. Corbett, he has the right to punish them."

Wortman paused, and then as if thinking out loud said, "I wonder what kind of balls this guy Sharpe has and if an aggressive attack at Discovery might scare him?"

The *Chronicle*, a competitor of the *Bugle*'s, assigned reported Joanne MacDonald to the story. When Wortman saw her name above a story about the suit he said, "Those fucks, what they didn't disclose to the readers was that MacDonald lives with Steven Jobb, and she's anything but neutral in her rants."

Dunlop, who was reading the front page article by MacDonald, said, "Judas Fucking Priest, listen to this patriotic crap, and whoever said it, I agree that the last refuge of a scoundrel is patriotism."

It was on the morning of that provocative *Chronicle* article by Joanne MacDonald that the *Bugle* lawyers submitted the first names of witnesses to Dunlop and Wortman, as the rules required. Among them was the name Reverend Michael Crossey Edwards of Capitol City, a retired Baptist Minister. Wortman, phoned Dr. Corbett to see if the clergyman's name meant anything to him. "Who is this guy and where does he fit in your affairs?" he asked.

Corbett was mystified too, "I don't remember him, but let me research it a bit because mystery witnesses are always unpleasant."

That same afternoon, Sergeant Jack Baptist called Dunlop, "Can you come to a meeting at Hoss Foley's after work? We want to discuss your law suit."

Dunlop said, "Ray and I'll be there, but I can't imagine how your case and this are related."

Baptist laughed softly and replied, “that’s what the meeting is about counsellor, to see if there is a relationship or a connector between the two issues.”

CHAPTER TWENTY-TWO

Tactics

"Delay is preferable to error."
- Thomas Jefferson (1792)

The pungency of the morgue, despite its being sterile, creates a dark, unpleasant aura, even in sunlight. At night the place is even less inviting, reeking of antiseptic chemicals, which coupled with the sparse, efficient, and colorless architectural design produces a feeling of depression.

Dunlop and Wortman arrived there shortly after six. As they entered the public waiting room just inside the big glass doors, they could hear a baffling conversation from Foley's corner office. As they moved forward, they could hear a combination of trash talk, gossip, and verbal jousting between people who obviously knew each other's foibles, real or imagined. Dunlop announced their arrival in a voice loud enough to carry over the din in Foley's office. In response, Foley's abrasive voice announced, "Prayer meeting has started. C'mon in."

Dunlop introduced Wortman, whom those assembled knew by sight and reputation, as his law partner. There was a brief pause in the banter as they settled in. Foley's combat-size jug of Newfoundland Black Rum stood conspicuously in the center of the desk, like a beacon, encircled by coffee cups situated in front of Kirk, Baptist,

Shirley, Foley, and Sharon Marshall. Sharon was on her way out but finished her drink standing up. Noel, nursing a Pepsi, sat next to Foley.

Wortman was curious about the liquor. Kirk, sensing that, said casually, "Rum, very mellow, overproof but delicate to the taste buds. Used mostly in Newfoundland by hunters who run out of kerosene."

Foley slopped at least three inches of the fluid he called Black Death into a cup and passed it to Wortman. He raised the cup, and as the first small wave of the liquor passed over his tongue, he gasped, sucking part of it up his nose and almost choked. He struggled for a breath as the abrasive liquid leaked down his throat into his stomach.

"Thank you, Jesus," he croaked among the roars of laughter.

"Prayers have commenced," replied Foley.

Baptist opened the serious purpose of the meeting. He asked Dunlop, "When you go about the discovery process and depose witnesses in a civil case, how much latitude do you have? Specifically, are there restrictions on who you can call or what you can ask?"

Dunlop realized Baptist had a reason for asking but could not imagine what it was. He tried to fashion an answer without it sounding like a law school lecture. "Discovery is governed by the *Rules of Civil Procedure*. Both sides can call witnesses to question under oath before going to court in order to uncover the truth or facts surrounding the dispute. It can be done in writing or in person by oral questioning, which is usually the most useful to lawyers, because often an answer will provoke another question, and that's how you root out the facts." Dunlop paused and then asked. "Does that answer your question, or have I made it too dry?"

"Yes and no," Baptist replied.

Kirk interrupted, "Why don't you tell him what you have in mind, Jack , so he can deal with a specific rather than an abstract question."

Baptist smiled, "OK, what I was hoping was that you could depose Sergeant Richard Murphy in your suit against the *Bugle*, and if you do, perhaps we'd learn something we could use in our investigation of the murders?"

Dunlop looked at Wortman who shrugged. He said, "I suppose we could depose him, but I can't imagine what we'd get unless he out and out confesses to something. As far as calling him, we likely could call anyone, save the President, but really there has to be some reason or connection to the issue even though a lot of depositions are nothing more than fishing expeditions."

Foley knew Baptist's idea grew from his feelings of defeat at making little progress on several investigations. "What have you got?" he asked Baptist, "No matter how weird or circumstantial it sounds."

Baptist revealed his frustration in the reply, "Just about nothing. We have hearsay evidence that maybe Murphy killed the Anslow girl, plus there's weak forensic evidence, which a good defense attorney would blow off in a New York second. Then there's a mentally disabled eyewitness to Murphy and some unknown person putting that trooper on the railroad tracks."

Wortman had not heard that the railroad death was being classified as a homicide. "Tell me about the dead guy on the tracks," he asked. "What I just heard is not what I thought happened. Are you saying that it was murder?"

"Yes, I am," Baptist answered. "I drove an eyewitness up to the state police headquarters today, and Lieutenant Folker explained that the man who was run over by the train was a state trooper who had been working undercover as a janitor at the police department looking into police corruption. For the record, the train didn't kill him. He was already dead when he was placed on the tracks."

Dunlop gave no indication what he already knew about that, or what he had heard from his former associate Lieutenant Folker. He stuck to the subject Baptist had raised, about deposing Murphy. "What real evidence do you have that might convince a grand jury to indict Murphy?"

Foley interrupted, "The bite mark on the Anslow girl's cheek is a poor match for Murphy's false teeth mold."

Dunlop looked shocked, "How did you get his dental plate impression?"

"I asked his dentist for it," responded Foley. "I've known him since university, and we're friends, so he gave it to us."

Kirk raised the question that was foremost in Dunlop's mind, "Is that a legal search, and is it admissible in court when you didn't have a warrant?"

Foley scoffed, "Bull feathers. What's the expectation of privacy on a bite impression voluntarily left in a dentist's office?"

Wortman came to life on that one, "I agree, but I'm not the judge. It's not like you searched his home without permission, but some feisty old judge will likely wrap that in the fourth amendment and pitch it out."

Foley was combative, "There's a Supreme Court decision where a woman allowed a search of her husband's car, and they found a weapon, and the court ruled the search was legal."

"Fine," Wortman countered. "Is Murphy married to the dentist?"

Dunlop joined in, "That's a chicken and egg law school argument, there's no expectation of privacy on one side, but you have the Fourth Amendment on the other, and God knows how different judges will deal with it as to admissibility as evidence. Let's not waste time; it might be useful, but you need more than that."

Baptist had endured the legal pessimism and was growing angry, "I only wanted to have you guys try a few hot questions on him at discovery, because if we question him, he'll either lawyer up or clam up. Or the press will hear rumors about it, and they'll try to dunk the whole department with an accusation of police wrongdoing."

Dunlop realized he was not encouraging Baptist, "Your strategy is great," he said, "but maybe we can rethink the tactics. For instance, we may be suing the police department on behalf of the Frank family for the false arrest and the rape of their son. If they proceed, we could depose Murphy and those other cops who arrested the Frank kid within a month. We would have a better chance of picking up a few crumbs from them if we depose each of them separately. You could give us a list of hot questions. We'd work them into the mix, and then you could compare the answers of each of them while looking to spot anomalies. If you find anything, you could try to flip one of them on the others."

Baptist replied, "We're going over the same issues repeatedly like a squirrel in a cage. We have to be very careful from here on in because these guys have killed already, and if the bank job was a hit, then we're dealing with some very desperate people."

Kirk had listened in relative silence until Baptist finished. He said, "Explain the bank business to me. Tell us all, what's your bank theory?"

Baptist outlined the robbery: that both Dale and the retired cop had seen spit-shined shoes on one of the robbers, and that the accountant, who had been murdered, resembled Dunlop in many ways.

Dunlop was still not convinced, "Your points make sense, but why wouldn't they go into the vault, even if it was a hit. The vault was open, and it would have provided them with a bigger payoff. Everybody likes money."

"Exactly," said Baptist, "they didn't take advantage of an open vault, because they were waiting for the guy they believed was you to show up, and one guy being in the vault would add an unknown time factor to their plan."

Reading agreed with Dunlop, "I'll admit it's strange, but anyone could wear spit-shined shoes, and not doing the vault suggests stupidity not necessarily murder."

Baptist pushed on, "Dale has stirred the pot, and they know about the Frank family mess. And the courthouse factor is another real question. What's going on in that place? Obviously there's something, because Dale has stirred Morash and crew into a frenzy."

Shirley suddenly remembered the day of the robbery. "Listen, I was on the Main Street road block the day of the robbery. Murphy, Clarke, and that weirdo Frank Nichols came through my checkpoint about twenty minutes after the robbery in a plain police sedan. They were all in civilian clothes. After listening to the rest of your speculation, this may be relevant to the robbery."

Bear had listened to the bank argument without comment, but he subscribed to Baptist's idea. "If you're wondering who the three were there at the bank, I know Kierans wasn't one of them, because he's in the hospital with complications from a bad case of adult mumps. He's almost always with Clarke, but not this time."

"What's so suspicious about Murphy and Nichols being in the company of Clarke in an unmarked car the day of the robbery?" Kirk asked.

Shirley answered, "They have no job-related contact or duties. Murphy floats around as the chief's Sancho Panza; Nichols runs the drug section like the Bat Cave; and Clarke picks his nose. In other words, what were they doing together on the day of the robbery?"

Bear's thoughts were more practical, "Jack could check the radio logs and the blotter to see if those three were sent on any calls, or if they were assigned special duties. That wouldn't prove much because they may have been going to church, but it would be a start."

Baptist agreed, "I've asked Sergeant Perry White to come over here around seven-thirty to work with us on the records that Taureen McIntyre gave Noel from the courthouse. If we can get him to compare all those with the disposition notices on the information sheets at the PD records section, it might open a door for us."

Bear was curious as to why Taureen McIntyre had given him the microfiche court records for Dunlop. "I'm surprised she would do that because her boss is such a tyrant that she'd get fired in a heartbeat, so what was her motive? Is she attracted to Dale or does she know something?"

The rhetorical question prompted Shirley to make a suggestion, "She's a woman, and she's not stupid.

Whether she knows anything or she's just after Dale, maybe Dale should take her to lunch or at least for coffee, because she's attractive."

"Done," Dunlop agreed. "I'll be like the CIA, the company lover."

Foley winced. "And humble too," he said as he offered the rum around the table again. Only Wortman accepted seconds. Simultaneously they heard the umpire-like loud, cigar-roughened voice of Sergeant White from the reception area.

"C'mon in, Perry," Foley shouted. The big guy ambled in like the sheriff of Dodge City but looked surprised at the assembled group around Foley's desk. Foley passed him a coffee cup half full of the black rum.

White tasted his drink and smacked his lips. "Holy shit, a guy would have to have a designated driver to have seconds of this stuff." He continued to sip it while Baptist brought him up to date. White sat spellbound. For what seemed like a long time, he made no response, then he spoke but almost sadly.

"I planned to retire in about a month. The department is a mess and the job is getting boring. I know it's likely just me, but I've started to feel useless. Yet, I can't leave with a mess like this going on. It would either look like I turtled or that I was too old to care. Besides, this might be my only chance to go out in a blaze of glory, so I'm in. What do you want me to do?"

Dunlop produced the bag of microfiche. "Maybe you can cross-reference these with your department information sheets and look for inconsistencies."

White agreed, "I know something's off at the courthouse. I doubt it's only incompetence, because their records suck. And then that fire at the record storage the other night is suspicious, and the fire chief told me late today that he's announcing it as arson tomorrow morning, because an accelerant was used."

Kirk sat impassively, listening to the exchange of ideas and the banter. "You know," he said to White, "once you're in this distinguished group of law enforcement junkies, you have to learn a secret handshake like the Masonic Lodge."

White smiled, finished his rum, and stuck a thick cigar into the corner of his mouth. "I know, don't light that thing in here. Well, you guys better get used to it. I'm off to start a cross-check between my records and those ones from that old bag Morash's fiefdom."

He turned to leave, but then paused, "I just remembered something about the dead janitor. I was talking to him on my way out one evening just as he was coming into work. I never would have guessed he was a trooper. Anyway, he told me one of our plain-clothes dicks had asked him to use his janitor's master key to open the record section the night before, but he had refused. He said the guy was really pissed and threatened to have him fired, and he told the guy his instructions were that nobody but me or my assistant had access, not even the chief. I asked him what the officer looked like, and he described someone who could have been that moke Stent who runs with Nichols. The janitor said he had no name tag, because he was in street clothes. He promised me he'd find out the guy's name that night, but I never saw him again before he was killed. I never figured out exactly if it was Stent or not, because all the dicks wear strange clothing these days."

Kirk said, "Everybody should remember what Baptist said earlier. I think we should take all these guys very seriously."

White replied, "Yes, I think this is serious shit, and obviously they have little to lose by killing somebody else, especially if they think it will keep them out of jail."

CHAPTER TWENTY-THREE

Courtship

"A common cause creates bedfellows."
- Redhorse (2000)

Dunlop dialed the county clerk's number and waited nervously, fearing the feisty Mabel Morash might answer and possibly recognize his voice. Taureen McIntyre picked up the call instead. She said mechanically, "Prothonotory's office. Ms. McIntyre speaking."

Dunlop took a deep breath and mustered his nerve. It had been a long time since he called a female for any reason except business, and while this was a social call, he did have a business objective too.

"This is Dale Dunlop speaking. I'd like to invite you for a quick lunch. Could you go today?"

There was a pause, a brief silence, just long enough to make Dunlop wonder if she would accept or refuse.

"I only have from twelve to one. Under the circumstances, I think it would be better if my boss didn't see me with you outside the office. I could meet you for a sandwich at the East End Dunkin Donuts at twelve-fifteen, if that's OK?"

"Sure," he replied. "That's cool," and then he almost hung up without saying goodbye.

Dunlop punched the number of Baptist's cell phone, despite the lack of security, because it felt safer than dialing into the police department system where all calls were recorded.

Baptist answered with a curt, "Yes." Dunlop did not identify himself by name, as he knew his voice would be recognized when he mentioned Foley's Newfoundland coffee party.

"I'm having lunch with our microfiche person today."

"Speaking of which," Baptist replied, "our in-house expert told me this morning he barely scratched the surface, and already he's discovered a pattern."

Dunlop was encouraged, "Can you run my lunch date's name and background through the federal system? I don't have her date of birth, but maybe you can pull that from the motor vehicle registry on the computer."

"Gotcha," Baptist replied, "I'll try to get my pal in Washington to run her name. I'll give you a call."

Three hours later, at ten minutes past noon, Dunlop drove into the parking lot at Dunkin Donuts on Minas Street. He saw McIntyre standing just beside the glass door as he approached. He noticed her auburn hair looking almost red in the bright rays of sunshine that shone through the plate glass. She was dressed in a green plaid skirt, with a white frilly blouse, and a short plaid jacket much like those worn by Highland dancers.

Dunlop was unusually flustered, hoping he'd be able to make palatable small talk to hide his nervousness. Taureen greeted him with a friendly, pixyish smile.

"You surprised me, Mr. Dunlop, when you called. I'm sorry to pick a place this far away from downtown, but I didn't think it would enhance my standing at the courthouse if Ms. Morash saw us together."

Dale smiled, trying to overcome the initial awkwardness that arose from his lack of practice, not having dated since his divorce. Now soon after starting a new private law practice, he had discovered this beautiful woman.

He spotted a two-seat table in the corner. Despite the noon crowd, they managed to capture the seats. Because of the lack of time, they decided on soup and sandwiches. Dale could think of no other way to start the conversation, so he commented on her wardrobe.

"Is your suit McIntyre plaid, your family dress colors?"

She answered graciously, "I believe in Scotland the main difference between a plaid and a tartan is that to be called a tartan it must represent a clan and be registered with the Lord Lyon in Scotland. This one is from my mother's clan, MacFarlane, the hunting tartan as opposed to the dress MacFarlane which is mostly red."

"My word," Dunlop said, "I guess that mistaking a clan or tartan would be about as stupid as identifying Noel Bear as a Sioux when he's a Seneca."

Taureen laughed, "That's an excellent comparison. I would think you could pick a row pretty easy in the old days if you insulted someone's clan, but my family's from Boston, and the only people we avoid insulting are the Charlestown Irish."

Dunlop had managed to get her to talk about herself. He was armed with a sketchy background that Baptist had provided him with over the phone en route to the meeting, but it was far from complete, because it was compiled so quickly.

"How long have you worked at the courthouse?" he asked.

"Just about a year. I arrived here just before you did."

Dunlop had dozens of questions but wanted to avoid sounding like a prosecutor. "What did you do before you moved here?" he asked after swallowing a mouthful of soup.

She did not act coy, yet neither was she expansive in her polite reply. "You know, the usual stuff: university, a bad romance, a bunch of dead-end jobs, and then a new start in Shiretown." Her next answer let him know she realized he was checking her out. She added, "I've never been married; I'm an independent voter; I'm straight, a respectful but agnostic Protestant, and I believe there is a real God besides Mabel Morash. What more would you like to know?"

"Busted," Dunlop sighed. "You're right. I was checking. I'm sorry but I was in law enforcement too long, and it's a bad habit, especially in social situations."

Taureen now seemed to toy with him, "And what did you find out when you checked on me?"

Dale wanted to deflect the question and avoid giving a direct answer, but decided to confess, thinking it was the only way to build trust. He said, "I found out you graduated from Harvard Business School and have an MBA from Wharton. You had three years in the US Army before Harvard on a tuition plan, and you're an accountant. I also found out that you lived in Washington, had a Virginia driver's license, and I doubt your career ambitions led you to apply for a receptionist-clerk's job at the Sussex County courthouse."

She remained silent for what seemed to be an uncomfortably long time to Dunlop. She said, "Well, I checked on you too, and your reputation is such that I'm authorized to tell you I'm a US Treasury agent on loan to the US Justice Department, and I'm here investigating embezzlement, tax fraud and civil rights violations in the Sussex County courthouse."

Dunlop was not shocked but surprised at her candor. Her background was inconsistent with her being a clerk at a courthouse. "Tell me, how come the feds are investigating a county matter instead of the state police?"

"It's the civil rights issue that concerns the Justice Department. After the Rodney King affair and the four New York cops who shot that guy who was just holding out his wallet, the heat's on. Municipal police forces have to play by the rules, and the public is riled up about police abuse. Some of the chicken-poop charges the cops here are pushing for the sake of getting fines generated are violations of civil rights. Aside from the possible RICO charges and tax evasion, these cops are falsely imprisoning citizens. Just like your guy MacDougall who was stuck in the slammer over night despite the fact he'd paid the fine, and they stole it."

Dunlop was impressed by her passion. "How'd this come to the attention of Justice?"

Taureen smiled, "A small incident set the whole thing in motion. A lower level clerk at the IRS became suspicious of a Shiretown police officer's tax return. I don't know if she was a super-efficient auditor or just an eager-beaver trying to impress the IRS supervisor, but she noticed the return of a cop who earned twenty-six thousand dollars a year and also had an equivalent investment income from Canadian sources. Now that could have passed muster with most auditors, because the taxpayer was declaring the income and paying the tax. There could have been numerous innocent explanations, like the guy might have won the Canadian lotto, or inherited Canadian assets, or maybe he was winning at a Canadian casino. But the IRS pain-in-the-ass auditor wondered where a poorly paid police officer got a big chunk of money that was invested in Canada.

Her next move was to check the returns of other police officers in the same department," Mac Intyre continued. "Auditors do that to establish a baseline term of reference for comparison of a suspicious taxpayer on an audit. Next, this auditor did an asset and net worth audit on these guys. She discovered they all had big lifestyles with expensive cars, boats, and toys like the rich and famous but on a lowly cop's salary. And not all of them were declaring income from their Canadian investments, but their banking records still showed regular income form Canada. Now that is too much of a coincidence"

McIntyre paused to take another sip of her soup before continuing. "So this tax auditor wins brownie points by causing a tax investigation, which quickly reveals more than a simple case of some shrewd fellows evading taxes. There's international money laundering here, and the source of their crooked funds spells bad publicity if those cops are tramping on citizens' rights. If the IRS ignored that aspect of the crime in the greedy pursuit of unpaid taxes, the public fall-out would be terrible. They had to report to other government agencies that something else was going on here, especially after some of the heavy handed methods used by the IRS were exposed in a Senate Hearing a few years ago. So, here I am but, so far, without great results."

Dunlop was still curious, "Is that why you helped us by giving Bear the microfiche of court records?"

"Yes. I figured when you started raising hell about the records that you must be suspicious, and you seemed honest, so I had you checked out. Then my supervisor talked with the state police who vouched for you and Noel

Bear. My problem was I couldn't go to the police department without blowing my cover, and who could I trust there? What I wanted to do was just what you're doing: check the records from the courthouse with the records at the department to identify discrepancies in reported fines."

Dunlop grinned, "Sergeant White already has identified some, and according to Baptist, he just started doing the comparison. Now, my next question. Who is involved, and who's the brain behind the whole scheme?"

"So far, I know two officers are definitely involved," Taureen answered, "Kierans and Clarke, and by process of elimination, I know Mabel Morash is also involved. But that's hardly evidence. She keeps control of the status reports that are supposed to go back to the police department on each charge they file. On the return-information sheets, it is supposed to show the result of the trial – such as guilty or not guilty – and the sentence, whether a fine or jail time. Nobody is allowed to touch those reports but her. The PD record guy, Sergeant White, can't get her to co-operate, when he calls for her to speed up the forms. She's always behind, because she shouldn't be doing the reports. It's a time consuming nothing-job that a clerk should be doing, yet she insists on doing it."

Dunlop was puzzled, "Does it seem to you that Morash and the two cops are the only ones involved?"

"It didn't seem possible, until I discovered that Kierans' wife is a niece of Mabel's. And Officer Kierans is thick as thieves with the others, which makes me wonder about all the connections. The reason I'm suspicious is that the courthouse bunch and the politicians are so damn incestuous in granting jobs in this city. The only reason I got this nothing job was nobody wanted it, and I had to apply three times to get in. Now I wonder how many henchmen they have on the pad. I know that's also hardly evidential either."

Dunlop was dubious that the scheme involved so few. "Everybody claims Morash and Goat Chase are lovers. Could he be behind this?"

She shook her head, "Not so far, but there are at least two other cops with illegal incomes according to the IRS: Stent and Nichols, but so far I can't find them on the courthouse pad. As to Chase and Mabel, she runs to him to bitch all the time. Sometimes when I call him he says, `Tell her I'm busy, she can fight her own battles.'"

"What about the prosecutor, MacAdam?" Dunlop asked.

"Good grief," she replied, "he's the thickest, most stupid person I've run into down there. How he got through law school amazes me. And Morash hates him. They never talk unless it's absolutely necessary."

Dunlop now asked her the question he knew would shock her, but he hoped she'd answer anyway. "Have you people considered wiretaps on Morash's phone or on the two cops who you know are involved?"

McIntyre displayed her coolness, with no outward emotional reaction evident to Dunlop who usually could read faces and body-English with accuracy. She replied, "I guess it's OK to tell you we already have wires on them. It may eventually cook their goose, but there's nothing so far, because they're so damn cautious and speak in mumble-jargon." She continued, "did you know your pal Bear is connected to the state police? So why don't you see if they'd file a sealed request for some wiretaps on the other guys you suspect?"

"Maybe," Dunlop said thoughtfully, "maybe that's a go, but it puts me on a spot, because I'm about to sue the police department for the Frank family and possibly for MacDougall, so it might look like I've got a personal agenda. But I'm considering leaving private practice to go back to the state."

She replied, "Then ask Bear to get the people you suspect wired. Ask Folker to arrange taps on them, and we'll compare notes. Anyway, I have to go. Incidentally, I knew the dead trooper slightly. He and I compared notes on what was happening in the department. He told me that Murphy was dirty and was involved in serious stuff with Nichols and Stent, plus he said Murphy was connected to someone with power, but he never said who."

She stood up, "I'm late, and I can't afford to get fired and ruin my cover."

Dunlop walked to the door with her. "Do you like movies?" he asked.

Taureen rolled her eyes in a suggestive manner. "If that means do I date, I would if asked. If it means at the theater, I'd sooner watch them at home, and if that means you're asking, the answer is yes," and with that, she hurried away.

Dunlop pushed the direct dial to Bear's cellphone. "Coffee, at Hoss' place at six-fifteen. Bring Jack and Shirley." He walked slowly to his car and was about to wave to MacIntyre who was driving off, when he saw Murphy drive in through the take-out lane. He ignored him but wondered if Murphy had seen them together. "Jesus," he thought; we both might get whacked for having soup together."

CHAPTER TWENTY-FOUR

Vultures and Eagles

"When you're hurt, don't give up. The other guys hurts too."
- Attributed to Hawkeye.

Ellen Anslow had slipped deeper into a quagmire of anguish and depression, since her daughter suffered the horrible rape and murder. Her appetite had waned; she'd lost weight; and she'd spent sleepless nights wrestling with her dark thoughts. She recognized her own symptoms but lacked the will to overcome them. At work her usual good humor and inspirational manner was noticeably absent. She had periods of silence when it seemed she had moved into an insulated private place, shutting out those around her.

Ellen Anslow's anger grew as she struggled with the gory memories. Her doctor suggested that the terrible shock of her daughter's death could have triggered a revival of the post-combat stress disorder she suffered, when she served twelve months as a combat nurse in Vietnam. The slow progress of the investigation, despite the great efforts of the police, triggered more frustration. She felt helpless, believing that she should do something to help, but knowing there was little, perhaps nothing, she could do to speed up the results.

On Monday morning after another sleepless night, she felt compelled to go to the department to visit Sergeant

Baptist whom she met during the course of the investigation. When she arrived, the receptionist in the investigation section called Baptist and then led Ellen to his cluttered corner office. He offered her coffee, which she refused, and then encouraged her to express her obvious frustration.

"I have a friend," she began, "at the telephone company, and I asked her to get a computerized printout of all calls to our phone number before Mary's murder. Eleven of those mysterious calls the week she was killed were made from the phone at the Lutheran Church. I want you to arrest that creep minister Solomon."

Baptist, despite his surprise at her words, maintained his usual stoic expression. He said, "We did the phone computerization too, but the phone at the church is available to dozens of people, so it's only circumstantial evidence that Reverend Solomon could be the perp. The problem is that we need additional evidence."

Ellen listened attentively, growing to believe the law and the system favored the criminal. "What about the bite mark on Mary's cheek? Did they do a mold of the mark?"

Baptist tried to hedge, but his sympathy for her exceeded his usual penchant for giving non-answers to questions about evidence and investigations. "We have a match, of sorts, but it's not flawless and would be subject to argument in court. But in a chain of evidence, it's useful but not conclusive."

She understood the general process but it added to her frustration. She said "What about the condoms they found at the crime scene?"

Baptist dreaded giving her another pessimistic answer, which would add to her discouragement, but he had to say something. "One problem is that the evidence from the condoms needs more testing because the contents are contaminated. Everything we have lacks any definitive forensic currency. We need a break, some small miracle to break the case open. We feel as frustrated as you do, but we can't seem to get a break."

Ellen Anslow was now hearing the words but not registering the meanings conveyed. Her innermost thoughts were re-focused on doing something herself to try and advance the case, to speed up the red-tape-infected legal system. She said, "I admit I'm frustrated and sticking my nose in won't help, but I need to do something positive on this mess.".

Baptist understood her feelings, "I'm as frustrated as you are, and yet I can't imagine what I can do to hurry up the results. I'm like the squirrel on one of those wheels, going nowhere fast."

Anslow stood to leave. "I have another concern. The money Solomon gave us at the church, I would use that money to help solve the case if it would do any good. I don't feel good about keeping it."

Baptist listened carefully, trying to formulate an answer. "Maybe at some point the money could be of some assistance, but I doubt it. I suggest you go see an attorney and see if there are any negatives to your just keeping the cash. You didn't seek the money, it was offered to you, and it was the chief's idea, so I can't see any need for you not to keep it."

Baptist's sympathetic ear made Ellen feel slightly better, even though the results was far from satisfying her anger and impatience. She left the department, drove downtown, and parked in the back of the Morse Building, where the office of Dunlop and Wortman occupied the second floor. She walked up the oak staircase of the old building and down the hall to their office, where a matronly, almost dowdy receptionist sat behind a small sign stating her name, Heather MacDonnell.

"I want an appointment with Mr. Wortman," Ellen announced in a firm no-nonsense tone.

The receptionist was not too cordial, but perhaps sensing Anslow's no-nonsense demand, was at least civil. She said, "Maybe you can see him for a few minutes right now, but you'll have to make an appointment for a longer visit if it's necessary."

MacDonnell then walked back to a frosted glass door at the rear and disappeared behind it, closing the door firmly so the glass rattled. When she returned, she said, "Mr. Wortman will see you," and then led her to his office.

Wortman recognized her name and knew of the murder of her daughter. Anslow related her experience, starting with the chief's call and finishing with the murder of her only daughter. She described how the possession of the money had come about and about the mysterious phone calls just before her daughter's death. When she told Wortman that she knew that eleven of those calls had originated at the Lutheran Church, his reaction was much like Baptist's. He said, "I think Solomon could be the guy alright, but It's only circumstantial evidence; as to the money, I'd forget that. The chief of police suggested you get the money, and you reported it to the investigating officer, Baptist. Plus, you're being prudent in seeking legal advice. There is no legal reason I can see why it's not yours to keep."

Ellen shook Wortman's hand, "How much do I owe you?"

"One dollar," Wortman answered. "That's just to make it a legal appointment of me as your attorney, so anything that has been discussed between us is confidential. As soon as you feel up to it, I'll buy you a cup of coffee."

Ellen felt some relief but was far from satisfied. She paid the dollar to the receptionist and, as instructed, obtained a receipt for the record. She walked back down the stairs wondering if Solomon was Mary's killer. Then, despite her long friendship with Joan Murphy, she admitted to herself that she was suspicious of Joan's notorious husband, who was rumored to be the police department's ladies man. She only heard that rumor after Mary's death. With those thoughts swirling around in her mind, she headed for home to try to sleep, because she was slated to work at the hospital on the midnight shift. Her urge to do something to catch her daughter's killer was temporarily subdued by the need for sleep.

Baptist's obsession to make progress on the case was tormenting him. The case was stalled, and each time they found prospective evidence it faded or fell short of being conclusive. Dunlop had clued him up on the previous day's lunch with Taureen McIntyre and her suggestion that Lieutenant Folker be approached to help obtain wiretap warrants.

Baptist called Folker for assistance, knowing that if Folker applied for the warrants in Capitol City, it would be easier to maintain secrecy.

Folker was under the same self-inflicted pressure as Baptist because of the murder of the undercover trooper. He said, "I'll consider any sensible and legal idea to advance the investigation, and I'll try to get you warrants."

Baptist was direct in his appeal. "We need your guys on the wire taps, because secrecy is at risk down here, because we don't know who can be trusted. I think the

McCurdy case would give you probable cause on a warrant application and we want taps on Nichols, Stent, and Judge Chase as material witnesses."

Folker listened sympathetically, "We already have taps on Solomon and Mrs Pineo, because we think they both have knowledge of the death of Major Brown. Getting the warrants isn't as much trouble as the lack of personnel. You'll need experts twenty-four hours a day. It would really require three people because wire taps are dull, sleep-inducing ordeals that wear out the listeners. They need breaks and relief. Frankly three people can't be spared. And McIntyre has a couple of fed taps going on in the courthouse investigation already."

Baptist pushed his request. "Listen," he said, "we can work around the relief problem by helping whoever you send us. ·But for God's sake, try to give us at least two people, so we can have one expert with one of us at all times."

"OK, I'll get you the warrants, and I'll find you two technicians. But you and Bear, or anyone else you decide on, will have to come up here to appear in the judge's chambers to support the warrant applications. I'll call Dunlop to grind out the paperwork, and you can bring the legalese with you. I think having a representative from both law enforcement agencies appear in the judge's office with the applications will strengthen the cause. What about this Judge Chase you want to tap? Is that necessary?"

Baptist understood the politics of the question. "I'm afraid it is. Someone is running this courthouse gang, and while I can't promise you it's him, I can argue that he has potential as a suspect."

Folker laughed, "Fine, I can see if this thing blows up I'll be assigned to a commercial weigh station on highway I-95, and you'll be a school crossing guard for fucking with a judge." Folker continued, "Now, for the worst news, your witness Feters is scrambled sometimes, almost as useless as a square rifle barrel, and nuttier than a squirrel hotel. Our shrink thinks he may straighten him up with medication. But for now, don't get your hopes up. He has about six versions of seeing Murphy at the railroad tracks. Three before the body was put on the tracks and three after. As to what some other bum told him he saw at the ballpark, that's hearsay. Bunk. Frankly, I think he has a hard-on for Murphy. His story's got more holes than a Vietnamese sandal."

"Shit," Baptist said. "I knew he was nuts, but when he first talked to Bear and then to me on the way up there, he seemed reasonably good. That's typical of everything we have seen in this mess."

Baptist signed off and headed to meet Bear at the morgue. Folker's help was positive, but his news was still bleak. Reality was bitter medicine, and Baptist found himself in a blue funk. As he drove towards the morgue, he decided not to spread his personal gloom to the others.

When he arrived, he saw by the cars that the others were already there. Inside, as he entered the antiseptic smelling morgue, he could hear an argument raging in Foley's office. Kirk and Hoss were toe-to-toe, yelling heated theories about the science of bite marks and molds as evidence. Baptist sensed their frustration was equal to his own because the two medics were acting like sandlot kids disagreeing about who was safe or out in a game played without an umpire. It was a chicken-and-egg argument of shouted empiric guesses punctuated with army style foul cuss words about false teeth.

"Listen," Kirk yelled, "you fucking thick-headed old shit. You're letting your law degree cloud your knowledge of street smarts. Stick to medicine, which you've practiced for years and listen to me. I don't care that some fucking textbook says a jury will not understand your theory about the mark on her cheek! The defense will crucify that theory by pointing out that false teeth can be exactly the same at the bottom regardless of which gums hold them in place. The reason is simple. The local dentist churns each set out with the same cheap false teeth stuck in different unique upper molds. The fucking defense lawyers will claim that anyone could have bitten her with a set of cheap store bought choppers."

Hoss screwed his face up in a sour lemon look and replied, "You mean cheap teeth are all the same at the bite level even though the mold which holds 'em is unique to the individual's gums, and your argument is that everybody's false teeth have the same size bite".

Kirk shook his head and sighed. He said, "I mean no such thing. I mean that the bite mark into soft flesh can defy accurate measurement, and the overall size will be difficult to prove. The teeth in hundreds of cheap false choppers will look exactly the same when they bite into a soft substance like flesh. You know goddamn well what I mean and some fuckin' defense attorney will stick those teeth up your ass in court. It won't be like arguing the unique, finger-print-like mold of natural teeth, which are all different sizes that are unique to each individual. Sure, some false teeth are unique to each person, but here we have a dentist who makes everybody the same cosmetic looking square, cheap choppers. Your theory may fly in court, Hoss, but I say we don't have much evidence, and if we look stupid about false teeth, it could kill all our poor circumstantial evidence."

Bear sat quietly listening, turning his head to one speaker and then the other like a tennis spectator.

Foley shouted back, "You know everybody's jaw structure and bite is unique to the individual, and so will the jurors all of whom watch TV crime shows. And they will believe that Murphy's plate and that bite mark on that little girl are one of a kind, and so do I. We can sell that to a jury, so where's the problem?"

Kirk pointed his finger. "I agree. The inside of the mouth and gums on all people are different, but both Murphy and Solomon have complete sets of false upper and lower teeth made by the same cheap dentist. Surely to God, you don't think any defense attorney worth his salt won't be able to sell the jury that some few false teeth made by the same dentist can look the same at the biting end. How they fit the gums is surely different and I'll grant you that, but each and every tooth in both sets of their false choppers are like fence pickets, exactly the same, uniform, generic, and cheap. You can certainly tell they're different on a lab table if you look at the jaw impression that holds them to the gums. But bites by picket-fence teeth into soft flesh may look the same. In fact, Hoss, that dentist likely has dozens of patients with the same awful cheap beaver-like choppers, and any defense attorney who figures that out will stick 'em up the prosecutor's ass right in front of the jury."

For almost thirty years, shouting matches between Foley and Kirk had been a hobby which they both seemed to thrive on. Foley now lowered his voice, because he knew Kirk was right about the jury destroying the false teeth theory. He nodded and said, "Yes, damn it, you're right and I fuckin' hate it."

Bear tried to wind them up again with questions designed to fan the debate's cooling embers, but they were too tired to continue.

Kirk spoke calmly, "What we need is a break, a wild, luck-inspired happenstance to shake up the suspects' complacency."

Foley perked up. He said, "What you're saying is right, for a change. It's like the eagle and the vulture."

"OK," Kirk said, "what the fuck is that theory?"

Foley looked smug. "The vulture sits and waits for its victim to die before it eats. That's sometimes a slow process. But the eagle strikes and eats sooner. That's why the vulture gets rotten meat and scraps."

Bear rose from his seat, "I have to go on that one, but I'll admit it sounds sort-of like Indian folklore."

Kirk responded with a chuckle, "Sounds like Indian buffalo shit to me."

Baptist came to life, "Not so fast" he said, "I called this bunch together to tell you we're all drafted to learn wire taping after Bear and I go with Lieutenant Folker to get warrants. They'll lend us a couple of electronic nerds, and we will have to help with the taps."

Bear replied, "I'm still going home, and yes you can count me in on the warrants and the listening."

Sharon Marshall shuffled through the office on the way to the side door. She said, "Some of us have ideas about how you could do many things, but I'm too tired tonight, and without Sergeant Reading here to take my side, you wouldn't listen anyway."

"Oh shit," Kirk replied, "poor you. I never knew you to hide your opinions since the army, so tomorrow night we'll give your shy-humbleness the floor."

"'Bout time," she said and disappeared into the night.

CHAPTER TWENTY-FIVE

Shadows

"Guilt turns shadows into monsters."
- Dismas Redhorse, Seneca shaman

It was an annoying, grating sound, disgusting and loud, more like an animal snorting than a woman snoring. She lay on her back, her head canted backward, her mouth wide open in her noisy struggle for air, which resulted from her swollen nasal passages and bad teeth. The snore emitted sounded like a muffled bagpipe from hell.

It was two in the morning and Reverend Ken Solomon was agitated and tired. He had been sleepless for two hours listening to her snoring. After twenty-plus years of sharing the same bed, he found her fat, repulsive, and sexless. Her bad breath, a result of bad teeth due to an abnormal fear and avoidance of dentists, was nauseating. His wife Rosealee was such a mess that his affection was long gone, strayed elsewhere, albeit unknown to her. His secret affairs with lonely women of the congregation satisfied his omnipresent sexual urges, but he had to continue the public appearance of married propriety, because that was expected and required for a minister of the ultra-conservative Lutheran Church of Shiretown.

Solomon quietly collected his pillow and one quilt and picked his way across the dark bedroom, out through the door and down the hall to his private study, where he often had to spend the night to avoid Rosealee's sleeping noises. He placed his pillow on the fat leather sofa in his den, spread the blanket out, half beneath him the other half as a cover, and was about to enjoy the silence and go to sleep when the phone rang. He quickly reached for the receiver on the nearby desk to prevent the bedroom extension from waking his wife.

Mustering his ministerial voice, he said, "Hello." At first he thought the call was a prank, perhaps kids trying some phone humor after a few beers, but it was soon obvious this was no ordinary call for assistance. There was an animated cackle, almost a witch-like laugh, and then a deep raspy voice spoke. It sounded like it came from an electronic voice-altering device like they sell in novelty or joke shops. But it became painfully apparent to Solomon that it was no joke.

The voice said, "I know about the Anslow girl and you feeling her tits and about the money you paid her mother and that you're a pervert."

Solomon's mouth suddenly went dry and his chest muscles tightened and he could not immediately respond.

The person on the other end laughed.

"Who is this?" Solomon demanded. "What kind of sicko are you?"

There was no reply, yet he knew the caller was still there, as he could hear breathing.

"I'll have the phone company trace this call," he threatened.

The voice answered in a raspy exaggerated tone, "I'm calling from Major Brown's new number in hell, and it will be hard to trace unless you visit him in person."

Before Solomon could reply, there was the distinctive click of a hang-up. Solomon panicked. Wild thoughts and fears crashed around inside his head and his objectivity deserted him.

"It was no joke," he thought. "Whoever it was knows. What do they want? Is it blackmail? And how did they know?" Solomon picked up the phone to call the police. Then he put it down. "No police. Not a wise idea to involve them."

He picked up the receiver again. He'd call the phone company, but just as quickly he placed it back down again. It would only open a can or worms. He sat on the sofa, sweat soaking his pajamas and his head swimming in confusion. Then it dawned on him. He'd phone Chief Pineo, who could check the call discretely. But it was two-thirty a.m., not a good time to rile up Pineo who would be dead tired and not receptive to hearing what could be a threatening call to both of them.

The call was dangerously accurate; the caller knew his dirty little secret.

Solomon decided not to call Pineo until morning. He lay back on the sofa but did not find the comfort of sleep. He lay wide-awake for a long time until the comfort of daylight was creeping through the window.

It was eight a.m., almost two hours later than usual when he walked down the back stairs of the old parsonage into the kitchen. Rosealee poured coffee and asked, "Are you sick, and you've cut yourself shaving, which you only do when you're upset? What's wrong?"

Solomon took a sip of coffee. "I've got a headache. I'm late. I'll have to rush," and then offering nothing more, he departed through the side door into the driveway where his car was parked.

At the church office, he closed his door and dialed the police chief's direct line. When Pineo answered, Solomon launched into a verbal tirade about the anonymous call. Pineo had to respond aggressively to shut him up. As a police officer, he knew telephones were less secure than gossip columns and Solomon was blabbing like a carnival pitchman over a police line.

"Shut up, Ken," he ordered. "I'll be right over," and hung up on him. He hurried to his car, and on the way to the church, Pineo damned the day he first met Solomon many years before.

At the church, he discovered Solomon sitting alone in the musty little office staring straight ahead. Before Pineo could close the door, Solomon started to babble.

"Someone knows about Mary Anslow and the money. The call was explicit and whoever it was disguised their voice." He rambled on and on and Pineo suddenly realized it was only a matter of time before Solomon went completely bonkers. Such an event would drag him down too. There was no quieting Solomon, and he ranted on, repeating himself as he illustrated that he was a confused slave of his own guilt.

Pineo had to intervene and try to convince him to keep quiet. "Stuff it, Ken. The call has done exactly what the caller wanted and that was to set you off into orbit. You're a danger to yourself and to me too. The call was designed to torment you, and it's likely based on speculation. It's not evidence, and if you shut up, it can't hurt you." But in his heart, Pineo had serious doubts about his own assertion of confidence, because someone knew the truth about his perverted pal's indiscretion, and that was serious trouble for him too.

Solomon nodded, "Yes, yes, you're right of course, I'll shut up about it."

Pineo knew Solomon was still out of control despite his promise to keep quiet. Solomon was a desperate man, and that required strong measures.

Pineo decided to buy some time. "I know how to find out who this is and how to stop it," he lied. "Now you have to trust me and do nothing more. If the person calls again, all you do it listen quietly and make no comments, because there's a good chance they'll be recording your response."

Solomon promised again. But on the way back to the department, Pineo knew in his heart that Solomon was a deadly threat, and if provoked by more calls, he would fall apart like Humpty-Dumpty.

Solomon was still upset after Pineo left, and despite the fact that he had promised he would follow instructions, he grew terrified as he contemplated the situation. Each time the office telephone rang, Solomon was fearful it would again be the phantom caller. The mere sound of the telephone became a trigger, and Solomon's heart would labor like a giant frosty hand had seized it - a Pavlovian reaction.

Finally, he began to tire and convinced himself to be more controlled, less agitated. Then the telephone rang again. He thought to ignore it and not answer, but morbid curiosity drove him and despite the foreboding, he picked up the receiver and said, "Hello." He expected to hear the weird tormenting voice again, but it was not.

Almost as terrifying, however, was hearing the voice of Steven Jobb. Solomon knew the most innocent press query could turn into a embarrassment. Jobb went directly to the purpose of his call.

"We've been reliably informed that you were involved in a sexual incident of a criminal nature with the young

Anslow girl, and that a senior police officer is involved in a cover-up of your misconduct."

Ken Solomon suddenly felt an agonizing tightness like a steel cable clamping around his chest. He struggled for air and tried not to be too long in answering lest he convey the wrong impression to the reporter.

"Mr. Jobb," he began in a weak, fearful voice, "I have no idea what you are talking about, and I'll bet your informative source was a poison anonymous phone call."

Jobb was taken aback. The tip-off call had indeed been from an unknown source, but he was not about to admit it. "Reverend Solomon, I know the Anslow girl worked for you in the church office, and I know she left suddenly, and then, of course, there was her tragic rape and death."

Solomon almost choked hearing his name mentioned in conjunction with the terrible crime. Maintaining politeness, he tried to defuse Jobb's accusatory questions.

"Surely, Mr. Jobb, such a scurrilous statement might amount to slander or libel if written. It's not true. While I'm no lawyer, I don't imagine your paper would welcome another legal battle on the back end of the suit by Professor Corbett."

Jobb silently realized Solomon was no fool and the veiled threat of another lawsuit struck its mark. "Reverend, I'm only asking questions or you in privacy. I'm attempting to find out your side of a potential story." He then paused for effect, hoping Solomon would be uncomfortable with the silence and reveal something. Jobb's interview style was always to keep the subject off guard.

Solomon now changed tactics. "It was a terrible event that the young woman suffered. The incident must be devastating to her family."

Jobb was not stupid; his years of experience provided him with a keen awareness that people often made statements as a diversion. "Why did Ms. Anslow leave the employ of the church?"

Solomon lied, "I have no idea."

Jobb tried to provoke Solomon to say something indiscreet. He was taping the call to catch Solomon in a contradiction despite the fact he knew the practice to be illegal in his jurisdiction. He believed the chance of being burned by the authorities for taping was less threatening than another lawsuit. Foremost in his mind was the sex scandal involving the President of the United States, who had been trapped by illegal taped phone calls by federal witness Linda Tripp. He felt smug because of the legal result in that case, when the authorities declined to prosecute Ms. Tripp although she publicly admitted her conduct.

Jobb thought, "She was guilty of taping facts relating to the privacy of the country's most important citizen and was let off, so what can happen to me?" He rationalized the risk, believing that a tape recording provided exact evidence of an interview to protect the paper in the event of a lawsuit. He had developed a telephone marketer's interview pattern using carefully crafted questions, innuendo, and the pretense of knowing more than he really did in order to stimulate his subjects to fearful blabbing.

He tried his best to provoke Solomon into giving him more. He asked, "What is your answer? Why did Ms. Anslow leave your employ? It's a shocking coincidence that she was the victim of a sex crime shortly after she left her position with you, is it not?"

Solomon was afraid. He was stressed and tired from lack of sleep, and he was angry about the impertinence of the mouthy reporter's comments. He decided to use his most professional clergy voice. He replied, "That calls for conjecture and my in opinion that event is so tragic that no more words should be uttered, because nothing I could say would give comfort to the relatives of the victim."

Suddenly Jobb switched subjects, "Isn't it true, Reverend Solomon, that Chief Pineo's wife is the church organist and is a friend of yours?"

Solomon answered shrewdly, trying to minimize what he knew to be a loaded question, "Mrs. Pineo is the church organist and has been for a long time. However, my wife and I are not social friends of the Pineos."

Jobb knew that the association of those two people, no matter how innocent or platonic, was one of those facts in a news story that added a stimulant to a reader's conclusions. He knew from experience that to plant a fact in the middle of a story provided any weak speculation with a hook, or better yet an anchor, which rendered the other weak facts more believable.

Jobb was growing frustrated and decided to use his ace in the hole, which was to lie boldly. He often made the subject of an interview panic by saying some outrageously untrue fact. He asked, "Isn't it true, Reverend, that there is to be an audit of the church's finances?"

"Not that I'm aware of," he replied truthfully, but in his heart he was terrified. He knew that any writer could even present silence so that it cast a shadow. Suddenly, Solomon could stand no more. He felt a cramp in his abdomen, a terrible spasm like a childhood pain resulting from eating too many green apples. He knew his gut was about to let go from the stress, because that had been a lifetime problem when he was severely agitated. He thought, "Oh God I'm about to embarrass myself within the hearing of a reporter." Solomon excused himself. "I have to run," he exclaimed in agony and hung up without another word. He turned in panic, and unfastening his pants, he rushed pell-mell toward the small bathroom, but it was too late to avoid a personal disaster of a most embarrassing nature.

CHAPTER TWENTY-SIX

Discovery, The Deposition From Hell

"A liar must have a good memory."
- Marcus Fabius (35 AD)

Dale Dunlop claimed with some currency that discovery, the give and take of questions and answers in an in-person deposition, is one of the greatest challenges in the legal process..

Dunlop said,"There are rules that govern that process, but they are far less restrictive than those of courts, particularly in the take-no-prisoners forum preceding civil litigation where both sides get to question the opposing sides' witnesses prior to trial."

And Wortman, who was a master of the practice, called it staged legal rudeness including bluff and fakery, sometimes resulting in blunders which dramatically altered more than one legal dispute. He said, "Go big or stay home in these discovery gang-bangs, because it may be your one chance to unnerve the bastards without some judge shutting you down first."

In the case at bar, *Corbett v. The Daily Bugle et al.*, Dale Dunlop, attorney for the plaintiff, was slated to conduct the first deposition in the boardroom of their second floor office in the Morse Building on Webster Street at nine-thirty Monday morning. Mr. Steven Jobb, accompanied by the paper's attorneys, Peter Sharpe and Mary Grassmuck Fox, would be deposed.

At nine-twenty on the appointed day, Jobb and his attorneys presented themselves at the reception desk at the office of Dunlop and Wortman. Sharpe announced their names and the purpose of their visit. The receptionist fairly fawned over them, bade them sit down, and offered coffee while they waited. Her courtesy was noted and it eased the tension.

At twenty minutes before ten, fashionably late, Raymond Wortman came out of the stairway from the street below dressed in faded blue jeans, a bright, hideous reddish-pink T-shirt, and Cordovan loafers. He looked dreadful, his ugly shirt wet with sweat. He completed his poor appearance by mopping his brow with a Willie Nelson-style red bandanna, adorned with white polka dots. He looked sloppy and apologized for his tardiness, explaining that his partner, Mr. Dunlop, had been suddenly called away to some emergency in Capitol City. "I did not think I would be coming in this morning, but this came up, so I shall conduct the deposition in Mr. Dunlop's absence."

Sharpe responded with patronizing politeness, because he was secretly pleased his dolt of a client would not have to deal with the tough and experienced Dunlop. Wortman, in Sharpe's opinion, which he whispered to his associate Fox, would be unprepared on short notice and that was a break.

Wortman seemed adversely affected by the temperature, and just before the group entered the boardroom, he instructed the secretary to adjust the thermostat.

It was no surprise to Sharpe and Fox that the offices of Dunlop and Wortman were a far cry from the marble halls of the huge Wall Street law firms. There were no paintings, not even prints by fashionable impressionists, no oak furniture, no comfortable chairs, and the place was stifling hot.

Inside the boardroom was equally unimpressive. A rectangular six-by-twelve foot table looked second-hand and was surrounded by old, used, and uncomfortable wooden chairs. The far side of the second-story room was a long plate-glass window overlooking Webster Street. The huge window had no blinds or curtains and allowed the morning sun and the noise of the street below to permeate the sweltering room.

A second, smaller table sat between two filing cabinets in the far corner for use by the certified court reporter whose electronic gear was situated there. Her name and credentials were read and accepted by the lawyers in the record of the hearing. The smell of lemon oil wafted through the room, leaving a sickening sweetness that was noticeably annoying.

Wortman sat down opposite Jobb where the two microphones, one pointed at each party, were located. He frequently wiped his forehead and arms with the bandanna and Sharpe seeing that was convinced that Wortman was unprepared.

Sharpe and Fox, in contrast, had prepared their client all the previous day, inventing tough questions and coaching him in devil's advocate-like rebuttals. Sharpe looked Brooks Brothers perfect in an expensive blue suit, four-button surgeon cuffs, a white silk shirt, and striped British regimental tie of hand-sewn silk. His Church of London wing tip shoes were highly polished.

Sharpe's partner Fox wore a short, deep gray, pinstriped jacket over a conservative length skirt and matronly English kid pumps. Her blouse was white silk with a frilly neckline resembling a Scot's shirt, and was adorned with a small gold pin bearing the scales of justice.

Wortman made a mental note that their combined wardrobes would cost more than four thousand dollars, which he considered a conservative guess. He chuckled to himself as he had bet the women in the office that the two would appear in typical Wall Street duds, where they all dressed like retired English military types. Wortman had wordsmithed a name for their sartorial deportment, which was patterned after stuffy English barristers' clothes. He called it their regimental dress, describing them as the Queen's Whoresars, a wordplay on the English regiment the Queen's Hussars.

Even Steven Jobb, who usually looked like the Salvation Army store styled his clothes, had dressed up. He wore a gray polyester suit, a blue shirt, a loud flowered tie, and leather shoes in place of his usual dirty white Reboks. His hair, however, still looked like he needed an oil change, but admittedly, he looked better than Wortman.

The recording equipment and the back-up system were tested, and the name of the case, the issue in dispute, the names of those attending, the time, and the date were read into the record.

The lawyers knew, and Jobb had been cautioned, that during a deposition the asking and responding could become animated and sometimes downright belligerent. Sharpe was confident that their work with Jobb had prepared him for the important questions and answers, and he had warned his client not to lose his cool under pressure.

Sharpe and Fox exchanged quizzical glances when the questions Wortman started with seemed obscure, not directly on point, and soft by nature. Fox noted to herself that Wortman was sweating profusely and concluded his questions were an indication of his preparedness. He seemed to lack a cohesive plan.

Wortman followed the standard Q and one question, then one response, then a supplemental question.

"Mr. Jobb, do you know Dr. Walter Corbett personally?"

"No, I've never met him."

"Did you interview Dr. Corbett by telephone?"

"No, I only analyzed his columns, not him personally."

"Did you attempt to interview Dr. Corbett?"

"No, I felt his written opinions were explicit, and I disagreed with his conclusions, and I made fair comment in rebutting his views. I found his words to be incomplete and circular in reasoning."

"What particularly bothered you about his written opinions?"

"He left out the topical case of Rubin "Hurricane" Carter who spent over twenty years in prison. That case wasn't solved by science, and therefore, it contradicted the opinion of Dr. Corbett about science reducing wrongful convictions."

"Did you write that Dr. Corbett was racially biased as the result of his not including Carter in his articles? Carter is black."

"I put that down as the only reason I could think of, because the case was so well-known and the movie had just come out with Denzell Washington, who is also black."

"Would you say that any white author who left out the case of a black man did so for racial reasons?"

"I would be inclined to do so if the author's reason was circular. Dr. Corbett used circular reasoning."

"And you concluded this without having ever met Dr. Corbett?"

"Yes, I did. I read his article. And that was my fair comment."

Wortman chuckled to himself. He thought, "Even though Jobb had surely been well prepared his answers were too legal. The use of the term 'fair comment' was a dead giveaway because it was right from a law book. Almost all lawyers know the important legal defense against a charge of libel is that the words were 'fair comment,' and Wortman knew Jobb had been over-prepared. Wortman decided to coast along and appear aimless in his questioning to see if and when Jobb's memory would fail him, and then perhaps he would stick his foot in his mouth.

"Have you listened to Dr. Corbett's speeches on radio or have you seen him on television?"

"No, sir."

"You are sure you have never seen photos or any pictures in magazines of Dr. Corbett?"

"No, sir."

"Did you discuss Dr. Corbett with your companion, Joanne MacDonald of the *Chronicle*?"

"Absolutely not. We don't discuss each other's business. The most we ever ask each other is how to spell a word or a word's meaning."

"So I can absolutely be assured that you knew nothing of Dr. Corbett before these articles he wrote?"

"Yes, sir."

"Would you conclude, based on your earlier answer that a white author who omits a black person from fair open discussion is liable to be biased, that a black author who omits facts about another black man would or would not likely be prejudiced or a racial bigot?"

"I think it's fair to assume that a black author who omits another black man from his writings wouldn't be motivated by prejudice, but he might be uninformed."

"And is calling a person uninformed less damaging than calling a person a bigot?"

"Uninformed is less damaging, I'd say, but if a person is a bigot, the truth counts and should be written."

"But you wouldn't conclude automatically that a black author was a bigot about another black man?"

"That's correct. He'd be unlikely to be racially biased."

Wortman excused himself, went to the boardroom door, and spoke to the woman in the outer office. "Adjust the temperature please," he ordered.

He returned to his chair and instructed the reporter to continue recording.

"Mr. Jobb, are you aware that Dr. Walter Corbett is a black man?"

Jobb appeared to panic and he turned to his lawyers, who sat passively and gave no response, perhaps because there was no adequate response. After a moment, Jobb answered in attack mode. He said, "I know your client is not an American citizen and I've found the old clergyman up north who can prove it. That shows what type of man your client is, so his reputation is at question because he's an illegal immigrant."

Since Jobb did not answer whether he knew if Dr. Corbett was black, it was fair to assume he wasn't aware of that fact. Wortman normally would not have given back any information, but Jobb's lack of ethics prodded him into breaking his usual routine to try to incite Jobb. He said, "You know about Dr. Corbett's personal problems, and you did a lot of tough research to find out embarrassing facts about him after you accused him of being a racist. You even found a witness who would not be easy to locate, but you didn't bother to research Dr. Corbett before you wrote the articles. I saw the mystery clergyman's name on your attorney's discovery list, and I expected something like this, so we researched him too."

Wortman was hot, sweaty, and angry looking. He stood up and walked to the door, the sweat beading on his face. "Adjust the temperature again," he commanded through the door. Then he strode back to the table and pointed his finger at Jobb's nose. He spoke in a loud voice, "Dr. Corbett was brought into this country as an innocent party when he was less than ten days old. Secondly, his parents are adoptive by construction, and he is adopted by estoppel. In the event, you don't understand that, it means it's a legal adoption and the Immigration and Naturalization people accept that. Adopted children of American citizens are allowed into the US. He is also a US Army hero and a decorated veteran of the Vietnam War whom the President of the United States asked Congress to make a United States citizen one month ago, and they did."

There was a brief silence. Jobb's face was scarlet in the sweltering heat of the room and the scalding words of Wortman. The sun had now reached a point above the bank building across the street, and its full power had turned the boardroom into an uncomfortable cooker. Sharpe stood up, excused himself, and removed his suit jacket and tie. Fox followed his lead, and Jobb sat silently, the sweat drifting down form his oily hairline.

Wortman again walked to the door of the outer office. "Bring me that package of tapes," he instructed, and then as if it were an afterthought, he turned to those sitting at the table, "Coffee anyone?"

They all declined.

Wortman's young employee brought in a shoebox-sized package labeled Steven Jobb in big letters, and when Wortman removed the top of the box, it was filled with tape cassettes.

Jobb stared at the box. It was evident by his countenance that he was curious and a little concerned. Wortman picked though the cassettes and then paused to wipe his brow with the polka-dot handkerchief.

Sharpe was as curious as Jobb, "Wait a minute. We have a right to know what this is about and where this material came from."

Wortman leaned back. "Damn the heat," he sighed, and then as if he intended to continue without explanation, "Let's proceed."

Sharpe leaned forward and for the first time, his facade of cool seemed broken. "Where did you get that box?"

Wortman said in a low even voice, "This is not a criminal trial, Mr. Sharpe, although it may very well end up with criminal charges being laid. As an attorney you know that there's no poison tree evidence protection or inadmissibility of evidence in a civil trial-discovery, and in some respects the courts are lenient on that score too."

Sharpe was slightly flustered and it showed. "Who gave you those tapes?"

"There is no property in a witness, sir," Wortman replied, "and you know any witness is fair game to both sides in court. Now, I'd like to continue with the Q and A, Mr. Sharpe, and if that's not satisfactory, we can do it before a judge, and your client will have to answer."

Sharpe said nothing more. Wortman decided not to ask again if Jobb had known that Corbett was black, as his original response to that question was more powerful than any lie Jobb would tell now that he knew he was trapped. Wortman opened a new area of questioning.

"Do you record all interviews, Mr. Jobb?"

"Well yes, but it's only for reference. We don't use them in a public sense."

"Are you aware, sir, that it is illegal in this state to record personal or phone conversations without permission?"

"It's a non-issue. We only keep them as a reference."

"Are you aware it is a crime to do that?"

"I thought if I didn't use them it was OK."

"How many tapes, just an approximate number, have you made, say over the last year without permission?"

"I have no idea."

"More than five?"

"Possibly."

"More than twenty-five?"

"Likely."

"More than seventy-five or one hundred?"

"Yes."

Wortman was completely in charge now and had reduced Jobb's smart-alecky attitude to red-faced discomfort.

"Do you and your roommate, Ms. MacDonald, compare notes or talk shop at home, and would she be inclined to tell anyone that you retain tape recordings of interviews?"

"I suppose she'd know, and possibly she would mention it because someone seems to have known about the tapes."

"Mr. Jobb, do you ..."

Sharpe interrupted. "Mr. Wortman, it is very hot in here, unbearable. Would you allow me to use a private spot to make a phone call to our client, the *Bugle* before we continue?"

Wortman agreed and led Sharpe to the spare office that also served as a lunch room and storage space. He left Sharpe at the desk and closed the door behind himself as he returned to the boardroom to wait. Fox sat silently except for tapping a pen on the desk like a drum. Obviously bored or curious, she asked which room her partner Sharpe was in and then headed to that office, leaving Jobb, Wortman, and the recording clerk uncomfortably alone in the board room.

Wortman made small talk with the court reporter, ignoring Jobb. The time passed with agony as the heat was sweltering. A half-hour, then an hour, and finally, looking only slightly cooler, Fox and Sharpe returned to the boardroom. Sharpe requested that the recording be stopped.

Wortman agreed, and Sharpe sat down.

"My clients," said Sharpe, "are prepared to settle with Dr. Corbett and make a public apology, issue correcting facts in a prominent article in the *Bugle,* and pay Dr. Corbett one hundred thousand dollars today."

Wortman responded aggressively, "My client has given me specific instructions in the event you wanted to settle. You will pay him two hundred and fifty thousand dollars. That is non-negotiable, and your firm will provide a guaranteed tax opinion that the payment is tax-free. The *Bugle* will run a full-page apology for three days on page one, on which we will have final say as to content. Nothing more, certainly nothing less is acceptable."

"Agreed," Sharpe said without hesitation. "Draw up a simple agreement and I'll sign it."

Sharpe and Wortman signed the one-page agreement at five minutes past one in the afternoon. Sharpe was the only one to shake hands with Wortman as the group departed.

Wortman closed the door to the stairs and then turned to his secretary. "Turn that frigging heat down now. How high did you have it?"

She smiled innocently, "I turned it up to eighty-five degrees from eighty on your last request, but I was scared as heck one of them would look at the thermostat and see that it was on heat and not a malfunctioning air conditioner."

Wortman headed for his office, "Hold my calls for fifteen minutes while I sponge off and put on my suit for my two o'clock client."

"What about that box of tapes?," she asked.

"Save 'em in the supply room. They're blanks."

CHAPTER TWENTY-SEVEN

Privacy

"There is no such thing as a secret. The walls have ears and that's why loose lips sink ships.

- sign at the British MI5 training center

According to the Police Department's policy manual, private mail and telephone calls are discouraged at the police station, because duty personnel do not have time for private transactions or personal relationships while they are at the station. Baptist said, "The theory is that an officer's full attention to the job is required." But he and everyone else periodically broke that rule because spouses, companions, and bill collectors cared not for what the department wanted.

Sergeant Richard Murphy had not ordered any products for delivery, nor did he ever have mail sent to the department address. But a boxed package wrapped in brown paper was delivered to him by UPS to the desk sergeant's window, adjacent to the small public area just inside the fluoroscope scanner. The prepaid waybill from UPS showed the sender to be John Dough, and the point of shipment was the courthouse at Capitol City.

Murphy finished his shift and retrieved his messages, which notified him the package could be picked up from the desk sergeant. He retrieved the package without comment and took it to the squad room where he sat in front of his locker.

He sat quietly, perhaps curious about the package, ignoring the bustle of police officers coming and going amidst a clatter of gossip and trash-talk.

Murphy, a solitary, private person and a loner, did not seek attention for his package, but it attracted a bevy of nosy onlookers, nevertheless. He was offered various unsolicited opinions and comments about the possible contents. He sat quietly as his colleagues, like smutty high school boys, suggested the box contained some secret sexual item such as a monogrammed dildo or a carton of assorted colored condoms or maybe a man's custom made red thong complete with a bullet-proof section.

As Murphy started to unwrap his parcel, the circle of curious onlookers grew larger. A plain shoebox emerged from beneath the paper wrapper with a note attached. It was printed in square black letters and stated "SOMEBODY KNOWS". Murphy removed the cover, and inside there was white tissue paper like that used in jewelry or china stores to protect and enhance the appearance of a special gift item. He carefully peeled back the layers of tissue and revealed two items: a short, stainless steel arrow from a small crossbow and a saw-tooth combat knife like those issued to military special forces.

Murphy made no comment, maintaining his usual silence. The onlookers were unusually quiet, but a murmur of curiosity mounted about the contents. Finally, Murphy, his red face revealing his discomfort, spoke, "I don't know if this is a threat to my life or a strange but admittedly weird and expensive joke?" He stood up clutching the box and said, "I think I'll see the chief to decide if this warrants an investigation of a dangerous situation or if we should just write it off as a nut."

He walked to the elevator carrying the strange items under his arm.

When Baptist heard about the parcel, he said, "gossip in a law enforcement agency travels at warp-speed, only equalled by barracks' rumors in the army." But when he went to see Sergeant Reading at her office, he speculated that the package amounted to an accusation of Murphy, who was noticeably upset as proved by his red face and nervous reaction. "Whoever did it," Baptist said, "has baited Murphy, and if he is guilty of anything he'll sweat or panic."

Reading was pensive, even more cautious in her analytical opinions than usual. She said, "Could be it's just a threat by someone who hates him, and that could be half this city."

Baptist ignored that issue and said, "Lieutenant Folker phoned Bear and told him the wiretap on Solomon's phone picked up a conversation from an anonymous source to the Reverend in the middle of the night. The caller harassed him about sexually touching Anslow girl and the money he paid Mrs. Anslow. Whoever it was certainly knew how to push Solomon's buttons. He panicked and must have called the chief from the church, which is not wired, because the chief went to the church to see Solomon the next morning. My question is, did Solomon phone the chief because Mrs. Pineo works at the church, or is there some other connection between these two, because it was the chief who suggested Solomon pay damages to the Anslows? But what's the connection?"

Shirley's view was more restrained, slightly more objective, even though she was also curious about the relationship. "It could just be that Mrs. Pineo works there, but there's no question that it could be there's some link."

Baptist did not argue the subject further, yet Shirley knew from her personal relationship with him and from reading his face and mannerisms that he did not agree with her watered-down theory. He stood up.

Baptist said, "While there is some momentum from this spooky package, I'm going to try and stir the pot by going to see the chief and add some misinformation."

As Baptist reached Chief Pineo's outer office, Richard Murphy was just leaving. They passed each other like ships in the night, nodding with an awkward courtesy but not pausing to exchange shoptalk. The secretary announced Baptist's arrival, and he was invited into the chief's large office. Pineo looked concerned. He said, "Murphy just brought me this package he received."

"Are you ordering prints checked?" asked Baptist.

"Yes, the ID guys are on their way up."

Baptist sat down and went directly to the subject of Murphy. He explained the conflicting stories of the road-agent Feters and the hearsay from him about Hicks seeing an officer, perhaps Murphy, at the ballpark on the night of Mary Anslow's murder. Baptist hoped to provoke a reaction from the chief but did not tell Pineo that he knew about him visiting Solomon. He sat back and waited for Pineo's reaction to the verbal probe.

Pineo was surprisingly cool, but he could hide his emotions under pressure, and Baptist knew that. Chief Pineo said, "Murphy is a good cop, but he is also eccentric. I know his wife well, and even she admits he is as mysterious as deep water. If you have to interview him to clarify anything on those circumstances, then do it."

Baptist was almost openly surprised. He noted mentally that the chief never mentioned Solomon, and it was no clearer if the anonymous call was the reason for the visit. He decided to try a rumor on the chief to see what his reaction would be. "I hear the state police like Reverend Solomon for Major Brown's murder," he stated matter of factly.

Baptist wondered if Pineo would give Solomon a heads-up on that, and if he did, the residence wire taps might pick it up, and that would be significant. But there were no taps on the offices Baptist knew, and that weakened their collection of evidence. The chief remained absolutely passive, showing interest but displaying no other emotion or reaction. Baptist finished his business and departed.

On his way to the ground floor in the elevator, Baptist decided to go to a payphone outside the department and call Lieutenant Folker to alert him about planting the rumor about Solomon on Chief Pineo. He left the building and walked to the Greyhound bus station and the row of payphones in the waiting room. He dialed Folker's number, and when Folker answered, Baptist outlined the developments about Murphy's package and the rumor planted on Pineo.

Folker was enthusiastic. He asked, "What's your take on the arrow and knife sent to Murphy?"

"Someone either suspects Murphy's involved," replied Baptist, "or is trying to scare the shit out of him. It may have worked because he seems spooked and ran to the chief."

"How do you read the chief on this stuff?" Folker asked.

Baptist said, "Pineo's reaction was bland, not defensive. But it will be interesting to see if he warns Solomon that you guys are looking at him."

"New subject," said Folker, "we selected two young cadets from the state Police Academy to run your wiretaps. They have extensive US Army training and experience in surveillance devices and wiretaps. They have rented an old house down there on Leverett Avenue, and the phone company has installed conduit gear for them. Plus, the warrant allows them to plant listening and video devices in the residences of the suspects but only if necessary as supported by other probable cause.. Some of their stuff is state of the art, voice activated, which is tough to detect. They will plant any on-site stuff by dressing as repairmen or telephone employees. The wire taps will be at the source with the phone company They'll need you guys to assist them at the house, because with only two of them, it means twelve hour shifts, and that's bad news on wiretaps, because sometimes there's no action for hours. Can you guys baby-sit them and keep them company? And they'll need food delivered."

Baptist was enthusiastic. "Absolutely," he replied.

Folker continued, "I told them Bear would visit them first because he's Native American, and they'd immediately recognize him. And then he'll vouch for the rest of you. By the way, these guys are gonna be stars, tough as combat boots, and they're electronic wizards, real academic nerds on that crap. They are also a tad eccentric, plus they are twins, thirty years old, Ernie and Bernie Blazek.

As Folker and Baptist conversed, in another part of the city, the man Bear and Reading suspected of being crooked, drug officer Sergeant Frank Nichols, drove into the parking lot of the expensive Oxford Place condominium complex where he owned and lived in the tenth-floor penthouse condo. Nichols was collecting his mail from the lobby mailbox. Two Bell telephone technicians dressed in blue company coveralls, carrying tools and electronic gear walked out of the telephone equipment room in the lobby.

"Hey, you two," Nichols called , and then flashed his gold shield, "how about doing me a favor? I work in the drug section and I worry that some drug moke will tap my phone or apartment. Maybe you guys could check the lines down here and give my condo a sweep too."

The two men exchanged glances. One of them said, "Gee, I don't know, mister. Without our security people giving us permission, we wouldn't dare," .

The second man was not so timid. "C'mon, for fuck's sake, he's a cop, and if he wants his own phone and apartment checked, it ain't like we're doing anything illegal."

Nichols stood by the elevator doors and held them open. "Let's go. Ride up with me. How long can it take to sweep the lines and rooms?"

The men both shrugged and got into the elevator with him. Nichols scanned his mail on the way up, and the two were silent. At the tenth floor, they followed Nichols across a spacious hall to a huge double oak door, which was marked only with a small gold letter "N". At each end of the hall there were floor to ceiling tinted thermal windows, affording a perfect view of the public garden on one side and the city clock tower on the other. As they entered the posh entryway behind the oak doors, it became apparent that cost had not been a restraint in the decoration of the interior. Hardwood floors, Persian rugs, expensive art and furniture adorned the living quarters, which occupied the entire tenth floor.

Nichols seemed to sense their reaction to the posh surroundings. He said, "I got this place for a song when the original owner went bankrupt." He led them to the kitchen and a room behind his built-in laundry where the electronic phone box was located.

"Perhaps you could sweep the lines, then the phones, and then the rooms," Nichols suggested, "and then I'll pay you."

One man shook his head. "No man, we'll give it a scan, but it'll take almost an hour, so you go about your business, and we'll yell when we're finished."

Nichols took his mail and went into his den. He leafed casually through the assortment of bills and junk mail, until he came to a flowered envelope addressed in square block letters to Sergeant Frank Nichols at his building and bearing a first class Statue of Liberty stamp. He thought it was feminine because of the flowers and the sweet smell of Obsession perfume which he recognized from his bar crawling.

He opened the envelope, which contained two pieces of fairly heavy white paper similar to the cover piece on the front of a writing tablet. Between the two pieces of protective cover there was a piece of colored paper on which three twenty-milligram Valium capsules where glued. Block printing on the feminine writing paper stated, "STOLEN FROM THE WALGREEN DRUG WAREHOUSE – EVERYBODY KNOWS."

Nichols' heart did a flip-flop. He reached for the telephone but then remembered the Bell techs were there. He put the envelope and pills in his pocket. He could feel his chest tighten but he had to remain cool. He waited.

It had been a long forty-five minutes when the two telephone men finally entered his den with a utility band 88-108 megahertz scanner and checked the room – walls, floors, furniture and phone – for electronic taps.

"No bugs, no readings on your phones or the box," one man announced.

Nichols showed them to the front door, attempting to remain calm, but he could hardly wait to get them out. "Let me pay you," he said, reaching for his wallet.

One man held up his hand. "Then it wouldn't be a favor; it would be selling a service we do not own. That's illegal. This way it's just a favor to aid law enforcement."

Nichols nodded, "At least tell me your names," he said.

One of the men paused, then took off his New York Yankees baseball cap and scratched his head looking puzzled, but did not answer.

Nichols said. "Geeze you guys are twins!"

"Yep," the man nearest the door replied. "Twins: Ernie and Bernie."

After they left, Nichols felt comfortable that his phone was safe to use because Ernie and Bernie told him so. He punched in the number of his partner Hunter Stent.

Stent's tired raspy voice responded with a gruff, "Hello."

Nichols said, "Meet me at Hooters right away. We got a problem."

Stent knew better than to argue with him, but he was tired and tried to beg off. He replied, "Is it really that important that it has to be right now?"

Nichols responded with anger, "It's serious like lung cancer, you fuck, so move your ass right now," and then he slammed down the receiver.

CHAPTER TWENTY-EIGHT

Ears and Eyes

"The hearing ear, the seeing eye, the Lord hath made even both of them."

- Proverbs

Sergeant Frank Nichols, a slow moving surly man of little mirth, was stressed and angry that someone was butting into his life, and mad as hell that he was under attack, harassed by some secret tormentor. He parked behind the Winn Dixie market and cut through the alley to Hooters to meet his partner. Stent stood just inside the side door and, before the door was all the way open, he said, "What's wrong with you? You were blatting into the phone and phone taps have done in more people than the holocaust."

Nichols frowned, in silence his mouth twisted in anger. His eyes scanned the parking lot in a brief, animated motion as if he was searching to see if he had been followed. He turned back to Stent and said in a half whisper, "Follow me into the can."

In the bathroom, Nichols checked the stalls to make sure they were alone and then snapped the lock on the entry door. He was fidgety, fumbling in his pocket, searching for the anonymous letter which had come in the mail. When he found it, he passed it to his partner without comment.

Stent surprised him with his response. "I got a letter too," he said, and passed a pink, flowery, scented envelope to the shocked Nichols. A female or someone who was trying to write like a woman had addressed Stent's letter in fine penmanship.

Nichols glanced at it and said, "It's clear the writer ain't worried about handwriting analysis." His eyes scanned down the single page, and he expected it to give the same message he had received. It was written on the same kind of pink flowery paper that matched the envelope, and emitted a faint smell of perfume.

Nichols said, "Smells like a woman or someone wants us to believe that. Or, if the letter is from a man disguising his writing, he's a master forger."

Stent replied, "I get the message even though it don't rhyme, and it's not impressive like Muhammad Ali's poetic ditties, but it sure as shit sends a stinging message."

COPS IN PRISON

Cops Nichols and Stent,
Are quite badly bent!
And soon they'll bend over,
Like cows in the clover!
For the Horney old bulls
Where they're sent.

Nichols' face on reading the rhyme was red and pained, a combination of anger and fear. He could not hide his feelings nor could he rationalize the fear with callous words. His squinted eyes and wrinkled brow were signs Stent recognized, because he had worked so long with Nichols. "The usual result," Stent thought, "is that he'll go nuts and do something impulsive, which will fuck us all."

Nichols finally let go, "Some rotten sonuvabitch is messing with us, trying to spook us, or trying to muscle us out and grab our pill-mine by using psychological warfare."

Stent was turning the words and the message over in his mind. He remained deadpan, thinking of how to calm down his partner. He replied, "It could be an attempted grab or maybe the bikers or even some kid Brown was punking, trying to stir us up for revenge. I think we should lay low. Brown stirred the whole city up with that stupid arrest of the Frank kid. Look at it this way, whoever whacked Brown did us a big favor. If we completely shut down right now, it will look like the drug business dies with Brown and we're home free."

Nichols listened and appeared to be digesting Stent's opinion. But he said nothing in response, so Stent continued, "Sooner or later that guy Dunlop is gonna sue the city over the Frank arrest, because people won't stand for that shit, and it'll all come out, and the heat's gonna be intense. Or, suppose this is the bikers trying to scare us off, let's give it to them. We'll offer them our inventory and fade into the sunset and then let the shit fly over someone else."

Nichols seemed to be receptive to that but added a note of caution. "Just remember," he said, "the bikers could snuff us like a candle if we get in the way."

"Exactly," Stent said, "so let's get what we can without pissing them off. What we want is out, no matter who is sending us the messages."

Stent couldn't get a response. He decided to ask the big question, "How did you and Brown get involved with the courthouse gang when you had a good thing of your own with no hassles."

"Simple," Nichols replied. "Brown was in the drug deal with me, but he was also in on the courthouse thing without me. The two things were quite separate, until he discovered that the janitor was an undercover trooper. He knew that was a potential threat to both deals, so Brown decided to whack the guy, and no amount of talk could slow him down. Next, Dunlop stirred up shit when that guy MacDougall got arrested for a fine violation when he had already paid it. Couple all that with the Frank kid, and then Murphy decided that Dunlop had to be eliminated too. He didn't ask for advice and fucked it up. His big snuff plan hinged on the fact that someone told him that Dunlop goes to the bank every Thursday to do his office payroll. Murphy planned the bank robbery to make shooting Dunlop look like a robbery gone bad and not a hit. But there was a major hitch, apparently Murphy didn't know for sure what Dunlop looked like. And some poor nerd in a lawyer-blue suit who happened to resemble Dunlop showed up and boom! That's it. Big mistake; big stink."

Stent was still curious, "But who runs Murphy and the courthouse scam?"

"First I thought it was all Brown's deal," Nichols answered. "But they got their dancing orders from someone else. I always figured it was Morash but it isn't, besides Brown hated her. I thought I knew who it was, but I've changed my mind half-a-dozen times. And I still don't know. But it sure isn't Brown's stooges Kierans and Clarke. All they do is provide a lot of minor arrests to generate fines, and fines are what they're stealing."

Stent looked serious, almost afraid as he spoke, "I'm sorry I ever let you drag me into this. I took a few bucks for a few favors and then bam, I'm in the pot with you."

Nichols look amused. He replied, "Just remember the conspiracy theory of crime, and you're up to your ass in it, just like me."

Stent moved his head in agreement because he recognized Nichols' mercurial nature and mood swings. He knew Nichols was dangerous, especially now that he felt threatened. Stent could imagine Nichols slipping out of control, going off half-cocked as pressure mounted. The anonymous letters had created a new threat from an invisible antagonist. Stent made up his mind that his own safety was as much at risk from Nichols' paranoid snit as from the letter writer.

Nichols only increased Stent's fear by frequently checking to see if they were followed. His fear of telephones too grew from normal caution to unreasonable theories of super-spy electronic gizmos. Nichols had gone over the edge and had developed a slight facial tick just below his left eye. It was involuntary and annoying as it twitched every time he became stressed.

"Be careful of your phone," Nichols warned Stent. "I just had mine swept by two Bell technicians."

Stent nodded. He was well aware of how often wire taps were used to secure convictions, but the fact that Nichols was overreacting worried him more than the actual wiretaps. It seemed more a manifestation of Nichols' mental instability than a real threat. He tried not to look at Nichols because the nervous facial tick was distracting.

"There's a lot going on," Nichols continued. "That fuckin' warehouse fire is a sure sign that the courthouse crowd has gone nuts, and they've attracted a lot of attention. Why the hell didn't they just quietly steal the records instead of burning the building?" he asked.

Stent said, "Let me talk to the bikers and see if they'll buy our inventory of pills, and then we can just fade into the darkness." Nichol's nostrils flared. He said angrily, "I'll contact the bikers, and you butt out."

At the same time that Stent was attempting to placate Nichols, the two state trooper technicians were putting the finishing touches on their wire tap operation at the old cape cod house on Leverett Avenue. Bear, Baptist, Sergeant Reading, and Sergeant White sat on dusty old covered furniture in the main room waiting for their indoctrination into the world of wiretaps.

Ernie Blazek spoke of realism and seemed to limit expectations. "It's state of the art equipment, but remember these guys are cops, and they won't likely blab much on the phone, so don't expect a miracle. They may not even give us a lead, and as far as probative evidence goes, it's highly unlikely. The best taps sometimes only give us useful intelligence data."

Sergeant White had similar realistic expectations based on experience. He said, "Even if we pick up a lead or a clue and no real evidence, it will help. As Blazek warned us, cops have a natural paranoia about telephones, and they'll be defensive in all conversations."

"What about MacAdam, our esteemed prosecutor?" White asked. "Has that McIntyre woman's investigator picked anything up on him?"

Ernie Blazek looked at his brother, "What did the Feds tell you about MacAdam?"

Bernie Blazek, who looked amazingly like his brother Ernie, except for a small red mark just above his right eyebrow, answered, "Some woman phones him for a meet several times a week at different places, but that's it."

"Maybe a love affair?" Baptist said.

"Maybe a married woman," added Bear.

"Sheeit," White said, "I don't think so, he's queer as a queen, and he ain't humping no woman, married or single."

"OK," Bernie said, "Who's gonna follow the queen to see who he meets?"

White smiled, "I know just the person. Sergeant Doreen Roberts works with me in ID. She has never been to court, so MacAdam doesn't know her. I'll give you her beeper number and set it up. Once you hear he's gonna meet and where, you can phone her."

Baptist said, "I talked to Dunlop today. He's going back to the state and they're gonna put him in charge of this prosecution."

"What about his practice and Wortman?" Bear asked.

"Professor Corbett is going to retire from the law school and join Wortman as a partner and they're going to sue the city over the Frank kid."

Bear laughed, "It's like hockey, Dunlop for Corbett and a player to be named later. That suit will stand the city on its collective ass."

"It can only help us," White said," because deposing all those cops may open it up a crack, so to speak."

CHAPTER TWENTY-NINE

The Owl

"..[H]abitation for dragons, and a court of owls."
- Isaiah 34:13

Skeeter Greene is a homeless man, a road-agent supreme, with a foul disposition and numerous eccentric and anti-social habits and idiosyncrasies. His very appearance advertised those traits without any additional explanation necessary. Green had not seen Noel Bear since Bear harassed him for information after the ballpark murder of Mary Anslow. Nor in normal circumstances would he ever want to see Bear or any other law enforcement officer again. "Because," he said, "they're all pricks, dangerous like Waffen SS Corporals. They are overcome with a little authority and they get off on hassling citizens just for kicks." But Skeeter had a strong motive to find Bear; because he was afraid.

Despite his unconventional, hermit-like penchant for a solitary existence, and his normally cranky nature, Baptist once said Greene was neither crazy, stupid, nor dangerous, only cantankerous according to the United States Department of Veterans Affairs. His aversion to soap, water, and society stemmed from a three-year stint as a POW at the Hanoi Hilton in Vietnam. Baptist said, "The VA reported Greene was fairly brilliant but strange."

Greene's opinion of the Veterans Affairs people was equally pointed and descriptive. His tirades against the veterans organization were like a cracked record, and his rhetoric never changed. He said, "The VA is a bunch of heartless bastards who've never been to Vietnam, and they make rank because they specialize in paying benefits to veterans. My theory," Greene said, "is fuck 'em all, save six for pall bearers, and one more to kiss my ass goodbye."

Greene lived in the murky world of the homeless, only surfacing periodically at the Salvation Army when panhandling was poor. Generally, he was dependent on himself. He survived by his wits, and he knew and frequented every warm secure sleeping place in the city. Not even experienced street cops knew all the hangouts where the homeless slept. And as a matter of practical fact, Skeeter was so big and menacing that he slept where he pleased, because no other road-agent wanted to experience his foul disposition. If he decided to sleep in a specific nook, under a bridge or overpass or in the courthouse park or behind the ballpark scoreboard, no other road-agent dared complain, because Greene was king of the homeless, and no one dared challenge him.

Greene was looking for Bear because he had decided Bear would be the safest to approach. Bear was new, he never roughed anyone up, and he had once paid Greene for information. It was a difficult decision. Contacting the police was not simple without going to the station or at least giving your name. Cops usually have unlisted personal phone numbers and hidden addresses for their own safety and neither are given out, especially to unnamed road-agents calling from a pay phone. But Skeeter was afraid for his life, and when he grew desperate, he waited behind a bush at the back fence of the police parking lot for hours hoping to see Bear. Greene's anger and frustration grew, and he said to himself, "You can never find a cop when you need one."

Finally, armed with anger, Skeeter dialed the number of the Shiretown Police Department from a phone booth at the Salvation Army. The response was the sort of canned, recorded, impersonal automated system that infuriated the public.

"Press one ... press two ... press my ass," Greene thought as he burned up quarter after quarter trying to reach the voice of a human being. On his fourth attempt, enraged, he hit the "0" and held the button in. A graveled masculine voice responded.

"Shiretown Police Department. Sergeant Thompson speaking."

Skeeter gloated silently about finally besting the impersonal Orwellian telephone system, "I'm looking for Noel Bear."

Thompson's authoritative, unfriendly voice was not much warmer than the recorded one. "Officer Bear is on patrol. Who's calling?"

"I need to talk to Bear, and I can't give my name," Greene responded. There was a brief pause as if Thompson was deciding what to say or do. Then he replied, "The best way to meet an officer is to come down to the station."

Greene tried to remain civil, "I can't do that. My safety is at risk."

Thompson seemed more detached and conveyed even less warmth than before. He said curtly, "Well, if you leave your name and number, I'll give Officer Bear the message."

Greene's short fuse did not allow him to suffer fools with patience. He yelled, "I don't have a number. I'm in a phone booth; I can't come to the station, and this is very important to Bear. Maybe you could get off your fat ass and contact Bear. Ask him if you can give me his cell phone number, and I'll phone him direct."

The response from the callous desk Sergeant did not strike Greene as helpful. Thompson said, "Give me your name, and I'll ask Bear if I can give you his cell number, but other than that I can't keep this line tied up any longer."

Green was furious, "Listen, honkie," he said, "this is a serious matter and I have important information regarding a major crime."

Thompson, who had almost three decades of experience dealing with the public's eccentricity, lost it when Greene insulted him. "Listen you mutha-fucker," he said, "I'm black, I'm no honkie, so don't let the name Thompson fool you."

Geene was no pacifist; Thompson had insulted him and the battle of insults commenced.

"Oh," Greene answered in a falsetto voice, "I guess that's where the expression Black Irish originated."

Thompson was beyond pretense, pissed off without bothering to hide it. "Leave me a name and a place Bear can reach you or fill your fuckin' boots. Give me something, and I'll give him the message."

"Oh goodie," Greene replied, "you're gonna broadcast my name and location over the radio, and every moke with a scanner will know just where I'll be."

That point obviously registered with Thompson, "Give me a nickname that Bear will recognize and a place, and I'll get hold of him."

Greene did not immediately respond as he considered the suggestion. The solution was far from perfect but at least it was something.

"Tell Bear Mary Anslow called. Ask him to drive back and forth on Memorial Drive next to Oak Grove Cemetery between two and two-fifteen. I'll be hidden and if I'm convinced no one is around but him, I'll make sure he sees me."

Thompson's voice softened only slightly but still had a detectable icy tone. "Two to two-fifteen on Memorial Drive by Oak Grove. Is that correct?"

"That's it," Greene said, "and two more points: contact him on his cell and not the radio, and you got an attitude problem, Sergeant."

Greene's final remark struck home, and Thompson mustered a dripping sweet phony reply, "And thank you, sir, for phoning the Shiretown Police," he said. But then, contrary to Greene's instructions, he wrote out the message and instructed the radio dispatcher to broadcast it by police band to unit thirty-two.

Memorial Drive gently curves two miles through Oak Grove Cemetery from South Street to Elm Avenue. The cemetery is an upscale and expensive private burial garden designed and occupied by the socially advantaged. On one side is the older section, dating from the Civil War, where a perfectly spaced lengthy row of oak trees border the sidewalk, providing shade and aesthetic comfort to visitors. On the opposite side, the newer section, Japanese yews and Mountbatten junipers follow the sidewalk as it runs parallel to Memorial Drive, providing a tastefully prepared border for burial plots.

Noel Bear turned his patrol car onto Memorial at exactly two o'clock as the dispatcher had instructed. He immediately saw a slow-moving, 1974 red Buick zig-zagging ahead of him. The movement of the old clunker seemed more consistent with an impaired driver than a citizen searching for a grave. And the registration sticker on the upper right corner of the license plate was green, meaning it was last year's expired sticker. Bear decided to check it out.

"Thirty-two to city," he said into the radio.

"Go ahead thirty-two," the dispatcher replied.

"Ten sixty-five expired tag number WHY one seven seven, state of Massachusetts, on a red 1974 Buick, four door. Copy?"

"Ten-four," the dispatcher replied. "Stand by."

Bear trailed slowly behind the car, keeping a decent interval between the two vehicles, as he waited for the dispatcher to run the plates through the computer.

"Unit thirty-two."

"Thirty-two," Bear answered. "Go ahead."

The dispatcher paused for a moment, "Say again the make, model, and color please."

Bear repeated the description, "Mass plate W-H-Y-one-seven-seven, on a red 1974 Buick Riviera."

"Negative," the dispatcher responded crisply. "W-H-Y-one-seven-seven, state of Mass, is from a blue 1998 Toyota registered to a Mrs. Marjorie Mosher of Haverhill, Mass."

Bear flicked on his roof lights as he replied, "Copy; it appears to have only one lone occupant, no visible passengers. I'm lit up and proceeding to stop the red 1974 Buick."

Once the flashing lights started, the Buick immediately pulled to the curb and stopped. Bear had an unusual feeling, almost a foreboding or premonition. He turned on the dashboard video camera to record the stop and got out, advancing cautiously toward the driver's window. The hair on the back of his neck quivered and a shiver ran down his back despite the midday heat. He stayed close to the side of the car and stopped just behind the front door post, after looking in the back window to make sure there was no hidden passenger lying in ambush.

Bear's position was textbook perfect, just behind the driver's door so that the operator of the vehicle would have to turn his head to the rear and look over his own shoulder to see Bear. It was an awkward position, which served to make an attack by a driver more difficult.

"License and registration, please," Bear instructed the driver, but the driver did not respond. Bear could not see the driver's face because his face was turned away. He repeated the instruction in a loud firm voice. "License and registration, please."

Suddenly, a Beretta nine millimeter was thrust out the window aimed backwards at Bear. Despite the driver's poor position, the gun was pointed above the bulletproof vest in the general vicinity of Bear's face.

In the same microsecond, there was a coincident noisy commotion from a huge bird, which had been flushed from the cover of an evergreen near the opposite curb. The big bird flew from Bear's left side directly at him, its wings beating the air in great arcs, sounding like the blades of a helicopter as it sought altitude. Bear involuntarily and instinctively jerked his head to the right, away from the surprising blur of the bird's noisy movement, which caused him to strike his right eyebrow viciously against the drain ridge above the car door. At the same instance, the Beretta fired a cannon-like deafening sound, sending a blinding flash near his exposed ear. It spewed powder, wadding and smoke in his face but the bullet missed.

Bear, dazed by the bump on his head and the roaring sound of the gun at close range, with blood oozing from his eyebrow, lost his balance and slumped to the ground just as the car took off in a tire-screeching lurch. Bear was stunned, confused and dizzy, and unable to get up, but he could see the sudden glare of the brake lights of the old car as it slammed to a stop about sixty feet away. Then, just as abruptly, the car's backup lights appeared and Bear knew the would-be killer was aiming to back over him and finish the job. He rolled over onto his stomach, raised himself to his knees, his arms supporting him in a half push-up as the noisy old car thrust backwards with squealing tires, aimed to kill.

Suddenly, behind him there were pounding feet, and then he felt powerful hands, one grabbing the back of his gun belt the other at the neck of his bulletproof vest, which heaved him like a laundry bag up on the sidewalk out of the path of the careening Buick.

Bear could see and smell the presence of Skeeter Greene as his savior, but he had no time for accolades. He rolled and then struggled to unholster his piece as the car performed a spinning bootlegger's turn up over the curb and screeched away in the opposite direction. Bear came up on one knee blasting away, the hollow points smacking into the metal of the fleeing car while Greene screamed obscenities. He screamed, "The tires, hit the fuckin' tires you asshole!"

Then the car was gone and Greene was leaning over him.

"You OK?" but before Bear could respond, Greene continued. "Call it in; call it in," he shouted. And then he turned his frustration on Bear shouting, "You couldn't hit a cow in the ass with a shovel. Some fuckin' scout you are."

Bear was a bundle of jellied nerves. He fumbled for his shoulder radio and said to Greene, "Where the fuck did you come from?"

Greene paced back and forth. "Behind that evergreen across the street. I wasn't showing myself till after you were done with the car. I must have spooked the big old owl when I hunkered into that juniper. Now for chrissakes, call the fuckin' number in!"

Bear was a mess, blood ran down his face and he seemed unable to function, but Greene's mention of the owl bothered him.

"An owl?" he asked Greene. "Are you sure it was a fucking owl?"

Greene displayed his usual impatience with detail, "Of course I'm sure. You think I don't know an owl when I see one? Everyone knows what a fuckin' owl looks like."

Bear shook his head in disbelief, "Well, here's a strange one for you, Skeeter. In some tribes, the Navajo for example, the owl is a powerful omen, a sign, big medicine."

Skeeter screwed his face up, "Fuck the owl stories, you got a bigger problem. Some cop heard we were meeting here and tried to have you whacked, and I'm on the same hit parade, so I'm outta here. Gimme your phone number, and someday I may call you about the ballpark pervert. Now, call this in."

Bear was slow and fumbled in his shirt pocket for a business card. He handed it to Skeeter as he called for back-up on his shoulder radio. He said, "My cell number's on the back, but you can't just take off."

Skeeter Greene shrugged, "Can't I?" he scoffed. "Read my cheeks and just watch my ass as it gets smaller and disappears across that burial ground."

CHAPTER THIRTY

The Halls of Power

"If you best a little man, you look bad. If he bests you, you look worse.

- Redhorse (2000)

Mayor R. Walter Finnie worked the room like the late Huey Long seeking re-election. The city employee's Christmas party was important in his political affairs. Finnie said, "I need them to respond quickly when I need the city works department to respond to voters calling for repairs of potholes in a street." To which the city works foreman said, "the fact is Finnie was elected by acclamation because nobody wanted the damn job."

Dick Newcombe, a local barber said,"the Mayor's self created image is about as impressive as the fact he spent a few months on active duty in the navy after ROTC training. And that was just prior to ear problems creating a medical discharge, and a veteran's pension for the pompous little asshole". And the city works department personnel, according to common gossip, did not disagree with the sage saber-tongued barber, nor did the police department.

The city Christmas party, like those held across the country by many organizations, presented career-ending opportunities for those unable to exercise self-restraint after too much eggnog. But the danger to the weak was free booze, skimpy skirts, and sheer blouses on female employees. There was also the chance that some person's repressed anger about their supervisor would be expressed without restraint by the tongue-lubricating Christmas punch. It was not unusual for overzealous employees at such parties to wakeup the next morning to social ruination.

Finnie sucked up to the city foreman, the city engineer, and the chief of police who had made only a quick visit. And there was a Twiggy-like secretary from the police department named Roxine Smith who seemed to grow better looking as the powerful Christmas eggnog worked its magic. There were the usual indiscreet pinches, the too-close dancing, the leering, and the broom closet diplomacy, all reported by longtime tax clerk Simmon, who as a teetotaler was a keen, albeit judgmental observer. He said, "Finnie had a knee-knocker in the standing-room-only closet in the hall with skinny Roxine. Sadly for Finnie, she just happened to be the girlfriend of police officer Tom Kierans, and according to Simmon, that fact started a public relations disaster.

Reportedly, Finnie's cheeks were flushed and his tongue flapped like a wind blown flag. His glad-handing presented a poor imitation of Jesse Helms running for re-election. Finnie did the rounds, kissing the foreheads of women he hardly knew, and the asses of those who managed the buttons of city power.

Suddenly it was midnight; the time had flown, and Finnie with thin Roxine in tow slipped away. He wheeled his big black Mercedes out of the city hall parking lot and headed down Roosevelt Drive to her apartment building on the corner of Park Street. A printed report late claimed that Roxine was snuggled close to His Honor with no seatbelt restraining her, apparently planning physical sexual relief for the Mayor while he drove. The car proceeded snail like from the street centerline to the curb in a snake-like pattern, as he drove in what he considered to be a safe and defensive manner.

The red-and-blue roof lights of the police car suddenly flashed behind them as they proceeded west on fashionable Roosevelt Drive, where anyone who was someone lived in expensive, old money mini-mansions. Finnie pulled slowly to the curb, jammed two pieces of Clorets into his mouth, and pressed the down button on the driver's side window.

Officer Tom Kierans accompanied by patrol partner Greg Clarke, known by Dick the barber as the James Brothers, because he claimed he paid them off on a traffic stop, appeared at the window of the mayor's car. There would later be several versions of what transpired: the police description, the mayor's version, and Roxine's version. And Judge Harold Chase likely had a version too, because he lived in the big house on Roosevelt where the stop took place. Disturbed by the police lights, he witnessed most of the events from his nearby verandah.

"Driver's license and registration, please," Kierans said.

Finnie fumbled in his wallet for the license while an embarrassed Roxine followed instructions and searched the glove compartment for the registration. Kierans glanced at the papers. "Step out of the car, sir," he ordered, and Finnie complied.

Despite the hour, several people had gathered on the sidewalk attracted by the red and blue lights.

"You smell of alcohol," Clarke commented, "and you had no seatbelts on."

Finnie was no fool. His power of communication and personality had carried him through university, the Navy and into the mayor's job without talent.

He said, "I think you are mistaken, sir; I unfastened the seatbelt when I stopped, because my license was in my wallet and I couldn't remove it with the belt on."

Kierans ignored the reply and stared daggers at his girlfriend Roxine. "We want you to do a Breathalyzer at the police station," he said.

Finnie again displayed sound judgment by not playing his trumps at the wrong time. He suppressed his anger and remained polite. He was also shrewd enough to speak in a fairly firm voice, so that the people who had gathered on the sidewalk, and Judge Chase on his verandah, could hear his side of the story.

"Well, I agree to the test even though it's unwarranted. I'll co-operate and go to the station with you."

He did not mention or draw attention to his friend Roxine, who now sat near the passenger's door making herself as small and unobtrusive as possible. A camera flash from the crowd indicated the likelihood of press attention or an enterprising observer who would sell or exploit a photo of the mayor and the police in a unique situation.

Kierans instructed Finnie to proceed to the back door of the police cruiser. He did not handcuff the mayor nor did he say anything else except warning the mayor to watch his head as he entered the caged back seat of the car. Clarke retrieved the mayor's keys, moved the car to the safety of the sidewalk, and instructed Roxine Smith that she would not be able to drive the car. She got out and, despite the hour, took off walking towards Park Street.

The police station holding-room, just behind the desk sergeant's caged area, is a social zoo of assorted drunks, petty criminals and, ne'er-do-wells, rounded up at local watering holes, traffic stops, and city streets at night. Officer Kierans paraded the mayor through the dregs of Shiretown and instructed him to sit quietly on a hardwood bench in the corner. Finnie was forced to sit next to a snoring drunk who had urinated through his trousers, down his leg, over his shoe, and onto the concrete floor of the holding room. It produced a repulsive smell similar to that in a bus station washroom where males always miss the urinals.

Finnie did as instructed and sat quietly, cooling his heels, not complaining, despite the fact he was seething inside about the treatment and knowing full well his detainment, an illegal arrest he would later call it, was because Kierans was sore about Roxine being in the company of another man. It was a jealousy-motivated traffic stop, and Mayor Finnie vowed silently to embarrass the police department when the time was ripe. He vowed quietly to make war on the whole bunch.

Two hours passed, and at each thirty-minute interval, Finnie announced the time or asked another person in the holding cell if they thought the wall clock was correct, all for the purpose of burning the time of his stay into their memories.

The desk sergeant, a gnarled veteran of twenty-five years, Sergeant Saul Lannon, realized from experience, that the potential for an explosion of media controversy over the arrest was great. It was especially a potential disaster if there was subsequent mismanagement of the matter at the police stattion. He walked to the detention cage and spoke to the mayor, whom he knew slightly.

"Shouldn't you call someone?" he said.

Finnie, recognizing the sergeant's attempt at reconciliation, replied quickly, "I'd like to phone the chief of police."

Sergeant Lannon unlocked the door, passed him two quarters, and led him to the payphone. Finnie dialed and waited. The tired voice of Pineo answered on the third ring.

"Walter Finnie here, Chief. I apologize for the hour, but I've been arrested by Kierans and Clarke, and I've suffered a two-hour wait with no Miranda, no Breathalyzer, and no phone call, until the desk sergeant intervened."

Chief Pineo's haze of sleepiness quickly cleared, "I'm on my way. Don't exacerbate the situation. Just wait silently." Pineo hung up.

Pineo's wife Ruth was used to ignoring late night phone calls, but she rolled over when she heard the chief's response, sensing a problem.

"What's wrong?" she asked.

Pineo pulled on his pants. "Two officers arrested the mayor, and apparently it's already been mishandled if nothing else."

Ruth, now fully awake and knowledgeable enough about police affairs to forecast trouble over a hot issue, understood the potential for bad publicity.

"Is the press involved yet?"

"I don't know," Pineo replied. "Assuming the worst case scenario we have to believe they know or soon will know."

Ruth swung her long shapely legs over the side of the bed, and as her feet hit the floor, she grabbed her silk

Japanese kimono and pulled it on over her sheer nightgown.

"Who was the arresting officer?" she asked.

"Officers," he replied, "Two, Kierans and Clarke," as he buttoned his civilian shirt.

Ruth's cheeks were flushed; she said, "The mess is getting worse, and you can't cut those two adrift because it's the mayor. But you can bet this is not going to pass with ease or speed."

Pineo started towards the bedroom door but stopped, turning to face her. He said, "I'll have to try and smooth it over, but the media may make that impossible. The problem is that the mayor could be the can opener if we drop the charges, because the papers will claims the fix is in. If we proceed, the papers will yell that it's another case like the little Jew. And it's the same two cops, and you're right, I can't afford to cut 'em loose."

Ruth covered the short distance to him and touched his cheek. She knew his weakness for conflict and she had to prop up his courage. "You go try and sort this out. I have an idea."

When she was sure he had gone, she picked up the phone. She was a cop's wife and did not trust phones because they were not secure, so she dialed a number, let it ring once then hung up. She counted to ten and then dialed it again.

"Yes?" answered a male voice.

"Thirty minutes," Ruth said. "The third place," and then hung up without saying goodbye.

It was a quarter after four in the morning when Chief John Pineo slipped through the back entrance of the station from the parking lot. He rode the code-card elevator up to the second floor to avoid any media people who might be at the front entrance. From the second floor, he descended one flight to the inside of the desk sergeant's cage, which was protected from public access by clear bulletproof glass panels. He peeked through the side window into the public lobby to see if the media had arrived . When he saw that it was clear, he approached Sergeant Saul Lannon.

"Where's the mayor?" he asked.

"In the back at the detention section," Lannon replied.

The chief was clearly upset, "Is he drunk? Would he blow an eight?"

Lannon shrugged, "Truthfully, I don't think it was a good call. He'd never blow an eight after this much time. They fucked it up from start to finish."

Chief Pineo looked directly into Lannon's eyes with a stare that left no question as to who was on the spot. "Then why did they bring him in and then leave him to sit?"

Lannon cleared his throat, "I purposely delayed the Breathalyzer when I found out why Kierans stopped him."

The chief's response was blunt, "And why did they stop the mayor?"

Lannon was just as blunt, "I think the mayor had Kierans' girl in the car and Kierans was pissed off."

Pineo could hardly believe his ears. "Is there anything else I should know?"

Lannon lowered his eyes, "It happened in front of Goat Chase's place, and he'd know something went down."

"Let me read the report," Pineo ordered.

Lannon passed it to the chief, "I never entered it into the system."

Pineo read the report and passed it back, "If it's your decision that it's a bum wrap, will Kierans and Clarke keep quiet?"

Lannon nodded, "Yes. If we enter a warning ticket for no seatbelt to the mayor in the blotter, it will cover our asses if Goat happens to ask."

Pineo replied,"Then get it done now. I'm going out to get the mayor. As for Chase, leave him to me." The chief disappeared into the holding area.

The mayor was sitting on the hardwood bench. Pineo motioned for Finnie to follow him back into the desk sergeant's area and then held up his finger to his lips indicating silence. Finnie did not speak.

The desk sergeant passed a slip of paper to the mayor. "This is a warning for driving with no seatbelt."

Pineo stood watching, wondering if Finnie would take the ticket and be smart enough to let the matter drop.

"I understand," said Finnie. "This is the end of it as far as I'm concerned, unless the press puts me through the grinder. If that happens, it's everyone for themselves."

Pineo put his hand on the mayor's shoulder. "C'mon. I'll drive you home. And if the press get into this, we all know it was a warning ticket – nothing more, and I hope you'll coordinate anything you may say with me, unless you're caught flat footed by a reporter."

Finnie followed the chief up the stairs. "You know what, chief? That fucker Kierans will ruin you someday."

CHAPTER THIRTY-ONE

The Tip

"The difference between a hooker and a reporter is that a hooker's honest about what she's doing to you."
- Hoss Foley

Tom Kierans was in a quicksand pool of his own making. On the night of the city employees' Christmas party, he had tipped Steven Jobb that he would bag the mayor for drunk driving, and Jobb had followed him, snapping a photo of the DUI stop as proof.

At four-thirty a.m., Sergeant Saul Lannon, trying to arrange damage control for a potential public relations disaster, informed Kierans and Clarke that if a member of the press heard about the incident they would be suspended pending a disciplinary hearing. He added that such a hearing might find their reason for stopping the mayor questionable – either frivolous or non-existent, and if that were the finding, they would be fired for cause and likely face a civil rights charge.

Kierans skulked through the PD parking area to the back lot behind the Salvation Army Center and finally across Webster Street to the payphones at Wal-Mart. He dialed Steven Jobb's home number and waited impatiently for an answer.

A female voice said, "Hello," in a scratchy, sleepy sounding voice. Kierans assumed it was Jobb's live-in squeeze who was a reporter for another paper.

"It's Tom Kierans. I need Steve, pronto."

"Hold," she replied curtly.

After what seemed a long time, Jobb was on the line. "What's up?" he asked.

Kierans did not waste words on diplomacy, "The shit hit the fan over the mayor and you have to kill the story."

Jobb did not sound agreeable, "You're nuts. They're putting the early edition to bed in about five minutes."

"Listen, shit-head," Kierans yelled, "This isn't any fuzzy freedom of the press issue; it's possibly a federal civil rights violation, and if you can stand another law suit then keep right on saying no to me."

Jobb was now giving him his full attention, "OK, OK. I'll have to handle it quick. I only got minutes left, so let me go."

Kierans re-emphasized his point, "I don't give a shit if you have to burn down the fuckin' paper. And that includes your girl friend's paper, the story can't run. Do you read me?" Without waiting for a reply, he slammed the receiver down so hard he broke it.

Back at the station, Clarke waited for Kierans to return, pacing back and forth like the floor was hot, losing his courage without Kierans' constant reassurance. Kierans returned from the telephone call and threw a thumbs-up sign to his partner. He said, "Let's go eat breakfast. We got an hour before the early edition of the *Bugle* hits the street."

At the diner across the street from the *Bugle*, the two wolfed down muffins and swilled coffee while they waited for the paper's birth. When the *Bugle* delivery truck arrived to fill the dispenser outside the diner, Kierans snatched a copy from the driver. He scanned the front page. No story about the mayor. He reviewed every page of the first section and was satisfied there was no story. His call to Jobb had done the trick. He turned to Clarke. "See, I told you, nothing to worry about. Let's go sign out, I'm tired."

It was hours later, after midday, and Kierans was off duty and asleep, the fitful sleep of all night workers trying to readjust their body clocks for rest before the next night shift. The abusive twitter of the telephone interrupted his tormented rest. His weak hello revealed his fatigue, but the message prodded him to attention.

"This is Shirley Reading," she said. "A formal complaint has been filed by the mayor against you and Officer Clarke, and I'm the officer on the rotation list who drew the complaint. I'm giving you notice in case you want your union rep to be present. I'll see you both in my office at four this afternoon. I've already notified Clarke."

Kierans sat up. He said, "The mayor shouldn't open this can of worms if he's smart. It'll end up in the paper and splash shit all over him and us too."

Shirley replied," You obviously haven't seen the afternoon edition of the *Chronicle*."

Kierans was short-tempered. "Well, tell me what it says for shit's sake."

"Hold your drawers," she said. "Here goes. The headline reads `Mayor Arrested for Drunk Driving,' and there's a photo."

"Awww, fuck!" Kierans said dejectedly. "What's the photo?"

Reading described the front page. "It's you, Clarke and the mayor standing next to a car; the door's open. His

Honor looks like he should have a lamp shade on his head, his fly is open and behind him on the car seat you can see some skinny blonde poised like a horny housecat with her eyes popped out like a ladybug."

Kierans was steaming, "Who's the reporter on the story?"

"The editor," Reading replied. "No reporter is named."

Kierans knew immediately that Jobb had double-crossed him by giving the story to his companion who then passed it along to her editor. He knew that having the editor on the story was a weak attempt to cover her ass and Jobb's manipulation. He decided at once that his only defense was that all of great spies who were accused of being double agents in passing information to the enemy: staunch denial. Deny, deny, and deny: known in the espionage world as the Kim Philby defense. He called Clarke, and as soon as he answered, said, "Listen to me, when they ask us if the mayor was pissed, he was, and other than that, we employ the Philby defense, and if we stick together it will blow over.

Clarke was trying to take it all in too fast. He said, "What the fuck are you raving about, and what is a Philby defense?"

Kierans had no time for fools. "Listen shit head," he said, "first read the *Chronicle*, and if you need a map then, I'll draw you one. And if you ever read a book, you'd know that Philby was a famous British agent who was also a Soviet mole, a double agent in the service of England, but working for the Russians stealing secrets for the KGB for over twenty years. He'd been the intelligence liaison officer at the British Embassy in Washington and purloined secret US data, which the Soviets used to trap and kill US agents behind the Iron Curtain. The United States became suspicious of him and pressured the British to confront him. After days of confrontational interrogations, Philby adamantly denied the American accusations. And the Brits couldn't charge him because he never flinched. Thus the denial-defense became known as the Philby defense."

Clarke had listened intently. "OK," he said," I get the message; there's no need to shit all over me."

But Kierans realized the one real threat to his plan of defense was his partner, a weak man. He believed Clarke was a fool who had no stones and had to be propped up by constant reassurances.

Baptist and the undercover group listened to the wiretaps of the conversation of Kierans and Clarke. Everybody remained silent after the tape played. Baptist spoke first, "I'd say that's probative evidence of misconduct and, if nothing else, proves they are not suitable for police work. And maybe the tapes provide enough evidence to get them for a civil rights violation."

At four p.m., Shirley sat at her desk when Kierans and Clarke arrived, as they had been instructed. Shirley was flushed, her facial expression revealing her displeasure, bordering on overt anger. "No need to stop here," she said, "the chief has turned the internal investigation over to Sergeant Murphy and has decided to ignore the procedure of rotating investigators for internal matters as set out in the regulations."

Kierans and Clarke exchanged sly looks. "C'mon," Kierans said, "let's go see Murphy."

Shirley was pissed off, her ethics offended. "By the way," she said before they were out of ear range, "you made the front page of the afternoon *Bugle* too."

Before they could respond she continued, "And for some worse news. That law professor Corbett who went into practice with Ray Wortman has filed the Donald Frank suit today against the city, the PD, the estate of Major Brown, and you two. And he and Wortman are representing Mayor Finnie in a civil rights suit against you guys." She cleared her throat and went on, "When those two attorneys depose everyone involved in this cesspool, it will amount to a wide open civil investigation of the police department."

Kierans no longer looked relieved. Wortman was a legal wolverine, and his style of cross-examination was fearful. Kierans could imagine, almost visualize, the weak-kneed Clarke folding under Wortman's relentless questions. It would be a deposition of doom if Wortman got his hands on Clarke.

Shirley pushed the paper across the desk to Kierans. There was the headline. "Mayor to Sue PD?" In addition, there was the mayor's official, obviously lawyered, public statement in bold black print surrounded by a dark wide border: "Mayor Finnie's Response to PD Action".

> I was stopped without cause. There was no reasonable suspicion. I was humiliated, photographed by a journalist who was tipped off in advance by one of the police officers, which denotes intent. Police procedure was violated. I was not given a roadside sobriety test, nor a Miranda warning about my rights, yet I was detained, which constitutes an illegal arrest. I was not allowed a phone call for hours until Sergeant Lannon intervened on my behalf. I was not given a Breathalyzer. When I was stopped I removed my

seatbelt to get my driver's license out of my wallet and subsequently was issued a warning ticket for driving without the seatbelt.

The photo, which appeared in the press, is contrived, poison tree evidence according to my attorney and yet the *Chronicle* claims they received it from an anonymous source. This amounts to malice or a civil rights violation when considered with the other prejudicial facts.

I am also informed that such actions by a police officer may constitute a federal crime of civil rights violation.

My attorneys, Wortman and Corbett, will be conducting all public response to these issues from this point forward.

R. Walter Finnie

Kierans stared at the paper for a long time. "This is all bull, posturing to cover his ass, the little prick. The stop was justified. Just look at the picture. He's pissed."

Shirley looked Kierans directly in the eyes, "Maybe so, but you can't stop people because they're shagging your girl. There are rules to follow. It sounds to me like his civil rights were violated, so you'd never get a conviction. Plus, there was no Breathalyzer done."

Kierans leaned over her desk. "Well fuck you. Why didn't they do a Breathalyzer here at the PD?" And then answering his own rhetorical question, he said, "Because they're all up his ass 'cause the 'Little Admiral" is the mayor."

Shirley said nothing more and watched the two men head for the elevator to meet Murphy in the chief's office.

She was less angry now after witnessing their abject attempt at face-saving but still disgusted that the chief had corrupted a departmental policy on internal investigation of public complaints. She punched in Baptist's direct line.

"Coffee," she said and clicked off and then headed to the back door, which bordered the PD parking lot.

When Baptist arrived at the car they drove off in silence. He knew she was fuming and he knew why. Everybody in the department knew the chief was trying to bury the scandal by whitewashing the two cowboy cops. Appointing Murphy was proof.

"Call Dunlop at this number," Baptist said as he passed her a slip of paper, and she took out her cell phone. "Lieutenant Folker wants us to keep him clued up, because he's been appointed special prosecutor on the PD case. I'll call Folker myself."

Despite the seriousness of the recent mess, Baptist was amused by Shirley's intense funk over the chief's crude politics. "You'll get the last laugh, so don't get your drawers in a knot. They're playing stupid games, and we're getting closer to proving our case."

Reading suppressed a smile. "Oh brother, listen to who's preaching to the choir. Besides, you were quite interested in my drawers last night."

They met Dunlop at the nearby Dunkin Donuts, and Baptist bought the coffee. Dunlop ignored the steaming drink and launched into the latest facts and theory of the case from his perspective.

"Blazek tells me Kierans called Clarke right after you sent for him. Panic is now driving Clarke. They were both pretty careless with their thoughts on the phone. We can take them out anytime; they're small fish."

Shirley was concerned, "We got two sets of wires running, the feds' and the state's. We got good people working around the clock on donated time, and Sergeant White has proof of embezzlement at the courthouse. His audit is evidential, yet all we got is two petty mokes as a result of a fluke bust of the mayor. How the hell can we move this along? Are we wasting our efforts?"

Dunlop understood her frustration from firsthand experience. He said, "I know you want McCurdy's killers and Brown's killers, and we all want whoever killed those two young women. Equally important, we want to clean up the PD, so don't for God's sake, get impatient or go off half-cocked at this stage. That courthouse mess is big, and we only know that Morash is involved, but she's not the whole gang."

Reading softened her attitude, "Young bull, old bull, right?"

"Exactly," Dunlop replied. "Walk, don't run, and do 'em all."

Baptist agreed, "What about MacAdam? Have the wiretaps turned up anything new on his meeting with the mysterious woman?"

"Nothing yet. We need a shadow for him. Someone who will sit on him with a connection to the wiretaps so they'll know when he's moving, then follow."

"Sergeant Roberts has agreed to do that," Shirley replied. "I'll take her up to meet the Blazeks so they can set it up like you suggested."

Dunlop finally took a drink of cold coffee. Baptist told him the details of Noel Bear's meeting with the witness at the cemetery.

"The witness saved his life, according to Bear. He almost got his burial flag. The guy says he's got evidence on the ballpark killer."

Dunlop perked up, "How good is Bear's witness?"

"Good news, bad news," Baptist replied. "He sounds like he's clued in, but he's not willing to get involved after the cemetery shooting. But he did tell Noel he'd think about phoning him."

Dunlop was intrigued, "See, we're making more progress than we realized before we got together. We should meet at the Blazeks' to check how we're doing on a frequent basis. If nothing else it boosts morale."

Baptist brought the conversation back to the courthouse fraud. "How big does McIntyre think the money is in that deal?"

Dunlop replied, "From comparing what she knows with Sergeant White's record analysis, they think they can prove over a million stolen so far,".

"Holy shit," Baptist said "Old Morash has to have partners if it's that big."

Dunlop stood up to leave. "What a collection of mokes. And then there's the weird Brown murder. I like Reverend Solomon for that but the troopers don't think so."

"What we need," Shirley suggested, "is a witness to roll. My candidate is Clarke."

CHAPTER THIRTY-TWO

The Deal

"- a deal of scorn looks beautiful; in the contempt and anger of his lip."

- Shakespeare

Sergeant Perry White, quoting Clint Eastwood said, "Frank Nichols of the drug squad was a legend in his own mind." He was the self-proclaimed brain of the squad who considered his own partner Hunter Stent a dolt, a gofer, and a gun bearer for the great himself. Nichols was an insecure person who trusted no one, especially his loose-legged wife Fay. Privately, Stent agreed with him about Fay, with a smile, because he knew from first hand experience. He said, "If she could hit like she screws, she'd be leading the American League batting race."

The wiretap run by Troopers Blazek and Blazek revealed that Nichols and Stent had shown signs of panic when they received anonymous letters suggesting they were involved in questionable conduct. Their telephone conversations had become defensive and evasive, and Nichols especially had shown signs of suspicion and paranoia. The troopers suggested that the chopped, coded conversations were evidence of misconduct, and Bear figured it was at least a good source of intelligence data, no matter how sparse. He felt it proved they were making some progress if fear was controlling the two humps.

In one taped conversation, Nichols said to Sten, "As to the business, I'll take the bike ride alone," and Bear guessed, correctly as it turned out, that it somehow involved the bikers, the Devil's Darlings.

Stent was now in a quandary. He realized he was helpless and couldn't control Nichols and had to protect his own interests. Worse, he believed his partner would sacrifice him without a blink. Proof in Stent's mind was his suspicion that only Nichols knew where the stolen drugs were hidden, so while he shared in the risk, only Nichols controlled the potential for profit. He confronted Nichols in a tirade and said, "You'll rue the day you fuck me over, because I know all your secrets, and I'm not standing by while you skate."

Nichols did not respond in kind. He tried to sound conciliatory. He said, "Listen, you make the arrangements for me to meet Bob Miller with no more than two of those bikers present, and when the time comes to do the actual trade, I'll set it up for you to do the exchange."

Stent was not sure of his partner's real intentions but did not reveal his feelings. He replied, "Ill get in touch with Bob Miller to make the appointment, but you better remember the Biker's Darlings are like tigers and can turn vicious in a New York nanno second."

Nichols already knew Miller was deadly, a vicious man behind a facade of civility. He was an unlikely looking dictator of a biker gang even in his leather biker's garb, and if he'd dressed in a business suit, which he didn't, he would have passed for an effeminate tax auditor. "The truth," Nichols said, "is Bob Miller looks more like a repressed closet faggot than the boss of the Devil's Darlings."

Usual gangland paranoia about telephones being wired was nothing compared to Miller's excessive fear of being convicted by a recording of his own voice. He warned everyone that complacency about wiretaps had done in the Teflon Don in New York, and since then, phoning him was a frustrating exercise in double-speak, half-truths, and grunts. Even in person Miller almost never spoke in complete sentences because he feared parabolic devices. Behind his back some associates called him Robbie the Riddler. Recording calls to Miller would provide little evidence of illegal transactions on his part; his distinctive grunts defied audio spectrograph analysis.

Stent placed the call to a cell phone number once give him by Miller. A voice answered with a curt, "Go", nothing more. Stent knew it was useless to attempt a transaction over the phone. They'd have to do it in person.

Stent said, "Visitor at the shed," because he knew Miller understood that to mean he wanted to meet Miller at an abandoned country farm, specifically in the small tool shed the bikers used to work on their Harleys.

Upon hearing Stent's statement, Miller paused long enough to make any police recording questionable by creating a brief silence on the tape; perhaps calling the evidence into technical suspicion. Then, when he answered, "OK", he also tapped the mouthpiece with something, causing a noisy clicking sound that would possibly add another element of potential confusion to any wiretap. He then hung up. Stent would have to see Miller in person to arrange for Nichols to deal, and no aspect of that was a comfort to him.

From experience, he knew that Miller would meet him outside the tool shed in the field and would run his motorcycle as they spoke to provide a noisy background for the limited conversation in order to distort any laser parabolic listening device. Stent was nervous himself, yet he knew how ridiculous it was to live in constant fear of recording devices.

He also knew that Miller was apt to produce a writing pad and pen and conduct the discussion in writing, because the mercurial paranoid Miller knew that pencil marks couldn't be recorded, especially if the paper was torn up and eaten after the writing was done. Stent was nervous, afraid, and deeply concerned about dealing with a whacko like Miller. But Nichols wanted the meeting arranged with Miller, and now Nichol's arrangements were completed.

Nichols drove up Willow and across the back road connector into the countryside, then down the long dirt road to the small shed, which had once been part of a long-gone farming complex. He parked his car on the low side of the building, in a ravine, to hide it from view and then walked up the side of the hill to where Miller waited astride his big Harley. The motorcycle chugged and putted in a distinctive gurgle, which reminded Nichols of a 1950s hot rod.

Miller reached into his bike saddlebags, produced a writing pad and pencil, and passed both to Nichols who took them and printed his message in block letters in straight lines:

> WAL-GREEN PILL INVENTORY
> MY PRICE $200,000.
> STREET VALUE up to $600,000
> INTERESTED?

Miller moved his head up and down signaling yes. Nichols again printed on the writing pad, like a child printing for a grade school teacher:

PAYMENT - CASH - $10 & $20 BILLS, $200K TOTAL
Miller held up his thumb to show his agreement.
Nichols continued printing in pidgin English,
WHEN AND WHERE CAN WE DO THIS AND PROTECT OURSELVES?

Miller now had to print an answer to the direct question. He took the pencil and printed slowly and mechanically,

PIECEMEAL, TEN PLACES, EACH PLACE TO BE DECIDED JUST BEFORE THE MEETING."

Nichols read the message and smiled. He liked the idea and made a motion with his hand in an agreeable fashion. He took the pad and pencil back from Miller,

FIRST DELIVERY RIGHT HERE IN ABOUT ONE HOUR. I'LL GO GET IT NOW.

Miller nodded. He gestured for the pencil and pad. He printed,

DON'T BE LATE. AND DON'T EVEN THINK OF FUCKING ME UP.

At that point Miller pointed to a huge bearded hulk of a man standing by the shed and printed,

HE'S RUSSIAN, A CRUEL MEAN MOTHER, AND HE'D CUT YOUR DICK OFF IF I TELL HIM TO.

Nichols understood perfectly. He printed quickly,
I HEAR YOU. I'LL GO NOW AND I'LL CALL YOU ON THE CELL JUST BEFORE I'M COMING BACK.

Miller tore off the sheet on which they had been printing and tore it into small pieces and then slowly chewed them up, devouring the potential proof of a criminal conspiracy.

"Sixty minutes," Miller whispered, "and I don't mean the Sunday night TV show with Mike Wallace.

Nichols drove the dirt road back, looking over his shoulder in the rearview mirror to make sure he was not being followed. He reached Willow Street and headed to the corner of the residential area and then doubled back, cutting across the Webster Street extension by River Street. He again took evasive action, covering and recovering his movements, checking and re-checking to see that he was not tailed. He reached Park Street by the longest route and then cut down Roosevelt. He glanced at his watch and realized he had already burned up twenty minutes, but he had to be sure there was no surveillance.

He cruised down Roosevelt past where he planned to stop and then turned back to make sure he was still alone. He slowed in front of an aged gray mansion, a giant of an old 1920s place, a popular and affordable style before the 1929 stock market crash and before the present-day rising costs of heating oil. He drove in the driveway, which curved around behind the house, and parked out of sight right next to the big three-car garage. The garage was an old-fashioned edifice with an apartment above it, which was once used to house the servants for the main house during the wealthy days of the roaring twenties.

Nichols unlocked the side door of the garage, first the padlock and then the Yale deadbolt, and went inside. The first thing he did was check the temperature. It was sixty-five degrees, perfect for storing the pills. He counted out ten cartons, worth twenty thousand dollars, his greed mounting. Then it dawned on him; ten was too many to fit in his car. He should have brought the van. Five boxes would have to do now, and even that would be tight. His doubts were at first just a ripple, hardly more than nerves. He was sweating, and his hands were covered with dust from the musty old garage. He started to wonder, "Would Miller believe the reason he only brought five?"

The exchange was proving more difficult than he had thought when he broke his promise to Stent and decided to do the deal alone. It would not be a simple over-the-counter transaction. He already had encountered two problems: time and space. He again checked his watch. Thirty minutes. Why had he arbitrarily set only one hour? It was already half gone. He was running late. The time was too short. Sweat, panic, fear, and hurry. Put the boxes in the car. His stress mounted. He checked the temperature again. It was still only sixty-five even though he was soaked with sweat. Nichols now lamented that he had not brought Stent along to help, but he didn't trust Stent. He hadn't even told him where the stolen drugs were hidden, even though Stent owned a half interest. Nichols didn't trust anybody.

He locked the door, checked it twice, and then walked to the car. He headed down the driveway. Suddenly fear gripped him. What if he had an accident? Or got stopped by some officer he didn't know well enough to BS his way out of the stop? Or, what if he had a flat tire in a tow zone?

"Why the fuck didn't I bring Stent?" he muttered to himself.

He hurried down Willow, across the connector, down the old dirt country road. He stopped to phone Miller and announce his arrival.

"Visitor," he said by way of greeting.

A voice with a thick accent replied, "Da, OK."

The daylight was shrinking fast. Nichols drove the last five hundred yards, thinking of the money. When he arrived he found the silence of the country unnerving. His thinking was frazzled.

He walked to the front of the little shack where the big Russian, a tall man, well over six feet, stood, dressed in biker's leather, next to three Harleys.

"Inside," he instructed Nichols. Nichols experienced cold feet and fingered his piece but it gave him little comfort. The foreign giant was right behind him, almost breathing down his neck.

Inside the shed Miller was sitting on a metal stool, sort of a kitchen telephone stool, which seemed strangely out of place in the musty old tool shed. The building was lighted by one Aladdin kerosene lamp. A third man, tattooed and muscled like a prison weightlifter, stood beside a crude workbench, which consisted of two wide planks spaced a foot apart and supported on each end by two carpenter's sawhorses.

Miller spoke first, apparently comfortable that no police recordings would occur in the shack. "We have a problem. Actually you have a problem. Word is that you're in trouble and on your way down the tube, so I figure it's a waste of money to pay a dead man."

Nichols controlled his fear and seething rage, curbing his urge to explode and blow the three of them to hell. He was on the spot with the big ape behind him. Any sudden move would be the end of him. He knew he couldn't take all three at once. He remained cool.

"I have five cartons in the car and you could hose me on those, but you'll never get the others without the money."

Miller stayed deadpan, no visible signs of his thoughts were evident. When he spoke he did not raise his voice or display emotion. Either by practice or by nature he did not waste words or make idle threats.

"Let me explain your situation, Frankie-boy," Miller said to Nichols. "The big man behind you is my Russian friend, a former KGB interrogator, and he loves hurting people. He can get answers out of anybody. Once he gets started, you'll tell us where your pills are hidden, or if he kills you, we'll get the location from your partner Stent."

Nichols knew it was no time to blink. Miller was using psychological warfare to play with his head; he knew the biker was quite capable of carrying out his threats. Nichols moved slightly and heard the big Russian shift behind him.

"Fuck you," he said to Miller, the hardness in his voice betraying no fear. He smirked, as if he had cards at cowboy poker. "It's a waste of time to ask Stent. He's a weak shit, and I don't trust him so I never told him where the goods were, because I knew he'd spill his guts."

Miller made a motion with his hand and Igor pounced. He grabbed Nichols from behind in a chokehold and relieved him of his weapon at the same time. Miller's voice was still calm, almost flat.

"No more talk. You say your partner doesn't know, so we'll have to get the answer from you." Then smiling as if he had a secret, Miller picked up the metal stool and placed it halfway between the two sawhorses that held up the two planks, which served as the top of the workbench. The third biker picked up a giant metal square-jawed vice, like those used in bending metal pipes, and placed it on the stool in the space between the planks.

Nichols struggled for air, as Igor's muscular arm was cutting off his breath, as it held him too tightly around his windpipe. The other man with the tattoos turned the handle of the vice, opening the jaws. He then walked over to Nichols, who was almost suspended in mid-air from Igor's forearm. He produced a long pointed knife, sort of like a chrome-plated bayonet, and pressed it not so gently against Nichols' soft belly just above the navel. He spoke with a Spanish accent, perhaps in a Colombian Spanish cadence, warning Nichols, "Stay very still, senior." And Nichols did not dare struggle; the slightest increase in pressure on the knife would penetrate his bowels.

The Colombian unfastened Nichols' belt, undid his pants, and pulled his trousers and underwear down around his ankles.

Miller seemed delighted as he watched. "Igor has great faith in his workbench. He claims it never fails."

Fear was now the master and Nichols lost control. His bladder relieved itself without his consent and splashed urine downward over his legs and into his crumpled trousers and onto his shoes and the floor. Igor roared but the Colombian was splashed with the urine and did not find it so amusing.

The Russian lifted Nichols off the ground, while the Colombian held the knife point pressed at his stomach to keep him from struggling. The two men placed Nichols face down on the two planks. Miller laughed and said, "Notice how your dick dangles through the space into the open jaws of the vice." Then Igor pinned Nichols down, while the Colombian slowly turned the vice handle and brought the jaws closer and tighter upon his dick while he screamed in agony.

"Don't move, my friend," cautioned Igor. "You are caught by your member and any sudden move will upset the little stool and the weight of the vice will rip your cock right off."

Nichols was still conscious but blubbered in distress. Suddenly he power-puked as the pain rendered him near unconsciousness. His eyes bulged, and he slobbered in absolute terror. Igor said, "His shrieks sound like the squeal of a wounded pig."

"The secret," said Igor, "is to make the vice so tight you cannot move, but not so tight that you pass out." Igor smiled a hateful, perverted, sick grin. He walked to the end of the makeshift bench where his head lay, so Nichols could see his Russian tormentor clearly.

He took the shiny knife from the Colombian and held it before Nichols' bulging eyes. "This is the answer, my friend," Igor said in a falsely solicitous voice.

Nichols grunted. He said between gasps, "Jesus Christ, if you cut my dick off I'll bleed to death."

Igor reached down and removed the handle from the vice so that it couldn't be opened. "No, we won't cut you're dick off. We'll put the knife in your hand and set the building on fire and you can cut it off yourself." Nichols was now somewhere between abject terror and insanity. He cried, begging for mercy.

Miller splashed gas from a five-gallon jerry can over the floors and walls of the old softwood building. Despite the open door of the shack the vapor and fumes hung inside the room slowly displacing the air and making it difficult to breathe. Miller said to Nichols, "Don't bet on someone seeing the fire away out here, because we're a good ten miles from the nearest civilization, and you'll be toast before the smoke is noticed."

The three bikers moved quickly to the door. Miller took out his Zippo lighter and stood outside the door looking in at the prostrate victim. He said, "That lamp makes the fumes dangerous, and it will ignite shortly, so I'll just stand here on the outside in case. By the way, do you want to tell me anything, Sergeant Nichols?"

Nichols had no more nerve for rhetoric or false bravado. "OK, OK for God's sake," he screamed, "I'll tell. The stuff is in my uncle's garage on Roosevelt."

Miller stood flicking the cover of the Zippo, open and closed, open and closed. "Pretty smart, that's a good place to hide the stuff. Nobody would think of that." He suddenly ignited the lighter and tossed it into the shed as he jumped away.

The vapor and the fumes burst into an explosive, oxygen-consuming flame in a blinding all-encompassing blast. Nichols' shrill terrible tortured screams and shrieks lasted only seconds before the flames engulfed him.

Hunter Stent stood outside, nearby but a safe distance from the roaring fire and waited for Miller. He looked at Miller and said, "See, I told you he'd tell. You over-estimated him. I knew he had no balls."

"And now no dick either," Miller added, and laughed a shrill feminine snicker at his own pun.

CHAPTER THIRTY-THREE

The News

"... the Phantom of Ourselves."
- Matthew Arnold (1867)

It was a provocative series of gossipy journalism, which according to Sergeant Perry White, mirrored the public interest in sex, religion, and scandal. It was a coup for the *Chronicle* that goosed the paper's circulation. It was conceived and authored by editor Allan Tobin, who prior to the series, many reporters had considered just a glorified spell-checker. The paper's torpid nature had suddenly changed, increasing its popularity with the public, and perhaps proving that the printed media was not yet slain by the Internet.

The first article of the series seemed, at first glance, to be an analysis of religious faiths. It leaned towards an explanation of the Church of Scientology, as its first example, because that sect, as the paper called it, was active in Shiretown. But that was only the foundation for the real purpose of the gossipy prose.

Sergeant White, who read everything with an analytical eye, correctly guessed at the start that the series was only using religion as bait.

"There's another goal," White surmised, and the theme, or hook of the story was soon apparent.

It was pure exposé journalism designed to sell papers, like the headlines of the *National Enquirer* or the *Globe*, which thrived on taking inconsequential facts and turning them into enticing leads to lure gossip hungry readers to buy the paper. But to those in the know at the PD, it was clear that someone had done some whispering into a phone and disclosed some inside information. There were some real facts in the *Chronicle*.

Sergeant White was a keen student of the news, a virtual fountain of facts and yet, unlike many fact-retentive folks, he did not bore people with unsolicited dissertations. The crucial question White put forth was, "Where did the paper get the facts to wash the city's dirty laundry in public?"

"The Church of Scientology," Editor Tobin wrote, "bases itself on the theory of Dianetics. And what is Dianetics? It's from Greek and means 'what the soul does to the mind.' And how does this relate to Shiretown affairs?" The answer was the main inspiration of the article. "Scientology" he wrote, "is an organized offshoot by adherents to the theory of Dianetics, a group of zealots who are carrying the religious theme to extremes and, coupled with personal motives, are corrupting the justice system for personal gain."

Sergeant White had a theory about that story. He noted that Tobin cleverly obscured any kind of even the remotest hint as to the sources for the articles. But yet, White said, Tobin managed to convince his readers that his information was from an authentic source. The editor was a talented wordsmith, and his facts seemed to ring true, leading even the most skeptical reader to conclude that Tobin was clued-up. Sergeant White noted, "I believe the accuracy is such that the source is from within the PD or someone close to it."

According to Tobin, as the articles played out day by day, each one enticing the reader to wait for the next like a TV serial, there was a rogue group of people in the justice system. He claimed they were operating like the Klan, dedicated to common social and religious beliefs that were advanced by their official positions and graft.

Then, a black woman, Eleanor Kennie, who was a contemporary Rosa Parks and made of the same gutsy stuff, wrote a letter to the editor's column in the *Chronicle*, supporting the paper's continued crusade about the justice system. She accused the city police department of civil rights' violations, and as an example, pointed to the arrest of young Donald Frank, a Jew. She also reminded readers that not too long ago more than half the police officers of Selma, Alabama were once members of the Klan. She threw verbal gas on the paper;s smoldering accusations by bringing the issue of race and prosecution of the socially disadvantaged into the open.

White disagreed. He said," Bullshit, I'm black and I can always smell race and this isn't race, it isn't politics, and it's not really religion, although the religious sect may advance their goals. This is plain old greed and graft by crooked officials."

Rabbi Aubrey Shane added credence to Tobin's journalism and Ms. Kennie's letter to the editor when he announced that the arrest of Donald Frank was pure anti-Semitism, and then he called for an investigation.

After he read the Rabbi's comments, White was less enthusiastic and more goal orientated. He said, "If these fuckin' sincere, do-good people draw too much attention to the mess it could ball up the investigation."

Bear was hung up on who the paper's source was. He said, "The specific details about the death of Sergeant Frank Nichols were not made public. Yet, Tobin printed a pretty accurate version in his paper, and that proves a police source."

Baptist replied, "Maybe it's not really a bad thing that the lid is off, and Tobin stirs the pot."

Shirley Reading sat listening to the discussion of the pros and cons. She said, "I hate to agree with you male experts, but it also seems to me that the source of the articles is in the know. But it may be someone from the county sheriff's office who is leaking this Nichols crap, because one of their deputies discovered the fire and Nichols on a routine patrol. Why don't we call Kirk and see what he knows. He finished the autopsy yesterday, and so let's see what he and Hoss think about today's news."

Bear phoned Kirk Donald's office, and Sharon Marshall answered. She was her usual matter-of-fact, opinionated self. She drawled, "Dr. Donald and Hoss have just left for the sheriff's office to discuss the Nichols' crime scene. Dr. Kirk wants you to call him on his cell phone."

Bear liked Marshall and her direct, to-the-point aggressive nature. She seemed to have a common sense solution to most problems and her opinions were presented bluntly, whether wanted or not. That included her opinion of the newspaper stories, which she said, "put all those courthouse mokes on notice that the skate is over." Bear had trouble getting away from her on the phone but finally signed off.

He punched in Kirk's cell number. The tone of Kirk's voice revealed the impact of the horrible crime scene. "I think we should involve Folker and the state people in this because the sheriff and your chief piss through the same quill and both of them talk too much." He paused only for a breath, and continued, "Let me tell you about Nichols. I just finished that mess. He's burnt to a crisp like he was barbecued. I know women say most guys are led into trouble by their dick. Well in Nichol's case that's true, because his dick was stuck in a vice that doesn't have a handle, and that place smelled like a gas station. Hoss claims Nichols got roasted by his own wiener."

Bear groaned, "Geeze," he said, "the usual compassionate humor from Dr. Hoss Strangelove, but that's more information than I need. Do you want me to suggest that Folker peek in or horn in?"

Kirk did not hesitate, "Hoss figures the state police can keep information from leaking, plus some of the sheriff's people are too tight with the Shiretown bunch."

Bear agreed, "I think I'll get Dale Dunlop involved now that he's prosecuting. He's got clout. Incidentally, he told me this morning that the lawyers for the defendants in the Frank suit got court approval to depose the witnesses before a judge in the civil suits brought by the Frank family and the mayor." Bear continued, "Apparently depositions done before a judge in cases of public controversy are based on the idea that a judge will run a tighter ship. But Wortman went bonkers and said it will produce restricted questioning and less information."

Kirk couldn't believe his ears. "Who's the judge? That's the question. If he's one of those political appointments he can be one-sided and curb the questions."

"Exactly," Bear responded. "Who the judge will be, and who can pull his strings will be the big question as far as fairness goes. I don't know who it is yet, but Dunlop will know."

Kirk's question about the identity of the judge in the depositions would not need to wait for an answer from Dunlop. The afternoon edition of the *Chronicle* announced that magistrate Harold Chase had been selected by the clerk's office to hear the depositions. The *Chronicle* explained how depositions worked and that it was a pre-trial method of giving both sides an insight into the facts that would be argued later in court, in the interest of court efficiency.

When Bear read Chase's name he went numb. He and Baptist had hoped the questioning of the witnesses in the civil suits would provide them with information to use in the criminal cases. In a panic, he called Dunlop.

"How the fuck can a magistrate who is not a real judge get selected to hear the depositions? That old bastard is twisted."

Dunlop did not disagree, "The clerk's office, specifically old Morash, has arranged that, or maybe that's a signal from up state that they're about to appoint Chase a trial court judge. He's been sucking around for that for a while."

Bear was steaming mad, "Can't you prod Wortman into raising hell about this or complaining to someone upstate and trying to get Chase pulled off this?"

"Already called him," Dunlop replied. "He's as pissed off as you are and wonders if the political fix is in."

Bear was no happier. He replied, "Maybe old Morash used her influence upstate or just stacked the judge's schedules on her own?"

"I'll ask McIntyre," Dunlop replied, "and if she thinks that's the case I'll call the Attorney General's office and see if it can be changed in the interest of procedural fairness affecting justice. The problem with that request will be that the Frank case is a civil matter, not a criminal one, and it will cause those guys at the AG's office to wonder why I'm meddling in it, especially with my former law partner involved."

Bear was still incensed. "What about the idea that the information we might get out of the civil case could be important to a criminal investigation?" Bear asked. "Are we going to be free to use it in a criminal prosecution?"

"Oh man," Dunlop replied, "that's a how-long-is-a-piece-of-string question. What the hell is a piece? Yes and no is your answer. The law books and the Restatement of Torts point out that free and frank testimony must be encouraged in civil suits without fear of civil suits for defamation. As to subsequent criminal prosecutions, facts can be used unless the court in the civil matter tries to grant immunity to a witness, and that becomes another legal argument. Except, perhaps, in Louisiana. But overall the information from a civil deposition is useful to an investigation even if some trial judge won't let it in later."

"Holy sufferin' double-talk, Batman," Bear quipped. "How the fuck can a poor country boy like me, or even some Harvard law student, figure out a definite answer from that lawyer's bull-kuzunka?"

"Forget it," Dunlop advised. "Let's not buy a boat until we're sure there's a river."

The PD dispatcher cut short the conversation with instructions for Bear to see Sergeant White at the tombs. Bear replied with a "ten-four" and headed for the station.

At the tombs, the omnipresent smell of White's Old Spice shaving lotion, mixed with the mold of old files and records, interspersed with cigar smoke gave the place a unique scent.

Bear could tell at a glance that White was wound tight and was pissed off with a capital P. "What's happened?"

White had a frown with furrows in his forehead like a ploughed field. Sergeant Roberts was trying to settle him down to quiet his marauding blood pressure.

"Someone tried to break in here. Only police officers can get into this part of the building, so we have to assume it was some twisted cop," White said bitterly.

Bear sensed that's White's outrage was more from the thought of a crooked police officer than from the insult of an attempted break-in of his scared records area.

"Did they get anything you were dealing with?" Bear asked.

White shook his head slowly. "Nope. The files from the courthouse are at Roberts' place. We committed all of them to disks so we could do the comparisons down here without putting the files at risk."

Bear looked at the jimmy marks on the cage door leading into the record section. "It looks like there's blood here. Did the perp get cut trying to spring the door?"

"Absolutely," White replied. "That's why I asked you down here. We got several good blood samples and I want you to take them to Hoss, so he can get the state guys to do a DNA."

"Did you report this?" Bear asked.

White flashed his seldom-seen smile. "Report my donkey. I'm not wasting time writing reports for Chief Ali Baba and his thieves. You give me a receipt, Hoss will give you one, and that's a chain of evidence if we ever go to court."

Bear took the blood samples and went down the stairs and cut through Reading's office on his way out. She was on the phone arguing with someone about not charging some girl who was legally a minor and had been caught shoplifting. When she saw Bear, she mechanically reached into her desk drawer and pulled out the late edition of the *Chronicle* and passed it to him, all the time continuing to debate with the person on the other end of the line. It was clear she was growing more agitated and frustrated.

Bear looked at the newspaper while he waited. The serialized article by Tobin was now approaching pay dirt. Bear realized the paper was giving internal police details that had never been officially reported to the media. Surprisingly, the autopsy of Frank Nichols, which had only just been completed, was reported fairly accurately. The crime scene description was amazingly complete, and the vague suggestion of police corruption appeared as part of the gist of the story.

Shirley completed the call and slammed the receiver down so hard it bounced out of its receptacle. "Ignorant tight ass," she muttered. "I can't talk him out of charging this girl. She's already been to hell and back and needs a break. If the SOB won't withdraw the complaint I plan to be sick the day it goes to court, and if I'm not there, the judge will kick it."

Bear smiled, an exaggerated grin, a sardonic sort of reaction. "Does that mean that as an officer of the law you'll purposely miss a trial?"

"You heard right. I'm trying to cut some slack for a young girl named Taylor who ran away from home because her stepfather pawed and abused her, and she was shoplifting to finance her escape. I got Social Services involved to protect her and now this creep of a manager at the store won't drop it, even though he got all the stuff back."

"Right out of Dickens," Bear said. And isn't Taylor the name of the girl Baptist is looking for to question in the Anslow murder."

"I thought so too," Shirley replied. "I've called him, and he's on his way, and she's in the holding cell."

"I have to go," Bear said, "so let me know later if he shakes anything loose from her."

Baptist arrived out of breath. "Let's talk to her in here," he said. "She'll feel more comfortable with you present."

When Shirley brought Diane Taylor into the office from the holding cell, the girl slouched like a cornered animal. She was not a pretty girl, nor was she particularly shapely. She tended to the pudgy side with a large bosom. It was clear that she was shy in the extreme, averting her eyes so as not to look directly at them. She nervously toyed with the pencils and paper clips on Reading's desk and acted like a child waiting to see the dentist.

Shirley broke the ice. She said, "I don't know if the store manager will come around or not, but I'm prepared to help you and speak up for you in court if he pushes the complaint. Now, I want you to meet Sergeant Jack Baptist. He's been looking for you and has been to your house quite a few times over the past few months. Your stepfather always claims you're not there."

Taylor perked up at that news. "The reason my stepfather says that is because after I went to the doctor, he figured the police would be coming to hear my story about him," she said.

Baptist spoke in a low comforting tone. "Can you help us with the murder of Mary Anslow? We need to know who was phoning her. Did she tell you?"

The question caused a pained look to appear on Diane's face, and she suddenly looked about twelve, like a child who shouldn't know of such matters let alone suffer sexual abuse.

She shook her head no in response, but did not deny she knew something. Baptist tried to win her confidence, "Diane, I read the complaint the doctor filed with social services against your stepfather. Not only has he been charged, you won't have to live there any more, so you don't have to be afraid. Was it your stepfather who was stalking Mary?"

She shook her head again in a negative response.

"Are you sure it wasn't him?" Baptist asked again.

"No it's not him," she said flatly, offering no more facts.

Shirley tried to convince her, "Diane, whoever did this must be stopped. Do you know who was phoning Mary?"

There was still no confidence evident on the face of the girl. She now sat with her hands in her lap, gently rocking back and forth while bending and unbending a paper clip.

"Yes," she finally replied, but added nothing more even though they both waited. Shirley believed she was seriously mentally ill and needed professional help at once. "OK, Diane, we'll respect that for now. We're going to get a police officer to escort you to social services, and they've arranged for two older, widowed sisters to let you stay with them for now. But we must talk to you again after you feel better."

Taylor suddenly looked horrified. She was panic-stricken. Baptist thought she would fall apart. "What's wrong? What is it that terrifies you?" he asked.

She looked directly into his eyes, and Baptist could again see the primal fear of a pursued animal. She said emphatically, "No cop. If Sergeant Reading comes, OK, but no other cop."

Baptist nodded knowingly, "Are you telling us it was a police office who was after Mary?"

"Yes," Diane stated but could not be induced to say more.

CHAPTER THIRTY-FOUR

Judgment

"Suicide ... being in fact the sincerest form of criticism life gets."
- Wilfred Sheed (1978)

Baptist was called out of court by one of the sheriff's deputies and told to phone his office. In the hall, on his cell phone, he received the information that would have caused a flock of press people to show up had the information been given over a police radio. A patrolman had phoned it in, and the dispatcher had exercised good sense in quietly notifying all the appropriate people, including Hoss Foley and Kirk Donald.

Baptist arrived to find a rookie patrolman trying to comfort the Lutheran church janitor, a dirigible of a man in a state of shock sitting on the back steps of the church. The man's huge jowls rested in his hands, supported by his elbows, which rested on his knees. His eyes were as big as silver dollars, his face an expressionless, chalk-white waxen mask. His lips trembled and quivered involuntarily and revealed great mental trauma.

"Inside the church office," the patrolman said and as Baptist entered the musty room, he could see it clearly.

The Reverend Ken Solomon hung by his neck from one of the ancient steam pipes, which ran exposed beneath the ceiling of the room. A half-inch nylon rope, secured to the pipe, was neatly and tightly tied in a strangling slipknot around his neck. It suspended his lifeless body almost two feet off the floor. His bloated and discolored tongue protruded from his gaping mouth, like a child's silly putty creation. His eyes were popped wide open in an exaggerated rubber Halloween mask with a horrible, inhuman stare. His arms dangled at his sides: his hands positioned slightly open, suggesting that perhaps his final decision was exercised without resistance. In death, his body was an advertisement against a life of debauchery.

By the time Foley and the crime scene techs arrived, the janitor's well-being was of more concern than the body. "Tell me what happened," Foley said softly to the shocked man.

The big man's labored breathing, complicated by his excess weight, made his speech difficult to follow. Between gasps for air he said, "I came in at eight. Reverend Solomon was already here at his desk. He was pale and his lips looked blue; he was sweating like a hog. His shirt was off and I could smell whiskey. He did that from time to time, and then he'd get the shakes, so I figured he was just sick with a hangover. I didn't stay in the office cause he was writing, and I knew he never wanted to be interrupted so I left." The janitor took a deep breath.

"Take your time," said Foley. "What happened next?"

"Solomon called to me around nine. When I went in he looked like he needed a doctor. He was stooped over, still white as a sheet and his eyes were like two pissholes in the snow. He asked me to witness his signature on what he said was his will. So I did, but I never guessed what was up. I should have guessed right then. I knew him a long time. He was OK, and I was stupid not to think what was happening."

Foley was moved by the old man's compassion and self-blame. "Don't sweat that. When they make up their minds, it's already too late. You can't blame yourself."

A bespectacled academic technician measured and re-measured the rope, the distance from the pipe to the lasso knot around Solomon's neck, the distance from the floor to his dangling feet, and the height of the chair that Solomon was assumed to have stood on before kicking it over on its side. Another technician photographed each area of measurement to create an evidential record for later assessment.

Kirk Donald arrived late as usual, because he did not think it prudent to endanger public safety by driving fast to examine a person for whom time no longer mattered. He took one look at the wheezing janitor and fished a yellow pill out of his medical bag and passed it to the man, instructing him to wash it down with water.

Kirk then walked to where Foley stood next to the body, crisply issuing orders like a seasoned petty officer on the burning deck of a boat, making sure all hands continued to perform their duties in a professional manner.

Baptist stood nearby scribbling notes into his book. He only interrupted his observations for a moment to notify the chief of police.

"What do you think so far?" Kirk asked Foley. Both Baptist and the technicians paused, waiting for the shrewd old pro to answer.

Foley cleared his throat and peered over his bifocals like a professor. "We're not sure of his body weight yet so we have to estimate it for the time being, but it looks like suicide. We'll computerize the exact measurements, the length of the rope, the tensile facts such as stretch features, which are provided by all manufacturers, and then use his exact body weight to produce numbers and compare the results. The computer will tell us exactly what should have happened in comparison to what actually happened. I'm betting from the estimates it's going to be a perfect match, a suicide."

Kirk expected no less from Foley; he knew he was too careful to make many mistakes. "What about a note? Is the fact there is no note a negative factor in deciding if it's a suicide or not?"

Foley continued to stare at the body. "Notes are often found, and some of them are quite strange. One guy I recall put a note on the cellar door telling his wife not to go downstairs, to first call the police and then their lawyer. Another guy put sheets all around to absorb his blood before he shot himself. Another unusual thing is they often lay down before they shoot themselves as if a fall would damage them. Strange shit. But no suicide note? Sometimes yes, sometimes no. This man left a fresh will leaving all his goods, chattels, and trinkets to his wife. So I guess that's a kind of note."

Kirk watched Foley stare at something about Solomon, which seemed to hold his attention. "What are the odds of a faked suicide as a cover for murder?" he asked.

Foley did not move his eyes as he answered. "Doesn't often work. Killers make glaring mistakes. For instance, if there is no ladder and the distance from the pipe to Solomon's neck was longer than to his arms, it raises the immediate question as to how he would have tied the rope. If the distance is too great, it proves someone else did it and then hoisted him up there. Plus, that would leave neck chafe abrasions in a wider pattern. It's pretty tough with today's science and the computer to fake a suicide. In gunshot deaths, for example, the blood patterns can prove scientifically the proper angles and marks to an exact degree."

Kirk was impressed with the answer but his curiosity was still running strong; Foley just stared at the fly area, just to the left of the zipper cover, of Solomon's dark clergy trousers.

"What the fuck are you staring at, Hoss?"

"A wet spot," Foley replied. "Something like a man with a prostrate problem makes when he dribbles urine. But is that urine?" He turned to the technician with glasses who had been taking the measurements. "Put some luminal on this and then scan it to see if it's blood."

The tech-nerd followed instructions mechanically. It seemed to take forever. Kirk waited impatiently as Foley continued his persistent stare.

"You're right, Hoss," the technician finally said. "It's blood."

Foley was not through. He said, "Now the question is, is it his blood and if so, where's it from? That's over to you, Kirkie, and it's your body now."

Motivated by Foley's curiosity, Kirk moved to the hanging corpse. He undid Solomon's belt, waistband button and then the zipper. He pulled Solomon's trousers and underwear down to the dead man's ankles to see where the blood had originated.

"Holy sweet Jesus," Kirk blurted as he stood looking at the minister's crotch area. "He's been surgically castrated. Look at those sutures. Whoever did this knew exactly what they were doing. The clamp marks are perfectly placed; the closing is neat and tight; plus the stitching is just as professional as my old grandma would do on a sewing machine. No amateur cut his balls off or he would have bled to death. The only blood is the little spot you noticed on his pants."

Foley was mesmerized. His profound shock was unusual. "Losing your jewels is serious shit, and I can only guess how much of an impact it would have on someone."

Kirk made a funny sound, a low guffaw. "I heard yours were like two old prunes, so what's the difference?"

Foley ignored Kirk's taunt but smiled weakly. "Is it be possible that he was done somewhere else while he was drunk, and when he woke up, he discovered it and came back here? Could he have made it here on his own after a trauma like that?"

"Oh yeah," Kirk replied. "I saw cases in Vietnam where guys with their balls mangled by exploding devices managed to travel over a lot of territory on pure bile and guts. Old Solomon likely had more mental anguish at the discovery than the actual trauma, even though he wouldn't feel great by any means."

Kirk walked slowly around the body. "Look here, at his butt. There's a syringe mark. Someone likely got him loaded and then shot him full of Pentothal, so they could operate without waking him up."

Foley looked away. "If you're through here, let's bag him up and move him back to the lab, so we can do his blood alcohol level and scan for chemicals, plus I want his accurate weight for the computer."

Chief Pineo arrived just as the technicians were undoing the rope. His reaction to the sight was not that of a callous, experienced police officer.

"What a way for some poor sonuvabitch to end up. I knew him for a long time, and he was far from perfect, but no one should end up like this."

Foley was sympathetic. He said, "You say knew him as well as anyone, Chief. Have you noticed anything different or troubling about him recently that would contribute to a suicide theory?"

Pineo's eyes and thoughts were glued on Solomon who was being fitted into a body bag by two hefty technicians.

"Yeah, Solomon had troubles alright. He had money problems, and he drank too much, and his dick ruled him, three issues which led him to misadventures in the past. And he talked of all three compulsively in the last few weeks."

Baptist listened to the chief's answer, knowing that he had neglected to include that he had arranged a pay-off to the Anslows for Solomon's sexual indiscretion. He said, "He was one of two people I suspected in the rape-murders of those two girls."

Pineo was not outwardly shocked by Baptist's statement. He said, "Well, Solomon seemed to have a fixation on young girls with big breasts, so it wouldn't be the first time his dick got him into trouble."

Kirk sensed the conversation was dead and not going anyplace else. He snapped, "Amen to him, his balls and this place. Move him out to the morgue."

CHAPTER THIRTY-FIVE

Puzzle Pieces

"[W]hen he hid himself away among women, ... puzzling questions are not beyond all conjecture."
- Sir Thomas Browne (1645)

Ellen Anslow's early morning appearance at the desk sergeant's office served as a prod, reawakening the police department's discomfort and guilty conscience about their failure to solve her daughter's murder. She identified herself to the surly sergeant. "I'd like to see Sergeant Baptist," she said.

When he asked for the nature of her business, she replied coldly, "The unsolved murder of my daughter."

The lights went on in the grumpy old sergeant's mind and suddenly that signaled action stations. A clerk nearby overheard the conversation and stood up and immediately left for the bathroom to avoid facing Mrs. Anslow. The corporal in the adjacent radio dispatch section suddenly became engrossed in an imaginary flurry of paperwork, and the patrol supervisor decided to go on patrol without finishing his coffee or morning paper.

The curmudgeon working the desk pushed the direct line to the investigation section only to learn the overworked Baptist was at the morgue on the Solomon case.

"Sergeant Reading is taking his calls," the secretary at the other end informed him, "but she's tied up in a meeting with Officer Bear."

The caustic sergeant couldn't abide her response. "Well, untie her," he growled, "and tell her I'm sending Mrs. Anslow to her office."

Ellen Anslow, still dressed in her hospital garb after the night shift, was guided through the busy building to Reading's desk. Brief and strained introductions were made to the two officers. Shirley Reading was gracious by nature and sought to put her at ease. But Mrs.Anslow started speaking while she was still standing, as if she was eager to get to the point of the visit. "I've met you before," she said to Shirley. Bear adjusted a chair for her. She nodded, a subtle, almost indistinguishable movement, which was so tentative it was difficult to ascertain whether it was intended as a greeting or to mark her disdain. Ellen passed the early edition of the morning *Chronicle* across the desk so both officers could see the accusatory front-page story by editor Allan Tobin.

"Police Incompetence" was the headline. The story featured quotes by the hospital's attorney Elias Fraser. Fraser claimed the murders of his niece Katherine and Mary Anslow were cold cases, and the police were either incompetent or covering up for one of their own. The words corruption and dishonest rang out with the clarity of a citywide alarm clock. Fraser also attacked the police for the unsolved murder of police officer Frank Nichols.

Bear spoke first. Initially Shirley was shocked by his candor, but slowly she came to realize he was empowering Ellen with thoughts and words, without overt instructions, hoping the exchange would bring about a positive result.

"Could I have your word that anything I say here will not be attributed to me as the source?"

Ellen looked surprised, "Of course. Besides, you have a witness who would support your version of this conversation."

"Mrs. Anslow," Bear said, "you have every right to expect the murder of your child to be solved. We are just as frustrated with our lack of progress as attorney Fraser. To bring you up to date, I'll tell you that I personally thought at first that it was Reverend Solomon who killed both girls. By the way, he killed himself this morning." Bear paused and waited for her reaction. There was none forthcoming. Bear thought her stoic reaction was maybe a result of her long-ago tour as a battlefield nurse in Vietnam, or perhaps the recent murder of her only child had buried her emotions behind a passive facade. Bear's very nature illustrated his sincerity. He continued, "I could be wrong because Sergeant Baptist was suspicious of young Diane Taylor's father, but he had an ironclad alibi for both nights. Baptist and Reading believe your daughter's friend Diane knows who was phoning and courting Mary, but she won't give us the name. Her reaction suggests it's a police officer she's afraid of."

Ellen remained cool and expressionless. Shirley thought she was possibly medicated but more likely was just exhausted after working all night. Despite her flat emotions, her words conveyed a provocative idea when she finally responded.

"Would it be possible that Richard Murphy killed my little girl and maybe, because of the similarities, the Fraser woman too?"

Shirley did not show excitement in her response. She asked, "Why do you think Murphy might be involved? Do you know anything that might assist us?"

"I work in the operating room with Richard's wife Joan. We go back over thirty years, first at nursing school then later in Vietnam. There are no secrets between us. Recently, she told me that her husband has a history of problems with other women, usually young ones who seem fascinated by his good looks and uniform. It surprised me to learn what a sorry twisted individual he is. Joan has caught him messing around before. Joan told me she had to send her daughter from her first marriage away to school when she was only fifteen, because Murphy pawed her every time he got drunk."

Bear had a sick feeling in his stomach as he listened. "He sounds like a profile candidate, but we'd need real solid evidence. Would Joan Murphy talk to us or maybe to Sergeant Reading?"

Ellen looked skeptical, "I don't think so. She's totally terrified of him, and she vents to me. I'll help you anyway I can about what she's said."

"Unfortunately," Shirley said, "that's hearsay and likely not admissible in court. We probably couldn't indict him on that, let alone convict him. However, it's very useful to us in trying to solve this puzzle."

Ellen was not ready to give up on Murphy. "How about the warehouse fire where the court records were stored. If I gave you something on that could you search his house or try to use it against him?"

Shirley sensed pay dirt. She said, "Please go ahead. Tell us what you know.."

Anslow cleared her throat and continued, "Joan told me that the night of the fire Richard called the hospital to tell her to come home. She knew there was something wrong so she went right away. It was four in the morning and he was in uniform even though he wasn't on duty. He was in the kitchen and his uniform shirt was torn below the elbow and there was blood all over the place. She said he smelled like gas and smoke. He told her to stitch up his arm. She pleaded like hell with him and told him it was a tough place to stitch, because there's not much flesh to work with beneath the ulna and she had no painkiller. She told him they'd have to go to the hospital. That's when he went nuts and made her do it in the kitchen with whiskey for the pain. She knew damn well that he'd been involved in something bad. Then he told her to burn his uniform shirt and went to bed. When she came back to work, she heard about the warehouse fire so she never got rid of the shirt."

"God almighty," Bear exclaimed, "you both have to be very careful that he doesn't think you're a threat to him. He sounds like he's psycho and could explode in a second. I hope she hid that shirt well."

"The shirt is at my place," Ellen said quietly. "I'll turn it over to you two. Joan kept it as insurance in case Richard ever became a threat to her daughter again."

Shirley leaned forward, "Are you positive Joan wouldn't testify or at least talk to us?"

Ellen shrugged her shoulders. "She might talk to you if you ever arrested him, and she felt secure, but she's afraid. She says he's been getting away with serious stuff for years, so she doesn't think he'll ever be caught. Another thing, he told her that wives can't testify against their husbands, and he said he'd kill her daughter if she tried."

"What other things did she say he was involved with?" Bear asked.

"Joan said he and those two who arrested Donald Frank, Kierans and Clarke, have made a ton of money stealing fines. They're tied up with someone at the courthouse, that old woman Morash, and maybe a few others. Joan knows how they hide their money."

Bear said, "Perhaps this won't seem important to you, but my curiosity drives me. It says on the front page of the paper that the hospital's lawyer made statements about his niece's murder, and Mary's murder, but then he makes a big flap about the death of Nichols who most of us know was dirty. What would be Mr. Fraser's reason for including that sleaze in his criticism when there are so many other legitimate beefs? Has Joan ever mentioned anything about Nichols being tied up with her husband?"

"Absolutely," Ellen replied. "She said Nichols often came to their house, and he and Richard would huddle and mumble secretly about something. Once Nichols left an envelope of money at their house when Richard was out. You know that that lawyer Fraser's sister is Frank's mother, don't you? Word was that Frank Nichols got his appointment the old-fashioned way before civil service exams. Fraser pulled strings for him, so naturally he'd crow about his nephew's death."

"Good grief, Charlie Brown," Shirley said as she shook her head. "This damn city has as many good-old-boys as Selma, Alabama had in the old days."

Bear steered the conversation back on track. He said, "What about any other facts or even gossip that Mrs. Murphy may have mentioned in passing that didn't seem particularly important at the time? There might be something we can use in our investigation. No matter how dull it may seem to you, it could help us."

Ellen looked thoughtful. "Well, Joan told me that Richard can't get along with anyone. He's got a serious personality problem. She claims his mother was a control freak and an abusive person, and that's made him suspicious and defensive about any criticism or confrontation. He's had trouble with many people over small things, including Dr. Donald's assistant Sharon Marshall. She was so mad at him once she threatened him with a letter opener when he gave her hell about a parking space at the morgue. He tries to bully almost everybody but Chief Pineo. He even had a fuss with that janitor from the department who got killed because he wouldn't unlock some station-house door for him."

Bear replied, "I heard something about a similar incident. Someone tried to break into the records section. They cut themselves trying to jimmy the door. We got a blood sample from that, so maybe we could get a DNA test done to compare it with his bloody shirt that you have."

Ellen continued, "I suppose petty gossip is not very helpful."

"Like what, for example?" Shirley asked.

Ellen looked embarrassed. She answered, "Stories like Chief Pineo's wife sleeping with Reverend Solomon and Major Brown. And there were jokes about that because Brown apparently was bi-sexual, and MacAdam was one of his lovers. And then there's the stories about Mrs. Pineo and MacAdam being tied up in that strange religion I read about in the paper the other day."

"You mean the Church of Scientology?" Bear asked.

Ellen nodded her head, "My neighbor is one of them, and she claims Ruth Pineo and MacAdam have gone beyond the principles of Scientology to weirdness. She claims those two envision a new world order run by auditing, which is their version of mental health. It sounds almost cult-like the way she describes Mrs. Pineo's theories."

"Yeah," Shirley muttered, "the cult of getting rich from auditing a never-ending supply of gullible suckers."

Ellen continued, "Joan says that Richard is pretty worried about that law suit in the Frank case. He's concerned that the discovery process will cause trouble, because that cop Clarke is a wussy and will say the wrong thing."

Bear exchanged glances with Shirley. "What about the mayor's case? There'll be a deposition on the same two officers for it. Did Joan mention her husband's reaction to the mayor's arrest?"

"From what she told me, he went nuts. Ranted and raved and yelled at Clarke and Kierans. Said they were facing two tough lawyers on both cases."

Shirley was amused that the deposition of a civil case would worry him that much when he wasn't even involved. She said, "We figured the deposition might help with a few pieces of the puzzle, but we hear the city will settle both cases before trial. Even if they don't, if the depositions ever get before Judge Chase it will be a poor show, because he'll favor the two cops."

Ellen perked up, "Joan says Richard only jumps for two people: Judge Chase and the Chief. He never questions them on anything."

Bear was excited to hear that bit of information. "What would he have to do with Chase?"

"Joan says he and Richard talk all the time."

Shirley was equally interested in Murphy's relationship with the chief. "Why are he and the judge so tight? Does Joan know?"

Ellen nodded, "She said the judge once fished Richard's chestnuts out of the fire on a lie in court. Chase buried it or Richard would have been charged with perjury. Ever since then, he and Judge Chase seem to have some mutual interest."

"What about the chief? How does she read him?" Bear asked.

"Joan says he's a dirty old man. He pinched her once ,and as far as the job goes, Richard thinks he's incompetent."

Bear was fascinated at the gossipy knowledge Ellen carried in her head. "Dr. Donald hates Murphy. Do you know why that is?"

"Because of how he treated Sharon Marshall and because of Joan's daughter. Dr. Donald heard about Richard pawing her and wanted to push it, but Joan asked him not to. She and Dr. Donald knew each other slightly in Vietnam and are friends. I also met Dr. Donald over there, but I realized he didn't recognize me the day Sergeant Baptist interviewed me at the morgue. I figured with my married name and glasses and an twenty extra pounds, he probably didn't remember me, but someday I'll remind him. We both worked on some guys under fire once."

"You must be exhausted," Shirley said. "I'll follow you home and pick up Murphy's shirt. If you think of anything else, write it down."

As they stood to leave, Shirley turned back to Bear. "Set up a meeting for our bunch with the Blazeks to pass along these new pieces to the puzzle."

Bear yawned and stretched, "Another long night, but at least we have something new, and that shirt of Murphy's may be a door-opener."

CHAPTER THIRTY-SIX

The Bear Pit

"Being deposed in litigation is like a rabbit in a bear pit and the lawyers are the bears."

- Redhorse, at the Native Council meeting Christmas 1999

Magistrate Harold Chase, who loved being called a judge, sat at one end of the grand oak table in the judge's conference room at the courthouse. A certified court reporter, who operated two simultaneous recording systems, was at a smaller table near the judge's chair. The recording device was connected to each position along the table by sensitive, voice-activated microphones. On the judge's left sat Peter Sharpe and Mary Grassmuck Fox, the attorneys for the defendants, namely the City of Shiretown et al. and the city police department. Further down the table was the first witness, the dour looking police officer Gregory Clark.

The plaintiff's attorneys, Raymond Wortman and Dr. Walter Corbett, representing the Frank family and Donald Frank, sat opposite Sharpe and Fox to the right of the judge.

Magistrate Chase, selected by the court clerk's office in response to the defendant's motion requesting a judicially supervised deposition, called the proceedings to order and instructed the recording clerk to commence taping for the record.

Chase said, "This will be formally conducted, because it is a deposition before me, as a judge. The rules as set out by the *Rules of Civil Procedure* will be exactly followed, and my presence as a judge is to enforce procedural fairness in the conduct of the examination of witnesses."

He then read into the record the date and the time, then the case name, court number assigned to identify the case, the issue of controversy, the litigants' names, and the names of the attorneys for each side.

Walter Corbett sat with his elbows on the hardwood table, his hands together and his fingers steepled. Wortman prepared by removing the last of their six soft-bound books of deposition questions, each one almost an inch thick, which contained hundreds of meticulously prepared queries, many of which contained subsidiary questions to be used depending on the witness' answers. The very sight of the abundant binders gave silent notice that this would not be a simple or short deposition.

Dr. Corbett first addressed the judge. "Your Honor, the defendants petitioned the court to hold the deposition before a judge and it was so ordered. We also filed a subsequent motion with you, the clerk's office, and the opposing attorneys yesterday, and we request that you rule on that motion."

Harold Chase's face reddened as if by magic, and he suddenly looked as if he had serious sunburn. In contrast, his cold eyes peered out from beneath his shaggy gray eyebrows conveying his turgid disposition before he even replied. He said, "Dr. Corbett, I deem what you filed yesterday, a letter, to be your opinion and not an official motion; and, therefore, I do not intend to treat it as a motion. The nature of the deposition, and the fact that there is not yet any controversy about the proceeding renders your letter as 'not ripe'; and, therefore, it will not be considered."

Dr. Corbett had spent half his adult life studying, practicing, and teaching law. His experience included prosecution, criminal defense law, civil litigation, and teaching at a prestigious law school. His tactics did not include personal animosity, and he only depended upon and argued the law. He had an extraordinary grasp of facts and an encyclopedic ability to recall *stare decisis* in detail and analyze the decisions. His very presence in a courtroom served notice to experienced judges and attorneys that slipshod or deficient presentations would be quickly exposed, dissected, and refuted without mercy.

"Magistrate Chase," Corbett replied in a flat but polite tone, "A 2001 case, *Hallett v. Hart,* is on point with the issues we raise in this case. The Supreme Court of the United States decided for the plaintiff, who claimed damage from forced anal sex, sodomy by the defendant Hart. It is a case where the underlying facts mirror this case at bar. The child Donald Frank suffered this same heinous treatment at the city jail by jailer Crowell Roscoe and Major Lester Brown, and through the negligence of the city police department.

"In that case the original judge who conducted the depositions refused to recuse himself and conducted a large portion of the hearing, eventually resulting in the appeal court ruling nine to nothing that the apprehension of bias by the judge denied the plaintiff a fair hearing."

Corbett paused for a moment before he continued, "Before the deposition in that case, the plaintiff requested that you recuse yourself on the grounds of the apprehension of bias. We requested that a judge from an outside jurisdiction be selected who had no association with anyone involved in the case. You refused to remove yourself as requested.

"In the Hallet case, the plaintiff filed an interlocutory appeal in federal court to remove the judge, but the judge continued before the higher court ruled.

"The appeal court granted the injunction because the apprehension of bias test requires only that a reasonable person would suspect or believe there would be bias. But in that case, the fact that the original judge started the case despite the motion for his recusal was the grounds for the decision. We therefore cite that precedent and request that Your Honor must respond to our motion for recusal."

Chase was not hardened to or experienced in the fractious nature of civil litigation, as he was almost never confronted by issues of law in the minor issues presented in his lower court. He did not conceal his anger nor could he hide his contempt, which of itself was proof of his bias.

"Dr. Corbett, the defendant petitioned the court for a judicially supervised deposition on the grounds it was an important public issue that required procedural fairness. Despite the load of cases facing the court, and a shortage of judges, which is a burden to judicial efficiency, they were granted a seldom-used procedure in civil litigation. I was selected by the court clerk's office on the basis of availability, because the calendar is full. Now you wish to remove me before I've uttered one word. I did not seek this appointment nor shall I allow the efficiency of the court to be impaired by your whims. Therefore, you will proceed, and I shall not recuse myself. You may seek an interlocutory injunction to have me removed, but until that happens, we will proceed."

Dr. Corbett remained calm and polite. "Is the recording equipment picking up the voices clearly?"

The female operator said, "Yes. I'm listening on the earphones, and the recording lights on both devices indicate they are functioning properly."

"Very well," said Corbett, "Let the record show that as attorney for the plaintiff we requested Magistrate Chase recuse himself and that he refused. Secondly, let our objection be noted for the record to preserve our grounds for appeal."

Wortman smiled to himself. "The question," he thought, "of Chase's impartiality has now been raised in the record. Walter's strategy has placed Goat in a position where either he will lean over backwards to be fair, or his anger will be so obvious that bias will be easy to demonstrate on appeal."

Chase instructed the plaintiff's attorneys to proceed. "And let's not waste an hour asking Officer Clarke background questions. Let him read his CV into the record to save time."

Wortman agreed, and Clarke started in a cracked nervous voice. "My name is Gregory Clarke," he began, and then stated his date of birth, exact age, social security number, education, work experience, and so forth: all droned into the record. Wortman did not waste time on the mundane facts Clarke provided. He went directly to the important questions.

Q: "What was the reason, the reasonable suspicion, which prompted you to stop and confront Donald Frank?"

A: "We were ordered by Major Brown to observe and detain him because Brown said he was selling drugs."

Q: "How long before the actual confrontation did Brown give you those orders?"

A: "A couple of days before, maybe three days."

Q: "What were his exact instructions?"

A: "As I said already, he said to catch the kid with drugs."

Q: "Did you investigate or observe or follow Donald Frank for any specific period?"

A: "No."

Q: "Did you interview his associates or classmates?"

A: "No."

Q: "So you did not see or hear or investigate him to find out if he was dealing drugs?"

A: "No, we acted upon what Major Brown told us, and that was all we knew."

Q: "How were you to recognize Donald Frank?"

A: "Major Brown met us at the school prior to the dance that Friday night and pointed him out to us, as he entered the auditorium."

Q: "And why did you not confront him then?"

A: "Brown told us to wait until he was off the school grounds and said that the boy always went to his uncle's restaurant after school dances."

Q: "What did you do from before the dance, when you were shown Donald Frank, until after the dance, a period of over four hours?"

A: "We sat outside the school auditorium in the police cruiser."

Q: "It was a Friday night, a busy police call night, and yet you sat idle outside the school for over four hours?"

A: "Yes."

Q: "How many incidents or calls would you respond to on the average Friday night shift?"

A: "A few, maybe three."

Q: "Would it surprise you to hear that on the twenty-six Friday nights you have worked, according to the desk sergeant's log, you averaged, in fact, five calls a Friday night between seven and eleven?"

A: "No, but that sounds about right."

Q: "But on this Friday night, you sat idle for over four hours?"

A: "Yes, that's what Major Brown told us to do."

Q: "Did your desk sergeant know that?"

A: "I don't know."

Q: "Would it surprise you to learn that the desk sergeant did not know and was so worried, because you did not respond, that he sent other units looking for you?"

A: "No, I didn't know that."

Q: "Does your police department have a drug section of trained officers?"

A: "Yes."

Q: "Are you assigned to that unit?"

A: "No."

Q: "Do you have the state-certified drug course for police officers?"

A: "No."

Q: "After the dance did you go directly to the restaurant?"

A: "Yes."

Q: "What happened next?"

A: "There was a homeless man who was pretty drunk, so we drove into the restaurant parking lot."

Q: "Did you arrest him?"

A: "No, we ran him off."

Q: "Was he not urinating in a public place with dozens of people looking on?"

A: "Yes, but we were waiting for the Frank kid."

Q: "Because that's what Major Brown told you to do?"

A: "Yes."

Q: "Now about procedures and the police manual. Are there written instructions and training classes instructing you as to what constitute reasonable suspicions and stops or searches?"

A: "Yes."

Q: "And what was your alleged reasonable suspicion to confront, stop, and subsequently arrest Donald Frank? Walking into a restaurant?"

A: "Major Brown instructed us to do so."

Q: "Are you familiar with the Supreme Court case *Terry v. Ohio*, which mandates reasonable police stops and pat-searches on suspicion?"

A: "Yes indeed. All police officers know that. It's known as the Terry Stop."

Q: "Did you see a bulge or anything suspicious around or on the person of Donald Frank or under his suit?"

A: "No."

Q: "There were no bulges in his suit because he was only wearing a T-shirt and jeans. Is that not correct?"

A: "Yes."

Q: "And were there still witnesses present when you confronted Donald Frank?"

A: "Yes."

Q: "And was Donald Frank intoxicated, acting strangely, suspiciously, or in an unruly manner?"

A: "No."

Q: "Then what did you decide was suspicious?"

A: "We had instructions from Major Brown."

Q: "So it is your testimony that you were acting under orders, is that correct?"

A: "Absolutely."

Q: "Officer Clarke, have you read or are you aware of the war crime trials held in Nuremberg after World War II?"

A: "Yes, I know of the trials."

Q: "Was it not the expressed defense of all the defendants that they were only following orders?"

Before Clarke could answer, Peter Sharpe shouted, "Don't answer that!" He then lowered his tone. "Your Honor, that is an outrageous, prejudicial question along the lines of, are you still beating your wife. I object."

Chase turned to Wortman, "Enough of that Nuremberg stuff, Mr. Wortman. The witness will not answer."

Dr. Corbett, who had been busy scribbling points on a yellow evidence pad, addressed the judge, "Let the record show that Magistrate Chase allowed the attorneys for the defendant to instruct their client's witness not to answer a question: a question that goes to the issue of why a Jewish child was confronted by the police, who claim by their own words that it was because they were only following orders."

Chase did not hide his animosity from Corbett. "No more of the Nuremberg stuff Dr. Corbett. It will be stricken from the record? Do you hear?"

Corbett remained placid, "Yes sir, I hear but we insist our objection be recorded."

"Absolutely not," responded Chase.

Corbett reached inside his suit coat to the breast pocket and removed a small but sensitive interview recorder and placed it on the oak table. "Magistrate Chase," he said firmly, "we ask that you reconsider your decision to strike our objection and ask that you instruct the court recorder not to delete it."

Chase stared at the small recorder on the table in front of Corbett. The question was obvious to everyone in the room. Had the small powerful recorder been running since the deposition started? Chase paused and drummed his fingers on the hardwood table, obviously cogitating.

"The objection will be left in the record," Chase finally ruled. "Now proceed."

Wortman cleared his throat and continued questioning Clarke.

Q: "What were your exact orders from Major Brown?"

A: "I told you. Find the boy and search him."

Q: "Was there a file or written report on Donald Frank in the drug section of the department?"

A: "I don't know."

Q: "Would it surprise you to know that this morning, armed with a court order, we compelled the drug section to reveal any file on Donald Frank. And the officer in charge swore by affidavit that there are no files or reports, and the boy is not a suspect in any matter?"

A: "I'm not surprised. A lot of information is passed verbally or in the pass along book."

Q: "But there were no reports you saw, and you did not see it in the so-called pass along book. You only had Major Brown's orders to search the boy? Is that your testimony?"

A: "Yes."

Q: "So you confronted the child Donald Frank at the restaurant door in the presence of his friends, with no other suspicion except Major Brown's orders to perform this rights' violation?"

Once again Sharpe interrupted loudly. "Don't answer that! Your Honor the question is another wife-beater type, and we want it struck from the record."

"Agreed, "Chase said, "strike it."

Dr. Corbett noted another objection for the record, and Wortman proceeded.

Q: "Is it your testimony that there were a number of witnesses to this confrontation?"

A: "Yes, I said that."

Q: "Describe what happened when you approached the child, Donald Frank.

Mary Grassmuck Fox spoke this time, "Your honor, Mr. Wortman refers to Donald Frank as `the child' and we object. That's prejudicial and we ask that he not use that particular term."

"Agreed," answered Chase. "Drop the term `the child' and proceed, Mr. Wortman."

Corbett did not say anything. Wortman smiled but also did not respond to Chase's ruling.

Q: "Repeating the thought then: What did you do when you confronted this underage person, Donald Frank?"

As Wortman spoke, Mary Grassmuck Fox leaned over to her partner Sharpe and made one of her piercing, coaching whispers. "I wouldn't object to that, because the record will be littered for appeal already." Clarke answered as he was supposed to.

A: "We approached him and asked him what he had in his pockets."

Q: "Did he answer or resist you in anyway?"

A: "No. He said he had eleven dollars and his driver's license."

Q: "And did you find that suspicious and grounds for arrest?"

Chase did not wait for or need Sharpe to interrupt or object. "Mr. Wortman, your questions are laced with sarcasm. Drop that attitude. The witness will not answer that."

Dr. Corbett stood up. Chase held up his hand. "I know, Dr. Corbett, you object that I wouldn't let him answer. Is that correct?"

"Yes, sir," Corbett replied. "I strenuously object."

"Noted. Proceed."

Q: "Did you read the underage boy, Donald Frank, his Miranda rights?"

A: "No, we did not plan to hold him or search him at the time."

Q: "Would it surprise you to know that more than one witness has sworn an affidavit that you threw

Donald Frank to the ground, handcuffed him, and that your hand was seen in his pocket?"

A: "I must have been checking for a weapon."

Q: "Was it not your earlier testimony that you did not suspect a weapon?"

A: "Yes, but Major Brown told us to search him."

Q: "Did you call Donald Frank's parents as required in the police manual?"

A: "No, we didn't have time."

Q: "But you obviously had time to call Major Brown who arrived fifteen minutes later?"

A: "It didn't seem that long."

Q: "And what did Major Brown do upon his arrival?"

A: "He put Donald Frank in the back seat of his car."

Q: "Did he read him his rights?"

A: "I didn't hear it if he did."

Q: "Were you at the jail when the underage person was taken inside?"

A: "Yes."

Q: "Was he searched?"

A: "Yes."

Q: "Were drugs found?"

A: "No."

Q: "Then why was he still kept in custody?"

A: "I don't know. Major Brown dismissed us then."

Q: "And you were only following orders?"

"Don't answer that," Fox ordered.

Wortman continued anyway. "And you didn't follow written police procedures as set out in the police manual, did you?"

"Don't answer that," Fox repeated. "Your Honor, that calls for opinion, as the police rules are not here to be examined."

"Agreed, strike it," Chase instructed the recording secretary.

Wortman now stood up. "Let the record show that Magistrate Chase has again agreed to prevent the witness from answering a question about police procedure. The police manual is hereby submitted in full, the relevant section being section one relating to arrests and procedures for preserving the suspect's constitutional rights."

"Noted," Chase responded. "Proceed."

Wortman sat down and looked back to Clarke. "Would it surprise you to learn, or did you know, that Major Brown was being investigated for drug distribution, embezzlement of fines, and various sexual allegations?"

Chase roared. "Don't answer that! This is a civil deposition, Mr. Wortman, and those allegations of criminal conduct are prejudicial to this issue. You have prejudiced the procedure with those speculative allegations."

Wortman listened calmly to Chase's outburst. Across the table, Fox continued her stage whispers, coaching Sharpe. "Don't get involved in this exchange. We don't want any comment from us on the record."

Wortman finally spoke. "Your whispers are about as subtle as broken glass, Ms. Fox. Likely the recording equipment is sensitive enough to pick them up. Are you aware that numerous attorneys know of your whispering habit and refer to you as Whispering Fox?"

"That's it!" yelled Chase. "This proceeding is closed."

Dr. Corbett passed papers to Wortman and helped him to pack the large legal brief bags.

"Your Honor," Corbett began, "I understand now that the recorders are off that it's my obligation to inform opposing counsel that the federal Justice Department contacted us this morning about possible prosecution of the various defendants for civil rights violations. They requested us to voluntarily turn over any investigative material we acquired to them. We informed them that to pass over that material voluntarily would be up to our client, and that under the rules of privilege and litigation procedures, we could not do so. We have contacted the state Bar and they suggested we should inform opposing counsel of the call, but we did not do so for the record, as we did not wish to have it sound like a pressure tactic."

At that point Dr. Corbett paused, but no one responded. He continued, "Consider yourselves notified." Corbett and Wortman headed for the door carrying their legal documents under their arms.

Dr. Corbett suddenly stopped, turned slowly and looked back to the table where everyone else sat in stunned silence. Wortman looked on in admiration at the man he likened to an African-American version of Gary Cooper, standing tall for the right things. When Corbett spoke, Wortman thought of Cooper's quiet but deadly impact in *High Noon*.

"Having notified you, I now inform you that we shall be available in our office for settlement offers between twelve noon and one p.m.," and then the two attorneys for the plaintiff departed.

CHAPTER THIRTY-SEVEN

Surveillance

"It's like fishing without worms and worms don't like fishing."
- Sergeant Doreen Roberts

Sergeant Doreen Roberts had spent every evening from six till midnight at the old house on Leverett Street where Troopers Ernie and Bernie Blazek were running the wiretap equipment. They waited impatiently for calls, especially for ones from the mystery woman to David MacAdam in hope they would reveal more about his possible participation in the courthouse fine embezzlements. MacAdam's homosexuality lessened the likelihood that the female caller, who set up secret meetings with him, was just a nervous lover.

There were few calls during the week, and time passed slowly for Roberts and the Blazeks. They spelled each other on the listening device while the others played cribbage, rummy, hearts, and even hand and foot. Periodically they were reduced to watching dull TV sitcoms, and when that became unbearable, they argued politics. People and not issues seemed to lead to the best arguments. Ernie Blazek wished McCain was President instead of Bush, but that was yesterday's news. His brother Bernie seemed to disagree with whatever his twin thought, and the fact they were identical twins and the same in many ways, did not prevent their having divergent, independent opinions. They were frequently umpired by Doreen Roberts who seemed to enjoy provoking both brothers.

Roberts had been a police officer for twelve years, a black marble, a keeper, a person with brains, horse sense, and beauty, and her five-foot-two inch frame carried her molded female figure like the classic work of a sculptor. She had proven her mettle on the streets.

With the advent of computers, it was discovered that she was a computer whiz who had achieved a degree in computer science on her own time. Sergeant White invited her to join his records and ID section. He was planning for her to be his replacement when he retired to hunt and fish. Roberts, who had a secret crush on White, scoffed at the notion of his retirement, telling him he'd die of boredom because fishing is so dull. When White replied that everybody liked fishing, her sardonic wit produced a memorable reply.

"I'll bet worms don't like fishing."

Over a period of time, Robert's silent affection for White grew, but his addiction to his work and his deep sorrow over the death of his wife ten years previously made him all business. He showed no social interest in Roberts or any other female.

In a minute of boredom and frustration, Roberts confessed to Ernie Blazek, "I've tried every subtle, refined thing I can think of to signal my interest to that black cracker but to him I'm invisible."

Ernie's solution was aggressive, if nothing else. He said with a straight face, "Have you considered disrobing and walking into his office?"

Roberts snorted, "All you guys think with is your dick, and White's dick is apparently brain-dead."

The long nights of listening, waiting, cards, and bad coffee provoked such weird but amusing time-killing discussions. Surveillance, according to the Blazeks, was like fishing without worms. Finally, they picked up a call from Magistrate Harold Chase to Chief Pineo at home just after the fractious courthouse deposition of Officer Clarke. Both Blazeks were excited.

Listen to these two good old boys. It may not be evidence of a crime for court but it sure displays white-trailer-trash thinking by a judge with no ethics."

Chase said to Pineo, "The deposition in the law suit was a disaster. I did everything I could do, but that spook Corbett's going to spray shit all over the department like a flying manure spreader. For shit's sake put the heat to the City Council who you control to settle. Pay the fucking Jews off first. Don't pay off that little LaGuardia prick Finnie first, or the pompous little shit will suddenly oppose their settlement because he hates Jews. He's only allied with the Franks for convenience, so keep him waiting till they are shut up."

Pineo was deeply concerned. He said, "I can handle Finnie and two others. Can you do anything to influence any of the other four councilors? We need two more beside the two we can depend on. Finnie will do as he's told on a tie breaking vote of council, because he'll want a future settlement too, so forget about him."

Chase felt he could help. "I know one who owes me. I'll deliver him, but don't dally. Let's get it done before the Feds get into the act. According to Corbett the Feds are snooping already."

Pineo agreed. "I'll get on it today."

"Holy shit," Roberts said. "Old Chase is just a twisted good-old-boy pulling strings behind the scene."

"Yup," Ernie replied, "more like Boss Hogg."

Bernie was more practical in his opinion. "I think they have a golden goose in the courthouse and they're all profiting. Old Chase is devious enough to recognize the goose could get cooked if the suits against the PD aren't settled quickly."

"It also proves he's unfit to be a magistrate," Ernie added. "He's messing around with justice issues, which is unethical as old hell."

"The recording of that conversation provides a lot of intelligence even if it's not all probative," Roberts interjected. "It seems useful as circumstantial evidence if we get enough."

"They're all telephone shy or paranoid. It's almost bull-gab," Bear said.

Bernie Blazek agreed. "You should hear the chief's wife on the phone if you think the others are careful. She uses double-speak and grunts even when she makes a hair appointment."

Roberts laughed, "She really doesn't know me, but the two times I saw her from a distance gave me the impression you northern boys sure pick your women in some strange way."

Ernie Blazek said, "All men pick women by tits and ass, and after they wed the reality of marriage takes over, and the average guy finds he's spending his life with the devil's sister."

Roberts suspected Balzek might be gay because of his effeminate mannerisms, so she prodded him, "and how do you pick your lovers Ernie? she asked.

Bernie interrupted before Ernie could answer, and spoke directly to Roberts. "Don't let my brother's faggy act put you at ease or fool you. He's conned more women into bed than Frank Sinatra, because some women think he's queer, and they want to screw him into a straight conversion."

Then the call came. The mystery woman with the disguised voice called MacAdam from a payphone.

The woman said, "McDonald's inside Wal-Mart, the usual."

Roberts rushed into action to reach the proposed meeting place. She drove to the East End Wal-Mart and hustled into the small McDonald's inside the store. She bought a cup of coffee and buried her head in a newspaper and settled into wait for Mac Adam and the mystery woman.

The time dragged and the frustration grew to silent anger. MacAdam never showed. She grew restless, then bored, and suddenly her analytical curiosity ignited. "If these people are nervous about being seen together and paranoid about phones or surveillance, or even if they just read too many spy novels, they could be saying one thing but meaning another by pre-arranged instructions."

She made a decision. "The meeting isn't here. They're likely at the opposite end of the city," she thought. "And at the other end of the city, K-Mart could be the real meeting place." Suddenly she was almost embarrassed by her own wild deduction. "I'm never telling anyone about this nutty goose chase, but I'm still going to check it out."

At K-Mart, when Doreen Roberts entered the Big K restaurant, she spotted them at once. MacAdam sat at an angle from the only seat Roberts could find. The woman's face was not visible as her back was to Doreen. All she could see was an expensive raincoat, likely English styled by London Fog. Her mop of dyed hair was modeled in the modern wind-blown style, which defied order. All at once they appeared to finish their meeting and MacAdam passed the woman a brown manila envelope as she rose and walked to the archway marked washrooms at the end of the restaurant. Doreen moved quickly to the arch, which entered a T-shaped hall. On the left end of the T bar, about twenty feet away, there was a female washroom symbol on a door. To the right at the other end of the T was the men's room, and in the middle was a small closet with an open door, a sink and some cleaning materials.

Roberts went directly to the women's room. There was nobody inside, the stalls were empty and there was no other exit door or window. No more than a minute had elapsed. Then it dawned on her: the men's room. She ran down the hall, past the arch, and towards the men's washroom, all the time fumbling in her pocket for her badge in case she was confronted by anyone.

She pushed through the door to see an older man dressed in coveralls with a weather-beaten face and a baldhead standing up to one of the urinals peeing a stream like a garden hose. There was no one else in the room or in the stalls. The old geezer turned his head over his shoulder to look at Roberts. "What are you doing in the men's room, sister?" he asked.

Doreen held up her badge. "Did you see a person in a trench coat in here?"

The old man completed his duty and zipped up his fly. "If I got a badge could I go into the women's room without a hassle? I always wondered what took women so long in those places." He walked to the sink to wash his hands.

Doreen was not uncivil but spoke pointedly. "Never mind the bull fuddle, Pop, just answer my question."

"Yes, Ma'am. A feller came out of that stall. He had bushy hair, funny moustache, and was wearing a raincoat.

Didn't even wash his hands. Went out that door just before you showed up."

Doreen pocketed her badge and turned to leave.

"Hey, Miss," the man called after her. "Can I borrow your badge a minute to take a scoot into the women's bathroom?"

"Dream on," she replied.

Doreen arrived at the surveillance house on Leverett for the meeting with the others. It was obvious to all present that she was in a foul mood, and her first sentence provided the clue.

"The bitch hoodwinked me. What I'll do next time is get my old clunker car and sit it on MacAdam's house, and I'll stay in touch with these two chipmunks here by cell. When they tell me she's called MacAdam, it will be easier to tail him to the meeting. Maybe we'll even get a picture."

Ernie responded first. "We'll all be as pissed off as Doreen is when she finally catches this mystery person and discovers it's some closet gay cross-dresser."

Roberts screwed up her face to suppress a smile and said, "If this wasn't Ms. McIntyre's first time here with this motley bunch of perverts I'd say something real smutty in reply to that bull feathers."

Bernie walked over to the electronics table where Bear sat listening to a tape on earphones. Sharon Marshall was talking to someone on the phone while Kirk, White, and Foley discussed the recent developments.

Bernie spoke out loud to everyone present. "We'll play some of the wiretap tapes for you, because we could be missing something that you people will pick up, especially if it jibes with some fact you know and we don't. Remember as you listen that even silence or a pause or nuance may convey something to you, so listen with an inquisitive mind." He paused in case there were questions but none were forthcoming.

Bear said, "I watched *60 Minutes* Sunday night about the development of a sign language by deaf children in Nicaragua and the theories of the American woman studying the evolution of that method of communication. She figured people have a natural, almost uncontrollable urge to communicate, and even without words, there will be information conveyed to a keen observer. I guess a shrewd interrogator or cross-examiner can read the subject's body language. Of course you can't see the person on an audiotape, but you can read voice inflection, nervous pauses and tone. In fact, those things may tell as much or more than the actual words. Sort of a silent vocabulary or signal."

"I'm convinced," White said, "but the judge will want facts not an interpretation of silence"

Bernie moved to the machines. "This is Stent and some unidentified male."

Stent's nasal voice was easy to recognize by those who worked with him. "Hello," he was heard to say in an aggressive tone.

The second man replied. "I don't trust phones so I'll be brief. We need to clean uncle's garage tomorrow. We want you to serve and protect."

Stent did not answer. His silence indicated either telephone paranoia or agreement.

The other man sounded annoyed, "Are you there?"

Stent answered, "I don't like that, unless uncle's at work, so he won't be disturbed."

"The afternoon is convenient. He's at his office."

Again Stent remained silent.

The other caller became more aggressive, "This is not a detail that can be ignored. You will be there. Do I make myself clear? Our cousin will be pretty fuckin' upset if you don't show." The caller hung up without waiting for a reply from Stent.

Shirley cottoned first to the meaning of the conversation because of what she and Bear had learned from Ellen Anslow. "I think the uncle is old man Fraser, the attorney who lives on Roosevelt. Nichols was his nephew, and my guess is they're planning to pick up drugs Nichols hid there from the drugstore warehouse robbery."

Bear agreed, "My theory is similar. I think Nichols and Stent did both Walgreen robberies and hid the pills in Fraser's big garage, and now the bikers want the inventory."

Sharon Marshall finished her phone call. She said, "I've been listening with one ear while I was on hold to the state crime lab. They just confirmed that the chemical on Murphy's shirt was the same accelerant used to start the warehouse fire. Also the blood on the shirt and the blood on the door of the records room were confirmed as Murphy's by DNA testing."

"What about the semen on the tissue found where the Fraser girl was murdered and the samples from the condoms at the ballpark?" Bear asked.

"Not possible," Sharon replied. "Even with the new science it couldn't be separated from the other material."

Dunlop arrived looking tired and stressed. "So now what?" Bear said to Dunlop.

Dunlop replied, "If nothing else, we have enough evidence to bag Murphy and perhaps get some satisfaction, but I want them all. The chemical and blood on the shirt would likely get us an indictment, but at trial he could argue he attended the fire while on duty and got the chemical and the cut innocently. We'd likely lose, and worse, he's probably guilty of murder, so we don't want to rush in and ruin a real case."

"OK," Baptist agreed. "But what about Stent? If we could land him with the bikers and some drugs at Fraser's garage tomorrow, it would mean a lot. Possibly we could even roll somebody if we catch them with the goods."

"I think that's a better place to start," Dunlop said. "If we get desperate we can always bag Murphy and try it, but this Stent thing could be good and might loosen his tongue."

Shirley had listened carefully to the conversation. "One or two things worry me. We don't have enough reliable bodies in the department to take down the bikers, if that's who Stent's playmates are; we really don't know who we can trust."

White stood up, "Roberts and I discussed it, and we're in."

"Us too," Ernie said, "You know like those guys on Bob Newhart's TV show about Vermont, my brother Darrell and I are in too." He smiled at Bernie, and added, "but we do need a sketch of that yard layout. How can we get that?"

"Simple," Hoss said. "Kirk and I know Fraser well from hospital volunteer meetings, and we can go over and offer our condolences on the death of his nephew. We'll likely be able to create a rough sketch of the backyard for you. If you have a Polaroid, we could take a picture of his roses next to the garage, so we'll have a good shot of the garage."

"Back to the sex murders and the trooper?" Bear said. "What do we do to try and solve those?"

Dunlop rocked back and forth in an old rocking chair. He replied, "You need to find Skeeter Greene, because Lieutenant Folker says that the other witness Feters is only useful if medicated, and that's a big risk. And if Jack Baptist or Shirley can convince that Taylor girl to say who was calling Mary Anslow and which cop she's afraid of, it would go along way to solving that mess."

"It's interesting that you have such a strong interest in Murphy," Ernie interrupted. "We have some tapes of him talking to a woman who calls him frequently from a payphone, but it means nothing to us. Maybe it would mean something to you people."

"Roll the tape," Bear said.

"Here goes," Ernie replied. "She uses a cloth or something over the mouthpiece. We traced all the calls back to payphones."

"Hello?" Murphy answered.

"Can you talk?" the woman asked.

"Yes, Joan's at work."

She said," You-know-who is suffering from depression and is drinking too much. Something has set him off and I can't find out what."

Murphy sounded guarded, reluctant to say very much, "How serious is it?"

She did not hesitate, "Maybe a threat. I've never seen him like this."

"Watch it," Murphy said.

She seemed to ignore his warning, "I have that book here. When and where do you want it?"

"Not the usual place. Never there again."

"Where then?" she asked.

"The cottage, two o'clock Thursday. Don't go direct."

"I hear you," was her reply before Murphy hung up.

Reading spoke first. "Well, first of all he's likely just boffing someone's wife and this may be nothing. The woman's voice bothers me. I can almost make it."

Sharon Marshall had listened intently. "Can I offer a suggestion?"

Kirk looked at her. "My word woman, you've worked with me since you got out of the army and I never knew you before to need an invitation to suggest anything."

"Hush," she said. "I think there's more to that meeting than the fact he may be porking her. When she spoke about a book that didn't sound like sex to me. What do you think?" she asked McIntyre.

Taureen replied, "You don't go to a clandestine meeting over a frigin' book and there's evasiveness in the conversation which suggests more. Conversely there isn't much heat in Murphy 's response to the meeting. But then most men usually think foreplay and sweet talk consist of about ten seconds worth of their presence. On the other hand, it may just be an afternoon delight, and she's worried her husband is suspicious."

Doreen, looking directly at Perry White, agreed. "I'm with Taureen. I know certain men whose head, both heads, must be brain dead." White did not seem to get the message. Shirley and both Blazeks knew it was White she was prodding with words.

"How can we find out what Murphy's up to on Thursday?" Dunlop wondered aloud.

"I have an idea," said Doreen. "It's a bit of overkill if Murphy's just screwing around but in for a penny in for a pound. So borrow me one of those anteater listening devices," she said to Ernie Blazek, "and then if Shirley,

Sharon, and Taureen agree to help, we can follow Murphy in shifts. We can put the listening device on the windows of the place they meet and find out if it's an orgy or a conspiracy.

Ernie nodded, "I've got an anteater. You can hear and record a conversation up to a mile away, even through a closed window. I can teach you to use it in a minute."

"Not so fast," cautioned Baptist. "Murphy's no fool. He's a schiztzo, and following him won't be easy. He might be able to make you out."

"Sheeit," Doreen replied. "With three old cars, a wig and some sunglasses I reckon four smart women like us could have followed Kim Philby without him noticing."

"Fine with me," Baptist replied. "But just remember, when you hunt the tiger, you better do it right, for you hunt him by day, and he hunts you that night."

"Holy shit, another poet," quipped Foley.

"I'm in," said Doreen.

"Me too," Taureen said.

"That settles it," Sharon said. "We'll work out the scheme tomorrow night for Thursday."

"Alright," Baptist said, "Hoss, you and Kirk go get us the layout of Fraser's yard, and we'll wait here to make the final plan to raid the garage."

Hoss turned to Sharon. "Remember this, Sharon, Doreen and Taureen are armed and you won't be. And Murphy's a mean sonuvabitch."

"Listen sonny," she replied. "I was a nurse in Vietnam and he's just a pimple compared to some of the boils I lanced."

"What about Skeeter Greene?" Shirley asked Bear.

"I'm indebted to him," Bear replied. "He saved my life, so now according to our customs he's responsible for me. But so far he hasn't seemed very impressed about his responsibility in that respect. And somehow I'm doubtful about being able to convince him in the future, since in our last conversation he told me to fuck off. So all I have do now is lure him out of hiding, and for that, I have a plan."

CHAPTER THIRTY-EIGHT

Dropping a Dime

"It now costs a quarter to drop a dime."
- Dismas Rhodes, Police Officer

It was a dull, muggy Wednesday. Joanne MacDonald, her reporter's mind stuck in neutral, sat at her desk sucking on a cigarette in the *Chronicle* newsroom.

Allan Tobin, the volatile and neurotic editor, was not exhibiting patience or understanding about MacDonald's lethargy. He was more obnoxious than usual, and even his bad breath seemed worse than normal as he pointed out what Joanne already knew. He said, "Your boyfriend Jobb at the *Bugle* is scooping you regularly with contentious, provocative, attention-grabbing, front-page quality stories. Even your one good story about the mayor was a gift from him.

MacDonald was nervous, because she worried that Tobin believed she might be referring good news leads to her lover instead of writing them herself.

"Bullshit," she thought. "No ego-mad reporter loves anyone that much." But she did not share that sentiment with the editor.

Suddenly, it was like the news-fairy heard her silent cry for news. The phone rang.

"Ms. MacDonald?" a soft male voice inquired.

Joanne was on the defensive, nursing the verbal bruising of her editor, yet she had the presence of mind to be polite and receptive. "This is she."

"Ms. MacDonald, if I were to give you a hot news tip for a good story, would you promise me not to drag an army of news shit birds with you to the scene?"

Joanne MacDonald was leery of anonymous voices with alleged news tips, which often seemed to turn out to be some nut or some old fart passing along a pain-in-the-ass tale of how his neighbor's cat was pooping in his yard. Skepticism was her initial thought, but she was too hard up for news to be rude or cynical.

"I'll certainly hear you out, and I promise you if it's a true story with any news merit, I'll attend the scene alone."

"It's two-thirty now," the caller reported. "You're fifteen minutes away from the big gray house owned by attorney Fraser down on Roosevelt. The police have just busted six bikers and a local police officer in the garage behind the house with the drugs from the Walgreen warehouse robbery in their possession."

"I'll be there!" MacDonald stammered before hanging up the phone.

Driving across the side streets in a rush, ignoring stop signs except for brief slowdowns at the intersections, she gunned her old Ford across the back side of the city and cut over to Roosevelt. As she approached the area she began to have doubts.

"It's an upscale neighborhood, not where the usual drug busts occur," she reasoned to herself. "Maybe it's somebody's idea of a joke sending me on a wild goose chase? At least I can show that creep Tobin I made the hunt whether I make a story kill or not."

When she parked her car, she saw Sergeant Jack Baptist as he walked up the driveway carrying a bunch of police leg-iron restraint chains for prisoners.

"Hey, Baptist," she called, "what's going down here on snob street?"

Baptist paused, "Hi. I can't make any public comment about this arrest because of an ongoing investigation."

MacDonald smiled as she neared him, a wily, knowing reaction to a typical police reply. "C'mon, Jack, I'll keep you out of it altogether, honest Injun."

Baptist smiled back, "You'd have to speak to Noel Bear about that," he replied, ignoring her question.

MacDonald shook her head, "No offence intended, just an expression. Let me get a few photos, and tell me what's the story."

Baptist remained distant, not enthusiastic at all. "How could I explain the pictures you'd publish? I'd be accused in court of polluting a crime scene because you were there."

"Jack," she whined in a pleading tone, "I'd walk back behind the fence outside the crime scene area and get my photos from there, but I need background."

Baptist continued to be nonchalant, but was surprisingly civil despite his reputation for not talking to the press. "I guess I couldn't stop that as long as you're outside the crime scene. I don't have enough officers to shut down the whole block."

MacDonald suddenly turned into a hound after a fox. "I still need background. How about it?"

Baptist was too shrewd and more than experienced enough to know not to blab to any media person. Like Noel Bear, he figured reporters had two tongues and no ethics.

"I might give you some background, purely on the basis that I wouldn't want any misinformation published, which would prejudice the case. There would be some stringent rules you'd have to agree to, and I'd need you to write them out in brief form and sign it."

MacDonald almost jumped at the offer. "Go ahead, scribble down the rules and I'll sign it for you."

Baptist looked stern, "I'm not an attorney, but if you sign the agreement and double cross me, it's likely grounds for a suit."

MacDonald was listening, waiting. Baptist continued.

"OK, now the ground rules. I'm an unnamed source: a source not referred to as a background provider and definitely not a police source. There will be no hint these facts came from a police officer. In fact, you can imply your own sleuthing ferreted out the details, and it will make you look smart. Next, you will write from your own personal perspective to prove it's your story, not our story. You cannot photograph the two troopers you'll see back here nor the federal agent who is wearing a ski mask for obvious reasons. You will mention that both state and federal agents assisted a Shiretown PD special unit in making the arrests. You can name the local police but not me."

He paused to give her time to write his rules. "I want the state and feds to receive their share of the credit."

"I agree," she said. "Now fill me in on what's happened."

Baptist cleared his throat, "Six bikers, members of the Devil's Darlings, who seem to control a large portion of the local drug business, were arrested here today. Those bikers include their leader, Bob Miller. Also arrested was a city police officer. This arrest resulted from an extensive investigation into the Walgreen drug warehouse robbery. They were found in possession of over two hundred thousand dollars and the stolen drugs." He paused gauging her reaction.

MacDonald scribbled furiously, "Who's the crooked cop? Is he the only one?"

Baptist was coy in his reply. "The officer arrested is Hunter Stent of the drug squad. And as to others, the only one we suspect right now is his late partner, Sergeant Frank Nichols, who was recently murdered. Our investigation continues."

MacDonald chuckled. Even when discussing background Baptists reply was a bland and canned speech like a recording. "What about the owner of this property, Mr. Fraser? Is he involved?" she asked.

That question posed a problem for Baptist. Any way he answered would produce more questions and maybe innuendo. At present, he was not quite sure of Fraser's role although he was not a real suspect. He decided on a soft, pliable answer. "Mr. Fraser is the uncle of Frank Nichols, the dead suspect. At one time Nichols lived in an apartment above this garage, and apparently he stored belongings in the garage area. We are not suspicious of Mr. Fraser."

Baptist hardly took a breath before changing the subject. "If I were taking pictures, I'd want the six bikers and especially that snake Hunter Stent. After we put these leg irons on them we'll stand them up for transport to the car so you'll be able to see their faces from behind that back fence, because we'll have them faced that way."

MacDonald, like any news hound, could smell the impact of the story. She rushed away, down the side of the Fraser property and cut in behind the backyard wrought iron fence. She peered through and discovered a perfect view of the seven suspects now standing with their faces towards her. Their legs were shackled with the leg irons and their hands were behind them, obviously restrained by handcuffs. She snapped picture after picture, making sure to avoid the troopers and the federal officer.

Baptist passed a list of other arresting officers through the fence to her. "These people worked hard for a very long time. Don't forget that the troopers and feds should also get credit."

"Deal," MacDonald agreed. "How do you suppose I received a tip to come here?"

"Someone dropped a dime, I guess," Baptist replied. "How would I know?"

He walked back toward the men in restraints. "OK people, load 'em up, except for Stent. Put him in Bear's car. The truck and the Harleys are now seized property of the Shiretown Police Department, since they were used during the commission of a felony."

While Baptist spoke with MacDonald, Bear called Dunlop. "The deed is done. We'll meet you at Hoss' place with Stent in tow."

Dunlop was curious, "Any action or trouble?"

Bear laughed, "A piece of cake. No shots fired except for Miller who shot his mouth off yapping that he'd kill the rat bastard who snitched on them."

Dunlop was amused, "He may have a long stay in the slam to plan it."

Bear rang off and went over to talk to Baptist. "Why not hint to MacDonald that we had a snitch among the seven arrested and create some internal strife in the biker gang?"

Baptist paused only briefly, "It's a good idea, but I don't want it to look like Stent was undercover because he's in a jackpot. Maybe I can sell the idea that it was one of the bikers who ratted, and that won't make Stent look good."

Small whispers into telephones start big stories, according to Sharon Marshall. When the crew met at the morgue the late edition of the *Chronicle* was filled with a bombshell featuring a front-page headline that stated "Bikers and Cop Busted for Drugs". A byline by Joanne MacDonald seemed to cover it all.

She wrote the story with a subtle suggestion that the tip-off snitch was one of the bikers. She told of the$200K in cash, put the street value of the drugs at $400K, and named the special task force of local officers.

There was no satisfaction at the *Daily Bugle*. They had been scooped, skunked, and shut out, and the boss was beside himself. Editor Parker Purves bellowed at Jobb, "Call the fuckin' police chief. Find out how the *Chronicle* got a leg up on this. Someone's fucking us because of that fight over the Corbett suit."

Jobb knew he had to make the call, but he didn't relish the task. When the chief's secretary tried to blow him off, Jobb knew he had to insist on speaking to the chief or Purves would have his balls for ping-pong practice.

"I don't care how busy he is," Jobb insisted loudly. "You tell him it's the *Daily Bugle,* and if he doesn't see fit to use us fairly, I'll write that fact on the front page."

The patronizing, sycophantic voice of Chief Pineo responded almost immediately to Jobb's threat. "Hi, Steven. How can I help you?"

"You could have helped me by giving us the same heads-up you gave the *Chronicle* on the drug bust."

There was an awkward moment of silence before the chief answered. "This was a task force operation, a combined force of officers, and not even I knew the details in advance."

The usual ass-kissing voice of the chief came through the telephone lines clearly. "We'll give you an exclusive heads-up on something real soon."

By the time Jobb finished his call, Purves was again standing next to his desk, still ranting. "Look at this," he said and passed a half-page advertisement across the desk to Jobb. It was a copy of an advertisement that appeared in their own paper.

Warning!
Skeeter Greene
Contact the Scout
You're safer with me
Than you are without!
Signed- The Owl

"What the fuck is this all about?" Purves asked Jobb. But before he could hazard a guess, Purves continued his tirade. "Some woman walked into the ad department and paid cash to run this. The stupid bastards downstairs only remember she was dark-skinned and that she paid cash. The name she gave was Mary Belacana and the address was the paper's street address. No one noticed it was our own fuckin' address!"

Jobb dared to ask a question. "Then why did Classifieds run the ad?"

The question pressed Purves' hot button. He leaned over near Jobb's face and shouted, "Because it's not indecent, it's not insulting, it's not libelous, and it was paid for in cash, which is what we're in business for! I want you to run this down and see what it's all about."

Jobb was dumfounded. "How the hell can anyone run it down when there's no address, and none of our people remember anything except she had dark skin? Does that mean she was black, brown, or beige?"

Purves leaned over Jobb's desk again, supported his weight on his two extended arms and said, "Why don't you try to find out who Skeeter Greene is first? Are you an investigative reporter or do you just re-write stories from real papers like the *Chronicle*?"

The phone on Jobb's desk rang, and he welcomed the interruption from Purves' tongue-lashing. He answered curtly, "Jobb here"

The voice at the other end said, "This is Dr. Walter Corbett from Ray Wortman's law firm. Do you remember me?"

Jobb was thunderstruck. He wondered if it was some sick joke. Finally he decided to answer. "How the hell could I forget you after Wortman killed me on that deposition? It was a stomach turner."

Dr. Corbett's voice was pleasant. "Mr. Jobb, let's bury the hatchet. The reason I called you is to make peace. We have two clients in our office who have sued the city. We'd like·you to have an exclusive interview, if you want to come over, because the city has settled with both parties."

Jobb was pleasantly shocked. "Indeedy, indeedy". He said, "Thank you Jesus and thank you Dr. Corbett. I'll be right over." He fairly flew out of the office and left Purves sputtering about real reporters and the good old days in the press room..

At the top of the rickety old hardwood stairs inside the door of the offices of Wortman and Corbett, the receptionist greeted Jobb and led him inside. Dr. Corbett held out his hand in friendship, and Jobb slowly responded. He secretly imagined sticking his hand into a tiger cage as he grasped the outstretched hand.

"Relax," Wortman said to Jobb. "We're not going to hurt you. Take pictures if you want." He called the Frank family into the room. "This is Mr. and Mrs. Frank and their son Donald." He stood back so that Mrs. Frank could greet Jobb.

"Here's a copy of my statement for the press," Mrs. Frank said. "The city settled with us for two million dollars, and we insisted it be made public. Now I'll turn it over to my son."

Donald Frank, a dark-haired, handsome boy, stepped up to Jobb. "My heritage, my religion, and my parents have taught me about overcoming adversity. We are donating the two million to AIDS research, ALS research, and to the search for an antibiotic that will not be resistant to TB."

Jobb was impressed. All his stereotypical opinions of Jews were destroyed in one generous swoop by a skinny Jewish teenager.

"The suit wasn't about money," the boy added. Jobb snapped pictures and the Franks, sporting sincere smiles departed. Then Mayor R. Walter Finnie entered. "The little Admiral," Jobb thought and marveled to himself at the physical resemblance between Finnie and the long-ago mayor of New York, Fiorello LaGuardia, known as The Flower. "Finnie is more like The Weed," he chuckled to himself. The mayor passed Jobb a prepared, typewritten statement, which was canned and unimpressive, but it was news.

> The city of Shiretown and the city police department humbly apologize to Mayor R. Walter Finnie for an unwarranted stop and search and the subsequent bad publicity caused by the actions of two city police officers and the jailer. The City Council has ordered the suspension, pending discharge, of both officers and jailer Crowell Roscoe.
>
> Signed - John Pineo, Chief of Police

Jobb snapped more pictures, secretly hoping the Finnie photo would look bad or not come out at all, but he was glad to have the story. First, it would shut Purves up, and secondly; it would make the late edition interesting.

Hoss Foley walked into Kirk's office at the morgue. "Fucking marvelous," he said, by way of greeting. "Everything I touch has turned to shit today and as the ball rolls down the slippery slope it gets larger and larger. But finally some good news, really marvelous."

Sharon Marshall rolled her eyes and in a caustic tone she asked, "And what is marvelous, Dr. Foley?"

"Why, me," he replied. "But I'm speaking about the arrests our guys carried out, and the fact that the city settled with the Frank family who gave the money to charity."

"What about Mayor Finnie's settlement?" She asked.

""Fuck him!" Hoss snapped.

"No thanks," Sharon retorted. "But I'll hold your coat if you want to."

Foley tried not to smile. "What I really want is to have a last look at you before you and those other three bust - kateers follow Murphy this afternoon."

Sharon sauntered away but could not resist her need to have the last word. "Up your bucket, Uncle Remus," she said.

CHAPTER THIRTY-NINE

The Chase

"Blessed am I in the luck of the chase when the deer comes to me."

- Native American song

Like the hounds before a foxhunt, Roberts, McIntyre, Reading, and Sharon Marshall were nervous and jumpy, anticipating the chase, thinking about the quarry: Sergeant Murphy. He was actually more a tiger than a fox, according to Kirk and Hoss who had known him the longest.

Last minute doubts surfaced, tempers flared from stress, and the usual array of latrine lawyer questions arose.

Was the fact Murphy had a strange telephone conversation with some woman anything more than a love affair, which was a private matter? McIntyre thought so.

Was there reasonable suspicion of illegal activity to justify the use of a portable listening device? Dunlop said yes, because the court had already found reasonable suspicion existed, or they wouldn't have issued a warrant for the wiretap.

Would some slick attorney be able to convince a trial judge that the evidence obtained from a listening device was inadmissible, because it was an invasion of the right to privacy if Murphy was recorded talking to another person not named in the warrant? Kirk pondered the invasion of privacy fears and answered with his usual logic. "I can promise you some two-tongued attorney will argue all those things, but we have to start somewhere, and this is the best chance we've had so far."

Hoss did not argue the legalities, despite his penchant for legal debate and any other argument he could get started. "I'm more concerned about the safety of the women. He's a psycho, and I think he raped and killed those two girls."

Baptist shared his concern. "Me too Hoss," he said," but we don't really have a lot of choice if we want to find out what he's up to. The women won't attract suspicion as quickly as we would, because Murphy is paranoid by nature, so he'd make the rest of us in a minute. Besides, Bear borrowed three old cars that the state police seized as property on drug busts, so Murphy won't recognize the vehicles. And man, do they look bad even though they keep them in top running order."

Bernie Blazek tried to calm Hoss too. "I fitted each of the women with a body wire, a cell phone, and a small radio set to a private band, so we can all stay in touch. We'll be on side streets and behind them as back-up from start to finish."

The disguises were left to the women. Sharon Marshall decided on a blonde wig. "Now I'm a black woman exactly like most of the other blondes in the city, a fake blonde."

Sergeant White, who sat listening to her, mumbled about the blonde Wig, "My God girl," he drawled, "you're the most unlikely looking blonde I ever saw. You look like Sugar Ray with a wig on." Marshall scowled but continued with the fitting, arranging and rearranging the ill-fitting hairpiece.

Shirley Reading added granny glasses and a long red wig to her duds. Taureen McIntyre wore a baseball cap with Red Sox on it, sunglasses, and a jeans jacket over her bulletproof vest to make her slender body look bulky. Doreen Roberts put on a snow-white granny wig and silver-rimmed glasses, causing White to say, "you look like a Q-tip."

Baptist was still concerned and giving instructions, "Sharon, you ride with Roberts, because she's going to bring the anteater and two women in a car might seem less suspicious then one."

Sergeant White was the resident authority on surveillance, "You look like you're appearing in a high school play" he said. "But you'll blend in and that's the secret of what is called alternating multi-vehicle surveillance. All that really means is switching the car closest to the suspect often enough to allay his suspicions. In the city where the chase starts, you'll have trouble keeping sight of the target vehicle. Trucks will block your view; cars will stop in front of you unexpectedly; buses will do exactly what the nutty drivers are known for, cut you off or crowd you out. There is the danger of detection if you stay too close, yet, in the city if you fall too far behind you'll lose him if he turns off."

He continued, "Most cops automatically check their rear view mirrors and Murphy will be no exception, out of habit. So you have to pull aside, and let the next pursuit car get in behind him every once in a while, to maintain his comfort level. Before you pull aside, make sure, by radio, that your partner is in position to see the target. Are there questions?"

No one spoke. White was not happy. "Well, there should be. The back-up cars will need you to give constant location checks because they have to travel different routes. Now let's talk about following a target on a state highway or a turnpike. If he leaves the city, and he very well might because he said they'd meet at a cottage, you might end up on small rural roads. You can usually keep the target in sight without getting too close, but you still have to alternate the cars. Where the real problem comes in is if he leaves a multi-lane highway and goes off a ramp to a country road. That makes it very difficult to follow without detection. You can only stay behind him for a mile, maybe two, in the same car or he'll get suspicious. The trouble is that a narrow two-lane road may have no convenient shoulder or place to turn off to allow a second pursuit car to take over. What I'm saying is, don't try to follow him more than a few miles on a back road. Break it off and come back, or he'll figure it out and might hurt somebody."

Bernie's instructions were just as simple but important. "You should all know how to operate this portable parabolic listening device, which we call the anteater because of its extended snout. Roberts will carry it first but someone else may be in a better position to use it efficiently. The long snout is pointed at the location you wish to listen to and record. There are earphones for you to hear exactly what the device hears, and you can make adjustments to alter the volume or tone just like a radio. There is a recording device located here in the pistol grip of the handle, so basically all you need to do is point and click it on. It will pick up conversation up to a mile away through glass and even through some building materials. The cottage, if it's like many, will not have thick walls so recording should work by sighting on the windows and walls. The sound bounces back from the target point, thus the name parabolic.

"I also have two simple point-and-click cameras for you to use. Marshall who is an amateur photographer gets one and Reading the other. Try and get pictures of both subjects arriving, leaving, and if possible together. But do not get closer than within fifty feet of the place, even if there are bushes and trees to conceal you. Last word, if you're discovered, pop the tape, shove it in your pocket and run. The device is not heavy, but it's not worth saving at the expense of your safety."

"Alright," Baptist announced, "saddle up. It's a little after twelve noon and we have to get located near his house soon in case he decides to leave early."

The three pursuit cars set out separately for exact points near Murphy's side street house on Place Lane. They parked at different locations so they could observe both ends of his street in order to follow him no matter which direction he decided upon. Roberts and Marshall had the best location on the street, which ran parallel to Place Lane. They parked in the neighborhood CVS drugstore lot, which offered a view of both ends of Murphy's street.

McIntyre parked around the corner on Hillview Drive so she could observe the east end of Place Lane. Reading was situated at the west end in the parking lot of St. Martha's Church, so she could move in either direction once Murphy's travel direction became apparent.

It was one in the afternoon. White cautioned the watchers. "Be ready for surprises and stay alert. Don't get bored and let your mind wander. It's important to be sharp because one distraction and you'll lose him."

At one-thirty White transmitted again. "The time might suggest he doesn't need much of a period to get to wherever he's going. That could be a break for us if he stays in the city instead of heading to some back road."

At one forty-five, Roberts sounded the alarm. "The bird is flying west. We'll play tag and then alternate from the rear, so we will be the last unit and can move in close to him at the end."

"I'll go first," McIntyre announced. "I don't think he's ever met me."

Murphy's vehicle moved at a steady pace through light traffic and headed west with no noticeable attempt by Murphy to conceal his direction. His initial route revealed no fear of being followed.

"Why is he acting so normal?" Reading asked. "Unless he's just going to meet his girlfriend."

White radioed back. "He may do something strange yet, so be careful. Or he may just be careless, even super spies get caught, and he's no super spy."

At the corner of Park Street Murphy, turned right on Train Street, which connected to old Main Street, a parallel route running to a dead end behind the outfield of the ballpark. At one time it had been the main thoroughfare through the city. It was now a dead end, since Park Street had become the main route through the city after World War II. It was an old 1920s-style street with tall stately trees and very old houses. At the end of the street was Woodlawn Cottages, situated among a growth of evergreens. The cottages were once a busy tourist attraction prior to the street becoming a dead end. Few people now knew of their existence because tourists traveled Park Street to get to the state highway, and Woodlawn had become a victim of progress. Visitors now consisted of permanently housed low-income families, and a few daytime lovers enjoying some afternoon delights.

Reading caught on first and transmitted to the others, "There's a good chance he's headed to Woodlawn. There's nothing else at the end of old Main unless he's running a diversion and going to double back on us."

White interrupted. "One of you pull off, turn around, or go in a driveway in case he does turn back. Roberts, hang behind Reading until you determine if he's going there. If he reverses we'll still have two unseen cars."

Bear broke into the transmissions, "I'm across the ballpark on the dirt connector and can back you up in two minutes if you need me."

"I'm behind the base of the triangle on South Park at the corner gas station about a minute away," Baptist said.

White spoke last, "I'm on Park Street at the corner gas station and the farthermost away. We're in good shape, so Roberts, you're up."

Roberts slowly eased her car forward, keeping Reading's vehicle between her and Murphy. Murphy pulled into the cottage yard at the first row of shabby cottages and left his car in plain sight. Reading broke off her pursuit and Roberts moved into the trees to the left, concealed by the busy evergreens. Marshall sat in the shotgun seat next to Roberts.

"Let's get a safe spot picked out," Roberts suggested. She announced their plan over the radio, and they dismounted and moved forward through the trees. Once out of the car they discovered that the black flies and mosquitoes were abundant, deadly annoying, and viciously hungry, and neither one of the women had thought to bring bug spray.

Ten minutes of scratching bug bites seemed like an eternity. Marshall saw the woman arriving to meet Murphy first. She parked at the end of the old driveway and walked without apparent concern toward the cottages..

"Bingo," Roberts whispered into the radio. "It's the same trench-coat woman who met MacAdam at the K-Mart."

"Go easy," White ordered. "Wait till she's close enough to get her picture."

Marshall aimed the camera but then suddenly gasped, "Oh my God," she announced into the radio. "It's Ruth Pineo, the chief's wife."

"C'mon," Roberts commanded. "Let's move up to that cluster of cedar bushes. We can aim the device better." The two women moved forward with the bugs following. They crawled inside the low cedars and propped the parabolic device on a flat slate rock before Roberts activated it.

The voices from within the cottage were as clear and distinct through the thin walls as if they were in the small room with the subjects. Roberts could hear Murphy's flat monotone. Despite his control and lack of emotion, she suspected his droning cadence concealed the fact that behind the facade there lurked a violent man.

"How much this week?" Murphy asked Ruth Pineo, and the recording device captured both voices loud and clear.

"Two K," she replied. "The heat's intense and everyone is too nervous to be greedy. We don't know what will come out of the Stent arrest or the suspension of Clarke and Kierans, so it's necessary to slow down."

Murphy seemed to ignore her answer. "That's a light take again this week. Clarke and Kierans will have to be looked after to keep their mouths shut, and we'll have to buy a big lawyer, or they're fucked. Once they think we've abandoned them, everybody's fucked."

Ruth was conciliatory, "Easy, Richard. Don't shoot the messenger. I don't write the mail I only deliver it."

Murphy was definitely not placated. "I can't guarantee the silence of those two without money, so you tell Morash, in person not on the phone, that I'll need big bucks to keep their confidence."

Ruth, always the politician tried to placate him but said, "You're in no position to push it. But I'll talk to Chase, not Morash. She's too difficult, and he's a nervous wreck, so he may get the message, but frankly, Richard, there's not much to connect the rest of us to the mess, so maybe you should try to handle those two."

Murphy was furious. "Not quite," he said in a loud voice. "I may look stupid to you fuckers, but I wore a body wire at every meeting. I have MacAdam giving me Chase's instructions to whack the trooper. I also got old Chase on tape trying to get me to do Major Brown, and when I wouldn't, I recorded him instructing MacAdam to do it. Chase told him that Brown was his lover and had become a threat to everybody, and MacAdam agreed to kill him. All those tapes are hidden securely and if I go down the tapes will go to the State Attorney with copies to the newspapers."

Ruth Pineo's voice now revealed her fear. "Richard, for God's sake, don't fall apart. We have another problem. Morash says that her clerk, McIntyre, in the courthouse snoops all the time, and she thinks she's an undercover state or fed officer. Chase says she's got to go and to make it look like one of those rape-murders so it doesn't seem connected."

"Fuck Chase," Richard retorted. "I burned the records they were stupid enough to keep, but I'm not capping anybody else."

Outside, Roberts was recording and giving a soft-voiced synopsis over the radio to the others. "They're done for," White said. "Make sure you have it on tape."

Marshall, scratching and swatting the bugs, said, "Why would a paranoid like Murphy be so careless as to blab this in the cottage?"

"Simple," Roberts whispered. "It's bare wooden walls; they only made their plans to come here yesterday; they're not on a phone; he's pissed off;and they apparently can't imagine we can get their voices through the walls."

Inside the conversation continued with Ruth Pineo trying to placate Murphy. "Come here," she said softly, "Let me ease your tension."

Murphy was all business. "I'm not in the mood. From here in I'm looking out for me. You tell Chase that I got ten years of tapes, and they love judge's ass inside the prisons."

Pineo tried again. "Come here," she offered in a sultry voice. "I'll put a smile on your face."

Murphy was still distracted by rage. "Not today. I'm not in the mood. You should be as worried as I am, because those three at the courthouse won't be worrying about you. Where does this put the Chief? Have you thought about that?"

Pineo hardly paused. "He's not involved. The worst he did is cover up Solomon's sexual assault on the Anslow girl, and you helped him with that."

Murphy laughed and replied, "Mrs. Anslow did better thanks to your husband than she would have in court."

"Well, I'm not dunking him in this jackpot. I got in this mess alone when MacAdam, Morash and I were raising money for the Church, and someone paid a fine in cash. We decided it was more useful to the church than the city pot. That's how it started, and then Morash got Chase involved because he needed money for his bad investments."

Murphy laughed again. He said, "Embezzlement because of a depraved need for Jesus. And Chase would be seen as greedy and violating his trust as a judge. Jesus saves, and Chase gambles in the stock market."

"Don't be sacrilegious, Richard," Ruth snapped with indignation. "You guys were quick to get in when MacAdam slipped you a few bucks after arrests."

Murphy was no longer laughing. "Get going," he said, "and carry my message."

Outside, Roberts spoke into the radio. "They're breaking it off. How do you want to play it?" she asked White.

"Everybody move in," he ordered. "Roberts, you try to approach them to delay them, but no confrontations. Just delay them if you can, and we'll move in quickly."

"Ten-four," she replied just as the cottage door opened. "Stay here," she ordered Marshall. "Shoot pictures. I'm going out there to slow them down."

Roberts moved forward, her head canted downward so that her white wig would detract attention from her face until the last minute. Roberts got close just as Ruth walked away from Murphy to head to her car.

Roberts said, "Mrs. Pineo? Could I have a word?"

Ruth Pineo's face revealed surprise to the point of shock but she looked to see who had called her name.

As Doreen moved even closer, Murphy rushed and grabbed her from behind. Sharon Marshall, upon seeing this, grabbed the anteater and charged forward, approaching Murphy from the rear. She banged him on the head with the listening device, and when he turned to see where the blow originated, she could see he was dazed.

Sharon continued to attack, kicking Murphy between the legs, high into his testicles. "Muthafucker," she yelled. "How do your crushed plums feel?" But Murphy, rolling on the ground in pain, could not answer.

Roberts crawled to the anteater and checked the tape. "It's OK," she announced as Baptist's car, followed by the others, screeched to a halt near the cottage.

McIntyre confronted Ruth Pineo shouting, "You're under arrest," but before she could administer the Miranda warning, Ruth threatened to report them all to her husband.

Taureen shoved her federal credentials in Ruth Pineo's face and yelled, "Shut up, you have the right to remain silent ... and you best exercise that right."

Baptist turned to Bear. "Murphy's your collar. You and Reading were smart enough to suspect him, so read him his rights."

Bear looked serious, "It's no joy to arrest a crooked cop," he said before turning to Murphy who was still on the ground.

"Richard Murphy, you are under arrest for violation of the federal RICO laws. You have the right to remain silent, you have the right ..." but Murphy was still preoccupied with pain.

Baptist and White realized the bust was good news, but there would be some long, rough days of investigation still ahead to convict the other conspirators. Then the battle of the trials would follow, and it would be a trench by trench lawyer's war.

Baptist used his cellphone to call Dunlop. "We need you to meet us at Kirk's place. We made two grabs. I'll clue you up in person. We're taking the two there until you arrive."

Dunlop was encouraged by the news. "I think I understand. I'll see you in a jiffy."

Shortly after he arrived at the office and listened to the tape, Dunlop was amazed. "Take them down and book 'em. Then let's meet back here because how we proceed on the rest of them may affect the trial if we're not careful."

Shirley and Bear paraded Murphy and Ruth Pineo, both in cuffs and chains, to Shirley's car and headed to the station.

Dunlop dialed Lieutenant Folker and briefed him on the tapes. Folker was excited.

"This will open up the case, but we got a long way to go yet, because the trial of prominent people will be an uphill battle against the best lawyers money can buy."

Dunlop agreed, "In my heart of hearts, I don't think Murphy did the rape-murders, but he definitely did the trooper, and we'll need you to keep that nutty witness Feters on his medication."

Folker was curious about Murphy's possible involvement in the rape-murders. "Feters' testimony on the tracks murder is probative, but his rant about the ballpark is hearsay, so you'll need more than that."

Dunlop was aware of this. "Bear has a great witness about the park. The bad news is we can't locate him."

Folker was concerned. "If you charge Murphy with the girls and the evidence is weak, it may serve to wreck the rape-murder cases by tainting the jury's opinion, because he is a police officer, and he'll have some sympathy in the public view."

Dunlop said good-bye and clicked off. "Jesus, now we have to phone the chief and report the arrests." Baptist said, and he screwed up his face. He added,. "I'll do it. It's my job and yes, it sucks because it's hard to say how he'll react."

Baptist called and got put through to the chief. He announced why he was calling and then waited for a response. Pineo was silent for a long time and Baptist began to wonder if the chief had passed out or was in a state of shock.

"Thank you for calling, Jack," the chief responded politely, "I'll have to get her an attorney and be prepared to meet the press."

Back in Kirk's office, Hoss was pessimistically arguing that the evidence was largely circumstantial if a Judge happened to exclude the parabolic recording from Woodlawn cotage because the warrant did not cover Mrs. Pineo, only Murphy.

Sharon Marshall, who had been listening, was hostile. "That sonuvabitch is a pervert and his balls run his brain. If he skates because of some judge's loophole there is no justice." Kirk looked sympathetic. "Relax Sharon, these things have a way of working out in some fashion so lets not waste anger at this stage."

Dunlop sat waiting for Shirley and Bear to return and amused himself by listening to Foley and Kirk debate the fourth amendment and the possibility some judge might rule that recording inadmissible. Every time the heat of the argument subsided, Sharon would throw verbal gas on the flames.

"What if Murphy didn't kill those two girls?" Dunlop interjected.

Sharon turned her head quickly and stared at him. "Whose side are you on?" she asked in a cold tone.

Dunlop was not deterred, "If we charge him without sound probative evidence on every count, it could prejudice the other good cases, so we have to be sure. That means finding Skeeter Greene, for starters."

"What should we do next?" Baptist asked.

"Go see a judge and get a warrant to search Murphy's house to find the tapes he boasted about when he was yapping to Ruth Pineo. If we find the tapes with what he claimed was on them, we got them all without the cottage tape."

Sharon was still grumbling, "I should have kicked that cracker's balls again and then he wouldn't feel like raping anyone else."

"C'mon," Baptist said to Dunlop. Let's go see a judge."

CHAPTER FORTY

Cases

"Circumstances alter cases."

- Judge Sam Slick (character of Thomas Chandler Haliburton)

Judge Fred Flinn, his imperious manner revealed by his caustic tongue and gratuitous remarks, was slated to be on the bench. His reputation and conduct created an aura of tension, defensiveness, and belligerence even among experienced, thick-skinned attorneys. When Shirley and Bear entered the courtroom for the arraignment of Murphy and Ruth Pineo, Dunlop, who was prosecuting, notified them that judge Flinn would be sitting.

Shirley screwed up her face in an uncharacteristic grimace. She despised Flinn because of his handling of an old case and felt he was both incapable of impartial judgment and ruled by his own bias and emotion. Bear had not yet experienced Flinn, but he noticed Shirley's reaction.

"What's the story on Flinn?" he asked.

Shirley was usually a cool person, not given to snap judgments or holding a grudge, but the mention of Flinn pressed her hot button. "There were twin fifteen-year- old girls sexually abused by a stepfather. They depended on each other, like most twins do. Both of the social workers recommended that the girls not be split up in separate foster homes. Flinn ignored the professional advice and ruled they should be separated, because placing twins together was an unnecessary burden for the system and separately they would have a better chance of adoption.

"Once the twins learned of his decision, that very same day, one of them hanged herself. I told the sonuvabitch about it, and he said he never second-guessed yesterday's decisions. The truth is that he's intellectually dishonest and never should have been appointed a judge. When he practiced law he was called before the state Bar accused of signaling witnesses. He used various methods including fake coughs. The court tapes proved he coughed in cadence, and the audio was unmistakable. But they let him off with a warning because he argued the evidence was flimsy and that he had a bad throat which made him cough."

She took a deep breath before continuing. "On top of that, he served in the Navy with Murphy and they used to whore around together."

Bear was mystified, "How'd he get to the bench then?"

"He gave money to the campaign of the current governor who just happens to be a cousin, that's how."

Just then the bailiff called for order. "All ... district court ... the Honorable Frederick Flinn presiding."

Flinn, a pale man with a jowly face and gray hair slicked down with bat-rum like Clarke Gable, spoke to the courtroom, "Be seated."

The case called first was the *People v. Richard Murphy*. A ripple of conversation swept across the packed courtroom. Reporters and the usual bored cadre of retired folks who attend such notorious events as the arrest of a police officer annoyed Judge Flinn with their noise.

"Hush," he commanded. "Any more disturbance or comments and I'll kick you out of here."

The charges were recited. The *People v. Richard Murphy*: murder, rape, bank robbery, conspiracy, arson, and a list of crimes amounting to operating a criminal enterprise.

Murphy stood next to his attorney, a man who spoke with a distinct gravelly voice interrupted by a hacking cough, which was the obvious result of excessive smoking...

"Barry Howe," he announced, "Attorney for Richard Murphy. My client pleads not guilty, Your Honor. I was only appointed counsel a few hours ago and have hardly had time to read the charges. I am also filing a motion for dismissal on the grounds that the listening device tapes proffered by the prosecution are poison tree evidence. We also request that Sergeant Murphy be ROR."

Flinn looked down at Dunlop, "Well, what say you, Mr. Dunlop?"

Dunlop, his face and manner placid, responded, "He's a flight risk, Your Honor. We have more evidence than the tape recordings. Sergeant Murphy is a dangerous individual, a threat to witnesses, and he is involved in numerous felonies."

Flinn looked back to Murphy's attorney, "Mr Howe," he said." what say you?"

"Your Honor," Howe said, "I won't bore the court or take up more of your valuable time. Sergeant Murphy is a decorated and respected police office and to place him in a jail will subject him to life-threatening actions by people he has put inside. I move that he be released on his own recognizance."

"Agreed," Flinn ruled. "ROR."

Howe turned and passed Dunlop a copy of his motion to suppress the tape from the listening device at the cottages. Dunlop glanced at it and placed it in his bag. They shook hands and Howe walked away. Dunlop turned to Bear and said, "Mr. Howe is as good as any lawyer ever gets, and don't let his appearance fool you. That's part of his Matlock character. He's over seventy, round-shouldered, and some people think he wears those tired, shiny, outdated suits, and dull shoes with run-over heels because he wants to impress the jury with the fact he's a county-mouse lawyer, a poor boy among the mass of slick, city- lawyers. The truth is he doesn't give a damn and is always himself. What you see is what he's about. Just look at that awful skinny necktie. I've seen better old rags from the 1960s on neighborhood garage sale racks without takers. And feast your eyes on that snow-white hair, which points in all directions, because he stirs it up like a brain stimulant when he's practicing for court."

Dunlop paused and the look on Bear's face revealed his curiosity. He said, "You mean this is not all an act, his self created aura, to win?"

Dunlop smiled and replied, "'fraid not Noel, and he's not only good, but most folks underestimate him, and that's a serious mistake. You just watch his facial expressions. His remarkable face speaks volumes, and he never offends a judge or jury with his low-key performance. He's very subtle, just raises an eyebrow, which signals his disbelief of a witness to all observers without uttering a word. His inoffensive pantomime in court keeps the jury spellbound while opposing attorneys are seeking their attention. And his most distracting habit, usually displayed when an opposing attorney is conducting a cross-examination, is to put on his glasses and then quickly remove them, then put them back on in quick succession. Or, he places them above his forehead in his unkempt field of hair and then conducts an exaggerated search for them. He pats his pockets, riffles through his papers, rummages through his old briefcase and then looks all surprised when he finds the glasses on his head. The discovery is always accompanied by a pure Colombo smile, which delights the jury and distracts their attention from the other poor bastard trying to make a legal point."

"Oh my God," Bear mumbled after hearing Dunlop explain the abilities and mystery of Barry Howe. Then he became more depressed as charges against Ruth Pineo were read.

Dunlop knew Flinn had social connections to the Shiretown elite and would not set excessive bail for Chief Pineo's wife, but he made the argument anyway. He said, "Mrs. Pineo poses a flight risk your honor."

But a high-priced attorney from the state capitol, Elizabeth Roscoe Stern, a trial lawyer who was an expert on wiretap evidence, presented herself to the court. She announced her arrival like a prizefight-announcer in a nasal tone, "Your Honor. Elizabeth Roscoe Stern as counsel for Ruth Pineo. We plead not guilty, and there is no evidence of a crime, and before the prosecution does more damage to her reputation, I would remind the court that Mrs. Pineo is a pillar of the community, a church organist, a humanitarian, and a person of high moral values. She is not a flight risk and is no danger to anyone. To suggest a prohibitive bail is an affront to her civil rights. We anticipate these charges will be dismissed without a trial."

Judge Flinn turned to Dunlop but did not allow him to offer a rebuttal and ruled. "Released on her own recognizance."

Dunlop wasn't surprised. He knew the legal trenches were dug and would be defended inch by inch with every conceivable obstacle by the two talented defense attorneys. He packed his papers and put them in the bag. Stern approached and presented Dunlop with a similar motion to Howe's.

"Here is a motion to suppress the tapes."

Dunlop smiled graciously, "It really doesn't matter because there is so much other evidence, which we will eventually show you, that even without the tapes we will convict."

Stern was surprised and her face registered it. Dunlop knew she would relay his story to Barry Howe for Murphy, and so he played tough legal poker. He knew his comments would worry them, and bluff was about all he had for now.

As she departed, it dawned on Bear that the trial would be a miserable, uphill fight, and to convict Murphy or Ruth Pineo would be difficult because much of the evidence, especially if the tapes were excluded, was largely circumstantial.

Bear walked to Dunlop, "It will be a ball-breaker. I thought we weren't going to file the rape and murder charges because the evidence was weak."

Dunlop shook his head, "I would never have filed those two charges on Murphy, but the Attorney General's office insisted after they reviewed the file. What I'm afraid of is a weak presentation on those cases may taint the strong charges. And the jury will let them off if they think we're stretching evidence to convict him, because the truth is juries like cops, even those accused of misconduct."

Dunlop paused and looked at Bear and Shirley, who had joined them. "Relax, this is just the usual BS, so don't get your shorts in a knot on the first day. You'll have worse days than this when we finally go to trial. Now go interview Joan Murphy about her psycho husband."

Bear and Shirley were now in poor spirits, discouraged and concerned about the impending trial. They phoned the hospital to make sure Joan Murphy was on duty. They knew that any interview at her house would be doomed to failure if her husband showed up.

"You do the interview," Bear suggested. "Not only do you have the experience, but she should be more comfortable with a woman. I'll make notes."

They parked in the no-parking zone in front of the Fraser and entered the automatic doors to the busy lobby. At the reception desk they made their request to speak to Joan Murphy and then waited. After twenty minutes, she appeared, dressed in operating room scrubs and held out her hand to shake.

"I've been expecting you," she said. "Ellen told me she went to see you." She led them into a small office situated off from the accounting section for privacy.

Shirley's manner and friendly approach were assets. She explained the necessity of reading Joan her Miranda rights, even though she was not under investigation. Bear sat quietly making notes on a yellow legal pad. He discovered it was not easy to record a verbal conversation with a pen. He was constantly behind.

Shirley added an extra explanation to Joan. "You don't have to talk to us at all. No wife can be compelled to testify against her husband, so if you don't want to continue, we'll understand."

Joan smiled sincerely, but her face looked tired. "It's OK. I understand, and I don't mind nor do I need an attorney."

At first Shirley kept the questions routine, relating to background, history, education, age, children, the marriage, and her armed service career in Vietnam.

She established a pleasant conversational approach and only slowly moved toward the subjects, which were more important to the prosecution of Richard Murphy. She played her cards fairly, open and above board. "Some of my questions may be offensive. I don't mean to be, and if you choose not to answer, it's OK."

Bear was impressed. Shirley not only asked questions that were vital, but she handled them in a very correct and professional manner. Joan Murphy did not seem defensive or offended. The objective, Bear learned, was to keep a subject relaxed and talking, which provided a profile of information as opposed to trying to illicit simple answers by the use of questions, which were offensive. "It's not a cross examination," they told him at the academy; "it's a search for information." Now he understood as he observed Shirley Reading in action.

As they talked, Joan almost seemed to be relieved to speak openly about her husband. Reading slowly moved to the real questions but remained low key.

Q: "Is your marriage a happy one?"

A: "No, never. I made a terrible mistake marrying him. I didn't really know him at all and by the time I knew better, there were children."

Q: "Does your husband abuse you?"

A: "Richard is an abusive bully, especially when he's drinking, and that's quite often. I married him right after he was discharged from the Navy. He'd been a Seal and I discovered too late hat he carried a lot of emotional baggage. He beat me for the first time when I was pregnant with our first child. I was stupid enough to ask him about lipstick on his shirt. That was over twenty years ago and it has never stopped."

Q: "Were there always other women?"

A: "Oh yes, dozens. He has a fixation on young women with big breasts. I gave up caring after our second baby arrived."

Q: "Do you think his interest in sex and young women with large breasts goes beyond what most of think is normal?"

A: "Perhaps. He collects porn photos of nudes, always young, always-big boobs. He's embarrassing to be with in public. One day at Wal-Mart I was convinced he was going to feel a woman's breast. The look in his eyes was scary."

Q: "Do you know if he had any connection of any kind to the Fraser girl or Mary Anslow?"

A: "He definitely knew Mary. He drove her home from the church when that pervert minister grabbed her. I couldn't read anything into that, but Ellen was nervous about him and asked me a lot of questions about his schedules, so I became worried about her daughter."

Q: "Did anything he or anyone else said worry you or cause you to think that Richard might be involved?"

A: "No more than usual. I always knew the young ones found him attractive in the uniform, despite his age."

Q: "Does your husband have a crossbow or any knives, perhaps from his time in the service?"

A: "Yes, he has a crossbow. The Seals use them for silent attacks and several of his pals kept theirs too."

Q: "What about the night you stitched up his arm; that's the night of the warehouse fire, is it not? Did you give his shirt to Ellen Anslow to hide?"

A: "Yes to both questions. His shirt was torn, and he was badly cut. He was a real mess. Some chemical was all over his shirt, but at first I didn't recognize the smell. Then it dawned on me; it was naphtha gas.

"His right arm had a vicious cut. I guess it was from glass. He insisted I sew it up in the kitchen with no anesthetic to work with. It was a helluva job, almost like trying to sew up a wounded man under poor conditions to keep them from bleeding out."

Q: "You were a combat zone surgical nurse in Vietnam."

A: "I guess the proper answer was that I was sent there as an Army surgical nurse, but the front lines changed so quickly we did operate under combat conditions."

Q: "Why did you give the shirt to Ellen Anslow to hide?"

Joan Murphy paused before answering, and Bear bet himself that she had decided not to answer the question. He lost.

A: "I knew he was off duty, yet he was in uniform. I could smell the naphtha and Ellen had called me about the fire. My bell rang. I just knew he was involved, and looking back there were other signs too. First, Judge Chase had come by the night before, and they had downed a whole bottle of Scotch downstairs in Richard's office. I heard them discuss the warehouse, while I sat next to the air vent in our den. And then he wore his uniform out when he was off duty. And later I cut off a piece of that shirt and dropped a match on it, and it ignited like magic."

Q: "Did you hear Chase and Richard discuss the warehouse specifically?"

A: "Definitely. Chase said all the records were there. And if they were gone, there would be no problems for anyone."

Q: "Did they mention fire?"

A: "No, but Chase said they needed a weenie roast and quickly."

Q: "Is there anything more you can tell us, or any suggestion you can make that would help our investigation?"

A: "Search our house. His closet has a false wall. There is over a hundred thousand cash in assorted bills in one box and twenty-five thousand in brand new hundred dollar bills still with the bank bands around them in another box. There is also a pile of dozens and dozens of tape recordings."

Q: "Do you think he was involved in the bank robbery?"

A: "Definitely. I heard them plan it through the air vent from the basement office where he and his friends drink. Nichols and Clarke were there. Kierans was in the hospital. They planned it in great detail but I couldn't quite hear why they were discussing a lawyer named Dunlop."

Q: "You realize that it your husband is convicted he may end up doing life."

A: "I made up my mind that when the kids grew up, I'd leave. My kids are in university, and I have the money now. It's been hell and I can't take anymore of it."

Shirley passed Joan her card. "If you think of anything else or if you need help, call me, night or day."

Joan smiled, a sick, worried look on her face. "I'm not about to cross Richard at this point but if I learn anything, I'll get a message to you."

After the interview, Bear and Shirley were back sitting back in the car, staring straight ahead.

"What are thinking, Chief?" Shirley asked. Bear was slow to reply. Then he said, "My God, a Navy Seal, a cop, a nice wife, two kids. All a guy could hope for and he pissed it away. Why?"

Shirley replied, "Flawed, insane, maybe screwed up by the service, or the streets. Maybe his mother was a matriarch who he hated. But definitely unsalvageable."

Bear was back to business. "Is it absolute, black letter law that a wife can't testify against her husband?"

"That's a question for Dunlop," Shirley replied. "As I understand it, any communication between man and wife is privileged unless the crime at issue is committed by one against the other. But, there may be a loophole. No spousal privilege if the spousal witness hears something said to a third party."

Bear smiled, "Like what Joan heard through the heating duct when Murphy talked to Chase and the others?"

"Possibly," Shirley answered. "I think it's a good maybe, but let's ask Dale."

Bear called Baptist, "What's up?"

"Sorry I didn't make it back to you," Baptist responded. "It took us a long time to get the search warrant. As a matter of fact, we're all here waiting for you so we can proceed with it."

Bear laughed, "Well, baby, have we got some pointers on that subject, but we'll share them in person."

Baptist was eager. "How close are you? We're all here and Lieutenant Folker has moved into the PD, and he's going with us."

"Two minutes," Bear estimated. "What about taking in the other birds?"

"After the house party," Baptist replied. "We might find something useful."

"Call Dunlop for us," Bear requested. "Shirley and I have an important question; it's a deal maker or a ball breaker.

CHAPTER FORTY-ONE

Searching

"Some circumstantial evidence is very strong, as when you find a trout in the milk."
- Henry David Thoreau

Baptist decided Sergeant White would be in charge of the search of Murphy's house because of his knowledge of search procedures and the proper methods of cataloguing, storing and establishing an evidential chain of custody pertaining to admissibility on court. White, according to his associate and not-so-secret admirer Doreen Roberts, was an organizational nitpicker, a compulsive adherent to proper procedure and efficient to the point of obsession.

White did not deny this. "Never had my evidence excluded by a court in over twenty-years," he said. Then his instructive sermon began, "By sticking to the book in collecting and preserving evidence we can keep some sleazy defense lawyer or nutty judge from giving these bozos a skate because of a legal loophole." He had not only had the FBI course on searches, he'd excelled in it. He also had common sense and his words of wisdom made sense. He said, "A house search is a serious undertaking. It's big and filled with junk. The search can be botched beyond repair if you're not observant and curious. Once a search takes place, the suspect is alerted and will dispose of anything not found on the first try. And before any subsequent search can be organized the evidence will be lost, so we have only one good chance. But strangely, criminals do keep a lot of stuff they shouldn't that links them to a crime."

"Basically," he continued, "the biggest problem facing you is that often you don't know exactly what you're looking for or what might be evidence. That's not as dumb as it sounds, because not every piece of evidence you find has a neon sign on it telling you its evidence. The easiest way to stay alert is to imagine a physical search like an index search in a book. Sometimes you have to use some imagination and try to match the issue to a range of what might be evidence.

"That brings us to what the FBI teaches in the class on searches for law enforcement people: 'the trout in the milk theory.' A trout is definitely out of place in the milk, so if you find something in unusual surroundings, it might be a clue for you to examine it. Look for anomalies: a document in a book for example or papers hidden behind pictures or under drawers. Believe it or not, many people hide evidence around or under their mattress or in the pockets of clothing in their closet. So the range of a good search goes from stupid hiding places to real strange places. I recall one at the school where a wise old cop saw that the screws in an old medicine chest had the paint chipped off them. He removed the screws and pulled the chest from the wall and found dope hidden behind it." White paused, and then continued, "Be through, and don't get bored."

When the group arrived at Murphy's house, the magnitude of the task made White's lecture make sense. There were abundant crannies in the large urban ranch-style house for someone to hide things. A thorough search would not be completed quickly.

Shirley and Bear accompanied White directly to the bedroom to examine the closet that Joan Murphy had informed them about. It was noticeable that the Murphys slept in separate rooms. There was nothing feminine in his room: no women's clothing, no make-up, and no jewelry. And the closet, which in most homes would be jammed with female items, only contained his clothing and shoes.

The closet was almost ten feet wide and paneled with cedar for moth protection. On the left end wall, there were shelves loaded with men's underwear, shirts, socks, and toiletries. There was a metal rod running from left to right where Murphy's uniforms and civilian clothes were hanging. Bear and White removed everything from the enclosure, searching all the items including the pockets, but found nothing. Shirley examined the back wall, tapping with a wooden coat hanger to see if she could hear a difference in sound, which would indicate a hidden space. She looked for a latch, lever, pressure spring, or electric button, which might open a secret compartment but did not find one.

Shirley called down the hall to Joan Murphy. When she came to the bedroom, she appeared nervous. She did not know Sergeant White and feared he could be a friend of her husband. White seemed to sense her discomfort. "I'm sorry we're rooting around in your house. I know you helped Shirley and Noel already, but we can't seem to find the compartment you spoke about. Can you assist us?"

Joan moved into the closet and faced the shelving on the left. One by one she slid them out and passed them to White. Behind the center shelf there was a hole about the size of a quarter in the panel. Joan put her finger in the hole and easily slid the panel, which was on a hidden metal track, to the right into an invisible gap behind the closet and the adjoining wall. There was the secret compartment: three feet wide, three feet deep, and eight feet high, compacted next to the space near the shower stall in the en-suite bathroom, which abutted the closet. It would never have been suspected without Joan Murphy's direction.

White was amazed. "I suppose you're all too young to have seen the movie *Treasure of the Sierra Madre*," he said, "but this is what Walter Huston called a man's poke, a hidden booty where people squirrel away their treasures. Maybe at heart we're all squirrels," he concluded philosophically.

There were one hundred and seventy-six thousand dollars in assorted denominations of cash, mostly older bills, untraceable, and safe to spend if you did it slowly and without too much show – like buying a yacht. There were twenty-five thousand in hundred dollar bills. It was obviously from the bank robbery: twenty-five packs in all, still neatly wrapped with paper bands bearing the bank name. The serial numbers were in sequence, which would make it easy to compare with the bank records, in order to link Murphy to the robbery and shooting. There were fifty-six miniature cassettes from a body-wire recorder, each bearing a tiny label with a name and a date. A double-edged, razor sharp, military assault knife and a crossbow stood next to a shoe box full of twenty-milligram Valium capsules on the compartment floor.

There was more: a shocking set of twenty-six, eight-by-ten color photos of nude young women, all large-breasted girls, all in sexually suggestive poses. The girls looked to be underage. Shirley recognized two of them from their appearances in juvenile court. On the back of each photo, in Murphy's distinctive handwriting, was printed the girl's name, address, and phone number plus a brief description of what kind of sexual acts she performed and enjoyed.

The miniature tapes held the searchers' interest as being likely to have evidential value for the arrest and conviction of the others involved with Murphy.

White whistled through his teeth. "What a stupid man. In his penchant for self-preservation, he may have provided us with what could be proof of his own crimes. The tapes will need professional analysis and an audio spectrograph to match and establish the voices of the speakers so some split-tongue lawyer can't claim the voices are not of his client."

White bagged and labeled the evidence. Bear continued the search in the en-suite bathroom while Shirley rooted around in the bedroom. She noticed something out of place with its surroundings – a trout in the milk – which was really a huge old Bible on Murphy's nightstand. Shirley couldn't imagine a scoundrel like Murphy reading the Bible. Besides, this Bible was too big and awkward to read comfortably in bed. She leafed through the first fifty pages but found nothing. As she turned to the next page, she found the secret.

From pages fifty-one to five hundred, the middle of the pages had been carved out with a sharp instrument to create a perfectly concealed, fort-like space in which Murphy had hidden a list of secret bank accounts, complete with the amount of cash in each one. The total exceeded four hundred thousand dollars.

Dunlop arrived at the house to advise the police on protecting the evidence and to supervise the labeling so that any legal challenges by defense attorneys at trial could be met by showing proper procedure was followed. He warned them, "It's a fair bet that the only hope the defense has is to try and get this damning evidence excluded by motion *in liminie*. And all judges prefer motions before trial, because it is more efficient and less troublesome than removing a jury from the court room when those dull legal arguments come up during the trial."

When Dunlop saw the twenty-six nude photos of the young girls, he took a deep breath. "This is serious and incriminating, but you can be sure Murphy's lawyer will argue that these photos are more prejudicial than probative, and they have no bearing on the bank robbery charge. And if Judge Flinn hears the case he just may exclude them too."

White was not happy upon hearing the Dunlop dissertation on evidence. He warned the others, "This stuff is impressive, but let's be careful and do a lot of interviews, including those young women, because Dunlop is likely right that the defense will throw up barriers to this evidence every inch of the way. Move the tapes to the Blazeks for analysis, but get evidence receipts for them, so there can be no court challenge claiming they were out of your custody."

Back at the surveillance house on Leverett Ave, there was guarded optimism as the crew arrived. Lieutenant Folker attended for the first time. He said, "It's no good for me to try and BS an experienced group of fact-seekers like you, but I'm impressed."

Foley took it upon himself to translate, "What he's saying is he's too experienced to try and bullshit a bunch of bull shitters like us."

Folker smiled, then continued, "First a word from our federal agent, Ms. McIntyre."

She stood nervously and showed she was shy before the group. "Here it is in a nutshell," she said. "My people in Washington have instructed me, and I agree, to stand aside and assist you all in the prosecution of these people. You now have sufficient probable cause to get arrest warrants issued for the lot. There are basically two reasons for this. First, it will be better community relations and will make the honest officers look better if the local PD and the state do this. Secondly, if you have bad luck and don't convict, there is no defense claim of double jeopardy if we prosecute them for civil rights violations under federal law, so we can get a second kick at the can."

Bear was still concerned and somewhat dubious about charging Murphy with the rape-murders. "It seems pretty weak evidence to me. I hoped Folker and Dunlop could talk the AG's office out of those charges, especially since we seem to have a chance of putting him away on the other charges with a lot of solid evidence. I think we should go for the solid charges and leave weak-evidence charges out."

"Dale and I will try again," Folker promised.

"We hear you," Kirk interrupted. "I'm no lawyer, thank God," he said throwing a sidelong glance at Hoss, "but how serious is the point Dunlop and Bear and White are worried about with this rape charge?"

Foley was fairly bursting to interrupt, "I think the fucker is guilty. He snapped. You guys sound like a bunch of latrine lawyers. It won't matter a bunch of snake shit if he gets off on the rape or not, because it sounds like you got more than enough to hang his guilty ass on the other stuff, so let's not waste more time on that subject."

Sharon Marshall, who felt she was only an informal member of the group, had remained silent. But the evidence argument provoked her sense of decency. She said, "I don't know squat about law or evidence, but this man Murphy is a social disease, and to hear you fools saying he might get off pisses me off. If all you smart lawyers and wise old cops can't get his ass with all the stuff you got, then I now understand why they lynched cattle rustlers without a trial in the Old West."

Kirk said, "Hear, hear, 'cause Sharon is right."

The long vigil of listening to the fifty-plus tapes of Murphy, Chase, and their minions – Clarke, Kierans, and Nichols – definitely implicated them all, including Stent and Morash. She had remained outside the evidence pot until the tapes revealed she was a major player.

The arguments, the coffee, and dispositions dragged the discussion down to inarticulate noise at the old house where the two Blazeks ruled with their listening devices. Dunlop, looking tired and drained, finally said, "Let's meet tomorrow to plan the arrest of these others. It should be done on Friday, so there's a chance they won't be able to make bail on the weekend. I'd also like to suggest that perhaps Taureen would like to be the one to arrest her grumpy courthouse boss, Mabel Morash."

He paused and looked to McIntyre for a reaction. She smiled, showing the satisfied look of a cat that had just cornered a mouse.

"Indeedy, indeedy," she said. "Just tell me the time you're taking down the others, and I'll bag that old bag with pleasure."

Dunlop closed the discussion, "Baptist and I'll get the warrants tomorrow morning. We'll meet here at one and go do it."

On the way home, despite his weariness, Bear allowed himself to feel a little pleased, because their efforts were starting to show positive results despite his worries about the trial. He parked in his driveway, unlocked the front door, and then double-bolted it after he entered. He stripped off his gun belt, boots, shirt, and socks, leaving them in an irregular trail from the hall to the bedroom. When he arrived at his destination, he snuggled in next to Shania. "Hey puddin'," he said, "are you awake?"

"You're about as subtle as a horny buffalo," she said. "I have news. Skeeter Greene has called here a dozen times tonight. Apparently you gave him our number on one of your cards. He's in a state of paranoid fear. Says he's being stalked. Claims someone's searching for him, and his life is in danger, and that ad in the paper really pissed him off. And then he said some new cuss words that beat any police vocabulary I ever heard."

Bear hardly heard her last words. "Life's a bitch," he mumbled, and before she could elicit more from him, she recognized his heavy breathing as a sign nothing would wake him until his own internal alarm clock kicked in.

To prove her point, she tried to provoke him, by gross exaggeration. She said in a loud voice, "And then Sketter said I was a great looking kisser, and he always wanted a squaw." But Noel Bear was off to the Land of Nod and didn't hear the baiting remarks.

CHAPTER FORTY-TWO

Future Prospects

"Whoever builds a house for future happiness builds a prison for the present

- Octavio Paz

It was a dull rainy Friday, a gloomy day when the weather set the mood. "Only a rainy Monday could create a worse attitude," Bear mumbled as he reached the department at noon, tired and groggy after several nights of too little sleep. Even though he was supposed to be off duty, he was center stage in the struggle, and he knew today would see the arrests of the courthouse gang, and he wasn't about to miss the action. There was an undeclared air of excitement in the squad room as the others drifted in for the pre-arrest briefing, all of them looking just as tired as Bear felt. The need for secrecy and low voices was apparent. Baptist sat nursing a cup of the bitter dark army-style coffee from the old copper, squad-room pot.

When Baptist saw Bear, he said, "Folker and Dunlop took hours on the paperwork and then went to Judge Freeman Gerald's office to get the warrants signed. They shouldn't be much longer."

Bear checked his watch. Time dragged. There was little conversation, and he checked his watch again. It hadn't moved, and he listened to hear if it was ticking. It was, and yet the time was hardly changing; it seemed like ages had passed. It was agony, boredom. He looked down at his wrist over and over again, acting like a child waiting for Christmas.

Dunlop barged in through the squad room door at a quarter to one, followed by Lieutenant Folker. "We got the warrants signed quickly, because we took the extra time to make sure the paperwork was perfect, so the defense can't find some technical loophole in court."

"A little irony for you," said Folker. "When we went to Judge Gerald's office, his secretary asked us to wait because he had a visitor. We sat outside waiting and you'd never believe who came strutting out of the office and grunted to us on the way by ..."

White interrupted, "Judge Harold Chase, of course."

Dunlop and Folker both looked surprised. Folker's expression was that of a guy at a party who thinks he's telling a super new joke only to be blindsided when some ignoramus tells the punch line before its time and ruins the story.

"How the hell did you know that?" Folker asked White.

"Sorry," White apologized. "Just an old cop's intuition. I know those two play golf together, and that Chase has been kissing Judge Gerald's ass trying to get promoted to the trial division since the governor is Gerald's brother-in-law."

Bear groaned, "Talk about judicial incest. Did he sign the warrant to arrest Chase?"

"Surprisingly, yes," replied Folker. "He read it, signed it, and then passed it back to us. All he said was that he guessed that Harold wouldn't be teeing off with him on Saturday."

"Rats and ships," Shirley said in a cynical tone.

"Exactly," Baptist agreed. "I hope they all abandon each other when we start questioning. As far as the judges go, most of them, including Freeman Gerald, were some politician's apple-polisher, and so I trust damn few of them."

"Drunks, fools, and neurotics, according to my experience," White added.

"Who's doing what today?" Doreen asked. "And do we treat Goat or MacAdam any better or more discretely than any other sleaze-bag when we arrest 'em?"

Folker smiled a crooked smile, giving his words impact, "Nope, just think of Wile E. Coyote and how he'd act the day he finally caught that beepin' road runner. But be careful: keep to the rules of legal procedure, but treat them just like the road-agents. If the press is around and ask, give them their names but only say the charges won't be known till arraignment. We don't want some defense attorney whining to the judge later and claiming we prejudiced the case by trying it in the media."

Taureen McIntyre arrived late, dressed in full combat gear including body armor, and displayed her federal badge over her heart on the bullet-proof vest. "Morash is in her office now, and the reception area is packed with people lined up to pay fines. I'd like to take Ernie Blazek for my back-up and arrest her now."

"OK by me," Folker said. "Just give us five minutes to settle who does what."

"Who is taking Chase?" Doreen asked.

"Bear and White," Baptist replied. "You and I'll do Kierans, Shirley and Bernie Blazek get Clarke, Lieutenant Folker and a man from the desk sergeant's office will arrest MacAdam, and the desk sergeant has a squad in reserve if we need back-up."

"Last word," Dunlop interjected. "Try to get as much out of your perp as you can before they lawyer up. Remember the Miranda requirement, but pump the hell out of them while they're afraid. If they do ask for counsel, Folker and I have selected one of Murphy's incriminating tapes to play for them, and that should come as a tongue-loosening shock to them. I already spoke with Stent the other day when we arrested him with the bikers. He's trying to bullshit me by claiming he didn't know all the courthouse involvement."

White snorted, "Stent is a disgrace and a rat bastard, and I'm glad we're not giving anybody a slide. This is a serious breach of public trust, and it reflects on all of us."

"I agree," Bear said, "and any deals or special treatment will not go unnoticed by the public."

Dunlop understood their feeling about being softhearted. He promised, "No get-out-of-jail-free cards from me. But we may have to make sentencing compromises to get what we need in terms of rolling some of them."

Baptist asked if everyone was ready, and when they all confirmed, he said, "Let's do it. Move out."

At the courthouse, Taureen McIntyre and Ernie Blazek walked into the court clerk's office. Taureen buzzed them through the security gate and into the administration space behind the counter. At least a dozen people were waiting in line to pay their fines. Taureen spoke to the girl collecting the payments.

"Where's Morash?"

The girl looked dumbfounded because she was used to seeing Taureen as a secretary and now, all at once, she was dressed like a SWAT team member.

"Ms. Morash is in her office and said not to disturb her."

MacIntyre smiled sweetly. "Please go tell her I need her out here at once, but don't tell her anything more. Is that clear?"

The girl shook her head in silent agreement and walked to the frosted glass door marked "Court Clerk," knocked gently and then entered. There was a brief, muffled conversation, and then the girl returned.

"She'll be right out."

Morash, displaying a stern, unhappy face like a drill instructor, strutted through the door, showing in her manner that she was not pleased by the interruption. When she spotted Taureen and Ernie in uniform, her mouth actually dropped open, proving her utter surprise.

"Mabel Morash," Taureen began in a mechanically firm voice. "You are under arrest for conspiracy, embezzlement, breach of trust, and felony murder. You have the right to remain silent, you have the right ... ," and a horde of nosey onlookers were absolutely silent as Mabel Morash, a graduate of Harvard Law School, received her Miranda warning and was led away.

Judge Harold Chase was in his small private office just to the rear of the courtroom bench, finishing his tea as the midday recess ended. He held an elaborate English china cup in his right hand and was raising it to his mouth just as White and Bear entered the room via the private door reserved exclusively for the use of the judge. The look on his face upon seeing the intrusion was difficult to read. Later, Bear would recount it might have been anger at the invasion of his space or the realization he had big legal problems. "Whatever the cause," Bear recalled, "the look on his contorted face was as sour as if he'd just tasted a green persimmon."

"Harold Chase," White stated in an authoritative tone, "you are under arrest for felony murder, conspiracy ... you have the right ..."

Chase's face was blood red as he was handcuffed. He looked like he might stroke out. Bear and White led him through the private door behind the bench, out into the courtroom, and down the aisle between the public seats. Dozens of spectators, witnesses, defendants, police officers, and attorneys were there in anticipation of the afternoon session. There were two reporters lounging around near the back of the room, each wearing a plastic press badge.

And there was silence, for it was not a usual sight to see a judge in handcuffs in the custody of two police officers.

And before court started, one reporter from the *Bugle* finally seemed to sense that this was a story with front-page appeal. As he snapped pictures with his camera, he activated his cell phone. "They've arrested Judge Chase." He said, and then he turned to Sergeant White as if to question him, but White ignored him like he was invisible.

Donald MacDougall, the man who had been wrongfully arrested for non-payment of a fine for which he had a receipt, was at the courthouse because he had received an anonymous phone call as a heads-up. It was ironic that his case and Dunlop's defense of it before Goat Chase had been the catalyst, a sort of legal blasting cap, that triggered the whole investigation. As Chase was led out of the courtroom in cuffs, MacDougall stuck his face almost nose to nose with Chase. He said, "Now, you old sonuvabitch, you're going find out exactly what Crowell Roscoe's cockroach hotel is like."

And Sergeant White, certainly understanding MacDougall's emotions, whispered to him. "And so will Crowell Roscoe."

It was three o'clock and the perps were booked, including Roscoe the jailer and sometime bailiff. All the others were seated in separate, wired interview rooms. At first there seemed to be more questions than answers.

In the police station, outside the secured area that housed the desk sergeant and communications section, there is a public lobby. As news spread through the grapevine, the public area was jammed with news people, TV apparatus, and photographers. The desk sergeant, Ralph Turner, was old school, callous, tough, and sensible, not given to explanations and generally unresponsive to the media, using evasive shrugs and grunts. Normally, he could paralyze reporters with his deadly stare and kill their questions with a frown. He asked that those assembled be quiet and orderly. He spoke even louder the second time to give the message more impact. "If you don't settle down, you won't be here when the department press relations office comes down to brief you."

A female reporter waved to get his attention, "Where's Chief Pineo?"

Just then Sergeant Shirley Reading, acting as press officer, arrived from the security elevator. She said, "Chief Pineo is on a leave of absence, which has nothing to do with today's press conference." Then she handed out a list of the names and the charges.

Upstairs, Bernie Blazek sat with Officer Greg Clarke, whose status had changed from suspension to arrest. While they waited for Reading to come back from the press conference, Clarke suffered fear, nerves, and stomach cramps constantly whining for medical attention. When Reading returned, she raised the issue of the probability of his going to jail. Blazek was even more aggressive, conjuring upsetting mental pictures with his words, "You know what cons do to police officers who end up in prison?" Before Clarke could respond, Bernie continued, "They make you some old wolf's love child and he punks you up the ass until he's tired of you, and then he rents you out to the others for cigarettes."

Shirley could see the hunted animal look creep into Clarke's eyes. She'd seen it many times in others when they realized they were in serious trouble and would be going to prison.

"Let me tell you what might be put on the table, before you lawyer up," Shirley offered. "We could try and persuade Dunlop, and the others, to see if they could arrange for you to be put into segregation out of the general population, if you give us some good stuff."

Clarke looked brighter, even interested, "Can you promise that?"

Shirley shook her head, "No promises before trial because the defense attorneys would claim we bribed you for your testimony."

Clarke knew how the game was played. "I'll have to discuss it with my attorney first," he mumbled.

Down the hall in interview room three, Mabel Morash demanded an immediate arraignment. Her dictatorial attitude and demands were as offensive when she was a prisoner without power as when she ran the courthouse with an iron, and usually unreasonable, fist. Dunlop was summoned, and when he entered, Taureen and Ernie were sitting silently being verbally abused by Morash.

Dunlop tried to reason with her, "Tell us who whacked the road-agent Hicks with the crossbow, and why?"

Morash twisted her mouth and raised her eyebrows but did not answer. Dunlop was not dissuaded, "Who decided to kill the undercover trooper?"

Again there was no reply as she sat looking hateful. Dunlop decided to change his approach and use a different tack. "I'm sure that as an attorney you realize that you were involved in a crime that resulted in those murders. That's felony murder, Ms. Morash."

She still did not speak but Dunlop was almost certain that he saw her flinch. He looked at Taureen and saw her wink indicating that she too had observed Morash's fearful reaction.

He continued, "There are no deals and there are no promises, but it might be easier on you if we could tell the judge that you helped us solve the trooper's murder and the death of Hicks too."

Morash decided to seek favor. "What can you promise me?" she asked?"

Dunlop scowled and stood up. "Nothing. I explained where you are, and in a few seconds I'm leaving here, so you decide now what you plan to do."

For the first time, perhaps due to Dunlop's curt yet professional I-don't-give-a-damn attitude, Morash seemed to acknowledge the mess she was in. "You know the law as well as I do. If one conspirator testifies against another, it's useless unless you have other evidence. So, my testimony may mean nothing to you, and then you could forget to try and help me."

Dunlop did not intend to reveal anything about evidence to Morash. "I guess we're through here," he said.

Morash came to life. Her attitude softened. "Murphy and Nichols did the trooper. The night they did it, they saw someone across the tracks, a witness. It was too dark to tell who it was, but later some homeless guy looking for a favor ratted and told Murphy it was Hicks. Chase ordered his murder. I heard it."

"Here's a pad and pen," Dunlop said, "Don't leave out the part about Chase."

In interview room five, MacAdam was maintaining an absolute, stone-faced silence. Lieutenant Folker had lost patience with MacAdam. He reached in his brief case and extracted a tape cassette. He said, "I want to play an excerpt from a tape that Murphy made of Kierans, and I want you to know some of the others are more co-operative than you, so if you continue with the attitude, you're only diddling yourself." He turned on the machine.

Kierans voice was loud and clear as he talked about a money split with Murphy and claimed that the payments from MacAdam, Chase, and Morash were too small. Folker removed the first tape and placed another in the recorder. He pressed play and the unmistakable voice of MacAdam was heard discussing an increased split to shut up Kierans' complaints. MacAdam now sobbed convulsively and started to babble. Folker let the tape run, and the voice of Murphy said to Chase that MacAdam had killed Major Brown. MacAdam asked for mercy or a deal, and even before Folker sent for Dunlop, he agreed to make a written statement acknowledging guilt and implicating the others.

Folker left and headed back to the interview room where Kierans was still playing sphinx. The room was damp, cold, and depressing. Outside, the rain beat against the window in a dull serenade like a stifled snare drum.

"I just spoke with MacAdam," Folker commented. "Now I've come to play you part of a tape that proves you killed Major Brown."

Kierans exploded, "He fuckin' killed Brown not me. He's trying to alibi out, but I'm not making any statement because I know how this interview shit is played, and I 'm not buying in."

Folker plopped another cassette into the player. Murphy's voice was heard talking to Chase. The conversation would sink Kierans, and he knew it. When the brief selection of shocking words was complete, Folker removed the tape and started out the door.

"Wait!" Kierans pleaded. "What could I expect if I co-operate?"

Folker kept walking. He paused only to have the final word. "That depends on what you tell Jack and Doreen. Personally, I wouldn't give you anything."

White and Bear headed for the interview room where Harold Chase had been placed and left to stew while they purposely ignored him. When they entered, Chase's face was still blood red from stress and he looked as if his blood pressure would burst the large blue vein in his temple. Chase was fuming. He was not used to waiting for anything or anybody.

"Let's not waste a lot of your time or ours," White began. "You know how the system works, and you're in the center of the shit-pile, so why not make it easier on yourself by co-operating."

Chase showed his contempt with a sour look and did not answer. Bear thought, almost sadly to himself, what a pathetic comedown; but Chase either did not recognize his predicament or decided to hang tough in the face of the accusations.

White tried again. "Bear will play you a portion of a tape recording, and after you hear it, I suggest you volunteer some help or else we're out of here and with us goes any hope of some consideration for your welfare."

Bear pressed play. As the incriminating sound of Chase's own voice drifted out from the machine, he appeared deeply concerned and looked even more pathetic. Bear exchanged a quick glance with White. He wondered quietly, "Had Chase blinked or was he still determined to remain silent?"

"Mr. Chase?" White asked, "are you aware that the Attorney General's Department has just instructed Dunlop to charge you with felony murder because of the tapes Murphy kept." Chase looked like the words struck home because his face reddened and his lip trembled. He asked, "Can I get a deal in writing if I cooperate?"

White stood up. "I think of the Chance brothers Mr. Chase, Slim Chance and No Chance. Now if you want to make a statement I can speak to Dunlop about trying to ease the road a little bit after the trial. But for now, Your Honor, there will be no deals before trial. Everybody runs the gauntlet."

Chase looked arrogant, his fear apparently subsided. "I'll take my chances then," he said.

"Let's go," White commanded. "We're wasting our time here." And then, outside the interview door, in a voice loud enough for Chase to hear, White said to Bear, "The wolves at the pen will like shoving it to him after he sentenced so many of them. Now they get a chance to fuck him back." And as they walked away they could hear old Chase screaming that he had changed his mind and wanted to cooperate.

It had been a long day. Back at the house on Leverett Avenue that night, the Blazeks were busier than usual preparing the technical reports and audio spectrograph analysis of all the tapes to support their admissibility as evidence. There was no jubilation and not a lot of conversation.

The trials, Bear thought, were an unspoken worry overhanging them all, and everybody seemed to sense the concern, but nobody wanted to reveal their uncertainty. He thought to himself, "Is it fatigue bothering me or some ancient superstition?" And he couldn't stop the thoughts, which plagued him. "Damn my ancestors and their old stories," he thought. "I'd be sick with concern everyday if I believed the superstitions of the old ways." Yet, he dared not tell the others lest they think he was a reservation idiot who believed in omens. The mental wrestling match had started on his way to the meeting. He couldn't explain that had driven through the graveyard in the hopes of seeing Skeeter Greene. It was a weak stupid idea, borne out of frustration, which he couldn't resist.

And then at the graveyard he saw it, the damn big owl. The elders' superstitions seized his mind. What was the ancient history of the owl? The owl was a powerful omen but what kind of omen? The conflict about the old ways was haunting him. He sat silently arguing with himself about the omen and then he cheered up as he thought of the day the noise of the graveyard owl had saved his life. Surely the owl could be a good omen, not just bad, and besides he was not a Navajo, and it was they who believed the owl was bad. He was a Seneca, and for them the owl was good. Gawd - almighty he thought, "I'm losing it, arguing with myself over an owl when I don't even know the significance."

Hoss Foley provided the first opening for Bear to voice an opinion, without mentioning owls. Foley had been unusually quiet, even Kirk's needling had not provoked a war of words. "This gawd-damn thing is not right," Foley blurted out just as Dunlop walked in. "Something's wrong. We got tapes; we got evidence up the wazoo, and it still seems too good to be true. I'm worried."

Bear admitted he was suffering the same dark thoughts. "Maybe it's just that I've never been in a huge legal fight before, but I have a foreboding."

"Very perceptive," Dunlop commented. "They just assigned that fucker Fred Flinn to try Murphy's case."

CHAPTER FORTY-THREE

Court

"Most people in government are fools; judges are the worst. If they weren't foolish when they went there, they soon turned that way."

- Redhorse

Legal scholar Walter Corbett was engaged by the State Attorney's office, at Dale Dunlop's request, to be legal consultant and second chair for Dunlop at trial in the prosecution of Richard Murphy.

At law school, Corbett had lectured to each class that while a trial in general resembles a chess game, in the initial stges, the opposing attorneys are closer to dueling male lions establishing a breeding territory by scenting, roaring, and aggressively prancing and pawing.

Corbett and Dunlop prepared their case in chief. "A fancy phrase," Foley explained to the arrest crew, "meaning the prosecutor has the burden to prove the guilt of the accused, and with Flinn on the bench, they better be well-prepared."

Dr. Corbett elaborated, "We'll have to be prepared to counter any shrewd defense theories and arguments. We won't know what they intend to argue until they stand up in court, because the rules of criminal procedure in this state do not require the defense to disclose their evidence list in advance like we do. They can move their case forward without prior notice of evidence or theory and then spring it like a trap. The best we can do is be ready for every possible scenario. That's where superior preparation shines. Dunlop and I will research the case as a devil's advocate, searching for as many possible theories and cases that the defense might use against us, so we can be prepared to counter argue."

Dunlop instructed all the officers who would later testify, so they would be coached and ready for a tough court session, making sure each would understand the legal process. It was necessary because several of them had no murder trial experience, and none had yet faced Barry Howe, the old legal fox in court.

When it was again Corbett's turn to speak, he said, "Dale's opening statement will inform the jury of Murphy's crimes and his guilt. The statement is crucial because some jury experts claim that juries almost always make up their minds on an opening statement and seldom change their opinions during trial. If that's true, we want everybody on the same page. The other reason the opening statement is important is that the defense will do it best to keep out as much of our evidence as possible or at least to have enough declared inadmissible to cast the remainder in doubt. They do that by filing a motion *in liminie*, which means the defense will try to raise legal roadblocks in advance of trial so the jury may never hear the best prosecution evidence. This will happen on the opening day before the chosen jury is allowed in the courtroom."

Bear grew more apprehensive as he listened to the two prosecutors explain the process with a law lecture. "How does the motion *in liminie* work?"

"I can read your mind, Noel," Dunlop replied. "We all know Murphy's guilty, but the defense will try to find legal glitches in our search methods or argue the evidence is more prejudicial than it is probative, or they'll object to its admissibility on constitutional grounds, claiming Murphy's Fourth Amendment rights on searches and seizures were violated. For example, they'll claim that our wiretap warrant did not include the portable listening device we used on Murphy and Mrs. Pineo at Woodlawn Cottages."

"It's a superior move to keep as much evidence as possible away from the jury rather than try to punch holes in the evidence after the jury's opinion is tainted," Corbett interjected.

White was familiar with court antics. While the others had all been through some general court procedures, most of them had not experienced an intense criminal trial involving a top-flight defense attorney like Barry Howe.

"Tell us how you'll counter the defense motions, because we're all worried about Judge Flinn," White requested. "He's connected, and this is his first big trial, and we wonder if he'll recognize the difference between shit and peanut butter."

Corbett was now in his realm, the area of law at which he excelled. His research, strategy, and counter-argument were thorough at all times. He warned. "If Howe files complicated and drawn-out motions, we will be prepared to argue them. But if we suspect that he is going to drag them out so he can win the trial on technical grounds before the jury trial starts, we will try to show the judge a better way to ascertain what is admissible in a closed session called a *voir dire.* All that means, and any pocket legal dictionary will explain it to you, is to speak the truth.

It's a hearing in advance of the trial without the jury present where the judge can hear the evidence and decide what is admissible and not prejudicial. It saves a lot of time when the real trial begins, because it cuts down on the interruptions. It's sort of a judge-supervised legal hair-pull between the lawyers who both try to convince the judge that their evidence should be admitted, and then the judge rules out some of the time wasters that would cloud the real issues."

Corbett cleared his throat before continuing to try and fortify the dwindling optimism of the officers who had worked so hard. "We can also file interlocutory appeals with the appeal court during trial on any of Judge Flinn's rulings that we feel are unfair. Usually the higher court will decide such appeals quickly because a delay could affect the lower court trial."

Dunlop now attempted to break the tension, "We're very lucky to have a man of Dr. Corbett's talent on this case. His advice and knowledge will drag us all through this with success, so stop acting like a bunch of rabbits."

White chuckled and then replied, "I've seen brother Corbett in court a few times, and what Dunlop says is very true, plus he isn't any cream -puff himself."

The next morning, before the trial was scheduled to begin, there was a long snake-like line of people winding down the block outside the courthouse, all hoping for a seat in the limited spectator section. Inside the building, the press had been allotted a small area of seats where note taking was allowed, but photos were prohibited. Dunlop had arranged with a deputy for Ellen Anslow, accompanied by Sharon Marshall, to be seated behind the prosecution's table.

Sharon leaned over and whispered to Dunlop. "I spent hours last night with Mrs. Anslow and Joan Murphy, who is in a terrible state, because her twenty-year-old daughter phoned yesterday and confirmed that Murphy has sexually abused her for years. The university psychologist had convinced her to reveal the details to Joan." She paused, correctly sensing Dunlop's revulsion. "I think Joan is an emotional wreck and is ranging between clinical depression and vicious rage. I also know she was always suspicious of her husband and young women, and that's why she sent her daughter away to school. My feeling is that she is powder keg that can blow without warning."

Dunlop almost choked. He scribbled a note to Baptist, telling him to get a statement from Murphy's stepdaughter and then charge Murphy with the sexual offence.

At exactly tenthe court bailiff called the room to order. "All rise, the trial court case number three-two-one-three, the *People v. Richard Murphy,* is now in session. The Honorable Frederick Flinn presiding."

Judge Flinn entered the bench area from the door behind the judge's chair. "Be seated," he said. "Are you ready for trial?" he asked, while switching his gaze from the defense table to the State's table.

"Yes, Your Honor," Dunlop replied.

Barry Howe stood very slowly and gazed at the jury for maybe half a minute. He was dressed in his usual shabby attire and looked like a blind tailor from a used clothing store had outfitted him.

"Howe is already getting sympathy from the jury, 'cause he looks like a runaway scarecrow," White whispered.

Howe cleared his throat as he started, "Your Honor, there are serious legal issues that must be decided upon before we can contemplate the allegations against my client, Richard Murphy. I have filed motions *in liminie* and would like to settle those questions about the prosecution's evidence and witnesses now, before the jury is seated, or the official trial commences."

Dunlop and Corbett had correctly anticipated that Howe's best chance to get Murphy off was to try and exclude as much evidence as possible and to cast doubt upon their entire case. The facts were probative, and if admitted, the evidence would be very damaging to Murphy and difficult to refute.

Howe continued, "First, there is the matter of the arrest of my client at the Woodlawn Cottages without a warrant, just based on information and recordings made by the police on a portable listening device, which we feel was not authorized by the police wire-tap warrant. Secondly, the prosecution has presented us with a list of evidence and witnesses as required by the rules. However, we note that there are two witnesses absent from the prosecution's list. We know the People are aware of the two individuals and have talked to both, yet they have not produced them. They have not revealed to us where these witnesses can be found, so I can only assume that their omission suggests that the witnesses possess exculpatory information that would aid the defense of Richard Murphy."

Howe paused to take a deep breath and then continued. "Third, the prosecution has presented us with a list of various items that were seized at the residence of Richard Murphy, which the prosecution plans to introduce as evidence. In the prosecution's affidavit supporting that evidence, they admit the items were acquired from a private compartment in Sergeant Murphy's closet. We ask that all these items be excluded and declared inadmissible based on the grounds that the discovery violated spousal privilege, resulting from private communication or conversation between husband and wife. The police had searched the bedroom closet and found nothing incriminating. Then Mrs. Murphy informed the police of the secret compartment in her husband's closet and how to open it, whereupon they discovered the various items on their evidence list. The People certainly cannot claim the items were in plain view. The fact that Mrs. Murphy told them where to look violated her husband's privileged and private communication with his wife and renders that evidence tainted and inadmissible as illegally obtained poison tree information.

"There are only two exceptions to the husband and wife rule, your Honor, in this State. One is when the spouse of the witness overhears a communication between the other spouse and a third party. That ends the privilege. The second exception is when one spouse commits an offence against the spousal-witness, and then a spouse is free to break privilege. Neither exception applies here, Your Honor."

Even Corbett seemed surprised at the daring legal assault Howe was claiming on the evidence from the Murphy house. Corbett whispered to Dunlop, "This is a tough claim to undue, because it is based on good law. If need be, just stall until I get to the pay phone to get some recent research from the Law School."

Howe continued without a break in his flow of words. "Your Honor, in *Harwood v. Tizard*, 446, US 39, 55 (1999), a case where Harwood, an alleged pedophile and drug user hid his cache of pornographic pictures of children and drugs under a kitchen drawer in a false compartment, the police did not find the evidence when they searched with a warrant. The spouse then led them to Harwood's secret compartment, and subsequently, he was convicted on the basis of that evidence. The lower court held that the evidence was admissible, because there was a legal search warrant. The defendant appealed his conviction all the way to the Supreme Court of the United States, and in late 1999, the court ruled that the evidence was inadmissible, because it was discovered as a result of Harwood's spouse violating spousal privilege. The facts in this case are on point with that decision. If this court allows that tainted evidence to be admitted, it will start spousal privilege, the private communication between husband and wife, down a slippery slope, which will further gut an already damaged Fourth Amendment."

Judge Flinn shifted his reading glasses down on his nose and peered over them. His face was flushed, but it was not clear from his expression if he was impressed, confused, or just frustrated, but he was clearly uncomfortable. Corbett got the impression that Flinn had suddenly realized that a promotion to the trial court required knowledge of law and carried with it an onerous responsibility to understand complex legal arguments as opposed to his previous mundane life on the lower court bench. He whispered, "Appointment by political party membership does not make a competent judge."

Judge Flinn responded, "You have the floor now, Mr. Dunlop."

Dunlop conferred briefly in hushed tones with Dr. Corbett and then turned his attention to the judge.

"There is a later Supreme Court case than the Harwood case cited by Mr. Howe. In *Crossey v. Edwards*, 625, US 44, 68 (2000), the court made it clear that the Harwood decision is not a binding precedent because challenging evidence on the grounds of a violation of spousal privilege, or what is more commonly called husband and wife communications, must be judged on a case by case basis. It appears that Mr. Howe has a number of thorny, perhaps controversial, legal issues he intends to raise, and before we argue the motions, the prosecution respectfully moves that the court conduct a *voir dire* to decide what is or is not admissible evidence, with the public, press, and the jury excluded."

Dunlop continued, "In the casebook 2001 *Criminal Procedures* by Khatto et al. at twenty-three, thirteen-seventy-nine to thirteen-eighty-one, there are reasons cited for the exclusion of the public and press from hearings or arguments to prevent extrajudicial press reports from reaching or influencing non-sequestered jurors. The fear of bias can be avoided, according to the casebook, by the court, which may take such action on its own motion or at the suggestion of the prosecution. We hereby move for a *voir dire* without the press, public, or the jury present prior to the actual jury trial."

Judge Flinn's relaxed facial expression now suggested to Corbett that Dunlop's idea was more acceptable than having endless arguments lead to delay, interruptions, and press judgments, and possibly interlocutory appeals. It would also afford Judge Flinn the time to have his clerks research the points made by both sides and that would lessen the possibility of his appearing to have shortcomings in his grasp of the law.

"It sounds like a plan to me, Mr. Dunlop. Do you have any objections, Mr. Howe?"

Howe obviously knew the rules of modern criminal procedure covered such a scenario. To oppose such an idea would send a negative message to the judge, and it would eventually leak to the jury that he was obstructing efficiency by dragging his feet and tying them up longer than necessary. In addition, he knew from experience that all jurors hate lawyers who dawdle through trials and impose upon their precious time with delay tactics.

"I agree, Your Honor, but I respectfully suggest that you instruct the prosecution to locate and reveal the two witnesses we know they left off the list. Those witnesses could be important."

Dunlop was quick to respond. "The names of the two witnesses are Diane Taylor and a homeless man known as Skeeter Greene. It is our belief that neither would be of assistance in an exculpatory sense to the defense, but we undertake to search diligently for them. I might add that an advertisement in the press did not turn up Greene, but we will try again to produce them for *voir dire*."

Judge Flinn, suddenly looking very relaxed and satisfied, tapped his gavel. "The *voir dire* will commence next Monday morning, the nineteenth, at ten a.m."

CHAPTER FORTY-FOUR

Voir Dire

"A legal mud fight."
- Sergeant Perry White

It was almost noon on the Sunday before the *voir dire*. Bear was sleeping like a tired lion in the back bedroom away from the chatter of the neighborhood kids playing road hockey on the residential street in front of the house. Shania was enjoying the twins as they displayed their football tactics on the rug while trying not to share a stuffed dog.

The front door bell made its annoying noise, and Shania moved quickly so it wouldn't sound again. She peeked through the lace curtains to see a scruffy-looking man on the front veranda.

"What do you want?" she asked through the glass.

He scowled back at her, the picture of grouchiness. "I had one helluva time finding where you live. Your husband needs me as a witness, but I don't need him, and I can turn around and hustle up the street if you don't call him right now."

Shania was not pleased with his answer. "Who are you?"

"Skeeter Greene," he said in a loud voice. "Now where's the Scout?"

She didn't want to leave the twins alone downstairs to go wake Noel. "Wait a minute," she instructed him and moved to the foot of the stairs. She shouted, her shrill voice carrying like an air raid siren.

"Noel, get up! You have a visitor named Skeeter Greene down here." In almost no time, she heard him thump to the floor.

Bear pounded down the stairs as if he was being chased, dressed only in his boxers and a T-shirt and still in bare feet. He yanked open the front door and ordered the surprised Greene inside.

"Sit down," he commanded, and don't start that mouth of yours 'cause I'm in a bad mood. I'll put on my pants and make coffee."

Greene sat on the hall telephone chair like a petulant child. He looked at Shania. "Maybe you could make coffee while Grumpy wakes up the other dwarves," he said.

Shania picked up the twins, one under each arm, and headed for the kitchen. Greene snuffed loudly as she left, "I hate kids, lady, so I wouldn't have touched the little pissers."

They were on their second cup as Noel explained what was happening and the need for Skeeter's testimony. Green sat stuffing himself with peanut butter cookies while Bear spoke.

"I'll have to call Dunlop to see where we can park you until he wants you in court."

Greene took a long drink from his mug and wiped his mouth on his sleeve. Now slightly mellower, he looked at Shania. "Could I have another?" he asked somewhat politely, and she took his cup to refill.

Skeeter turned his attention to Bear. "Listen, Scout, you call and ask the prosecutor when he wants me there, but you're not parking me anyplace."

Bear attempted to convince him otherwise. "We'll put you up in a motel with a police guard. The chief is staying in that one down in the east end so it's safe."

Greene became agitated, bordering on overt anger. "No motel; definitely no police. I don't want to end up like Lee Hicks. I'll pick my own pad, thank you, and that's that."

Now it was Bear's turn to be upset. "You know, Skeeter, we could always bag you and stick you in a cell until Dunlop wants you."

Greene took the coffee refill from Shania. "And I could develop one helluva case of amnesia in the cell. By the time you got me on the stand my silence would be profound."

Bear was now out of arguments. "I hear you, but I got to call Dunlop to see when he wants you." He picked up the phone and dialed Dunlop's number. When Dale answered, Bear explained that Greene was back on the scene and passed along his ultimatum.

"Fine," Dunlop replied. "We don't have a lot of choices so tell him Tuesday morning at nine. Monday's out because of Howe's motions."

The twins were becoming fussy and Shania was trying to placate them. "Naptime," said Skeeter. "Give me a handful of those cookies and a few quarters for the payphone and I'm history."

Bear rounded up the quarters and passed them to Green. "Where will you go?" he asked.

Greene rolled his eyes like it was a stupid question but replied, "With your owl."

Bear shivered. "That damn owl again," he thought.

Geene laughed knowing the superstition of the owl because of Bear's nervous prattle the day of the attempt on his life at the graveyard. "Forget that Indian crap, Scout, the only things owls make is owl shit," he said, and then took a handful of Shania's cookies and was out the front door like a breeze.

Shania watched him depart from the upstairs window and yelled to Noel, "Why does he call you Scout?

Bear laughed, "It's his idea of an insult. I don't know if he means an Indian Scout for the Army or Tonto's horse but it sure isn't a compliment coming from Greene."

Monday morning arrived with a mental thud after a weekend of anticipating excitement at court. The witnesses, including the police officers, were kept in the hall outside the courtroom, supervised by deputies to make sure that neither the case nor individual testimony was discussed. A hulking deputy secured the courtroom, and no one was permitted into the closed session except the lawyers, the defendant, the judge, and witnesses when specifically summoned. A court reporter would preserve the record and transcripts.

At ten a.m., Judge Frederick Flinn emerged through the door behind the bench. "Don't stand up. Now here's how this will run. Mr. Howe can argue his motions first and Mr. Dunlop can counter. When one side finishes the initial arguments, either side can rebut or summon a witness. We will listen to everything without restrictions, and in the case of the witnesses, I may exclude them from the actual jury trial but not until I've heard what they have to say. I'll rule on witnesses as we go but on the motions, I may reserve judgment. The jury trial will start next

Monday so that gives you both an entire weekend to adjust your presentations."

Howe stood up. "Your Honor, we asked for two additional witnesses to be summoned: Diane Taylor and Skeeter Greene. We'd like to add Chief of Police John Pineo to that list and ask that the prosecution be ordered to respond to that request."

Flinn looked down at Dunlop. "Mr. Dunlop?"

Dale stood up also. "Greene will be here Tuesday. Sergeant Reading has served Diane Taylor who will appear, and we will send an officer to see Chief Pineo, who is presently on a leave of absence for his health. Subject to Your Honor's blessing, we will ask the chief to come here Thursday, so he doesn't have to sit around the hall waiting for the others to testify."

"Agreed," Howe interjected.

"So ordered," Flinn declared.

Barry Howe now commenced arguing his motions to try and suppress the prosecution's evidence. He looked like a Southern Baptist prayer-tent deacon. "The arrest of Richard Murphy was conducted without an arrest warrant. The arrest and the recordings made by the police with their portable listening device are a serious violation of my client's constitutional rights, particularly the Fourth Amendment. I have outlined the cases supporting my contention in my written brief. The Supreme Court of the United States has ruled that such police activity is subject to close scrutiny, and the exclusion of illegally obtained evidence, poison tree evidence, will act as a deterrent to improper police action."

Dunlop interrupted, "Let's stick to some organized form here Your Honor. This is not his first motion, besides the arrest at the Woodlawn Cottages resulted from Richard

Murphy attacking Sergeant Doreen Roberts in a life threatening assault. Sergeant Murphy's attack created exigent circumstances, and such circumstances do not require a warrant, especially if it occurs in the clear view of a police officer. Now, to the use of the parabolic device and the recordings which Mr. Howe is trying to exclude as inadmissible. I have presented Mr. Howe and the court with a certified copy of the wiretap warrant issued by Judge Chipman which covers a number of suspects, including Sergeant Richard Murphy. On page two, paragraph one, it states `surveillance and recording of any or all conversations, by any means whatsoever, except those of a personal matter, may be conducted by any mechanical device whatsoever.' And that would include the portable parabolic device. I note Mr. Howe did not argue that discussing murder and crime was in any way a personal discussion. Your Honor, we have listed dozens of cases supporting the use of portable listening devices." With that, Dunlop sat down.

Flinn cleared his throat. "Mr. Howe? He makes a point about some order in your motions, so before I get to that is there an immediate rebuttal you wish to make here?"

"Only this, Your Honor. If you allow this evidence to be presented to the jury, it gives license to police to eavesdrop on conversations, and there will be no place where a citizen can be sure he is having a private discussion."

"Noted," said Flinn. "Now, Mr. Howe, you argued on Friday that the search of Sergeant Murphy's closet and the evidence acquired by the prosecution during that search should be excluded, because the suspect's wife violated the husband and wife communication privilege when she informed the police where the evidence was hidden. Lets deal with that motion first. Do you wish to call witnesses or make further presentations on that motion, before we jump into other issues?"

"Yes, Your Honor," Howe replied. "We call Joan Murphy."

Dunlop bounced to his feet. "Your Honor, Mr. Howe is arguing that Joan Murphy violated spousal privilege, and now he's trying to call her to testify."

Howe responded immediately. "This is a closed session to seek the truth. We feel her role should be heard to confirm she violated a confidential fact, which originated in a confidential conversation between husband and wife."

"Agreed," ruled Flinn. "Call Joan Murphy."

The deputy returned alone. "Joan Murphy is not present, Your Honor."

Dunlop stood. "Well, the defendants were planning to examine her, and we weren't, so its Mr. Howe's responsibility to summon her not ours."

"I'm sorry, Your Honor," Howe apologized. "There must be a glitch with the process server. May we call Robert Feters instead?"

"No objections," replied Dunlop as Flinn looked to him. Instructions were issued to the deputy.

Feter came forward and was sworn in. He was a different man than he used to be when he lived on the street. He was clean, presentable, his clothing decent. Howe had to try and discredit Feters as his evidence was potentially damaging to Murphy.

"Mr. Feters, where are you employed?"

Feters smiled a sincere smile without malice. "I am unemployed, homeless, and I haven't worked for twenty years."

"Why are you unemployed?"

"Because I am manic-depressive and have just been diagnosed."

"Are you currently on medication?"

"Yes, three types of pills. I have a doctor's letter explaining the medication."

"Who provides you with your drugs?"

Dunlop objected, "Not drugs, Your Honor, medications. Anyone reading the record on appeal might be misled."

"Agreed," Flinn nodded. "Strike drugs. Say medications, Mr. Howe, unless you are accusing Mr. Feters of drug addiction."

Howe smiled politely. "Of course. Medications ... who buys your medications?"

"The state police bought my prescriptions."

"Very kind of them to buy your med-i-cation," Howe commented in a sarcastic tone. "Are you employed by them?"

"No, sir."

"How long have they been so kind, Mr. Feters?"

"About three months," Feters replied.

"Tell us what happens to you if you do not take that medication, Mr. Feters?" Howe asked.

Feters was embarrassed. His face showed a slight flush. "I get depressed," he said.

"Mr. Feters, I'm going to read you the symptoms of your disorder as stated by the *American Medical Journal*, which outlines the sufferer's problems if medication is not taken. They are depression, paranoia, confusion, tremors, inability to remember things, and in some cases, hallucinations. Are any of these symptoms present when you don't take your medications?"

Feters looked down, "Yes, sir. Pretty much."

"And were you taking medication on the night the man was killed on the railroad tracks?"

"No, sir."

Howe made an exaggerated gesture with his hands. "Your Honor, this man's testimony, by his own admission, is without credibility and would be prejudicial and inflammatory."

"I agree," said Flinn. "Mr. Feters' testimony is excluded."

Dunlop stood up. "We object for the record, Your Honor."

"Noted," Flinn replied, "but you didn't counter-argue, that's hurts an appeal."

Howe proceeded. "Call Ellen Anslow please, Your Honor."

Ellen Anslow walked slowly with the deputy to the witness chair where she was sworn in. She looked pale and gaunt and seemed listless. The murder of her daughter continued to traumatize her.

Howe was solicitous, at first. "I'm sorry about your daughter, Mrs. Anslow. My job is to defend my client, and that causes me to ask some tough questions. Forgive me; it's my job. First, how old was your daughter?"

"Sixteen."

"Describe her appearance, please."

"A pretty girl, nice-looking, very pleasing."

"Would you say she was sexy, Mrs. Anslow?"

"Attractive," she replied.

"Mrs. Anslow, I want to read to you from a list of descriptions of your daughter complied by some of her classmates."

"Objection," interrupted Dunlop. "What kind of evidence is this, unsworn opinions of school kids? It's the worst type of hearsay. Mr. Howe is trying to impeach with hearsay."

"Mr. Dunlop," said Flinn, "any reasonable thing will be allowed in, and if it's biased, I'll strike it. Now proceed Mr. Howe."

"Here are the opinions," Howe continued. "A sexpot, she looked twenty-three or twenty-four, sexy woman, big boobs, great shape, liked older men, bragged about seducing older men." Howe paused. Mrs. Anslow looked horrified. "Mrs. Anslow, do you think your daughter looked older than sixteen, old enough to lie to a man about her age?"

"Objection," shouted Dunlop. "This isn't a statutory rape trial nor is the dead person's age relevant or evidential to a murder charge."

"Overruled," Flinn said. "I'm trying to ascertain if the witness' testimony is inflammatory or probative."

Anslow sobbed silently, the tears running down her cheeks, yet Howe pressed on. "She attracted, no, she trolled for the attention of older men like Reverend Kenneth Solomon who hanged himself over her. I can give you list of the other older lovers, but I think you already know most of them. You knew them, and you hated them because your daughter attracted them, is that not true?"

Ellen Anslow's face was buried in her hands, and she sobbed convulsively.

"Your Honor," Howe turned to the judge. "This witness is biased. She would incite false sympathy, not reasoning, from the jury, and anything she said would be prejudicial instead of useful. I read her statement on Sergeant Murphy that she gave to the prosecution and it is all hearsay, some of which came from Sergeant's Murphy's wife. That also violates husband and wife communication. I have additional questions for Mrs. Anslow, especially about a shirt she claims is Sergeant Murphy's, which she turned over to the police, but I don't think she is able to continue so I reserve the right to recall her. Perhaps we could recess until tomorrow morning?"

Dunlop was furious but did not object to the recess. He needed the time to try and rehabilitate Mrs. Anslow.

"No objection, Your Honor."

Flinn announced the recess. "Ninetomorrow."

Dunlop walked to Ellen Anslow and led her to the prosecution's table. She sobbed, muttering bitterly about Howe's mean-spirited comments in regards to her daughter. Dunlop called Shirley on his cell phone. She was just outside the courtroom in the hallway.

"Bring Sharon Marshall and come in here for Ellen Anslow," he requested.

The courtroom had emptied and the two women tried to soothe Ellen's grief.

"Listen," Dunlop whispered to Sharon, "and this is off the record, if ... if you and Ellen were to go see Joan Murphy before she testifies, you might consider cluing her up as to what to expect from Howe, so he can't badger her into tears."

Sharon Marshall drew her mouth into a thin line. Her chin quivered with emotion. "I should have kicked Murphy's balls flat the other day when I had the chance. He's a predator, and that's the only way to solve that kind of perversion."

CHAPTER FORTY-FIVE

Defense

"Legal questions are verbal tricks by lawyers to confuse witnesses."

- Sergeant Perry White

It was nineTuesday morning, and Judge Flinn appeared from behind the bench. Howe stood quickly, almost before the judge was seated.

"Your Honor, I wonder if Mr. Dunlop would agree to a slight change. As you can see, Sergeant Murphy is absent today. There was a call on my voice mail from a Ms. Smith informing me that Sergeant Murphy required medical attention in the night and would not be able to attend today. What I'd like to do is call Diane Taylor first, then Skeeter Greene and delay re-calling Mrs. Anslow until Sergeant Murphy returns. I think also, that the two witnesses will be important in forming other questions for Mrs. Anslow."

Dunlop objected. "Mrs. Anslow has suffered a great deal with the loss of her daughter, and then Mr. Howe upset her badly yesterday. To ask her to sit out in the hall for hours waiting for more abuse is too much to expect. She shouldn't be asked to wait, and Mr. Howe should not be granted his request."

"Mrs. Anslow is late," Howe informed the judge. "She's not here, the deputy told me."

"Mr. Dunlop, if the next two witnesses bring some explanation to the court that is relevant to Mrs. Anslow's testimony, you should want to hear it," Flinn said. "I'm granting Mr. Howe's request."

Dunlop did not pursue the issue. There was no point of law involved.

Diane Taylor was first. The deputy led her in and she was sworn and then seated. She was very young looking, child-like, and it was apparent by her features that she was afraid.

"Ms. Taylor," Howe began, "were you a close friend, a confidante of Mary Anslow?"

"Yes," she replied softly. "We were good friends."

"Did she tell you her secrets?"

"Yes."

"Did she tell you about her men friends?"

"Yes."

"Were you close to her mother, Ellen Anslow?"

"Yes, sort of, kind of friends."

"And what did you and Mrs. Anslow talk about?"

"School and Mary."

"Did you talk on a regular basis?"

"Yes, I guess you could say that."

"Did you talk about her daughter's boyfriends?"

"Sometimes."

"Is it true you told one of your school friends, Sue Reeves, that Mrs. Anslow paid you to spy and report on Mary?"

"I don't remember."

"Ms. Taylor, I can call Sue Burton in here, she's in the hall. Now, did you tell her that?"

"I guess I did."

"And is it true that Mrs. Anslow paid you?"

"Yes."

"And did you tell Ellen Anslow that Sergeant Murphy was one of Mary's boyfriends?"

"Yes."

"And who else did you report to Mrs. Anslow as being one of Mary's lovers?"

Diane sat quietly, looking at the floor, avoiding Howe's piercing stare. She did not answer.

"Come now, Ms. Taylor, we're waiting."

Diane fidgeted with her ring and turned it around and around on her finger in a child's response to the confrontation.

"I told Mrs. Anslow that Chief of Police John Pineo was also one of Mary's lovers."

Howe slammed his fist down on the table. "Good grief," he shouted. "Did you invent any others? Did you invent lovers to earn money from Mrs. Anslow about her daughter? How about President Clinton? Or maybe the Governor, or how about the Prime Minister of England? The Chief of Police, indeed. That's a beauty of a lie. Isn't it true that you are nothing more than a paid informant, a snitch who will invent anything to tell a worried mother in order that she would go on paying you?"

She hung her head in silence.

"Your Honor," Howe said, "I tender the witness to Mr. Dunlop, but her testimony should be excluded from a jury trial. She's a liar for hire."

"Your witness, Mr. Dunlop," said Flinn.

"No questions," Dunlop replied, because Howe had impeached her successfully rendering any of her testimony as questionable.

Flinn nodded, "Call Skeeter Greene. What is this man's proper name, Mr. Dunlop?"

"Peter Greene, Your Honor."

The deputy walked to the door and opened it. "Call Peter Greene," he bellowed into the hallway. Both Dunlop and Howe held their breath wondering if Greene had shown up.

Skeeter Greene followed the deputy up the aisle to the stand and was sworn in. He looked different. Dunlop realized Greene had combed his hair and shaved, but his clothing was still the same numerous layers of throw-aways he obtained from the Salvation Army.

"Your Honor," Howe began, "I think Mr. Dunlop should start this witness and we will be satisfied to cross-examine him."

Dunlop stood slowly, his face revealing his contempt. Your honor, Mr. Howe called Sketter Greene, so why should I question him, before I have a chance to see what is the burr under Mr. Howe's saddle? We did not have Mr. Greene on our list, even though we wanted him, because we were not sure we could find him, or if he'd show up. Mr. Howe asked the court if the prosecution could produce him, and we were not sure, but we managed to find him, because we did as the court instructed us to do! Mr. Howe now wants us to do the minefield exploration, so he can walk safely in his attempt to impeach Mr. Greene as a witness? If that's the plan, then our response is that we have no questions. If Mr. Howe decided to question this witness, then we may have some rebuttal questions."

Flinn smiled, a begrudging concession that Dunlop had out-maneuvered Howe. It left Howe to ask the questions or dismiss the witness, and Howe was certainly anxious to have Greene on the stand.

"You're up, Mr. Howe," the judge instructed. "Here's the witness you wanted."

Howe had no choice. He got up very slowly, searching through the pile of papers on the defense table. "I wonder if he's not sure how to handle Skeeter," thought Dunlop. Knowing Greene's nature and acerbic manner would present a challenge amused Dunlop, as he watched to see if Howe could match wits and words with the rapier-tongued Greene.

Howe started off with the usual background questions, but Greene cut him off. "Let me save the court's time counselor," he replied, "I served in the armed forces of the United States Army, like thousands of others. I served honorably. When I got out I decided to live free, without restrictions, and I do that. I don't get a veteran's pension. I never got one, even though I got a hole in my guts you can put a fist in, and I can't eat right. I don't steal or use drugs, and I don't rape children. Now let's get to the crux of your questions, lawyer, because I got other places to be."

Howe looked a little startled, but he moved on to his other questions. "Mr. Greene, do you know Sergeant Richard Murphy?"

"Yep, he's not here."

"When was the last time you saw Sergeant Murphy?"

Greene smiled. Dunlop wasn't sure if it was a smug smile or whether he just dreamed he saw it.

"When he was driving an old red clunker of a car backward at the graveyard trying to run over Officer Bear, after he missed shooting him. The car's license plate was W-H-Y 177, and it's now junked and sits in Cleveland's scrap yard."

Dunlop snorted softly, "A perfect legal squelch," he whispered to Corbett.

Howe was put off his game and surprised. He cleared his throat and cleaned his glasses with the wide end of his ugly necktie. He had to find another approach, a new tack.

"Mr. Greene, are you being paid by the police or anyone else to testify here?"

"Yes and no," Skeeter replied. "I got six quarters from Officer Bear's wife for my use if I had to make an emergency payphone call for help, because I knew someone was after me. I saw them."

"Were you promised money after your testimony?"

"Nope. I was offered a motel room and a police guard, both of which I refused, because I didn't want to end up like Lee Hicks."

"Did you see Sergeant Murphy on the night the man was killed at the railroad tracks?"

"Nope, but Hicks, Feters, and another person did."

Howe smiled, a self-satisfied grin at having elicited an answer he seemed sure he could discredit. "But Hicks is dead, and Feters is not fit to testify because he wasn't on his medication at that time, so that leaves your hearsay, and your assertion that some other person saw Murphy. Who was the other person, and what did they see?"

Skeeter did not hesitate. "Those people saw Murphy and another cop named Nichols put the body on the tracks. That live witness made me promise not to reveal their name until the trial starts and then to give it to Mr. Dunlop. I hear that when a witness' life is in danger, that's acceptable to the court."

Howe was not pleased. His manner bordered on overt anger, but he managed to restrain himself. "Your Honor, if he knows the identity of a witness, and I doubt that, he should be compelled to testify now."

Greene turned his head and focused both eyes of the judge like a poised cobra. "Your Honor, we can sit here for a week, and you can throw me in jail, but I gave my word. One witness has already been murdered, and if I go to jail. I'd feel compelled to tell the press whose car I saw at a certain place Thursday nights."

Flinn appeared to ignore Greene's words, almost as if he didn't want to hear them. "Strike Mr. Greene's comments about jail and the press," he instructed the clerk. "Now, my ruling is that Mr. Greene is concerned for the life of a witness, and I accept his word. He can speak to Mr. Dunlop, and as prosecutor, he can inform Mr. Howe next Monday before court."

"This ... this is an outrage," Howe stammered.

"No, Mr. Howe," Flinn replied. "It's my ruling."

Howe turned back to Skeeter. "Are you aware of the murder of Mary Anslow?"

"Yep, I know about it."

"Howe did you learn about that murder, Mr. Greene?"

"I saw it. I was there in my usual place behind the scoreboard. Hicks and I used to sleep there a lot. I was there when I heard a car drive up, around midnight, I guess; I don't have a watch. Two people got out. They put a blanket on the ground, and it was all lovey-dovey at first and none of my business. I thought they were just hauling each other's ashes, and I was sort-of trapped like being a prisoner at a sex show. It was a little embarrassing. I didn't say anything. Then it got weird."

"What do you mean, weird? What happened?" Howe asked.

"Well, there was no rape, she was as game as heck at first, and they were grunting like hogs, but then he started biting her and getting rough. He got rougher and rougher. He bit her face, and she yelled."

"What happened next?"

For the first time, Skeeter's voice softened. The belligerence was gone, and he answered with emotion. "My God, it was awful. It happened so quickly we couldn't move fast enough to stop it. He plunged a big old combat knife up under her rib cage at the tope of her stomach. He was cursing and swearing, calling her dirty names. He kept saying a lot of cuss words about her boobs. What he did was unbelievable. I saw a lot of guys all mangled up, but this was worse. He hacked her tits off. He was yelling and cutting, and I thought everybody in town would hear him. But nobody came. Jesus, it was awful."

Howe paused before continuing "What did the man do next?"

"He pulled his rubber off and pitched it on her chest. Then he took off his overalls, you know like the ones mechanics wear, and threw them down. Then he went to the car and got a five-gallon plastic gas can and poured it all over her and the blanket. I could smell the fumes from the scoreboard. Then he lit a match and threw it and poof! It all went up like a small explosion. I saw his face then, in the light. He watched a minute or so, then he walked to his car as cool as an Eskimo pie, did a U- turn, and then drove off. I got the plate number though. S-P-D 000."

"Who was the killer, Mr. Greene?" Howe asked, sure of the answer he was going to receive.

Skeeter was back to his usually aggressive self. "It was Chief of Police John Pineo."

Flinn cleared his throat as the impact of the words silenced all those present.

"Your Honor," Howe broke the quiet. "Might I suggest a fifteen-minute recess here?"

"Granted."

Dunlop quickly dialed Baptist on the cell phone and explained the situation. "Go to the Mayflower Motel, and ask the chief to go to the morgue with you. Keep him busy until I go see Judge Flinn for a warrant. Don't go alone. Take Bear or someone else."

"Copy that," Baptist responded. "Listen, Shirley is on her way in there from the courthouse hall to tell you something. Stall the court if you have to, but wait until you talk to her before the hearing proceeds."

Dunlop clicked off as Shirley hurried up the aisle to whisper in his ear. He listened intently and then nodded. When Judge Flinn re-appeared, Dunlop stood up.

"Your Honor, the police have just informed me that Sergeant Richard Murphy has been found dead at the cottage at Woodlawn."

"Was it a suicide?" Flinn asked.

"It does not appear to be, Your Honor. The ME suspects that he bled to death after a castration. There was a note at the site. It read as follows:

A sick twisted man who molested
Little girls, including his own stepdaughter.
His crimes were many and justice
is too slow.
This is what he deserves.
Justice is done.

Judge Flinn tapped his gavel. "This case is moot, thereby we are adjourned. Mr. Dunlop, you'll want a warrant. Come into my office."

CHAPTER FORTY-SIX

Just Desserts

"Justice is the art of the good and fair."
- Anonymous

Dunlop entered the morgue with the arrest warrant for Chief of Police John Pineo. Baptist and Bear had not yet arrived with the chief, and neither were Foley and Kirk present. Shirley sat drinking coffee with Sharon, who reveled in the gossip of the hearing and Murphy's just desserts. An hour passed. No explanation for the delay was forthcoming from Baptist, nor did the police radio provide grounds for intelligent guessing.

Baptist and Bear finally arrived with Kirk and Hoss just behind. Hoss looked solemn.

"No sweat about Pineo," Foley began. "He got the same treatment as Murphy. Kirk's initial opinion suggests that he bled to death after the castration. The bus is bringing his body in."

There was an uncomfortable silence before Kirk broke it. "Whoever did it used the same MO as was used on Reverend Solomon. A needle in the neck to put them to sleep, then a real pro job cutting out the nuts like a surgeon. But in the cases of Murphy and Pineo, the person made sure the bleeding didn't stop. I'd say the operations were definitely done by someone with medical or surgical experience. It had to be someone they all knew to get close enough with a needle."

Shirley was motivated by her nature to ask questions. "Any idea on the time of death?"

"Likely eight to ten o'clock this morning," Kirk replied. "Six or seven hours ago."

"Anyone see any visitors near the motel room?"

"None," Baptist answered. "There was a Do Not Disturb sign on the door, but around noon the maid decided to check his room, and she found him. There was blood everywhere."

Dunlop picked the early morning edition of the *Bugle* from Kirk's desk. "Look at this headline, `Police Chief Linked to Sex Crimes'. That's a public notice to a vigilante."

"Where'd they get that story?" Baptist wondered.

"His wife talked to the media : rats and ships," Dunlop replied.

"Tough case to solve," Baptist said. "Tough to try too. Besides, I have too much on my plate to spend much time on this."

Dunlop nodded. "Right now we want to concentrate on convicting the courthouse gang."

"What about the evidence seized at Murphy's place?" Bear wondered.

"All admissible, according to Judge Flinn," Dunlop replied.

After everyone else had departed, only Hoss, Foley, and Sharon remained. Hoss broached the subject of the castrations again. "How many people out there, who aren't medically oriented or surgeons, could do that cutting so professionally?" he asked Kirk.

Kirk chuckled, "There are eighteen thousand Vietnam vets in this state and at least two percent would be combat medics. I know of three right here in Shiretown, including my esteemed assistant here, Sharon Marshall."

"Who else?"

"Joan Murphy and Ellen Anslow both served as surgical nurses in 'Nam, and both learned a lot of stuff by necessity that most nurses never see except in a combat zone."

Sharon Marshall listened to their exchange. She took a long sip of coffee. "Are we likely to do long drawn-out autopsy reports with a lot of theory on those two castrations?" she asked.

Hoss looked at Kirk for an answer. Kirk yawned. "This is one of those times when less is more. We don't have to say very much. Does that bother you, Hoss? Because it looks like this case and all its issues are closed."

Hoss looked bored, "Nope, not one bit," he replied.

Kirk got up and walked toward the door of the morgue to start the autopsies. He mumbled, "Ius est ars boniet aequi."

Hoss and Sharon exchanged quizzical glances." My Latin sucks," Sharon said. "What the hell does that mean?"

"I'll re-phrase it," Kirk said. "As to these two dead eunuch perverts, frankly my dear, I don't give a fuck."

defacto-Justice

By Donald F Ripley JD

Epigraph

Payback is a bitch.
Author Unknown

BIOGRAPHY

Donald F. Ripley has covered a lot of territory since his childhood. Found in a trashcan in Buffalo New York he was adopted first by parents who abandoned him to burn in a fire. Finally he was adopted by Frank and Lucy Ripley of Canada and grew up with a keen understanding of the culture of Canada and the United States. He played senior hockey in Canada and semi-pro baseball in the United States before joining the US Army. Because of his birth mother's Native American heritage, he is a US citizen. In the service, he divided his time between playing baseball in the Japanese Central Service League and learning surveillance tricks as a member of the Security Division.

After a long illness arising from the service and exacerbated by being fired by an Investment Dealer, Don decided to fulfill a lifelong dream and go to law school, becoming possibly the oldest student to graduate from the New England School of Law at 63. He also found time to write two books, one on a Canadian TB Sanatorium, a history - *Thine Own Keeper,* and *The Home Front,* about small town life in a community near an Infantry Training Centre during World War II, and a political biography of Canadian Senator the Honourable John M Buchanan. He's now turning his hand to fiction, taking advantage of his own experience in the law and his son's knowledge as a law enforcement officer.

Don lives in Florida and Massachusetts with his wife of 46 years Frona and takes an interest in helping veterans navigate the legal system when not interfering in the lives of his four children.

Printed in the United States
2688